THE HANGED MAN

Praise for *The Hanged Man*

"Edwards skillfully blends rigorous characterization with political intrigue, action, and haunting worldbuilding in the exciting follow-up to 2018's *The Last Sun*. Edwards conjures a believably dangerous setting filled with tarot imagery and supernatural menaces. Series fans and new readers alike will be hooked."

—*Publishers Weekly*

A thrilling and satisfying follow-up to The Last Sun, The Hanged Man proves that K.D. Edwards is the real deal. The story shines with unique and complex world-building, stellar writing, and a fast-paced plot that is rounded out with humor and heart-felt emotional moments. I didn't want the book to end!"

—Tammy Sparks, BOOKS, BONES & BUFFY

"Much like The Last Sun, The Hanged Man is a quest story, and yet it is much more than that. It is theater of the mind. It is the finest form of escapism I have ever read. There are no proper terms to express how powerfully this book affected me . . . *The Hanged Man* receives 5 out of 5 Sigils!!!"

—Ben Ragunton, TG Geeks podcast

Praise for *The Last Sun*

"Edwards's gorgeous debut presents an alternate modern world that is at once unusual and familiar, with a grand interplay of powers formed by family and the supernatural. Intriguing characters, a fast-paced mystery, and an original magical hierarchy will immediately hook readers, who will eagerly await the next volume in this urban fantasy series."

—*Library Journal* STARRED review

"Edwards's debut combines swashbuckling action, political intrigue, and romance into a fast-paced and enjoyable adventure . . . Intriguing worldbuilding and appealing characters set the stage and pique the reader's interest for sequels."

—*Publishers Weekly*

"Jaw-dropping worldbuilding, fluent prose, and an equal blend of noir and snark make for that most delicious of fantasy adventures, an out-of-this-world tale that feels pressingly real. A smart and savvy joy."

—A. J. Hartley, *New York Times*–bestselling author of
the Steeplejack series and the Cathedrals of Glass series

"A fast, fun urban fantasy in a wonderfully original world, full of slam-bang magic and interesting characters."

—Django Wexler, author of *The Thousand Names*

THE HANGED MAN

THE TAROT SEQUENCE | BOOK TWO

K. D. EDWARDS

Published 2019 by Pyr®

Cover illustration © Micah Epstein
Cover design by Jennifer Do
Cover design © Start Science Fiction

Inquiries should be addressed to
Start Science Fiction
221 River Street
9th Floor
Hoboken, NJ 07030
PHONE: 212-431-5455
WWW.PYRSF.COM

10 9 8 7 6 5 4 3 2 1

ISBN: 978-1-63388-492-2 (paperback) | ISBN: 978-1-63388-493-9 (eBook)

Printed in the United States of America

"Dedication #1: Ground Zero of
~~*Dedications: For Mom and Dad"*~~

Dedication #2: For my sister, Stacy, who was my hero before I even had a grown-up understanding of what that word should really mean.

CONTENTS

PROLOGUE

For my kind, the first sign our world was ending came on October 24, 1946.

Over the White Sands Missile Range in New Mexico, a V-2 rocket shot sixty-five miles into space to take the first-ever, grainy, black-and-white photo of the curvature of the earth.

As humans celebrated their milestone, my people brooded over what it meant. We watched with mounting unease as satellites and rockets were invented and launched, greedily capturing images of the planet's continents and waters. The turning point—the final failure of our magics and illusions—came when Yuri Gagarin, a Russian cosmonaut, circled the earth in Vostok 1. From that unimaginable distance, his human eyes succeeded in doing what so many others had not: they pierced our veils. There's reputedly a sound recording of Gagarin accused of being drunk when he told someone to run and grab a damned atlas.

What he saw was an enormous North Atlantic island, more or less on the same latitude as Massachusetts and Maine, about the size of Japan maybe a little smaller than the state of California.

Atlantis.

So the gig was up, and Atlanteans knew it. My people decided to put on their finest, drop the spells that had kept the homeland hidden for millennia, and reveal themselves to the world.

Have you seen the newscasts? Read about the riots? Watched footage of the crowded churches and highways?

The existence of Atlantis changed humanity's perception of *everything*. We'd been the root of so much myth and legend. Forget Zeus and Odin and Shiva—we were the tricksters and thunder gods, the fertility deities and battle crows, the sorcerers and shape-shifters. We were the fae, and vampires, the weres, the undead. Humans had even pinched the names of our leaders and repackaged them into the mystical equivalent of playing cards. There really was a Hierophant and a Fool, a Devil and the Wheel of Fortune, Temperance and Justice. They are, collectively, called Arcana: twenty-two ancient men and women, each with the firepower of nations.

Humanity beheld our freakishness in all its glory, and decided the most sensible course of action was to destroy us.

The Atlantean World War was brief. The cost was high.

Magically radioactive wastes in the Pacific Northwest and half of Poland; the near-extinction of dragonkind; a viral plague that decimated the Atlantean homeland. A hundred thousand headstones, trillions in damage.

At the end, both parties sat down and signed a peace accord.

Flash forward to the late 1960s. By then, the last of the Atlantean race had gathered as refugees on an island off the Massachusetts coast, where they'd been steadily and secretly buying land since the 1940s. The settling of Nantucket (privately called the Unsettlement) would last three decades. In displays of magic unprecedented before and since, the Arcana came together to translocate abandoned human ruins from different parts of the human world. Virtually overnight they created a patchwork Gotham of brilliant, dense, staggering architecture. This vertical sprawl has become known as the city of New Atlantis.

Now, in the modern era, New Atlantis has settled its bones. It has become a world-class city with a world-class economy, powered by the talent and savvy of long-lived beings.

My name is Rune Saint John.

I am, before anything else, a survivor: of a fallen house, of a brutal assault, of violent allies and complacent enemies, of life among a people who turned their back on me decades ago.

Among those who matter I am known and notorious. I am the Catamite Prince; the Day Prince; the Prince of Ruin. I am the last scion of my dead father's dead court, once called the Sun Throne, brightest of all Arcana, now just so much ash and rubble.

These are my accounts.

SUN ESTATE

"—ing, testing, testing, one, two, thr—" I stopped talking in the middle of the word, but moved my lips. I tapped the ear bud with a badly exaggerated gesture.

Across the weed-choked parking lot, Brand stared at me.

"Did I break up again?" I asked innocently. "Sometimes it does that."

"Rune, oh my fucking gods, you will *not* pull this shit with me."

"What?" I said.

"You will keep that thing in your ear, and you will maintain a running commentary, or we will have *words*."

I didn't want to have words. I wanted to use walkie-talkies, like we always did, which made it easy to edit out the parts I didn't want to share with Brand. But Brand's fascination with headsets and "running commentary" was a new thing, now that we had money to afford the equipment.

"Okay," I said. "I promise. But I think the problem may be—" I stopped. "—ive solar interference."

Brand dropped the duffle bag he was holding and started walking over to me.

I decided to move to the other side of our beat-up old Saturn so that its hood was between us. When he was close enough that I could see his genuinely pissed expression, I held up my hands. "I promise."

"What are you planning?" he said.

"Nothing."

"*What?*"

"Fine," I said. "There are going to be monsters. There are always monsters. I don't want you running after me because you think I can't take care of myself. We've talked about this, Brand. You don't walk onto haunted ground, not like this, not unless you've got sigils. And I don't have the right spells stored to cover both of us. I'd spend as much time watching you as I would watching my own back."

"How is this new?" he said in exasperation. "You know I won't run after you. How many treasure hunts have we done?"

Past us rose the iron gates of Sun Estate, topped with rusting fleur-de-lis. A graying sky framed the blunted tips, announcing dawn.

"Sometimes it's worse than I let on," I finally said. Which was true, if not the real reason I was being so uncooperative today. "But it's nothing I can't handle."

"You think I don't know that? Rune, keep the damn earbud in. I know you can do the job."

I lowered my head into a nod, and stepped to the edge of the rough cobblestones. Once, it'd been the visitors' lot. Dead weeds had long since cracked the rock. It was the closest I could get to Sun Estate without actually being on its land, which made it a good staging area for my periodic scavenging forays.

"It's dawn," Brand reminded.

"Yeah," I said.

"So are you ready, or just fucking waiting for a little kid to start singing nursery rhymes in a spooky voice?"

I smiled at him—a real smile. He rolled his eyes back at me, which was his real smile.

I touched my mother's cameo necklace and released its stored spell. Magic shivered loose, tugging at my arms and hair, fluttering my T-shirt beneath my leather jacket.

One step into midair became two, and then three, and then I floated over the two-story fence.

Sun Estate had been one of the very first translocations to Nantucket, decades before the mass translocations of the 1960s and 1970s when Nantucket became New Atlantis.

My father had stolen a Long Island mansion called Beacon Towers back in the 1920s, bewitching land developers into thinking they'd bull-dozed it. This was back in the days when we operated in secret, before the human and Atlantean worlds collided.

Atlanteans had always had a fondness for old, ornate buildings. It took decades of emotional trauma to ripen stone. What better, then, than a mansion from Long Island's Gold Coast? Beacon Towers had been the inspiration for Gatsby. It'd been home to Vanderbilt and Hearst—storied American families who bled unrest.

The original structure was more than 140 rooms under a gothic, tur-reted roofline. Victorian sensibility bred with Moorish citadel. Even in ruin, it was gorgeous.

Every year or two, I made an armed foray onto the abandoned grounds, looking for useful salvage before the specters and wraiths got too stirred up. Nice clothes, preserved in cedar; an undamaged painting worth a year's rent; a set of tarnished silver hidden beneath a floorboard under the butler's desk. Once I'd found a sigil hidden in the dead seneschal's nightstand. I keep that particular sigil concealed under my pants legs, though.

I wasn't there for a treasure hunt, though. Not today.

It's only why Brand thought I was there.

I hovered above a knot of peeling brown roots, once rose bushes that framed the servant cottages, and stared at the gilded remains of my birth-right. The mist had broken up, the closer I got to the mansion. It was an arresting image.

That's as close as I planned on getting to the main house, though.

As soon as I was out of sight of the visitors' lot, I floated down an access road that ran by the beach. The passing years had caked it in sand and dirt, recognizable only by the parallel line of scrub on either side.

The tide was out, the waves lost in a bank of fog as thick as walls. Only the weakest of spirits fluttered about me. Dawn was a time of day called the gloaming, when the more serious spectral threats were crawling in or out of bed. These harmless ghosts simply flickered in my peripheral vision, trapped in their last moments.

I avoided looking at them.

The carriage house was on the north side of the estate, near an ornamental lighthouse. Its stucco had gone gray, peeling in large, scabrous chunks. The line of stable doors had rotted and fallen into the dune grass. The main room—the base of a two-story, crenelated turret—sat behind a rusting iron door.

I hovered above the dirt path that led to it.

And couldn't make myself go closer.

In all my forays, I'd never come to the carriage house. I'd always known I'd need to; but even now, two decades after the slaughter of my father's court, after the night I'd been held and tortured, the memories were too raw.

Three months ago, I'd discovered the identity of one of my abusers from that night. He was dead now, but the revelation was a loose thread, begging to be tugged on. I'd become convinced that I might find something inside the carriage house that would give me more threads to unravel.

And yet, I just stood there, and continued to stare at the iron door.

"Rune?" Brand said in my headset.

"Sorry. I need to be quiet for a little while. I'm trying to maneuver toward that attic stairway. Give me a minute?"

The earpiece went mute.

The door . . . I wouldn't even need a spell, it was so brittle. I could break through with a good kick.

They'd kept me in there for hours while the staff was slaughtered. Women and children. All the live-in help. People I'd known my entire life. *My father.* Barely identified by dental records.

I hadn't been spared violence, but I'd been spared. Why? I hadn't been tortured for information. I'm not even sure it had been entirely for their pleasure. I think they had me there for a reason.

I couldn't move closer to that door. Just stood there, floating. I tried to move forward, but I couldn't. What had happened in that building had infected every part of my life. Everything—everything good, everything new, every success and defeat—existed only in the context of that night.

"Minute's up," Brand said.

His voice was gentle, which instantly had me on alert.

"I'm fine," I said, clearing my throat. Maybe he sensed my hesitation through our Companion bond? He was good at picking up nuances, if I wasn't shielding tight enough.

"Rune," he said. "You know I won't let you go in there, right? Not without me. That's not something I'm going to let you do alone."

I rolled my eyes upwards, as if I could see the earbud. "You know where I am?"

"Of course I do. I've got a GPS app on your phone."

"Oh. Wait. *What?* When the hell did that start?"

"Just since fucking forever."

I ripped my phone out of my pocket with such force that I almost dipped onto the dirt-covered road. I didn't throw it, though, because all my games were on it. I turned it on and swiped through all the apps.

"Do you honestly think you're going to figure how to reprogram it?" Brand said.

"Spying," I said, with four syllables worth of outrage.

"How about we discuss that later. Rune . . . If you try to go in the carriage house without me, I'll be one step behind you with a sledgehammer and matches. There are better places to look for stuff. We don't need to go in there."

I sighed and put the phone back in my pocket. At least he didn't suspect *why* I was there. Our Companion bond was getting stronger as we aged, but it still wasn't telepathy, no matter how good Brand was at reading it.

"Okay," I said. "I'm going to go back and see if there's anything in the attic."

* * *

I covered the ground back to the mansion in half the time. Half an acre ahead of the visitors' lot, I made a soft turn and climbed higher, putting the dead shrubs of a hedge maze underneath me. Not much stirred except for those glass-like ghosts I'd seen earlier, though I checked them out anyway to make sure they weren't something more dangerous. Daytime haunts were almost always translucent, unlike the lumbering, obvious threats of night haunts.

Before I got within twenty yards of the mansion, *almost always* churned out an exception. A daytime haunt—a physical, shuffling creature—staggered around the frame of a greenhouse. I moved a finger over my gold ring, and waited.

If it sensed me, it was indifferent. It was a rare type of skeleton—the proper name escaped me. Formed of the bones of mass murder victims from noble houses, it walked in an unending loop, passing by all the places its component parts had died. I saw the rib cage of a child; the hipbone of a woman; the rawhide skull of what may have been a large man.

"You stopped moving," Brand said.

"I will throw it away and get a burner," I said in exasperation. "Just see if I don't."

"Are. You. Okay."

"There's a . . . go-ryo. A go-ryo. I didn't know the estate had one."

"What's a go-ryo? Is that bad?"

"No. It just is. It's not a threat." I realized—if I had the stomach for it—I could get a better sense of where my people had died by analyzing the go-ryo's bones and comparing them to the places it paused. It was an idea of grim forensic value.

I continued along the outside of the mansion. Salt flavored the morning mist, sharp on my lips. I brushed hair out of my eyes, hesitating, and then turned back toward the go-ryo.

Something—some back-of-the-brain awareness—was niggling me. I didn't know what, until I saw that the go-ryo's uneven gait was caused by the bones of a clubfoot.

A stable boy. He'd tended my father's horses. A bully, in truth, who'd made my life very difficult until Brand became a bigger bully. Those were the bones of Gregor.

There was no easy value in knowing that.

I moved my hand to the pewter ankh around my neck. A touch sprang the stored spell loose. The magic shivered around my fingers, making the knuckles swell. I held out my hand, and magic streamed at the go-ryo.

The spell made a sound like cracking glass. Not a shattering, just a single, sharp, fragile snap. The go-ryo fell apart into pieces. The remains rippled and dissolved, and the wind carried them away as bone meal.

During my time in the Westlands a few months ago, I'd left a lot of ghosts in my wake, but also accrued a lot of favors. I'd bartered one of those favors for an audience with Lady Priestess, the ruling Arcana of the Papess Throne. She'd taught me a deceptively simple spell—at great expense—to lay shades to rest.

It had taken me the better part of a day to duplicate the magic. Each use contained only a single charge. It was not a practical defense for an estate as haunted as mine. Nor had it been a practical bargain. But I was not always a practical person.

"You've stopped again," Brand complained. "This shit is getting old. Is this how you always work when I'm not around? Did you find a sofa?"

"I put the go-ryo to rest."

"I thought it wasn't attacking?"

"It wasn't. I used a spell Lady Priestess taught me."

"Why didn't you save it for something that was attacking? You're not even inside the mansion yet."

"I just wanted to see if I could do it."

Through the Companion bond we shared I felt the echo of his emotions. Anger. Resignation. Maybe a little shame.

"Rune, you've got eight sigils," he said carefully.

"I do."

"You wasted one of them on something that wasn't even a threat. That's . . . I know you're upset, but you don't have the luxury of wasting spells."

Most scions stumbled through life with an armory of sigils behind them. My own ragtag collection was small. "I'm here," I said, floating up to a weathered green door draped in rose vines.

"I can change the subject back just as fucking easily, you know."

"If I run into trouble, I'll abort. I won't take any risks. I promise."

"You'll abort if our connection fails, too."

"And I'll abort if our connection fails," I agreed. "I'm heading in."

We owed this approach to Max, our teenaged ward.

A couple weeks back—insisting he wanted to be more useful to us—he researched old, undigitalized blueprints of Sun Estate in the New Atlantis Archives. He discovered that a structure we'd always assumed to be a shed was actually the entrance to a back stairway that led straight to the smallest attic. In all the decades since Sun Estate fell, I'd barely made forays into the first two floors. I'd never got as far as the attic level. The very nature of the estate's haunting limited my excursions to only a handful of minutes.

The back stairway was both a plus and a minus. On one hand, it gave me direct access to an unplundered level. On the other hand, while I was in it, I was more or less boxed into a fifth-story coffin.

Excepting Lady Priestess's spell, I'd filled my sigils with some of my more aggressive magics. I was confident I could get out of a tight spot, but smart enough not to be cocky about it.

The warped, peeling door cracked open with a tug. Autumn sunlight fell into a narrow space, tangling in spider webs and clouds of dust. I murmured a cantrip—a quick, common form of magic—and a ball of butterscotch light manifested above my head. I sent it up a flight of rickety stairs that were nearly as steep as ladder steps.

Other than my sigils, my most powerful weapon was my sabre, one of the few weapons I retained from my childhood. It was currently curled around my wrist in the shape of a wristguard. I shook my hand, and the wristguard softened and stretched, scraping over my knuckles. I shaped it into a sword hilt. As it settled in my palm, I extended a blade of garnet-colored metal. Innate fire magic made it spark with fat, drifting embers.

"Still with me?" I asked, as I used the sabre blade to burn the cobwebs from my levitating path.

"Still with you. Any beasties?"

"No." I peered upwards to where the stairway switchbacked. "If this works, we may have to start paying Max an allowance."

"Let's see what's in the attic first. If we're taking this risk for an armful of old *National Geographic*s, I'm going to be pissed." There was a pause, and Brand swore softly. "I've got movement from the drone."

"The what now?"

"I bought a drone."

I stopped floating up the stairs. "You're spying on me with drones too?"

"Are these really the questions you need to be asking right now? There are ghouls in the orchard. Doesn't look like they know you're here, though. And I'm not spying on you, I'm watching your *back*, you ungrateful shit."

"I can't believe you bought a drone without telling me. How much did that set us back?"

"Well, I bought it at the discount department store down the street, not the one in 19-fucking-89. Do you even know how cheap drones are now?"

I continued floating up the stairs, slowing at all the turns. The blueprints were right so far; there was no access to any other floors. "Attic door ahead," I breathed.

"The ghouls still aren't moving. I'll keep an eye on them. Sound off every thirty seconds, okay?"

"Roger." I tried to open the door open-handed, but it was jammed in the frame. "I'm touching down. I can't do this while levitating."

"Roger," he said back at me.

I drew the Levitation spell back into me, and lowered to the ground. As I connected with the dusty floorboards, I kept my senses—my will-power—extended, trying to see if anything had reacted to my presence. Nothing pinged. I put my hand back on the doorknob and applied my shoulder. The top panel made a brittle splintering sound, but I was able to scrape the door halfway across the threshold.

A home as big as Sun Estate had more than one attic. This was the west wing's attic, above the family suites. Brand and I had had rooms on the third floor, once upon a time. My father had opted to occupy a tower on the other side of the compound. I'd heard my mother had lived in this wing, too; but she'd died before I was even capable of conscious thought. I had little of her in my life, not even a memory. Just a sigil shaped into an antique, yellowing cameo necklace.

The attic was at least a hundred feet wide. It was the smallest of them, but you could have still stacked ten of my current bedrooms side by side, with space to spare. It wasn't sectioned—just a wide, cavernous space rising to a crossbeamed peak. The hardwood floor was littered with dirt, animal scat, and mice skeletons. The walls were shadowed with water stains. Mother nature hadn't been as hard on the roof as I'd feared; there were no outright holes.

I wondered if the estate would ever be anything other than salvage. The effort to reclaim it was so far beyond my current resources, I didn't even know the shape such a recovery would take.

"Did you find another goddamn sofa?" Brand asked.

"No. Just checking for exits."

"Sure you are."

"Three doors. The one behind me; the one that leads down to the fourth floor; and the servant stairs. The servant stairs are blocked. Looks like a beam fell. See. I was checking. Tell me you're impressed."

"Not everything you do needs to be stuck on the refrigerator with a fucking magnet." But I sensed a warm flicker of approval through our bond.

K. D. EDWARDS

I whispered a cantrip to send two more balls of light above my head, and ran a gaze across the sparse clutter. There didn't seem to be much except two rows of cedar wardrobes, likely for seasonal clothes. I went to the first one and tested the door. It opened in a waft of worm-eaten wood and mothballs. Winter jackets—expensive felts and furs—were arranged on cedar hangers.

"Clothes. Many clothes," I said. "We need a coat for Max, don't we?"

"We're not risking your life for a coat." He paused. "Is my old leather jacket there?"

"The one that made you look like an extra in an '80s action movie? With lots of power ballad soundtracks?"

He ignored me. "Any chests or strongboxes?"

"Oh, tons of them. I just decided to check out the coats first."

Then I reached the end of the wardrobes and saw three cast-iron, filigreed chests. They could literally have been a Wikipedia picture in an article on buried treasure.

"You just found chests, didn't you?" Brand said.

"Three of them. It looks like there are . . ." I bent down and looked at the latch. There wasn't a traditional lock, just a shallow indentation on a deceptively fragile clay disc. "Bloodline wards. They're sealed with bloodline wards."

My mouth went dry. Bloodline wards were expensive ways to seal family secrets. I can't imagine any of my father's people using them, and it was my family attic. Which meant these chests likely belonged to my father.

"Wait!" Brand said, as I transmitted my sabre back into a wristguard, to free up my hands. "Could they be trapped?"

"I'm not sensing any. Just the ward. Why trap it? Only someone keyed to the bloodline can even open it. I'm going to try."

"Be careful."

I put my finger on the clay disc. The hard surface seemed to warm and soften. I pulled my finger away, and saw that the clay retained the oils of my fingertip. I heard—or felt, really—a whirring. The chest clicked.

21

"It worked," I breathed. I put my hands on either side of the chest, and pushed the lid up.

The air inside was not stale. It smelled, for just a moment upon release, like the last person who had sealed the ward, and the last day on which it had been sealed. Freshly cut grass and rosewater cologne.

I gently ran my hand along the top of the contents. There wasn't much. No precious gems, or stock certificates, or bars of gold. Yet for all that, it was a treasure of sorts.

There was a strange sort of pillow, with a belt-like elastic strap. There were crisp, sepia photographs. Some beaten brass jewelry—old, old things, from the days when metal was as rare as diamond. They didn't have the tingling hum of sigils, though. I experienced a brief, stuttering disappointment. What would it have been like, to open a chest filled with sigils?

"Rune?"

"Just . . . mementos, I think. And some old jewelry. I only opened one chest."

"You should open another. You can come back for mementos another time. *Shit.* The ghouls are moving. I'm firing a distraction. Get ready to run, just in case."

From my crouch, I shuffled to the next chest, but only after I pocketed a couple pieces of the jewelry.

"Launched," Brand announced. He'd come armed with a grenade launcher filled with flesh-bombs we'd borrowed from Lord Tower's head of security, Mayan. Flesh-bombs had as much stopping power as water balloons, but were filled with bits of blood and fat from the butcher shop. They hit the ground and created a very intoxicating blast radius for things that didn't get fresh meat often. "They're pulling towards it. You've got to start making your way out."

"Just let me check the other two chests," I said. I disengaged the next bloodline ward, and opened the lid. Snow? It smelled like snowfall. And . . . ambergris cologne?

My father's scent. The flesh on my arms tingled. I flexed my fingers nervously, as if they'd gone numb.

Inside were stacks of clean, manila folders. The tabs were numerically coded.

I picked a few at random and fanned them open. Copies of property deeds—long since irrelevant, in the aftermath of my court's fall. Copies of reports from the Arcanum.

A photograph fell from the third folder. It landed faceup. My brain had trouble making sense of what I saw, because it was Brand, but he was much older than we were now. And then I thought that maybe the picture had been age-progressed, which also made my brain hurt, because it was a stupid thought.

I picked up the picture and realized I was staring at a photo of someone related—biologically related—to my Companion. I thought I was looking at a photo of his father.

I opened the folder.

Reports from private investigators. Medical records. Birth certificates. *Addresses.*

"What's happening?" Brand demanded. "Rune, you're freaking out. Tell me what I'm feeling."

"I . . ."

"Rune!"

I shut the file and took a shaky breath. "It's okay. Just . . . a lot of pictures. There's a picture of my father."

I hesitated for a moment, then kept the file before sealing the chest shut. I shoved the file down the back of my pants, and pulled my shirt over it.

"We . . ." Brand trailed off. He wasn't very good at verbalizing sympathy. "I know it's tough. But you don't have time to linger. Pull out."

"Roger," I said, and leaned over to shut and seal the first chest too. It wasn't a good angle, though, and I pinched my finger in the lid. Swearing, I shook my hurt hand, just as blood began to well from the cut.

"Oh shit," I said.

I could almost feel the house vibrate. It was not a physical sensation; it was just the way my willpower interpreted the stirring of spirits. The ghouls outside were very suddenly the least of my problems. There were things inside the house that smelled my blood, and now knew I was there.

"I cut my hand," I said, springing up. "It's bleeding. I'm not going to be alone for long."

"*Extract*," Brand ordered.

"Tell me twice," I said, running for the stairs. I squeezed through the half-open door and began to skip, sideways, down the steep steps, the better to keep my balance. At the first switchback, I came to a dead stop. My magical senses were useless—I'd stirred up too much activity to spot any single threat. But my normal senses told me all I needed to know. From somewhere below me—and not far—came ragged breathing. There was a gentle scraping sound, like broken fingernails running along wood grain.

If I needed another sign, spiders and beetles began skittering up the stairwell, disappearing into the safety of the attic.

I ran back upstairs with them. I could hold my own in a firefight, but the mansion couldn't. Needing to blow a hole in the stairwell wall would only hasten the ruin.

Since the servant stairs were blocked, I jogged toward a larger stairway that led down one floor, transmitting my sabre back into hilt form as I did. I ran through the floor plan in my head, the memory of it cleaner and brighter than the reality of the molding wallpaper and rugs. At the bottom of the steps, a wide hallway lined with tarnished light fixtures led in two directions—a small schoolroom and chapel on one end; a desanctified sanctum and conservatory on the other end. I started toward the conservatory. There were windows there, a good egress.

As I passed the larger stairway that led to the third floor, a wight crawled up the rotting green runner.

Wights were decaying corpses, undead creatures that enjoyed a sort of painstakingly conditional immortality. They survived as long as they fed. The abandoned estate had no shortage of vermin, though, and the wight had eaten recently. Blood smears from a messy feeding had rejuvenated whatever skin it touched. The decaying monster had smooth, red lips; a single dimpled cheek; and one clear green eye opposite a shriveled socket.

It saw me, and sprang.

I ran a finger across my white gold ring, releasing the Fire spell I'd stored in it. I threw a sphere of superheated air in front of me. The wight passed through it, and its hair and clothing burst into flames. It hit the ground in a panicked roll.

"Wights," I said, before Brand could ask. "If there's one, there will be more. I'm going out a window."

"Go," Brand said.

I ran for the conservatory, hearing coughing gasps from the stairway behind me as more wights closed in. The hallway veered left, and brightened with a tepid gray light. Through a doorway ahead, I spotted a bank of dirt-stained windows. One out of every three panes was broken and covered with dead ivy.

Before I could cross the threshold, my foot broke through a bad floorboard. I managed to recover in a roll while brushing fingers across two of my sigils—my gold ankle chain, the circlet attached to a leather strap around my thigh. The sigils' stored spells flooded loose. Flight and Shield—their release balancing into a gassiness crossed with a bright, fractal light that shimmered around my body. I drew the Flight magic into me for later use, and let Shield sink into my body with a warm glow.

I shifted Fire into my sabre hilt, bolstering its own innate fire magic, so that when I shot the nearest wight with a firebolt it had the potency of a blowtorch flame. It went through the creature's head and it dropped like an emptied sack.

Six other wights, including the one I fought first, were crawling over each other in a seething, cautious approach.

I shot one in the heart; another through the mouth. More wights staggered from the bend in the corridor, joining the mob.

"The ghouls are moving toward you now," Brand said. "They know you're there."

"Almost out," I said. There were too many wights for combat. I scooted back from the threshold, into the conservatory proper. With a raised hand, I peeled the Shield magic from my body and threw it across the open doorway, fastening it to the worm-eaten wood.

I'd have to make my exit from this room. Easy enough. Walls were just a suggestion, really, when you were strong enough to blow them apart.

I ran a finger across my emerald-diamond ring. The Shatter spell slid loose, vibrating along my fingernails. I studied the bank of windows as I walked toward them, hand outstretched. The broken panes had already done enough weather damage; fingers of mold and fungus spread from the openings.

Behind me, the wights beat against my Shield. Their blows made faint crackling sounds.

Lifting my arm, I punched through the wall with Shatter in an explosion of brick and metal and vine. Glass shards sparkled in the light of the rising morning. In the smoking aftermath, fresh air seeped into the room, and I walked to the opening I'd made.

Before I reached it, someone coughed.

Sitting at a leaf-strewn desk at the back of the room was a wight, a very old one. Its posture was prim and unnervingly proper, as if it waited to conduct a lesson. It possessed a vanity unusual for wights—it had spread blood across its entire face, restoring it to a full, mocking beauty. Violet eyes narrowed at me.

It launched itself with the speed of a bullet.

I barely had time to pivot. It landed on the wall, clawed hands and fingers digging into the soft wood. I sent my willpower into my sabre. The garnet blade extended. The Fire spell made it burst into flame, setting floating dust afire.

I ducked under its next leap, bringing my sword in a backhanded slice. A line of fire cut across the creature's rags. It shrieked and hit the ground in a crouch. Before I could regain my balance, it jumped at me. Its claws raked along the sleeve of my jacket. The wards in the leather held; but the wight's nails created deep, bleeding wounds along my wrist and the back of my hand.

My blood spattered the dirty floor. Something in the distance screamed. I felt the focus of the estate's diseased life pressing in on me.

I grabbed my sabre with both hands for a powerful downward thrust. It sliced along the side of the wight's head, shearing off an ear, cutting through brittle skull. The wight went batshit. Pain drove it to abandon all caution, and it came at me with claws extended. I let my sabre blade crumble into a stiletto for close combat and stabbed its neck, then its collarbone on the back draw. Its claws dug flesh out of my own neck, but snagged in the collar of my jacket.

I finished it with a quick thrust through its withered heart. It fell to the ground. Its hands, covered in my blood, clung to the hem of my jeans. As I watched, the skin brightened until they were smooth and lovely, like a concert pianist.

There was a creaking sound. The wights outside the room were digging around my Shield, crumbling the old wood of the lintel.

I reached inside me and brought out the Flight spell. I let the buoyancy surround me. My clothes fluttered, as if caught in a strong wind.

I moved to the hole in the wall, stepped onto the sharp, broken rim, and shot into the air like a superhero.

"*Fuck*," Brand said when I landed in the visitor's lot. He was standing next to my car, putting a cat-sized drone into the duffle bag.

"I've had worse," I said, gingerly touching the gashes on my neck. I transmuted the sabre into wristguard form to free my other hand.

"You've got a Healing spell?" he said.

"I do," I said, and ran a thumb across a platinum disc slotted to my leather belt. I touched the wounds on my neck and hands, wincing as the flesh reddened and sunburned, and itched shut.

Brand studied me quietly.

"I've had worse," I said again. "It's okay."

"We can't do that again," he said. "Not without backup."

"I got out. It's fine."

Brand climbed on top of the hood of my car, ignoring my sounds of protest. He clambered to the roof, and shaded his eyes with his fingers to stare at the mansion. I didn't have to ask what he was looking at. He'd have seen the wall explode from here.

"Aren't we planning on living there again?"

"The windows were already broken," I protested.

"That's your room now."

"It's the *conservatory*. The windows were already broken. It . . ." I sighed. "You're right. It's all going to hell in there, Brand. The mansion is breaking down. I'm not sure it'll stand much longer."

"So we reclaim it."

"How? You just said yourself I can't go too deep into it without backup. One big fight, and it all falls down."

Brand looked down at me, eyes still shaded. He gave me a rare, small smile. "You'll find a way. You're a stubborn little shit when you want to be. Come on, let's go home. I bet Queenie baked cookies."

HALF HOUSE

Companions, an ancient institution, have lost favor in the modern world. As with most things—human and Atlantean—instant gratification is a cult following, and Companions are a decades-long investment.

It worked like this:

You find a good human candidate. An infant. You gamble on this infant by learning as much as you can about its genetic lineage. You gamble that it'll be a perfect match for your own infant. You gamble that it'll be the perfect friend; the perfect advisor; the perfect killer. Then you stick this candidate—this baby—into your own child's crib, speak a few powerful verses of magic, and metaphysically duct-tape them together for the rest of their natural lives.

You don't see many Companions today, except in older Atlanteans from the greater houses. Addam's brother had a Companion. Lord Tower—my benefactor—had a Companion. I had Brand. But even in these cases, the utilization was so *different*. Lord Tower's Mayan was the head of Lord Tower's security division. Christian's Eve was his formal consort. Brand was my partner. But one thing that tied all Companions together was that they were, without compromise, deadly. From childhood, they trained as lethal bodyguards.

Whatever my father had meant Brand to be, Brand had become more. He was more than just a Companion. He told me otherwise—he insisted that being a Companion was his purpose. If that's true, then so was the reverse: he was my purpose too. My first idea of the world was a soft mattress and wooden bars—and Brand, there, right next to me, the biggest thing in all of Existence.

He'd saved my life, over and over. He'd saved me from things worse than death. He'd saved me from myself.

I always knew he'd come from somewhere. That was the nature of

Companions. He came from a human family. But the details of his lineage, outside anonymous medical records, had always been beyond my reach.

Now I had a file that told me *everything* about his past.

There were medical histories in the records, stretching back three generations. Pictures of male relatives from both his maternal and paternal line. Dozens and dozens of pictures, from various points in their lives.

It made me sick. It literally made me ill. The files treated him like a thoroughbred. The details—the comparisons they made against his living relatives, to hedge the gamble on how he'd mature—were filled with violations. The quality of his relatives' teeth. How they aged. Hereditary diseases. The size of their dicks.

The file indicated where he was born. An address where his parents lived. It was over thirty-five years old, but it'd still provide a starting point, if we wanted to look deeper.

I wasn't sure I could do that. Because I was a selfish, selfish man.

I put my finger on two of the pictures and stared at them, feeling a hard, frightened lump forming in my chest.

Brand's older brothers looked like him.

I woke the next morning when something heavy landed on me. I blinked myself into a bleary awareness as Brand kicked off his running shoes and buried his head in my comforter.

"There's light coming through the window," I said, clearing my throat. "That means the sun is still on the wrong side of the sky. Why are you waking me up while the sun is on the wrong side of the sky?"

"I thought you were up already," he said.

He most likely had a five-mile run under his belt; had made breakfast; and probably been through one or two training sessions. But, on the plus side, he always got sleepy again late in the morning right about the time I was banging on my snooze alarm, so it offered me the illusion that we shared a wake-up time together.

"I think you should go to your own bed," I decided. "This never ends well for me. You sleep for ten minutes and then start talking about painting the living room."

He pressed into the cool corner of my pillow and shoved me toward the edge of the mattress, just like he'd done when we were kids.

I stared down at him, thinking about the file I'd hidden in my bureau.

Why did his parents give him up? Did they do it willingly? Did my father *buy* him? What would I find in the records, when I had the balls to read further?

"The *fuck* is going on with you," he muttered into my comforter.

"Nothing."

"Rune."

"Just a dream."

"At this hour, it's called a daydream, you lazy ass. I thought you were already up and bitching about coffee? I want you to go through your sword stations today. I can't believe you let a wight lay hands on you. A *wight.* They're like the cannon fodder of the undead world."

"It was an old wight. An ancient wight."

"How is that better? Something that gets discounts at fucking matinees, and goes to early bird specials?" He pulled the pillow out from under me and threw it clear across the room—which, granted, was only nine feet away. We lived in a sliver of a brownstone on a twelve-foot-wide property. "Wake up!"

"I am. You've got me thinking about coffee," I said.

"He's going to start demanding an allowance if you use him as slave labor," Brand warned me.

"The barista?"

"Max."

"What does Max have to do with the barista?"

"Who's talking about a barista?" he said, shifting so he could scowl at me.

It suddenly felt like we were having two different conversations. Only, Brand wasn't looking puzzled. Brand had gone very, very still.

"Rune, did you text Max and ask him to get you a coffee?"

"Max said I sent him a text asking me to get him a coffee?"

"I saw it," he said. "He ran down to the corner."

"But—"

Brand launched off the bed. His bare feet were already slapping down the metal rungs before my heart even had a chance to start beating hard.

I jumped up and swiped my thigh circlet off the bureau, along with a leather bracelet fitted to hold a sigil shaped as a platinum disc. They were the only sigils I didn't sleep with; they snagged on the sheets. Wearing only boxers, I ran down the stairs after Brand.

I didn't stop for boots. Or my pants. I flew out the front door, passing by our housekeeper Queenie, who stood in the kitchen archway with kitchen gloves, a dripping sponge, and an astonished look.

Brand was already halfway up the cul-de-sac. I panted a cantrip, and a burst of adrenaline tightened my calves. By the time we hit the main street, we were abreast each other.

"Stop," I said. "Brand, stop!"

He gave me a wild look, but stopped, scanning either end of the busy avenue. We were a dozen blocks away from the skyscrapers of downtown, but it was still pure city congestion, and there were multiple coffee shops in either direction. Max liked the one with fat yellow sofas in the lobby, though.

Before Brand could take off again, I whispered another two cantrips, hardening the skin on our soles. Cantrips were barely parlor tricks; but they'd keep our feet from getting sliced open too badly.

"We need to think this through," I said. "If someone is trying to snatch him, he may not even be in the coffee shop."

"How many spells do you have on you?" he asked.

"I didn't refill all of them yet. Just Shield and Heal. And I've got Exodus."

"Fuck. We want to find Max, not turn him into a crater."

We began jogging toward the nearest coffee shop, which gave me enough time to complain. "We live in a nine-foot-wide house. Why would you think I'd *text* Max?"

"Because I've fucking met you," Brand said. Frustration tightened the fine wrinkles around his eyes. "Is it the Hanged Man? Do you think it's the Hanged Man?"

"I don't know," I said. "We've heard nothing from his court. This wouldn't be his first move on Max."

"Who else would take him? Lure him outside?"

"Anyone who's met us?" I said. "Maybe it's not about him at all. Maybe someone is getting back at us."

Brand's pocket began to sing Green Day's "Basket Case." His eyes widened and he pulled it out, sliding a thumb across the screen and putting it on speaker.

Quinn didn't even wait for a greeting.

"Find him," the teenager said. "Hurry. You don't have much time."

Quinn was a prophet who usually spoke in riddles with messed-up verb tenses. It never boded well when he made clear-cut sense.

"Who has him?" I said. I took advantage of our pause to tie the leather strap of my thigh sigil around my leg. "Where is he, Quinn? We need information."

"The scarred man's people. He's being taken to a black car." Quinn paused, then added, in his much more normal voice, "Sometimes the black car is a helicopter, but the scarred man usually doesn't want to spend the money on that, because he thinks you're really stupid."

"He'll find out how stupid we are," Brand promised. "Who—"

"Oh! Park! Trees! There are trees in a park, and Max, and the crowbar. The crowbar's there!"

There was a public park behind Half House, in the other direction. Brand and I turned and ran like hell. On all sides of me, I noticed that people were stopping and pulling out their phones. I was going to go viral, in my boxer shorts, which was perfect, because there wasn't nearly enough gossip about me.

We ran off the street, down an alley that led to one of the park's side gates. Summer had cooled into autumn, and the concrete was littered with the first bright leaves of fall. People were milling around for an early lunch, blocking our path. We dodged around those we could, and sent others flying.

"If they're moving to cars, they'll be there or there," Brand said, finally sounding a little winded himself. He pointed to the access roads that criss-crossed the walking paths. "Quinn? Are you still there?"

"I need to hang up," Quinn said. He sounded like he was running too.

"Help us first!" Brand said. "Where is he?"

"Um . . . Go toward the road where the oil is shaped like a garden rake."

"We are going to have such a *talk!*" Brand said. "Try harder!"

At that point, I tried to run around a pebbled asphalt golem, and tripped over someone's duffle bag. I stumbled and hit a cashew vendor with the edge of my shoulder. The entire cart groaned and overturned, sending boiling peanut oil across the pavement. The spill made splatter patterns, one of which looked like a godsdamn garden rake. It pointed to the access road on our left.

Brand grabbed my arm and pulled me to my feet. We ran in that direction.

"There!" Brand said.

A football field's length away, two SUVs were parked along the side of the access road, near a huge fountain pool that had yellow warning tape around it. A group of men in tactical black was herding someone to the cars. Max's white-blond hair glowed like a bull's-eye in their center.

"Too far," I said.

They outnumbered and outgeared us, but the cars were the real threat. We needed to stop them from getting in those cars.

Or, at least, we needed to stop the cars from leaving the park.

I turned in a quick circle. People. Vendors. Children. Lots of children, milling around with parents and school groups. And running through them, toward the cashew cart mess, a guarda patrol officer in his green and amber uniform.

Before Brand could yell at me to move quicker, I nodded at the approaching guarda officer.

"What the fuck will the guarda be able to do that we can't?" Brand said.

"You'll see." I ran up to the official. Before the young man could ask what the disturbance was about, I said, "An underage scion is being kidnapped. Initiate the child abduction protocols."

"E-Excuse me?" the guarda official said, caught between affront and surprise. "Who the bloody hell are—"

"I am Lord Sun, heir to the Sun Throne, and you will *initiate the protocols NOW!*"

New Atlantis was not a democracy. It was a hill. There were people on top of the hill. There were people afraid at the boulders that could be rolled down the hill. The guarda official didn't waste time with guesswork; he recognized my standing, stared off into the near distance, and acted.

Whatever signal he sent to the protective wards happened almost immediately. Magic erupted around us, a sourceless, electrical feeling that came from every direction at once. The wards, hidden beneath the soil lining the park's perimeter, exploded into barriers of pale lavender energy. It was as good as a cage door swinging shut. No one would be allowed to pass through until a full guarda patrol was onsite.

I shook my wrist, transmuting my sabre into hilt form. With a flicker of willpower, a smoking garnet blade extended from the hilt. The guarda official blinked at it with an expression not unlike relief, because no average scion would have a weapon like that, which meant he was right to trust me.

"Stay with us," I told him.

"Can—my lord—I should radio it in."

"Radio it in, then. Send help to my side. Then follow." The man fumbled for the wireless radio in his belt, and trailed us as we began to run to the SUVs.

By the time we were abreast of the cordoned-off fountain, we could see the kidnapper's frustrated expressions as they stared at the barriers. Their confusion didn't last long, though. One raised a shout and pointed toward me. Five of them pulled bladed weapons and stood their ground, while two others grabbed Max by the arms and hustled him down a walking path away from the cars.

"You're faster," I said to Brand. "Go after Max. I'll handle the others."

"There's five of them," Brand said calmly. His face had gone blank, and he had a switchblade in hand. I don't even know where he'd hidden it in his running shorts.

"So? You need me to take your guys, too?" I asked.

He gave me a cool look, but peeled off and ran to flank the men who had Max. He could hold his own against two men, especially if Max was able to grief the person restraining him. I'd have to trust in that—I needed to focus on my own fight.

None of the men coming toward me had guns—just knife blades and a single sword. The one with the sword ran in the lead. I held up my garnet sabre blade and met his swing. My blade sheared off the last foot of his blade, leaving him with a small, broken edge. The man swore and backpedaled. I didn't follow. I let the moment settle, to see what they'd do next. I also ran a finger across my thigh sigil, releasing Shield. Faceted light spread—and sunk—into my skin.

"You will yield," I told them. "It's as simple as that. The boy is mine. He is under my protection. Do you know who I am, and what I could do to you?"

The man with the sword—average face, brown hair, brown eyes—gave me a surprisingly heavy look. "Yes, sir, I surely do. We don't have a choice in this, though."

He held up his hand and twisted his fingers in quick gestures. Two of the men veered off to my left; two went right; and he stayed in front.

Two came at me first, one from each side. I jumped at the one on my left. He dodged my sword and swiped at my wrist tendons. My Shield deflected it with a sizzle. I blocked his next thrust with a Shielded forearm, spun back, and parried the second kidnapper's stab. They disengaged immediately while a third kidnapper danced in with a slice, withdrawing before I could counter. My Shield sparked and saved me, filling the air with a smoky leak of energy.

They were weakening my Shield with multiple cuts. Professionals. Professionals wouldn't break easily, which left me with so few options.

I ducked around one, changed my sword beat, and hit him with a compound attack that sliced open his cheek and sent his knife flying. Before he could recover, I speared him through the heart. It would have taken too long to pull my blade free, so I let it dissolve with a fiery hiss. When the leader came at me with his broken sword, I shot him with a firebolt. He swerved, taking only a singeing shot across his bicep.

Another came at me from the side. I dodged his swipe, pushed in, and put my sabre hilt against his throat while extending a new molten blade. The garnet blade foamed out his head. He dropped and slid off my sword. I spun to block another advancing kidnapper.

My bond with Brand went cold—frosted by the very unique adrenaline surge he got when he engaged. I tried to set my anxiety for him aside, but I'd never managed that battle fugue as well as he did. So I turned my worry into anger, and my anger into fuel.

The remaining three pressed in. I dropped into a defensive stance, backing into a line of shrubs. The shrubs protected my rear but limited my mobility.

Then I stumbled. I fucking stumbled and went down hard. My bleeding foot was caught under a loop of tree root.

A kidnapper swung back for a vicious downward blow. My hand landed on a metal rod as I scrabbled. I wrapped my fingers around it and swung up. The shock of metal against metal sang up my arm. I surprised a moment's hesitation out of the man, but I was still sprawled on the ground.

My Atlantean Aspect—the physical manifestation of my magic and bloodline—answered my desperation.

Sunlight-colored fire raced along my arms. Flickers of it danced under my eyelashes. I pumped it full of willpower, and the light blazed so bright that it spotted the kidnapper's vision. When he staggered, I put a firebolt through his mouth. The man screamed flames, and fell.

I stood up and dropped the metal rod. As it hit the ground, I saw it was a crowbar.

"Enough!" I said, and it was as if I exhaled fire. *"Yield!"*

"That we cannot do, sir," the leader said hoarsely, and unsnapped a sphere from the back of his belt. He pulled a pin and tossed it. For a moment I thought it was a bad throw—until it dropped into the fountain and exploded in a huge, angry geyser.

A creature shot from the depths like a startled cat. It—she—landed on all fours. Her weed-like dreadlocks, serrated like alligator tails, dripped onto the flagstone patio. She was Jenny Greentooth, a dangerous water hag.

Jenny Greentooth spun in a furious circle. The first thing she saw was the guarda I'd spoken to, who was running up to help me. He'd drawn a gladius, but didn't even have time to raise his arm before Jenny Greentooth was on top of him, digging hunks of flesh out of his cheek with her mossy claws. Fungus spread from the touch, killing healthy tissue in horrific fast-forward. By the time the man dropped, he didn't have enough face left to scream.

The last two kidnappers took off at a run. Before I could go after them, Jenny sprang. The leader was able to get clear, but his partner staggered to the ground under Jenny's thrashing fury.

Brand was somewhere fighting. The leader was getting away. And a very pissed-off water elemental wasn't going to stop with two deaths. Too many things to handle at once.

Then I heard the high-pitched screams of nearby children, and knew I didn't have a bloody choice.

"Stop!" I roared at the elemental. "Look! *Look!* That man—that was one of the ones who hurt you. No one else!"

Jenny hissed from her squat over the now-dead man, and turned to me. She smelled like crushed dandelion stems. The grenade had left a long cut along her side that bled green.

"There will be consequences, if you hurt anyone else," I warned her. "Be smart. Go back to your den."

"Two-legged-air-sucking-*infestations!*" she screamed.

"Go back to your den," I repeated.

She shrieked at the ground while curling her claws into fists.

I knew she'd made up her mind a half-second before she vaulted toward me.

My Aspect flared, broiling the air. I rolled away from her leap, and fire trailed me in thick tracers. Jenny Greentooth's hair melted with a fatty popping sound. She rolled into a ball, regained balance, and charged me. I lifted my sabre hilt and shot three firebolts into her gut. She dropped in her tracks. It was not a killing blow, but it was fire, and water elementals had a weakness to flame.

Hunched over her injury, she stumbled toward the edge of the fountain and dove into its shallows. She didn't resurface.

Through my bond, I felt Brand. It was a staccato thrum of victory, the way he always felt when he took down his enemies. Brand didn't tend to leave survivors, either. He didn't like that movie shit when they jumped back up after you thought they were dead. Which meant we'd probably killed anyone who could tell us what the hell was happening.

Except for the two last kidnappers who'd run away from me.

I took off after them, glad that whatever metaphysics powered my fiery Atlantean Aspect kept my underwear from burning away too.

The men had parkoured over shrubs and stone benches, and made a beeline for a crowded area of the park. The abduction protocols were still active, so they'd be looking to lose themselves in a mob.

I ran, and tried not to feel how much my feet hurt. I could just still see the kidnappers ahead. *Too far.* They'd gained too much of a lead.

And then the violet ward by the main gates parted like a curtain. A phalanx of guarda officers rushed through. Striding in their lead, a sword in hand, was a tall, handsome man with sandy blond hair.

Addam touched a sigil on his belt and pointed at the two men. Stalagmites burst from the earth underneath them. One of the kidnappers was tossed in one direction while his severed leg flew in another. The other kidnapper—the leader—backtracked to his left and ran into the mouth of a hedge maze.

I was closer now. Addam would have my back in a minute, but a minute might give the kidnapper enough time to go to ground.

I ran into the hedge maze.

The startled pedestrian chatter was immediately muffled by leafy branches, which rose a good foot above my head. The path was swept clear—nothing to track—so when I hit the first fork, I had no idea which way to go.

I've never had a luxury of sigils, not like most scions. In a way, though, that made me better, because desperation taught me to use my own magic in very economical ways.

With a burst of willpower, I pulled Shield off my body and slammed it onto the ground in front of me. I stepped on a circle of vibrating air, and forced the Shield into a rising pedestal. I jerked upwards in stages, arms thrown out for balance, until I was above the top of the hedges.

The kidnapper was only one row away, doubling back on a parallel path.

I jumped off the pedestal, clearing the row. I managed to grab the collar of his black jersey and knock him off his feet. We hit the ground and rolled, only an arm's length apart. I swung up my sabre hilt, just as he swung his broken sword. The blade caught the hilt guard. Neither of us had good footing. Both sword and sabre flew into the foliage.

The man went for a blade in his chest holster. I touched a platinum disc looped by a leather thong around my wrist, the only spell I had left. Sunburn-warm magic covered my hand.

Like I said, desperation had always been my angry teacher. Even healing magic could be a weapon, with the right mind-set.

I slapped my hand over his right eye and focused the Healing into a pinpoint. The normal burning sensation that accompanied aid dug into his skull like a laser. He'd have the eyesight of a teenager when he was able to stop screaming in pain.

I grabbed my sabre hilt while he rolled around the ground in agony. I put the hilt against his forehead and said, "Stay still, or die."

The man stopped thrashing, biting down so hard that his screams distorted his throat.

"Is the Hanged Man moving on me?" I asked. The man kept his jaw clenched, spit making his lips slip against each other. I dug my sabre hilt into his forehead. "Is he?"

Turns out, it wasn't spit. It was foam. Green foam.

The man kept convulsing for seconds after he was dead. I sat back on my haunches in disbelief and stared at him.

"Rune!" Addam shouted. He ran past the row I was in, slammed to a stop, ran back. Three members of the guarda were on his heels. They came to an unsure stop and looked at the dead body.

"Poison tooth," I said angrily. "What sort of 1950s James Bond crap is that?"

Addam—who was sort-of my boyfriend—helped me up. His eyes flickered across my injuries. Bleeding feet. Blistered and bleeding hand. Bleeding shoulder from the cashew cart.

He said, in the faint bite of a Russian accent, "Your boxers have little smiley faces, Hero."

I was too upset for a comeback. And I was worried about Brand, even though I knew he'd survived his fight. I looked behind Addam, at the guarda. "My Companion, Lord Brandon Saint John, went to fight my ward's kidnappers. I need to know if they're both okay."

"Another unit already radioed in, Lord Sun. They're fine, and moving this way."

I gave the officer a small nod, and let Addam help me out of the hedge maze.

While we walked, I said, "Quinn?"

He nodded. "We were eating nearby. I was with him when he called you. What has happened, Rune? Who tried to take Max?"

"I don't know. I don't . . ." Two of the guarda were following, while the third had stayed with the body of the kidnappers' leader. It would be fantastically unwise to even breathe the Hanged Man's name in mixed company.

Three months ago, I'd learned that the Hanged Man, Arcana of the Gallows, had a prior claim on my ward. But with the fall of Max's court, the Lovers, I'd hoped the Hanged Man would lose interest in the association.

"I don't know," I said again. "And hey. Thanks for coming to my rescue. I could get used to this."

"You appeared to have the matter well in hand."

We left the hedge maze. Addam's brother, Quinn, stood by an oxidized copper fountain—not the one with a pissy elemental—throwing pennies into the water. When he saw us, he frowned. There was a mustard stain at the corner of his lips.

"Where's the crowbar?" he asked. "Didn't you beat him to death with the crowbar? You almost always do."

I said, "It bothers me you always think I'm going to pick the most violent possibility."

I looked in the direction Brand had gone. A small crowd of guarda was coming toward us, and in their middle I saw Max's pale head, and Brand's black hair. I turned to the guarda with the handheld radio. "Are you taking the bodies to the morgue? I want to know if anyone claims them. I want to know if you find any markings, anything that may identify them."

I had power. I had plenty of power. But that didn't mean I had position, which was always a problem when matters got political. I caught the guards trading looks between me and Addam—who came from a court with much more administrative power than I did. I said, pointedly, "I'm happy to have Lord Tower make the request, if you want."

The man blanched. "No, Lord Sun. I mean, yes, Lord Sun, I'll pass along word of your request."

I started toward Brand.

He wasn't limping, but there was blood on his thigh. I'd have to rely on Addam for a Healing spell, since I'd used mine. I knew Addam had Healing spells without asking. He'd told me recently that the daily storing of Healing spells was only one of the small ways I'd changed his life.

Brand strode ahead of his party and glared at my injuries. "You fucking led me to believe you could handle a half dozen men."

"I lulled them into a false sense of security with my bleeding. Your leg?"

"Fine."

"Any chance you left some men alive for questioning?"

"Why? So they could pop back up and stab me when I'm victoriously pumping my fist in the fucking air?"

I smiled, but only for a second. "Max?"

"He's shocky. We need to get him home. We need to figure out what the hell just happened. What's going to happen."

I looked behind Brand, toward Max, whose beautiful fae features were filled with the hollow remains of spent emotion. I went up to him and put my hands on his shoulder. When he wouldn't meet my eyes, I pressed my thumbs along his jaw and gave his chin a little shake.

He blinked and said, "I dropped your coffee."

Then he started to cry. I pulled him into me.

Behind me, Brand said, "Maybe we should call the Tower."

And I heard Quinn say, miserably, "No. Not yet. He never likes what you do next."

JIRVAN

Months ago, I'd been involved in a raid that took down Lady Lovers, a corrupt Arcana. Through a series of events that didn't reflect poorly on me at all, I'd found myself chained in a secret room while Lady Lovers decided whether I was worth the effort of reprisal. In the end, we'd made a deal. For one of her sigils, I would safely deliver a package to a destination of her choosing. She promised it would not interfere with my benefactor's agenda in any way, nor would it intrinsically cause harm to me or mine. I accepted that sucker bet, because my personal armory of sigils was catastrophically limited, and owning another one was a life-changing opportunity.

The "package" turned out to be her seventeen-year-old grandson, Matthias Saint Valentine. And Max's "destination" was his age of majority—four years in the future.

Vows among Atlanteans carried power and consequence. I hadn't known—still didn't know—if breaking that vow would rebound on me. But over the last few months, Max had become a part of the household. He and Brand sniped at each other with the affection of brothers; and anything that put more love in Brand's heart was something I'd fight to preserve.

The loose thread to the arrangement was the Hanged Man. We'd learned that Max had been promised to him as marital leverage between the Heart Throne and Gallows. I suspected—based on absolutely no evidence or fact—that Lady Lovers' deal, arranged in the last moments of her court, was an attempt to spare her grandson this future. I'd like to think some shred of decency had illuminated her mistakes in the end.

The Hanged Man's court operated on the fringes of Atlantean society. Once upon a time, the Gallows had served a purpose. Much in the same way that Lady Lovers' Heart Throne had served a purpose, before she corrupted it with rape and human slavery. The Gallows had been the patron of victims, and a recourse for the wrongfully accused. It had treated death with honor and reverence. It had believed in justice.

In the modern age, it had become its reverse. The Hanged Man was a killer. He'd left his humanity behind centuries ago, and, in the days before Atlantis was revealed and a peace treaty signed, was linked to some of the worst human myths.

He was surrounded by no great houses. His rule on his court was absolute and unchallenged. He was a monster to monsters, even in a city like New Atlantis.

But I'd survived monsters before.

We accepted a ride in one of the guarda cars.

Addam sat next to me in one of the two backseats. His hands kept itching toward his platinum disc sigils, the way he always got when he wanted to maul me with a Healing spell. "Your hand looks very bad," he said, concern sharpening the consonants of his Russian accent. "And your feet are black."

"Cantrip blowback," I said. Another side effect of quick, cheap magic; I was losing the outer layer of skin. "It'll hold."

"Heal him," Brand said from the front seat.

Addam touched his sigil. The warmth of the spell filled the air, then he set about sunburning my injuries back into health.

We soon pulled up in front of Half House. In silence, we got out, and filed into the narrow townhouse. Queenie was waiting in the living room, twisting a dishtowel in her hands. She took one look at Max, and grabbed a blanket off the sofa.

"You look cold?" she said, in her halting way of talking.

Max sat down in an armchair and buried his head in his hands.

"Tell me what's happened, Rune," Addam said, now that the door was closed behind us. "Quinn only mentioned a—Quinn? A scarred man?"

"It was the scarred man," Quinn said. He was wiping away the mustard stain with the end of his tongue.

"Who does the scarred man work for, Quinn?" Brand asked.

"The Hanged Man. But you guessed that, right? He and the Hanged Man overlap in almost everything, except for their legs." He gave Brand's eye roll a stubborn look. "It's clearer than you think."

"It really isn't," Brand said.

I didn't say anything. I just stared at Max, trying to figure out an easy way to snap him out of his fugue. An easier way than what I intended to do next, at least.

As Addam activated a second healing sigil to deal with the cut on Brand's leg as well as his own black feet, I started upstairs. Instead of going to my own room on the fourth floor, I stopped on the second. On one end was a bathroom. On the other was Max's room.

I went into Max's room and began, methodically, to tear it apart.

I tried not to fling everything into chaos, but I needed to be thorough. By the time the second drawer bounced on the mattress, Brand was standing in the doorway. Max was behind him, face alternating between red and white.

"What are you doing?" Brand demanded.

"Looking for the letters," I said.

"What?" he said at the same time Max whispered, "Rune."

"The Hanged Man is old guard," I said. "There are rules. Where are they, Max?"

"I," he whispered. Brand turned to drill him with a look. "I didn't want to put you in any . . . I . . . You've done so much already."

"None of that was your call to make," I said. "None of it. I am your guardian. I was just forced to *kill* for you. An officer of the guarda *died* for you. *Where are they?*"

Max stumbled over to his desk. He reached under the drawer and pulled something loose with a ripping sound. A bundle of letters—heavy, expensive ragcloth—were circled with a piece of torn masking tape.

I yanked the bundle apart. I handed half to Brand, and took the other. I ordered the shell-shocked Max downstairs to be fed and watered by Queenie. Together, Brand and I started to read through the numerous, increasingly less vague entreaties, in which the Hanged Man's people asserted his claim on Max.

It took the better part of half an hour. By the end of it, Addam, Brand, and I had moved to the third floor, which was a single open space I'd turned into my sanctum. Sanctums were the heart of every major Atlantean household; a blessed and highly personal space where we meditated over our empty sigils, filling them with magic.

"I don't know the rules," Brand said, running a tired hand over his face. "Are these important? We already knew the Hanged Man was interested in Max. He sent that letter months ago, remember? And Quinn's hinted that we're going to need to face him eventually."

"But he hadn't asserted his rights in that letter we saw. Max hid these—hid the formal claims."

"So what does this mean?" Brand asked.

"It means we've lost time," I said. "No more grace period. We're well into stage two, which involves dead men and screaming children."

"But if he's moved against you . . ." Addam said. "That is actionable, yes? That permits you to act."

"It would, if we could prove the kidnappers operated on the Hanged Man's word. Do you think we'll be able to prove that?"

"Quinn saw it," Addam said, but hesitantly.

"I will not involve Quinn in this." Which opened up a whole other can of worries. "Don't get me wrong, Addam, I am grateful as all hell for what he did today. But he's supposed to be medicated. This isn't healthy for him. How did he see all this through the drugs? As clearly as he did?"

"You're important to him. He says important things still break through the medication. He is . . . most evasive on this point." I could tell that it bothered Addam—or that something about it bothered him—but filed it away for future consideration.

Brand stared at me. "Are you honestly telling me we can't make the first move?"

"Not the kind you want us to make," I said. I sorted the letters in my hand. One of them had a simple red and black business card folded into it. I showed it to Addam. "Jirvan. Do you know anyone called Jirvan, related to the Hanged Man?"

"I do not. I know very little of—him—or his associates."

Him. That's the sort of Arcana the Hanged Man was. People hid from him with pronouns.

Without another word, I left the sanctum and climbed the stairs to my bedroom. Brand followed, and Addam behind him.

My phone was charging on the bureau by the window. I picked it up, glanced at the business card, and dialed. It was answered on the second ring.

I said, "We will parlay on neutral ground. Today."

Magic is infinite. Our ability to tap into it is not.

My own resources were more stretched than most of the ruling class. When my father's court was destroyed some twenty years ago, all of his wealth vanished with it. That included his sigils—the most powerful device a scion possessed. Using them, we were able to store, and re-store, single-use spells through highly individualistic acts of meditation. While most Atlanteans were capable of cantrips—small, showy parlor tricks—it took a sigil to focus truly strong acts of magic.

As a lost art, the number of existing sigils—and their overpowered cousin, the mass sigil—was fixed. I retained only a handful from my youth, a ragtag collection composed of a white gold ring, a gold ring, a cameo necklace, a pewter ankh, a circle attached to a leather strap that I kept on my thigh, and a gold ankle chain. I'd obtained a seventh sigil from Lady Lovers, Matthias's deposed grandmother. And I had an eighth as a gift from Quinn, for saving Addam's life.

Lost art or no, most greater houses were swimming in sigils. Arcana courts had *armories* of them. Just about the only edge I had was my own innate ability. While the potential for sigil magic was the same for any scion, the power to utilize that potential was not.

I was a very, very good magic user. I was my father's son. My throne may have toppled, but not the skill and bloodline that had raised it in the first place.

I picked the park as neutral ground. Literally, the spot of my fight. Not only did it seem fitting, but also it allowed for showmanship. By the time Jirvan arrived I was bending over and staring thoughtfully at a bloodstain.

The Atlantean who approached us—Jirvan—was scarred. He was *very* scarred. Healing magic had reconstituted as much as possible, but every inch of exposed skin still had the shiny, plasticky uniformity of old burns. Underneath that, he was an average-looking man, almost elderly. He walked with a pronounced limp in his left leg.

Quinn had mentioned something about a leg, hadn't he? That was the thing about Quinn's prophecies: you could never tell when you needed to take something literally or metaphorically. Sometimes Jell-O just meant Jell-O, and sometimes Jell-O meant the ectoplasm of monster dinosaur ghosts.

I'd dressed in a creased, button-down shirt and black pants. Brand was wearing tactical leathers, including a chest holster lined with vulcanized coal knives. He stood a short ways off, unblinking.

"Lord Sun," Jirvan said, without offering his hand. "It's a pleasure."

"Tell me who you are in relation to the Hanged Man," I said. "I will not speak to a puppet."

"Of course, my lord," Jirvan said. "Shall we sit?"

"No. I asked you a question."

"I am Lord Hanged Man's seneschal. In this matter, I speak with his voice."

"This matter," I repeated, rolling the word around. "I'm curious what you think this *matter* is. Are you referring to the Gallows' very mistaken claim on my ward? Sending messengers and letters to my home without my knowledge? Or today's attempted kidnapping?"

"My faith. Kidnapping?"

I stared at the bloodstains on the ground, patiently.

The seneschal gave a nearby bench a plaintive look. He sighed. "I'm afraid I'm not prepared to speak about any *kidnapping*. I am, however, happy to talk about Lord Hanged Man's pending nuptials."

Behind Jirvan, I saw a look of utter fury cross Brand's face, but kept my own anger in check.

"Why," I said, without the lift of a question. "That's what puzzles me most. *Why*. Matthias's court is gone. Lady Lovers is in exile. He no longer offers a connection to the Heart Throne. So why *him*. One might suspect it's a move against the Sun Throne."

"Lord Sun," Jirvan said, with a regrettably apologetic expression. "From a certain perspective—and I say this with all respect—the Sun Throne offers as few connections as the Heart Throne, if this was just a political matter, which it is not."

I continued as if Jirvan hadn't spoken. "The Hanged Man has never met Matthias. There have been no formal introductions. Matthias comes with no personal wealth, no sigils, no assets. He is unschooled. He is without prospects. So still I wonder: why."

"I wouldn't presume to speak about Lord Hanged Man's affections. I'm not even sure they are relevant to this discussion. There is a contract, Lord Sun."

"There *was* a contract, when Max—Matthias—was an adherent of the Heart Throne. Now he's mine. He's my ward. He's my responsibility. He's under my protection."

"The terms of the marital contract are very clear. It remains precedent, no matter which court Matthias belongs to."

"How much—" I began to say, but Jirvan raised a scarred hand.

"Apologies. I think it's in our best interests to be clear that this is not a negotiation. Lord Hanged Man's mind is set."

I didn't speak for a full ten seconds. I just let the weight of my regard build until the seneschal began shifting weight off his bad leg. I said, "Let me *be clear* as well. I have told you that Max is under my protection. Harm to him must pass through me. And I consider the Hanged Man's attentions very much a form of harm. Knowing that, will the Gallows still pursue this ridiculous claim?"

"I'm afraid the Gallows finds this situation anything but ridiculous. Knowing *that*, are you prepared to step aside, and send the boy into Lord Hanged Man's custody?"

"We will send him your head," Brand whispered.

"That would be a bitter start to the formalities between our courts," Jirvan said, and damn if he didn't even flinch.

My eyes wandered across the scars on his face. A man who had known such pain wouldn't be easily frightened.

"Very well," I said. "Rules."

Jirvan raised an eyebrow. He folded his hands in front of his stomach, and waited.

I said, "Matthias is not the sole resident of my home. Others live there. The presence of you or your men, the deluge of secret messages, can—and will—be construed as aggression. It will allow me to act."

"By all means, please accept my deepest apologies. We were led to assume you were aware of our advances. We believed we were acting with full transparency."

"And since I'm only becoming aware of the official claim today, the formal notification period begins now."

Jirvan hesitated. He shook his head faintly. "While we respect your . . . lineage, Lord Sun, you are not an Arcana. The notification period has ended."

I smiled. "My seat on the Arcanum exists, it's just empty. Perhaps you would prefer I claim it?"

Jirvan went still, except for one finger tapping against another. Finally he said, with a much less uncertain headshake, "That seems a rather dramatic course of action. And unnecessary. Our claim holds. That will not change."

I took a thin, long breath, and remained unprovoked. "You're the Hanged Man's seneschal, Jirvan. Advise him well."

Jirvan smiled at me. He smiled at Brand. With a final nod, he turned and left.

Brand waited until the man was far out of earshot. Then he said, with heartfelt emphasis, "Fuck."

"Could have gone worse," I said.

"No, I mean, *fuck.* This is going to be all about protocol, isn't it? That's not my world. If it can be stabbed, I take the lead. This is all words. Fucking protocol."

"Don't worry," I said, staring at the scarred man's receding back. "Protocol will only get us so far. There will be things to stab soon enough." I closed my eyes and rubbed them. "We need to prepare, Brand. We're out of time."

Later that night, after everyone had gone to bed, I went downstairs and sat on the sofa.

There was something about a house at midnight that always reminded me of sanctums. The refrigerator hissed as the ice tray filled; floors and walls groaned; distant traffic ebbed and advanced like an ocean tide. It was easy to slip into a meditative fugue.

I thought about things. Like Jirvan. I wondered how he'd been scarred, and if it had been in the Hanged Man's employ. I was surprised by his age, too. A seneschal is a high-placed position, especially in a court like the Gallows that had so few centers of power outside the Hanged Man's immediate circle. I would have expected him in better health and rejuvenated to a younger age.

Tomorrow, we'd need to start researching Jirvan. We'd need to research the more obscure clauses governing marital claims. We'd need to tap our contacts, and likely shore up a monetary fund for information brokering.

I let my thoughts flow in that direction while I waited.

I'd have guessed I'd be there until two or three in the morning, but Max was impatient. He barely waited until half past one before he snuck downstairs.

He made it to the door before I cleared my throat. He jumped in the air, then caught himself with that useful fae agility.

"No handkerchief," I said. "In all the stories, the kid runs away with a handkerchief tied around a fishing pole."

Max sighed and took a step closer, until he didn't have to squint to see me. His face was drawn into tight, unhappy lines. "This isn't a story. And I'm not a kid. I'm a grown man who has put everyone he cares about in danger, and has a responsibility to do something about it."

"I'll tell you when you're acting like a man," I said.

Max stared down at the duffle bag in his hand. Brand had got it at a tradeshow. The logo for the crossbow company was bright florescent yellow. Matthias had never been very good at picking the right colors for sneaking around.

"Sit down," I said.

"I can't put you through this," Max whispered. "I can't."

"We're already in it. We have to see it through."

"Don't make this any harder."

"Max, I swear on the River, if you try to leave this house, I will fall on you like *thunder*. Sit. The fuck. Down."

He didn't sit next to me. He chose the armchair I usually sat in. He put his duffle bag on the ground between his feet.

"I will have your word," I said. "Now. Your word."

"About what?"

"Max."

Max glanced at the door, and dropped his head again. "I won't leave if you can promise me that you see a way out of this. Do you?"

"There is *always* a way out. Give me your word."

"I won't leave," he promised.

I stayed silent, to see what he'd say next. Most people didn't let silence sit for long, and Max was more nervous than most. Sure enough, after a few seconds, he said, "Will you let me help?"

I thought about that, and said, "Yes."

"Will you let me fight?"

"If it comes to it. And Max?"

"Yes?"

"You have to . . . We . . . Look. I know there are bad things in your past. And you know I know they're there. I haven't forced the question; I've tried to let you decide when you were ready to talk about them. But the time is rapidly approaching when we'll need to have the conversation."

"I don't—that's done. All of that is behind me." He swallowed, on the edge of panic. "Do I really need to talk about it? Does it do you any good to talk about *your* past?"

"It's not about what's good for you. It's about arming Brand and me with every bit of information that may help."

"There's nothing there that will help you. My past has nothing to do with what's happening now. My uncle—"

He stopped talking as if he'd bit his tongue. I watched the emotion shut down his face. Brand and I already suspected that Max's uncle— who'd been his primary guardian—hadn't been a kindly influence. We weren't entirely sure if the man had survived the fall of the Heart Throne. We *were* entirely sure that, if we ever found out he had, he wouldn't survive much longer.

"It's been a long day," I said, "and there's a lot we need to do tomorrow. Why don't you go to bed?"

He nodded and got up, hefting the duffle bag. At the bottom of the stairs he turned around and, jerkily, hurried back to me. He bent down to kiss my cheek.

He whispered, "I love you and Brand and Queenie." Then he ran upstairs, his footsteps making the spiral stairway vibrate.

I didn't get up yet. I sat on the sofa and waited. About ninety seconds later, sure enough, a key scraped the lock, and the front door opened. Brand came in with an aluminum baseball bat against his shoulder.

I stared at it curiously. "Would you really have hit him with it?"

Brand said, all formal, "I was prepared to demonstrate my disappointment with his fucking martyrdom. You talked him out of running away?"

"He promised he'd stay."

Brand nodded. He was about to close the door behind him when—to both our surprise—Quinn poked his head in. It was windy outside, and his blond hair stood up in cowlicks.

"Hello," he said. He nudged the door open with a paintball gun.

I pointed at Brand, delighted, and said, "You didn't know he was out there, did you?"

"Shut up. He's a seer—he probably knew where to sit where I couldn't see him. Shut the fuck up!"

"Quinn," I said. "Please tell me Addam is out there too."

"Do you want me to call him?" Quinn asked helpfully, missing the point entirely.

"No. I want you not to be outside, in New Atlantis, by yourself, after midnight. Addam is going to kill you." I pulled out my phone and texted Addam.

Quinn said, "I didn't want to wake him up. Most of the time he's dreaming about circus tents, which is weird, but it makes him happy. He hasn't been sleeping very well. It's hard to run his business without business partners, even ones who try to kill him."

My phone chirped. I looked at Addam's response and said, "He's sending a car. He wants me to tell you that this is worse than the papaya incident."

Quinn went a little pale. "Oh, that was bad."

"I'm telling him not to send a car. You can bunk with Max. If you kick Max a lot in your sleep, preferably in the ass, I'll even make you breakfast tomorrow."

"So Max isn't running away anymore?" Quinn asked.

"No. And I thought you couldn't see what was going to happen anymore?"

"It's not so bad right now," he said, a little too evasively. "The medicine . . . takes a lot away. I can look, but it's not . . . like it was. I only see important flashes. You'll get in a fight near a boat soon."

"Is this a real boat or one of your not-really-a-boat boats?" Brand asked.

"I don't know what that means," Quinn said, with a lot of dignity.

"It means last week you told us to watch out for a *very very dangerous dog* when we infiltrated that warehouse. And the only dog was a picture of a hell hound in a frame on the wall."

"But it was a hell hound," Quinn pointed out.

"In a fucking picture," Brand said.

"Was the glass cracked? Did you maybe come close to standing underneath it?" Quinn asked.

Brand said, "Give me the paintball gun." Quinn held it out. Brand took it and fired a bright pink shell into Quinn's leg. Quinn was too stunned to even yelp.

Brand said, "And while we're on the subject, if you knew Max might run, why didn't you just call and tell us? You need to start fucking communicating better. If you 'see' anything, you tell us. Period. Do you understand?"

"I'm just trying to help," Quinn objected.

"So are we," I said. Brand was right. This was too serious to leave alone. "Quinn Saint Nicholas, look at me. Brand is right. We need you to work with us on this. Not go rogue. I would like your word."

"I do. I will. I give it," he said, and wiped at the paint on his pants. He gave us the sort of wounded look only a fifteen-year-old could do so effortlessly.

The smell of toast woke me the next morning. Since Queenie had the day off, I was curious, so I threw on a pair of sweatpants and padded downstairs.

Brand was standing by the kitchen counter with his arms crossed. He was showered and combed, and wearing a tight T-shirt that said, "Jesus loves you except when you act like an asshole."

When he saw me, he rolled his eyes and tipped a plate of toast into the trash. "It was bait," he said to my outraged expression.

The toast had landed on old coffee grounds. And the bag on the counter only had two end pieces left. "What the hell," I said.

"I don't have all fucking day for your four-hour morning routine. We need to plan."

I lowered my head in resignation. It was going to be another long day. Leaning against the refrigerator, I gave Brand my best serious look, and plotted my next move. "Tell me what you've come up with."

He opened his mouth, then closed it. "Rune, so help me, if you don't stop thinking about fishing that piece of toast out of the trash, I will punch you in the eye."

"I just don't understand why you needed to throw it away," I complained. "And while we're on the subject, have you noticed how much stronger our Companion bond is getting? I'm not used to you reading my mind this well."

"I don't need telepathy to guess what you're like before you have coffee. Sit the fuck down and get your shit together." But I think he felt bad about the toast, because he went toward the coffee pot and began brewing some. He even used an extra scoop.

"I keep thinking about what you said yesterday," he told me. "To that Jirvan."

"Which part?"

"About Max's lack of prospects. About *why* the Hanged Man wants Max. Do you know what it reminded me of?"

"It's the same thing we wondered when we got Max," I guessed.

"Right. Lady Lovers' little drug-rape kingdom was falling around her, and one of her last moves was to find Max a home? We never figured out why."

"The Tower once told me that when Max was born, his grandmother had—" I bit my lip and glanced over my shoulder. This wasn't the sort of conversation I wanted Max to overhear.

Brand snorted. "They're still asleep. They were up all night bitching at each other. Max even came downstairs for a while in a fucking lather because Quinn moved the wardrobe in front of the window."

"The wardrobe?"

"Max said that Quinn said that sometimes Max stepped on Quinn's face climbing out the window. Which, if we didn't have enough to worry about, means that we need to have a stronger talk with Max about the value of a fucking promise. His grandmother what?"

"She had high hopes for him. Max was supposed to have potential. When he didn't meet her expectations, she pawned him off on her son— Max's uncle."

"Max has plenty of potential," Brand said angrily.

"He can shape-shift, but it's transformationally limited. He's got fae genetics, but he's not full-blooded. He can use cantrips well enough, but he doesn't yet have the knack or training for sigils. There's nothing wrong with him, but he doesn't show the sort of innate ability an Arcana would look for in an heir."

"And that's what he was born to be? The heir scion?"

"I don't know. My point is that—for whatever reason—his birth was important to her."

"So are you saying we need to look into that? Figure out what made Max important?"

I wasn't sure what I was saying. That was the whole problem. We didn't have a starting point. If we spent all our time chasing down one lead, we'd be ignoring a whole other branch of possibilities. "I don't know," I admitted. "I could be completely off target. Maybe it has nothing to do with Max at all. Maybe the Hanged Man just has a bug up his ass about losing a potential consort. There's a lot of talk about his consorts—he has a thing for them."

"What *thing?*" Brand asked.

"He likes pretty young men and women—late teens, but younger than their majority. He marries them, and then removes them from the public eye. He keeps them in his compounds, completely covered in robes, like a religious order."

"Removes them from the public eye?" Brand repeated. "What the fuck. Are we sure he's not mounting their heads in the room at the end of the hall like fucking Bluebeard?"

"I haven't heard anything like that," I said. "People would talk if they vanished altogether."

"Then what's with the robes? Could—" Brand's fingers twitched in and out of fists. "What if they're all scarred under the robes? Like Jirvan?"

"I don't know," I said quietly.

Brand closed his eyes and took a few breaths. When he'd steadied himself, he said, "So he's got a harem. So Max may or may not have potential. Does knowing that help us?"

"I don't know what's helpful at this point. That's the problem."

"No. Follow me. So what if Max has hidden gifts? So what if the Hanged Man has a taste for teenagers? It doesn't change the fact that he's after Max. I think we'd be wasting our time figuring out the *why.*"

After a moment, I nodded. "We need to worry about the how, then. We need to figure out a way to make him relinquish his claim. We're back to politics."

"Maybe," Brand hedged.

Something about the way he said it made me narrow my eyes. "This is usually the point where you tell me you've already figured out our next step."

"Maybe," he said again, only less confidently. He went over to the butcher block. A nylon accordion folder I'd never seen was on top of it, leaning against a bowl of bananas. He picked it up, and sat it down next to me.

"What is this?" I asked, pressing on the clasp. The snap released, and the top yawned open. There were about a dozen manila files inside.

"People who want to hire us. The cases we haven't officially picked."

"We have cases we haven't picked? When did we get this organized?"

"*We* didn't get organized. I've seen your closet. Play to your fucking strengths, Rune."

"Okay. When did *you* get this organized?"

"After you blew up a cathedral in the Westlands. Your name was in the papers. *Pro bono* shit came out of the woodwork. People who can't afford to hire the big firms."

"I have many questions," I said after a pause. "I could be eating toast while I ask them, but I'm not, so how about you just skip ahead to the good stuff."

Brand pulled a file out of the portfolio and handed it to me. "I think this is our entry point."

I opened it. Inside was a printed email from someone called Corinne Dawncreek. I'd barely scanned two sentences before the Hanged Man's name jumped off the page. "Brand?"

"This woman is the caretaker of three kids. One of the kids is a runaway. A nineteen-year-old. He was last seen spending time in the Gallows."

"Why . . ." I shook my head. "Brand, I told you, this is political now. There are rules. We can't go after the Hanged Man openly yet."

"But you can investigate a runaway who may have vanished inside the Hanged Man's court."

"I'm not sure I can. It's too thin a cover."

Brand hesitated. "Read the second paragraph."

I looked back at the printout. The second paragraph said,

Until the death of your father, I served as Companion to one of his loyal supporters. We were members of your Court in good standing. My Companion is gone now, but his children are my responsibility, and I'm not too proud to make use of this old connection. I need help.

I'd barely made it past the first sentence when I stopped breathing. Now, light-headed, I took a noisy breath. "Oh."

Brand came up next to me. He stood so that our arms were pressed together and said nothing.

I closed my eyes. "I don't know how I feel. I don't know how this makes me feel."

"You don't have to," Brand said. "I wish I didn't have to spring this on you."

"This . . . these are my people."

"They *were* your people. I know that means something to you, but don't make it mean more than it needs to."

"What does that even mean? How can it not mean more than it needs to? They're my father's people, and they're in trouble, and I didn't even know they existed. I never—I don't—I never *think* about them. I never think about the houses who lost my father's protection when his inner circle was killed. I never think about where those families ended up."

"Rune, trust me, there are a hundred fucking things you should feel guilty about. I'll make a list. But this isn't one of them. You want to feel something? Feel good that you're in a position to help these people now. Feel good that helping them may help us."

"Maybe." I looked at the letter. Which of my father's supporters had this Companion been bonded to? What would she even think of me? I hadn't been strong or old enough to raise the Sun Throne's standard after my father died. I hadn't been able to reassemble a court out of the impoverished remains. "Or maybe I should be examining a more direct approach. Maybe I could seek an audience with the Hanged Man."

"That's one idea. But first, let me tell you a story that will demonstrate my thoughts on the matter." He put his mouth against my ear and said, "*No!*"

I glared at him and wiggled a finger in my ear. "It may not be the best choice, but it's a choice. We don't have any *time*, Brand."

"We still need data. We need to understand our enemy. A case like this will bring us into the Hanged Man's sphere without the appearance of a direct attack. Right? It'll give us cover?"

It could at that. I could very easily twist the case into a shield for our own agenda.

Since I knew Brand better than I knew myself, I said, "What time did you set up an appointment with Ms. Dawncreek?"

"I wanted to check with you first," Brand said, all innocence.

I stared at him.

"Fine," he said. "One o'clock."

I tucked the folder under my arm. I'd read it in my sanctum while I prepared my sigil load.

"Um, guys?" Queenie said from the back porch. Her nose was pressed up against the screen door. She wasn't allowed inside on her day off—for her benefit, not ours. She said, "I smelled toast? I was wondering if, um, Rune was using the stove?"

Brand grinned at me, because I got no credit, and they both treated my cooking like vaudeville. I ignored them and went into the living room, just as Max and Quinn thundered downstairs, each of them trying to push into the lead.

"He moved my wardrobe," Max said.

"To keep you from climbing out the window," I said.

"To keep me from *maybe* climbing out the window," Max argued. "Just like maybe sometimes Brand is a girl, and maybe sometimes you only wear tuxedos made of plaid flannel."

Over the last few months, Max and Quinn had developed a complicated relationship. They were nearly the same age, and both of them, in their own way, were outcasts. Quinn adored Max, in much the way Quinn adored anyone who didn't treat him like a freak. Max, though, had a tendency to be jealous at the space Quinn took up in my life. Sooner or later he'd realize that Quinn had somehow become his best friend.

I wasn't about to get sucked into their argument. I narrowed my eyes at Quinn and said, "Did you call your brother?"

"Oh no." Quinn shook his head emphatically. "He's very mad at me."

"Well, yes, I suspect he is. That's my point. You need to call him."

"I called him earlier," Brand said, coming up behind me. "He's already on his way."

"But," Quinn said, his face falling. "That wasn't the plan. Sometimes I stay all morning and there're waffles."

"There will be waffles either way," Brand said. "Queenie is making breakfast. She's giving up her day off, *again*, because Rune and Max are spoiled and don't know there's such a thing as fucking cereal."

"Okay, everyone outside," I said. "Max, set the picnic table. Quinn, pull some extra chairs from the shed. Go. I need coffee and quiet."

I let Quinn scurry past, but grabbed the collar of Max's T-shirt at the last second and pulled him against me I leaned into his ear and whispered, "I am your guardian. Your vows are my vows. If you break your promise, it will be as if I did, and my magic will suffer for it. Would you do that to me?"

"No," Max stammered. "No! I won't. I promise. I just want to help."

"Then I better not hear any more about climbing out of windows. Go. We'll be outside in a moment."

I let him stumble off as the doorbell rang, followed by a firm, polite knock. I went to the eyehole—set apart from the fake eyehole—and spotted Addam on our doorstep. A black town car idled at the curb.

I opened the door, and he smiled at me. I smiled back at him, because it was hard not to smile back at Addam. His burgundy eyes crinkled as he slowly leaned in for a kiss. "Hero," he said against my neck.

"Sorry about the Quinn thing," I said.

"He and I will speak later about it. I've brought his medicine."

A month ago, we'd hired an alchemist recommended by Ciaran, a powerful principality who'd become a friend. Principalities were the island's version of courtless Arcana—all the power, none of the burdens or blessings of a throne.

Ciaran's alchemist had tailored an elixir that dampened Quinn's prophetic magic. It was the best option we had for keeping the teenager sane. Prophetic magic—especially his kind—was a cruel gift, slowly grinding the idea of a normal life to dust.

"It makes me not want to eat," Quinn complained loudly from the kitchen. He came into the archway with a bag of paper plates.

"Your appetite will return," Addam said patiently.

"But there are waffles," Quinn said. "We don't have to go before waffles, right?"

"We can have waffles first, if Rune and Brand have offered."

Quinn gave him a guilty look. "Thank you. And I didn't mean to worry you. Are you very mad at me? This really wasn't as bad as the papaya incident. I didn't go to a foreign country at all."

"As I said, we will speak later," Addam told him.

Quinn sighed and went back into the kitchen. From the other side of the archway, I heard the clatter of pots, and the click of the gas burner. A classical radio station was turned on—Queenie's polite way of offering us the illusion of privacy.

"Have you made any decisions?" Addam asked quietly.

"We're debating whether to find a sneaky way to investigate the Hanged Man, or whether the direct approach is better."

Brand bristled. "No, we're not. You're not making an appointment with him, Rune. That piñata is fucking dead. Move on."

Addam said, "This sneaky approach. How will we proceed?"

I stumbled a little over the *we*. Addam was the son of a different court; my battles were not his battles. His mother, Lady Justice, would not thank me for drawing her son into the Hanged Man's orbit.

"I have become familiar with that expression," Addam said, pointing at my face. "I am in your life, Rune. This involves me."

"You have obligations. Political boundaries. I need to respect them."

"I do have obligations. You are correct. But you do not seem to understand what they are." He gave me a cool look. "Quinn can wait. Perhaps it is you and I who need to have a talk."

"Okay," Brand said, "I'm going to find somewhere else to be, and let you think I haven't already made the decision for all of us." He went into the kitchen.

"I know you can handle yourself," I said. "You know that, right? That's not what this is about. But . . . Addam. We'll be challenging the *Hanged Man*."

"I will not stand aside."

"I'm not asking that. Not really. I just . . . For now, I just want to limit your involvement. Can I do that, at least?"

"And what are my," he said, and now his accent came out like a tiger's single, popped claw, "limits?"

"Brand and I are going to meet with someone this afternoon who could provide us indirect entry into the Hanged Man's court. I don't want Matthias to come with us, and I don't want to leave him and Queenie alone. Will you stay here and watch them?" I put my hands on Addam's arms as he opened his mouth to protest. "Their safety means *everything*. You have no idea how much it means, that I'd trust you with them."

Addam continued to stare at me for a good five seconds, but finally dipped his chin.

"Come over here," I said. I slid my hands down his arm until our fingers touched. I led him over to the wall, and lifted his palm so that he was touching it. "In the basement is my mass sigil. I store a powerful defense spell in it. You remember?"

"Of course. You saved our lives with it, in the Westlands."

"Can you feel it? It's buried. Search it out."

Addam furrowed his brow. I felt the faint buzz of his willpower. After a moment or two, he nodded at me.

I covered his hands with my own and said, "I share this sigil with you freely. Its will is also your will."

The connection between me and my mass sigil flattened and expanded, until our willpower was a triangular circuit. Addam gasped a little, surprised at the power of the stored spell, and at my willingness to share. Ownership of sigils was a very, very personal thing for Atlanteans. They were rarely co-opted outside families.

"It's there if you need it," I said. "I trust you."

"Rune," Addam breathed. He shook his head. "There will come a point where my involvement should not be limited. When you'll want my strength at hand. Yes?"

I stared at him and said, "Yes. Thank you, Addam."

THE DAWNCREEKS

Addam offered his town car, which glided away from the curb with Brand and me in it. I gave an unseen driver instructions by intercom, and settled back to screw around with the air vents.

Brand went into his bodyguard mode, swinging a critical eye from window to window, never forgetting to look over his shoulder. He liked mixing up our transportation in order to stay unpredictable, which is probably why I got a town car ride without an argument.

After a while, he asked, "Would it be so bad?"

"Yes," I said, because it was the safest answer to any question Brand would start that way.

He shoved at my arm. "The throne."

"The *throne?*"

"Inheriting your throne. Would it be so bad to take a seat on the Arcanum? A lot of them owe you favors. You're not entirely disliked."

"The problem is that I'd need to depend on those favors to *hold* the throne," I said.

"The Tower would always have your back."

Brand never asked stupid questions, which was why I was caught off guard by his interest. "I'm . . . Arcana courts are . . . Gods, Brand. They've got hundreds of sigils. They've got *compounds.* They have household guards and courtiers. We don't even own a houseplant."

"Things change. How are you going to get courtiers until you have a court? If you had a seat on the Arcanum, we'd be in a better position to defend ourselves. We'd be able to make alliances."

"Alliances are about teamwork. Do you remember when we played dodge ball when we were kids? The first thing you did was take out your own teammates before they could stab you in the back."

"That's a damned exaggeration," he said, nearly offended. "And you're conveniently fucking forgetting that I took out *our* teammates and then stood in front of you like a human fucking shield. And that was just a game. Our lives aren't a game. I'll do whatever it takes to keep you safe."

"And I'll do whatever it takes to keep you safe, but swimming in the same pond as Arcana won't do that. I can't believe you of all people are raising this subject. Where is this coming from?"

"I . . ." He made a frustrated sound and slouched back in his seat. "I've always known you were powerful. I've always had respect for your powers. You know that, don't you?"

"You threw away my toast. Right in front of me."

He gave me a look, something balanced on the razor's edge of seriousness and nervousness. "Last summer," he said, "you faced an army."

"The recarnates? Lord Tower helped me."

"Lord Tower showed up at the last second and finished them off. But you were the one that marched outside the defense wards on your own and *faced an army.* There were a hundred fucking zombies in front of you, and you faced them by yourself, and you turned two-thirds of them to *ash.* You turned them into cinders, Rune. You are not your average fucking bear."

"I had a mass sigil," I protested. "Any—"

"Anyone *couldn't* do it. Anyone wouldn't have had the fucking balls. It's the sort of thing Arcana do. Can you honestly tell me you're not aware of that?"

I let my reply lapse. I couldn't lie to him, even if I wanted. I remembered what it had felt like, walking onto the battlefield with the explosive energy of a mass sigil leashed to my hands. And I remembered what it felt like to unleash it.

"Maybe you're not ready for the throne today," Brand said. "Maybe not this year. But you're moving in that direction. Right?"

"Sure," I said. "I just think it will take longer."

He was quiet for a second, swinging his gaze from front to back. Then, almost suspiciously, he said, "How much longer?"

"I don't know. I always expected it'd take a century."

His eyes snapped toward mine. He tilted his head to one side, as if bewildered, and then a flush crept up his neck. "A century. Of years. A hundred fucking *years*."

"I sense disagreement."

Every one of his body parts got bigger—his eyes, his mouth, his waving arms—as he yelled, "Are you shitting me? A hundred years of your dirty socks? A hundred years of finding fucking boxes of fucking ho-hos stuffed in air vents? A hundred years of you getting pissy and blowing holes in fucking walls? A hundred years of you using every new power as an excuse to fucking nap more? *Are you shitting me?*"

"It almost sounds like you're in this for the money," I said.

"Are you—? Is that a fucking—? Rune Saint John, I will turn this back seat into a fucking pinball machine. Are you shitting me? How . . ." His anger fell into loud despair. "How am I supposed to keep you alive for another century?"

I started laughing. What else was I supposed to do? Everyone should have a Brand.

I said, "I really love you."

He threw himself into his seat and began staring at the ceiling. He even forgot to look out the window to check for missiles or train robbers.

A few miles from the Dawncreeks' neighborhood, he muttered, "A century." A mile later, he punched me in the thigh and gave me a Charlie horse. And then, as we pulled up to a curb, he said, "*Fine.* But I am making some new fucking house rules. And maybe a fucking chore chart."

It'd started sprinkling while we drove. It had got to the point, these last few months, where people didn't even bother with weather reports. Temperatures and cloud cover had been schizophrenically uncertain since the events in the Westlands—the last vestige of the weather magic spell screwing up the atmosphere.

I may have ended the weather spell, but I hadn't been the one to start it, which might have been the only reason I hadn't been hauled before the

Arcanum on charges. Interfering with the weather was forbidden magic. Like all forbidden magic, the potential for creating a global domino chain of catastrophe was a starkly real possibility.

I stepped through a puddle of oily water, which shimmered into a rainbow. In other parts of the world, a neighborhood like this would have been called rundown. Beautiful houses with old paint jobs; heavily subdivided lots; cracked sidewalks held together with weeds. New Atlantis, though, wasn't the rest of the world. Economic cycles were fixed—the poor would always be sequestered in the same exact blocks, and the rich would always have their same armored rat holes. Nothing changed, except ownership of the corner bodegas.

Brand told the limo driver to turn the car around so that it faced the way we'd come, because that's the sort of thing Brand thought about. I waited and stared at the narrow Victorian in front of us with itching discomfort. One of the curtains on the second floor fluttered, hiding everything but a cap of shiny black hair as someone ducked beneath the sill.

"The Warrens are down that way," Brand commented, coming up next to me. "Bad area."

"I'm not so sure about that," I said. "There are wards in the sidewalks. I can feel them. I bet you'd find a lot of families in this neighborhood are distantly connected to formal houses. Or maybe were once houses, but down on their luck. It's a smart place to live, actually. You get the table scraps of protection."

We started up the walkway. The concrete had powdered in places, but the grass on either side was green and mowed. Halfway up the veranda, the front door opened. Someone immediately stepped back into darkness, snatching a brown hand from the knob.

I stopped on the welcome mat and shaded my eyes, until the shadows unblurred into the form of a girl. She was maybe eleven or twelve, with glossy hair and strong native features. I didn't really have an eye for American ethnicities, but I knew a lot of Wampanoag blood had made its way into the Atlantis gene pool centuries ago. I had a fair amount myself.

"Hi," I said, when it became apparent all we were getting was a glare from the curtain of black hair.

"There are lots of articles about you," she said.

"Of this I am aware," I said.

"That's your Companion," she said, and raised a finger in Brand's direction. "Like my aunt. Make him prove it. Tell him to throw a knife and break that ward in half." She pointed to a scuffed ward nailed above the doorbell.

"Excuse me?" Brand said.

"Go ahead—it's already broken. I bet I could do it. I bet I'm as good as a Companion."

"If you were, you wouldn't be telling fucking strangers that your defense ward is broken," Brand said.

I slapped a hand over my eyes.

"What?" Brand said.

"We have a swear jar," the girl told him. "It counts even when you're on the porch."

Brand had the sensibility to look abashed. I said, "Try not to put them through college."

"Okay, enough of this," he said gruffly. "You're Annawan Dawncreek. This is Lord Sun. I'm Brand. Get your aunt?"

For a second she didn't move. Then, hesitantly, she pushed her long hair behind her ears. One side of her face was scarred—no, burned. Those were the long-healed, contracted scars of a burn injury.

I gave Brand a quick look, thinking about the seneschal Jirvan. Annawan misunderstood the glance, because her face fell into an expression of familiar guardedness, like a muscle memory. "I just wanted you to see," she said. "Now you don't need to stare. Okay?"

I really did try not to stare, but it was hard, because she was a child, and I didn't like seeing injured children. But even worse than that, something unpleasant began stirring in the back of my mind. Something not unlike accountability. This girl was the child of one of my father's people. And she had scars.

Brand walked up the steps and gave her a cool nod. His casual reaction was the right response, because she nodded back and withdrew into the house.

The door opened into a living room. Velvet sofa with threadbare spots; cracked, clean walls; polished mirrors; dusted blinds. The household wards were cheap but working—the allergen ward smelled like pine with a faint undertone of tar pitch. Overall, the room had a patched sort of dignity, which was something I could relate to.

An older woman bustled into the room, shaking water from her hands. "My lord. Sorry, I was doing dishes." The upper half of her body jerked forward, like she was about to offer her hand, then realized they were wet and wasn't sure how polite that was. She put her hands on her ward's shoulders instead, pulling the girl in front of her.

Corinne Dawncreek had blunt nails, and training callouses on the back of her hands. Her eyes were the color of faded denim, milky with cataracts. Her face was wrinkled, but not in the places where you'd expect them—like the laugh and frown lines people spent a lifetime carving. It was deeply unsettling—aged features on a face that should have been young and rejuvenated—and I expected it had to do with the severing of her Companion bond.

Companions grew old when the Atlantean they were bonded with died. And they grew old quickly if they'd had rejuvenation treatments before that point. For all I knew, Corinne had been my age just a couple years earlier, when her scion was still alive. Now she was aging in fast-forward.

That thing in the back of my head—that nascent guilt—stretched and yawned and ran claws along my brain.

"Brand," Brand said. "This is Rune."

As nervously as Corinne regarded me, the look she gave Brand was much more measuring. Her eyes flicked up and down his body, most likely to size up the number of weapons he carried.

"I've made coffee," she finally said. "Unless you'd like tea? I could find some tea."

"Coffee is fine," Brand said.

"Please. Make yourself at home. Anna, come help me. Come, now." She shushed her ward out of the room, vanishing down a scuffed linoleum hallway that led to the back of the house.

We sat down, side by side, on a sofa that sagged in the middle. My knees came up to my lap. I started to look around the room again—and my gaze caught on a glossy tumble of hair peeking from the archway to another room.

I cleared my throat.

The mop of hair jerked out of view.

Brand and I waited until, slowly, a boy's face slid back into the archway. He was much younger than his sister, maybe five or six, with coppery skin and straight black hair.

"You're Corbitant?" Brand said.

"Corbie," the boy told us. He had a low, hoarse voice.

With inching bravery, Corbie sidled into the living room. He was wearing a florescent purple shirt many sizes too big. Skinny legs stuck out of shorts that came to his shins, and he had a candy necklace wrapped around his wrist.

He stood there and swayed, studying us. "Do you wear socks?" he finally asked.

Brand and I looked at each other.

Corbie said, "I wear socks too." He stuck out a foot to show that he was, indeed, wearing socks.

Having established common ground, he fled. I heard his muffled footsteps punch up an unseen stairway.

"You see the knife?" Brand asked.

"What knife? When was there a knife?"

"The girl had it hidden up her sleeve."

"You're making that up. You're not? That doesn't seem like a good thing."

"I'm pretty sure it was a fucking butter knife. But still." Only he was Brand, so he said it like it was, in fact, a good thing. Brand's approval ran in dark directions.

My eyes slid to the fireplace mantle, to the family photos. In younger photos, the girl only wore pigtails, and her complexion was smooth and unmarked. I said, quietly, "Her face."

Brand sighed. "I know."

"That sort of burn . . ."

"We'll ask questions. We'll listen to the answers. We'll find out."

"But—"

"It was my court, too," he said, unexpectedly. "I was supposed to protect them too. We're on this ride together, okay?"

I closed my eyes and nodded.

When I opened them again, Corinne was gliding into the room with a bamboo tray balanced on one palm. She moved with trained grace, like Brand; and, also like Brand, her eyes danced around the room as if she hadn't just been in it, mapping potential new threats. The girl, Anna, wasn't with her.

"It's instant," she said, with a little color in her cheeks. The tray had mismatched mugs and packets of fast-food sugar. A ceramic creamer held something too thin to be cream.

That little pitcher snagged my attention. It came from a formal service: expensive and vein-thin. I lightly touched the rim of it. "This reminds me of something my father used."

"Does it?" she said. "It must have been a favorite pattern. He gave it to my Kevan when he married, many, many years ago. We kept this piece when the rest of the set was . . . lost." She busied herself with the mugs, putting one in front of each of us.

When there was nothing more to distract her, she sat in an armchair.

Stuffing leaked from its seams, and the cushions, as she settled into them, gave a fat, gusty sigh.

"Well," she said, and tightened her fidgeting fingers into a loose fist. She looked down at this—at the unguarded display of emotion—and blinked away sudden tears. "I am out of my mind with worry. It's hard to think straight. I don't even know where to start."

"I'd like to know more about you. And the scion you were bonded to. I'm ashamed to admit that I don't recall your name. I'm sorry."

She waved away the apology. "My Kevan worked for one of your father's larger houses. You wouldn't have had much reason to know us, not at—well, not at the age you were, before the Sun Court fell on hardship."

"Hardship," I said, but smiled to take the sting out of it. "My father's court didn't fall on hardship—it just fell. Which of my father's greater houses did Kevan Dawncreek work for, Corinne?"

"The Ambersons. They managed your father's magical studies branch. Lord Amberson was the one who elevated the Dawncreeks, and made us a lesser house."

Memories flared and died like match strikes. A big man with a beard the color of rusting steel wool. A peculiar obsession with home-brewed beer. The Ambersons, as I understood, had not survived the fall of Sun Throne. They were no longer a named house.

"Kevan must have been very talented. That's not something Lord Amberson would have done without good reason."

"I suppose that's part of what I need to tell you," Corinne said. "We . . . That is. Well. Lord Sun, do you know how it was, after your father's death? For the houses in the Sun Court?"

The unknown raiders hadn't just killed my father's inner circle; they'd drained our bank accounts, and claimed our sigils, and destroyed our artifacts and art. The throne became insolvent, and hundreds of debtors darted in to peck what remained. The greater and lesser houses would have splintered. They would have been bought by other courts; at best solicited into better employment. They would have been extorted, or threatened, or bribed. That was *if* they had marketable skills. Without any quick and liquid value, they would have fallen themselves.

I said, "If Kevan was talented, other Arcana courts would have pursued him. The Hanged Man, then?"

"The Hanged Man, eventually. But not at first. There is a cutthroat market for unaffiliated lesser houses. Lord Amberson could not retain us, so we joined the swarm. So many houses, at once, cut adrift and jockeying for sponsorship. Alliances failed quickly. Lord Sun had been a good ruler for generations, so for those like us? We were unprepared for the vicious tactics."

I was trying hard not to get swamped by my reactions. And of course Brand knew that, because he leaned forward and gave Corinne his best glare. "There a reason for all this?"

"Would you rather I continue to explain, or explain why I'm explaining?" Corinne fastballed back at him.

"You know what I am. I know what you were. You know as well as I know that it's not just our job to protect them from knives and swords."

"What I *was*," she said. "I didn't just stop being a Companion when Kevan died. I'm still very good at my work. For instance, I wouldn't have sat there, like you, in the spot the sun will hit in fifteen minutes. And that jacket? You buy from Morrickson, don't you? I used to, when I could afford them—but I'd always have to reinforce the side knife pockets, they get the most tear because of the angle. I always needed to add a double row of stitches." She gave Brand's neat line of single stitches a plain look.

"We're not doing this," I said, and held up two hands, one to either of them. "Please go on with what you were saying, Corinne."

She held Brand's eyes a few seconds longer, and nodded. "For a while—quite a while, years actually—Kevan remained unaffiliated. He commanded a small but interested market. We may have lasted like that indefinitely, but his wife, Mariah, had medical problems after giving birth to Corbitant, my—her youngest. She passed away after many months in the hospital. The hospital bills drove Kevan to find sponsorship, and the court most interested in sponsoring him was the Gallows. The Hanged Man has an interest in mutilation magics."

"Mutilation magics?" I echoed. "Corinne, what sort of magic did Kevan practice?"

"Immolation," she said. "You're familiar with it?"

I leaned back into the cushions. It was a form of death magic, sure, but at least there weren't any zombies or dead cats. Immolation was on the veganism side of death magic. It harmed no one except the caster, and relied on manipulating the life cycles of bacterial and viral life. Most practitioners cultivated non-contagious forms of illness, colonizing their body in advance of heavy spells. They then used their innate magic to eradicate the microscopic life, and draw power from the death.

The Hanged Man was a recognized master of death magics. Immolation was an obscure form of it. I could see how someone like Kevan Dawncreek may have piqued his interest.

"I'm familiar," I said. "And I'm aware that the Hanged Man doesn't take no for an answer."

"He does not at that," Corinne said quietly.

"And Lord Dawncreek didn't welcome Lord Hanged Man's attentions?" I guessed.

"He did not," Corinne said. "My Kevan had dignity and values. Which, perversely, appealed to the Hanged Man even more. And . . ." Her hands continued to curl in and out of fists. "Do you know the only thing that appeals to someone like the Hanged Man more than a man with dignity?"

I shook my head.

"A man with dignity and three beautiful, young children."

The armor cracked. Manners failed. I could not, I would not, hear more. I just couldn't.

"Excuse me. The bathroom. That way?" I stood and pointed away from the spot I was sitting in.

Corinne started. Brand half-rose.

I walked away.

* * *

I closed the door behind me, and sat down heavily on the toilet. The plastic hinges had cracked. I tilted sideways as the seat skated off the marble rim. I got off the toilet seat, lowered myself to the ground, and focused on my breathing.

For a good, long minute I just breathed, staring at the blue plastic fishes on the closed shower curtain.

Years. I had spent *years* distancing myself from anything like what I'd survived as a teenager. Years spent burying every road, every path, every godsdamn breadcrumb that led to anything that resembled what I'd been put through. I did not take cases like this.

And then I'd met Max, who'd survived something not completely unlike my own trauma.

And then I'd met the lich, who had pulled my own memories out of my head and used them as catnip for his demented attentions.

And then . . . What? Now this? Was I going to find out the Hanged Man didn't just pursue young men and women, but children as well? Was I going to find out that this family—who had once been under my father's protection—had faced such predation?

When I had my pulse under control again, I got up and bent down to flush the toilet as an excuse for the delay. My sunglasses slipped from my breast pocket and plopped into the water.

I stared at them and said, "Fuck you, Universe."

Someone gasped and slapped a hand over their mouth.

I reached out and slid the shower curtain sideways, sending the cheap plastic rings skittering. The boy—Corbie—was sitting, fully clothed, in the dry tub with both hands on his face. A bag of gummi bears dangled from his fingers.

"Should I ask?" I asked.

Corbie opened his fingers wide enough to say, in that hoarse voice of his, "Ask what?"

"Why you're in the bathtub?"

"I'm hiding stuff."

"I see."

"Don't tell anyone," Corbie said. While keeping one eye on me, he slid his bag of gummi bears behind a bottle of off-brand shampoo.

"I hide my snacks, too," I said. "Apparently badly. I'm pretty good at making excuses for it, though."

Corbie nudged the conditioner next to the shampoo bottle. Satisfied with his concealment efforts, he climbed out of the tub. He was so small that he had to throw one leg entirely over the lip, pull himself on top, and lower himself down the other side.

I thought that was the end of it, but then he leaned back into the tub and turned on the water. I watched, puzzled, as he let a good inch pool before turning the faucets off again.

"Now that, I don't do," I said.

"It's so it doesn't burn," Corbie said.

"The tub?"

"The *candy*. Water doesn't burn. So my candy won't burn."

"Is this because of me? I'm a little concerned you think I'm going to burn your snacks. You know I'm not *really* the Sun, right?"

"I know," he said. "But people sometimes visit, and then sometimes other people come back and make things go on fire."

"Oh," I said.

Oh.

"It won't burn, right?" he asked worriedly.

"No. No, it won't. You shouldn't be worried about that."

"So it won't be like last time?" he asked.

I swallowed. "No. Not like last time. So there was a fire, when people visited?"

"Our house got broken and we had to move. And my . . . my papa . . ." He blinked at his feet. "Anna was burned, too. And my voice went funny. I drank too much smoke. Auntie says I'm very, very strong, though."

"I bet you are. And it's a cool voice. Sounds like you have a pack-a-day habit. Very tough."

He squinted at me for a few seconds, trying to puzzle out my meaning. "I'm only allowed two sticks a day. Not a pack. Auntie hides the rest of the gum."

"Companions," I said. "What are you gonna do?"

Brand, of course, was standing outside the door when I came out.

"Corbie, do you mind giving us a second?" I asked.

"I was going to ask if you'll have a glass of soda with me."

"Maybe later."

"Okay," he said, and let out a small sigh. "But it'd be rude if I had one and you didn't."

I smiled at him. "It's okay. I don't think it's rude."

His eyes widened and he took off like a shot.

"So?" Brand said.

"Do kids drink soda?" I asked, now unsure. "Did I just do something wrong?"

"Rune. So?"

"What? I didn't know he was in the bathroom. I wasn't really using the bathroom anyway. It's not as weird as it looks."

"Shut up," Brand said. "What's going on?"

"Nothing. And your phone is ringing," I pointed out.

Brand kept me pinned with a gaze while he pulled his phone out of his pocket. It was Max's ringtone. He didn't bother looking at the screen—he just flicked a thumb and said, "We're working."

He listened, closed his eyes, and started breathing through his nostrils. "No. No, that's not what it means. Max—just because Quinn says you someday might rub a ferret in his hair doesn't mean you *own* the ferret, and it doesn't mean you need to *own* that ferret *today* while we're fucking *working.* I'm hanging up now."

"At least Quinn is distracting him," I said afterward.

"You didn't answer my question."

"What question?"

"It's like you're not even worried I'm going to hit you," Brand said.

"Nothing is—" I grunted as he jabbed two stiff fingers into my gut. I waited until my breathing evened out. "I'm fine. I just needed a second to get my head on straight."

"Is it?"

"Yes. Pity party over. I don't have a monopoly on bad memories. Sometimes I forget that."

"It's not a contest. You're allowed to say it's too much. You're allowed to say if this is too much."

"It's not too much. Let's go hear what Corinne has to say. Did you write down that tip about the double-stitching?"

His mouth opened in outrage until he realized I was kidding, and even then it took an effort of will not to tell me to mind my own shit.

He followed me back to the living room. We passed Corbie in the kitchen. He was cradling a two-liter of soda as if he'd just dug up buried treasure.

"Corinne," I said, when we were back in our seats in the living room. "What happened with Lord Hanged Man?"

She shook off whatever thoughts were making her stare blankly at the table in our absence. Her face drew tight, pulling the deep unnatural wrinkles into sharp creases. "We tried to evade his attentions. Kevan accepted the odd job in lieu of formally pledging himself into that man's service. He tried to buy time until we found better placement elsewhere. But the Gallows was insistent. They hounded us."

"You . . . implied earlier. About the children. You . . . You must know my story. You know what happened to me when I was fifteen—nearly the same age that your oldest ward is. This is not an easy topic for me, but we should stop circling it. What did the Hanged Man do to the children?"

"I suppose the word is groomed. The bastard groomed them. Or he groomed Layne, at least. You've heard about his . . ." Her lips worked

around a word in disgust. "His *marriages.* To all those young lads and
ladies. When it became apparent that he had such designs on Layne, we
broke all ties. That was two years ago. Within a month of our rejection,
our home caught fire. Kevan was killed. Little Anna was horribly burned.
We—everything. We lost nearly everything. That man is poison. That
man is a fucking monster."

She stopped the conversation altogether for a moment—busying
herself with reaching a hand into her jangling pocket, and dumping a
handful of spare change on the scratched coffee table. As she counted out
two American quarters with the tip of her finger, I could see her struggling to blank out the tension in her lips, the tightness around her eyes.
Just like Brand did. When her emotions were emptied, she cleared her
throat and looked at me.

I said, "You're sure the Hanged Man was behind the fire?"

"I'm a Companion. I know my monsters."

"What happened after that?" I asked.

"I thought the bastard's revenge was complete. I didn't realize his
attention had merely shifted. Layne is . . . he glows. He lights up the room.
A more beautiful boy you've never seen. And the Hanged Man's people,
without my knowledge, remained in touch with him. They . . . *courted*
him. Seduced him with money and promises. Two weeks ago, the day he
turned fifteen, he ran away. I'm certain that he's vanished into the Hanged
Man's court."

Corinne looked between Brand and me, then shifted her full regard to
me. "Are you in a position to take on that bastard?"

"Corinne, you're a trained Companion, and I have an awesome respect
for what that means. But you don't really know the kind of monster the
Hanged Man is. You don't know his magic, and his resources, and the
ramifications of breaching his sphere of influence."

"Are you saying you won't help? That you can't?"

"Can't? No. I may have lost my throne and my court, but not my
power, not my legacy. I can help you—but I need you to be sure you're

willing to walk through that door. Because you haven't lost everything yet."

She looked at the floor for a few moments, and nodded to herself.

She said, "I will walk through that door."

"We'll need information," Brand said. "Information on Layne. His friends. Places he likes to go. Does he have a bank account? A credit card? A cell phone? Anything would hel—"

"I have a folder in my room. And more. One of his friends, a—" She started to censor herself, then shoved quarters to the middle of the table. "A damned whore, a good-for-nothing little bastard who works the Green Docks. Sherman. Sherman has information, but he wants a thousand dollars for it."

"Rune and I can visit Sherman," Brand said.

Corinne gave Brand a hard look. "If he could be beaten into compliance, I'd have done it myself. He's slippery and good at finding bolt-holes. But he's greedy, and that's the opening. I'm working to sell a few family effects. It'll take another day or two, but I'll have the money soon."

I exchanged a look with Brand. He gave me a small shrug. "We'll get to that in a moment," I said. "How did Layne become involved with this Sherman? Did . . . was Layne . . . I mean, did Layne—"

"I don't know," she said, and her cheeks reddened. "I would have cut out a person's tongue for suggesting such an insult a month ago, but I've learned things since. I know he's been skipping school and spending times at the Green Docks."

The Green Docks were New Atlantis's red-light district—a floating armada of derelict boats and ghost ships docked off the northern shores. Quinn said we'd be in a fight near boats.

"The Hanged Man has warped Layne's mind," Corinne continued. "Made him put distance between him and his family. The bastard—that unholy bastard—is taking my family apart."

"We'll write you a check," I decided. "You can go to our bank and get a cash withdrawal. For the information."

"I can't ask that of you," she said.

"Would you have said no to my father?" I asked.

She paused a moment, and nodded. "Let me get that folder. I'll be right back."

When she'd stepped from the room, Brand said, "Are you sure?"

"I'm sure."

Corinne came back with the promised folder several minutes later. She held it out to us with one hand, while shrugging into a jacket with the other.

Brand's eyes tracked Corinne's movements with suspicion. "What are you doing?"

"I'm going to cash the check and get the information."

"We're going right now?" he said, like he already knew her answer.

"*I'm* going now. Sherman will never see me if I bring you along."

"What about the kids?" I asked, with my own growing wariness.

"Corbie at the Green Docks?" she snorted. "He'd either run off a pier, or invite half the whores home with him for milk and cookies."

The truth loomed like the shadow of a falling piano.

She gave me a guilty look. "I can't be sure they're not in danger as well. Not until I know what's happened with Layne. I can't imagine there's anyone I'd trust more to stay with them, Lord Sun. You're strong. You can protect them. And I'll be back as soon as I can."

Within minutes, Corinne had run out of the house with a check Brand wrote her. It wouldn't devastate our bank account, but it'd put a rolling stop to the extra cash we'd lived off since the events of last summer. I shut the front door, and sighed. "She found the right button to push, didn't she?"

"The right button? You're a fucking elevator panel. *Only you can protect them, Lord Sun.*"

"Swear jar," I said.

"I'll add it to my to-do list. Look—someone needs to watch the kids, and someone needs to hole up and do research. We should—"

"Oh *absolutely not*. That is not how this is going to go down, Brandon Saint John!"

He exhaled through his nostrils. He said, "Fine." And then we both took a few seconds to stare uselessly around us.

Annawan—Anna—stomped into the living room before we could decide what to do next. Her hair was knotted into a braid, and she'd changed into dark clothes, not unlike a mini-Companion.

She put her hands on her hips and said, "Do you have pets?"

"Do we have pets?" I said.

"Simple question."

"We do not have pets," I said. "But there's talk of a ferret."

"How would you feel if I came into *your* home and fed *your* ferret drugs and then left *you* to deal with it?" she asked.

Corbie screamed and ran into the room. He jumped on the sofa. He jumped on the coffee table. He jumped on the armchair. He yelled, "Lava! The floor is lava! The floor is lava!" He did a rather remarkable leap to a wooden chair by the archway, and pounced into the carpet in the room next to us. His footsteps pounded up the stairway.

"Where do you live?" Anna demanded.

"In my defense, he tricked me about the soda," I said.

"He's *five*. Aren't you supposed to babysit? Have you fed him yet? If I'd been allowed to babysit, I'd have fed him."

"I'm thinking we wait and see if your aunt comes back soon. She didn't say anything about feeding you."

"So you're going to let him go hungry?" Anna asked. Her fists went right back to her waist. "This isn't my mess."

I glared at Brand, mainly because he wasn't saying a damn thing. He assumed his bodyguard pose and blinked back at me. I said, "Can we call for pizza?"

"Pizza! Pizza! Pizza!" Corbie thundered down the stairs, ran around the polished dining table in the next room, and catapulted back up the stairs.

"Can't you even make spaghetti?" Anna asked in exasperation. "Everyone can make spaghetti."

"That seems like it should be true," I said. "Okay. I'll make—"

"You can't cook," Brand said.

"Can't I? We must have cooked before Queenie, right?"

So Brand and I went into the kitchen, while asking Anna to check on her brother. I stared at the old, smudged cabinets. I tried to remember what we did before Queenie came along. Jars and jars of peanut butter came to mind.

I took a deep breath and walked over to the stove range. "I'll boil the water." I shook my hand and focused, transmuting my sabre from wrist-guard to sword-hilt form, and leaned in to light the gas.

Brand said, "How much damage do you think you'll do before you figure out it's fucking electric?"

I turned my sabre back into a wristguard. "Are you going to watch me do this? Or help?"

"I'll stand watch. Like a good bodyguard."

"Corbie!" I shouted.

The last syllable was still vibrating in the air when Corbie ran into the kitchen, across the kitchen, and into the kitchen wall. He fell onto his ass and rubbed his forehead. "I had a little crash," he said hoarsely.

"Good news then," I said. "Brand wants to give you a piggyback ride!"

They both shared a surprisingly similar expression of shock, before Corbie started bouncing around Brand, and Brand stared daggers at me. Sixty seconds later, Corbie was giddyupping Brand to the other side of the house, while I figured out how to turn the oven fan on.

Lunch went well. The spaghetti turned out exactly like spaghetti was supposed to turn out, and I didn't summon any evil spirits with my spice combination. Every time Brand took a bite, I smiled at him and nodded, because I could read his mind, and knew it didn't suck.

"Stop that," he finally said. "You weren't always this needy for approval."

"And yet."

"Fine. We've eaten worse."

"What are we doing after this?" Anna asked. She was rolling a quarter along the back of her knuckles—back and forth, back and forth. It was an old Companion training trick, and I saw Brand eying it with interest.

"We usually have dessert after dinner," Corbie said. His eyes lit up. "Cookies? Did you make cookies?"

"Do you smell cookies?" I asked.

He narrowed his eyes and tilted his nose in the air, sniffing deeply.

"There are no cookies," I said. "Okay, look, we're going to play a game now." I pointed to the hutch behind the dining room table, which overflowed with coloring books and broken crayon stubs. "The first person who draws me a picture of a dragon eating a pegasus in a lightning storm wins."

"Those are *Corbie's* crayons," Anna said. "I'm twelve."

"I'm five," Corbie said excitedly. He began to sing, "Corbie is five. Anna is twelve. Layne is fifteen. Layne will always be older than Anna, who will always be older than Corbie. That's true, right?"

I saw Brand's mind working. He didn't always respond appropriately to rhetoric. I said, before he could speak, "Dragon. Pegasus. Lightning. Brand and I are going to look at Layne's room while you draw. Your aunt said it was okay. We need you to be *really, really* quiet while we look for clues, to help figure out where Layne is."

"I can help," Anna said immediately.

While I tried to think of a polite way to keep her from underfoot, Brand just said, "Okay. But after. We need to form our own impression first. Do you understand?"

She hesitated, then gave him a tight nod.

We climbed the stairs while she found a clean sheet of paper for Corbie. Old shag carpeting muffled our boots as we made our way down an upstairs hallway, peering through open doorways as we went, matching rooms with occupants.

"You're good with Anna," I told him.

"Why do you say it like that?" he asked.

I was getting a lot of glares from him today. "Like what?"

"Like the bar is set at me not stabbing children."

"Corbie says that Anna will always be older than him," I said. "Is that true?"

"Unless she dies, then he'll catch up," Brand said.

"That's now the bar," I said. "Don't say things like that. And I was complimenting you, you ass. You were good with her."

For a second—just a second—another thought slithered through my mind. I remembered the folder, and Brand's siblings. The safe human life he might have had without my father's interference . . .

No. Not the time, not the place. I needed to focus.

There was a closed door ahead of us. We'd passed a bedroom filled with adult weapons; a bedroom filled with safe child-friendly weapons; and a bedroom filled with stuffed salamanders and octopuses. It was a solid assumption that Layne's bedroom was what remained.

We stopped talking, opened the door, and went into search mode.

We started by getting a general sense of everything that Layne wanted people to see. His own tastes were reflected in cheap posters, magazine cutouts scotch-taped to black wall paint, and the favorited links on his desktop computer. Like many young men his age, he pushed against the boundaries of respectability in very predictable ways. A mix of goth, gender fluidity, carefully fabricated media antiheroes.

Holding his own personal tastes together were signs of the quality of his caregiving. He had more than one pair of shoes, for different seasons; there were coats and jackets; clean sheets; no dirty laundry.

Once we looked in all the obvious hiding spots, we split up. I searched the hollow spaces in furniture and fixtures; Brand poked behind the room's basic infrastructure—electrical outlets and light panels, loose molding and cornices.

He stumbled on something before I did: a small leather pouch stuffed behind loose molding above the closet. He pulled three matchbooks out of the pouch, holding them up to show me.

"Old school," I said. "Is there a phone number written inside? Be careful—sometimes it looks like a date, but it's actually a safe combination."

He peeled back the plain brown lid of the matchbook. He bent one of the matches out at an angle and sniffed it. "Drugged. They pass these out at one of the Green Docks bars. The smoke is a mild sedative, nothing too batshit."

"How did you know that?" I asked, and, just as quickly, decided that I didn't want to know. There were few things Brand and I didn't share, and this was probably one of them. I knew he took nights off every now and then, and I'd always got the sense he didn't lack for casual companion-ship during them. The Green Docks was a very easy place to find casual companionship.

He opted to get exasperated instead of replying directly. "I know about poisons and red-light districts the same way you know about pen-tagrams and fire elementals. We had different fucking training classes. Keep looking."

The next find went to me.

Searching the hollow spaces in bed frames was always a bitch. It made my shoulder hurt to lift up the frame while pulling the cap off the leg. But Layne was clever, and my efforts were rewarded. He'd stuffed something in the middle of the tube of the back left leg. A thin sewing thread, tied to the object, dangled to the bottom, allowing me to tug everything into range of my grasping fingers.

It was a large piece of real velvet, carefully cut from something like drapes or a throw pillow. I unrolled the crushed red fabric and revealed a stack of small instruments and tools. Clean razors; Band-Aids; a tiny spatula that may have been part of a cheese and cracker set. There was a small, travel-sized tube of antibiotic; cotton balls; three sealed sanitizer napkins left over from a fast-food restaurant. And most importantly, there were two sealed vials.

"A cutting kit," Brand said from behind my shoulder. "He cuts."

Brand reached for a sealed vial, but I gently pushed his hand away from it. "It's bacterial."

"What?"

"Raw chicken juice, maybe. Or fecal matter. This isn't a cutting kit, it's an infection kit. Layne inherited his father's necromancy. He knows immolation magic."

In the movies, you stopped searching when you found the Big Clue. In real life, that'd be a stupid risk. So Brand and I kept trudging through implausibly long minutes with nothing more to show than inhaled dust, scratches on the backs of our hands, and spider webs on my sleeve. We found nothing else of note.

We headed back into the hallway. I said, "Looks like we're going to the Green Docks. The bar with the matchbooks is a good place to start. And I can find out if any other bars specialize in necromancy."

"The bars there . . . They're more brothels than bars. The Green Docks is—it branches." Brand looked uncomfortable even saying that much.

"It branches?" I said.

"It starts safe, and then branches in different directions according to whatever you're in the mood for. It's like a fucking floating rabbit hole. Quinn said that we'd be in a fight near boats—and some of those brothels aren't the types of places we'd want to get in fights. We can't go there until you spend time in your sanctum."

"Agreed. I've got some spells in mind. The brothel with the match-book—which direction does it go in?"

"It's high-end. In the safer parts. But the ones with necromancy? I know fuck all about that direction. It'll be deep into the docks."

"Well, that sounds about right, for our luck. And I think Corbie is eavesdropping." I nodded my chin down the hall, where a fringe of black hair snatched itself out of sight.

"Once we actually say your name, that doesn't work anymore," Brand called.

Corbie poked his head back into the hall. He was in the bedroom filled with stuffed animals, a piece of paper clutched in his hand. His eyelids were getting droopy, which I hoped meant he was crashing from his sugar high.

He came over and handed me the paper. I stared at the crayon monsters and said, "Nice. But you forgot the lightning storm."

He gave me a shrewd look, and pointed to a blank space in the sky. "Lightning bolts are white. It's right there."

"Well played. You look like you need a nap."

He gave me another shrewd look. "I take naps while watching TV."

"That sounds completely believable," I said. "We'll give it a shot."

He turned and bolted to the stairway. I began to walk after him, but Brand laid a finger on my shoulder. He said, though not to me, "Always pay attention to nearby light sources. If one is behind you, no matter how faint, you're going to cast a shadow."

Anna stepped out of her bedroom, a tight expression on her scarred face. She nodded at Brand.

"You said you wanted to help," Brand continued. "Where else does Layne hide things? Other than his room."

She held Brand's gaze for a good ten seconds. Whatever calculations happened in her head, they summed in our favor. She pointed to an open bathroom door. "Sometimes he spends a long time in there. The shower isn't running, but there are shampoo drips on the counter."

"I see," I said, because I didn't want to explain why a fifteen-year-old boy spent time in a locked bathroom when the water wasn't running.

Brand played it straight. He went into the bathroom, leaned into the shower, and picked up a bottle. The plastic was semitransparent. Brand held it up against the window, tilting it back and forth, until we spotted a dark object at the bottom.

I stopped him before he squirted it into the sink. People didn't buy off-brand shampoo because it was easily replaced. We found an empty container on a shelf in the closet. The container smelled like coconut, the same as the shampoo, which made me think that this was Layne's trick to fishing the object out, pouring the shampoo from one container to another.

Some mess later, I had a bronze stone in my hand. I smeared my thumbprint across the surface of it. My finger buzzed against its magic. Not a sigil. Similar to a ward, but not powerful enough. "A key," I decided. "It's a key. A wardstone. It interacts with a specific ward."

Anna edged around me and frowned at my palm. She gently put a finger on the wardstone. "It's just . . . humming. How do you know what that means?"

"I've always been good at sensing magic. Not many people are."

I watched her watching the stone, thinking to myself that, no, not many people were.

"Would you use this on your seal?" she asked. "Maybe that's what it's for."

"My . . . seal?"

She looked over her shoulder, back into the hallway. We followed her to a closed, narrow hallway door that opened to a closet. Blankets were stacked on the top shelf; towels on the middle shelf; and the lowest shelf had been removed to make room for a large bronzed sun.

"Oh," I said, but softly.

"Does that coin do something to this? We don't have anything else magical in the house. But this hums too. It didn't melt in the fire—it's magical, isn't it?"

"It is," I said. I lowered myself to the ground slowly, so that my knee made a drawn-out, popping creak. I ran my fingers across the stylized brass sun. The emblem of my house. Every family under Sun Estate's rule had had one of these, once upon a time. Kevan Dawncreek would have had one, certainly.

They were old devices—ritualistic, really—from the days before photographs and social media, when people didn't necessarily recognize the famous on sight or easily trust what they were seeing.

"No," I finally said. "That wardstone has nothing to do with this. This—these emblems—were owned by every house under the Sun Throne. Really, every house under *every* throne, though the emblems vary. They're a type of blood ward. They respond to my family's blood. They were used to confirm the identity of the rulers." And thinking about this blood ward, so soon after finding the one in the attic of Sun Estate, made me uncomfortably close to remembering all the photographs and reports in Brand's folder.

I distracted myself by putting a fingernail against my gums, and pressing roughly. When I tasted copper, I moved my fingertip to the emblem, and sent a small burst of willpower through it. The emblem recognized my blood and my magic, and awoke. A warm amber glow flooded the hallway, thick as sunset.

A shiny black head pushed under my armpit. Corbie stared at the glowing emblem with eyes as big as dollar coins. His lips moved for a few seconds before he greedily breathed the word, *"Nightlight."*

"You already have a nightlight," Anna said.

He stared at her, thinking furiously. "It broke. This morning!"

"It did not, and you are not using it as a nightlight," Anna said firmly. Corbie ran into his room and slammed his door.

"It only lasts a day," I apologized. "A full turn of the planet. Unless you keep adding my blood."

"You will kindly keep that fucking detail to yourself," Brand said. "Last thing we need is him following you around with a pair of safety scissors."

"You swear a lot," Anna said. "I won't tell if you let me swear."

"I won't make you go babysit your brother if you let me swear," Brand countered.

From behind Corbie's closed door, I heard what may, or may not, have been the crunch of plastic.

* * *

We'd barely made it downstairs when the front door opened and Corinne Dawncreek came in. I caught a split second of her weary face before she spotted us, and slid her features into a resting blankness.

"It makes me nervous that I can't see Corbie," she said.

"He's in his room," I told her, as Anna said, "They gave him lots of soda."

Corinne smiled at Anna for a moment, then let her coat slide off her back. She caught it with her left hand, and hung it on a hook by the door.

Brand gave Corinne a hard look, and lowered his gaze to Anna. "I need to speak with your aunt. Go check on your brother."

"Why can't I stay and listen?" Anna asked seriously.

"Because it's your aunt's place to decide how much to tell you, not mine."

Anna nodded and went upstairs.

"How hurt are you?" Brand asked Corinne, when he was sure he couldn't be overheard.

Corinne gave him a mulish look.

He waved at her right hand. He'd have already noticed she was right-handed, but had taken her jacket off with her left.

"Just a sprain," she admitted with a grudging sigh. "The little beast grabbed it and ran, and threw a chair in front of me. *Amateur.*"

"He took the money?" I asked. "Did he tell you anything?"

"He got away before I could question him." She went over to an arm-chair in the living room and, with careful motions, lowered herself into it. "If I start swearing, I won't stop, and I don't have that many quarters left."

Brand went and sat on the sofa opposite her. It was a straightforward motion, but it also felt a little like he was circling prey.

He said, "Why didn't you tell us that Layne was a necromancer?"

It looked as if he'd slapped her. Her face whitened, wrinkles and battle scars standing out in pale relief.

"You didn't know," I said suddenly. "Did you? We found a kit in his room. It's an infection kit. Do you know what that is?"

Corinne stared into her lap, horrified. "I remember something similar. From Kevan. Bloody fucking hellfire *shit*. Where? Where was it?"

"Very cleverly hidden," I said. "We also found a matchbook from the Green Docks, and a key to a ward. I'm not yet sure what the ward is, or where it is."

"I . . . the matchbook. I'd found that. Not anything else. I'm a fucking fool."

"Searching for things is what Brand and I do for a living," I said. "Do you have any idea where we might find Sherman?"

"I talked with people, after he got away. He's been working on an upscale ship. Maybe even the one on the matchbook. But wherever it is, he was fired, and couldn't find work near the lights."

Brand said to me, "That's jargon. The safer bars and brothels are near the dock lights."

"They think he's gone deep into that jungle." She gave a guilty look toward the stairway in the adjoining dining room. "But there is one thing to follow up on. He'd got the job at the upscale bar because his cousin works there. I've heard of that one, through Layne. We need to look for a blond, freckled male whore."

"Anything else?" Brand asked.

Corinne hesitated, and glanced between us. "Sherman . . . lives hard. He's always been on the edge. He's lived on the edge as long as I've known of him. But getting fired? If something has pushed him into freefall, I don't like that it's happened at the same time that Layne's gone missing. I don't like it at all."

"We'll find him," I promised.

THE GREEN DOCKS

The Green Docks was a dense, schizophrenic arrangement of wooden piers that stretched a mile into the ocean. It forked and overlapped on itself like a hedge maze, trapping hundreds of ships in boardwalk cages. There were old boats with wooden masts and hemp netting; rusting oil tankers; modern yachts with clean satellite arrays.

Every one of the ships had disappeared without a trace at some point over the last few hundred years.

I have no idea if the human world knew we'd taken these ships. Even if they did, I suppose it was easy enough to say we'd reclaimed them from the ocean floor, where they'd sunk in perfectly normal circumstances. What human would want to believe there were kraken the size of skyscrapers? Or creatures who were more interested in dinner than the material contents of the hold?

If I relaxed my eyes just *so*, I could see the energies that haunted the docks. I could see broken masts, and rogue waves, and claw marks as deep as a man's arm. I could see the transparent panic of inexperienced sailors, and the fury of insane captains.

Since relaxing my eyes just *so* wasn't important to the matter at hand, I shook my head and tried to ground myself in the present.

Brand and Addam locked the car and gathered their things, while I walked ahead, tilting my nose into the breeze. Addam had insisted on coming with us, which added a crapload of sigils to our general defense. I may have still hesitated at this, but Brand overruled me. Whatever he knew about this pirate's cove made him convinced we'd want backup.

The Green Docks didn't smell like the average New Atlantis dock. The area was so potent with energy that I wasn't even sure what I smelled was a smell at all. It was as if sounds and imagery got jumbled into odor.

The Green Docks smelled like neon. It smelled like 356 quadrillion tons of Atlantic water slapping against wooden hulls.

And Brand spent time here, I reminded myself. Brand *knew* this place, and visited these brothels. Thinking that was uncomfortably like tapping my finger next to a live wire. Uncomfortably close to the memory of that damned folder. So I shoved the thoughts as far down the fucking Nile as they'd go.

"Eh," I said, when Brand came up behind me. "I'm not impressed."

"You need to take this place seriously," Brand warned.

"Remember that time we fought a lich? I bet the Green Docks doesn't have a lich."

"The Green Docks has plenty."

"They're selling T-shirts over there." I pointed. "And souvenir shot glasses."

If Brand had really believed I wasn't taking this seriously, he'd have been pissed. But whatever he felt through our Companion bond let him settle the matter with a single eye roll.

"I wish we'd had time to do more research," Addam said. He unwound a scarf from his neck and stuffed it into his pocket. It was a chilly night, but he had a necklace made of sigils, along with a leather belt filled with sigil platinum discs. I liked that he exposed them without me having to ask. In a place like this, a show of force meant everything. "I would have preferred to learn more. I have little experience with this place."

"Brand does," I said.

And the Companion bond told Brand something about that, too, because he narrowed his eyes at me. But he let it drop, and nodded his chin past me. "We're going there. *The Honey Pot.*"

We headed off the main dock, up a set of wooden stairs that brought us level with the decks of the taller ships. The pier was sturdy and well built, but even so I could feel the roll against the planks.

Brand had dressed in lightweight cargo pants fitted with ceramic trauma plates, and a tactical chest harness lined with blades. My eight sigils were filled with a balance of aggressive, defensive, and stealth spells. Addam—who had three times as many sigils, courtesy of his family armory—complemented my limited load with spells I didn't have space to store, along with several copies of Telekinesis and Shield.

As we walked, I looked around me. "Why is this area even called the Green Docks?"

Brand scuffed a rubber-soled boot against the wooden deck. "Used to be painted green. You can still see the flakes if you look."

"That's it?" I said, unimpressed. "I kind of imagined dragon scales or dryad venom or something."

"Would you stop trying to stir shit up," Brand said.

"I never," I said. "Are you always this cranky when you visit here? They probably charge you extra."

That last bit didn't sound as lighthearted as I'd intended.

Brand stopped walking. "Do you have any questions you want to ask?"

I shook my head.

He said, "I'm allowed a night off now and then. If you want to know what I do when I come here, just ask."

"I'm not asking." I dug my back molars together to keep my stupid mouth shut.

Brand continued to stare at me for another three beats, then let the matter go, like I knew he would. It's not the type of thing he'd ever let distract us, not when we were on the job.

Then Addam went and said, "I'll ask. It may help to know. Have you been to this *Honey Pot*, Brand?"

"A lot of people come here. It's well guarded, and they don't put up with rude shit. It's safer than the places further along."

"Do they . . ." Addam deliberated his phrasing. "Cater to anything in particular?"

"Yes. People with lots of money. If this Sherman is as much a wreck as Corinne says, I'm surprised they even hired him. Rune, did you learn anything more about Sherman's cousin?"

I relaxed. The conversation had steered itself onto safe ground. While we'd prepared for our trip, I'd spent a half hour online researching some of the more popular dock brothels. The *Honey Pot*'s website was exceedingly customer-friendly, right down to a staff page that read like a restaurant menu. None of the pictures I saw showed a heavily freckled man, though.

I shook my head. "No. I printed out some names, just in case. We'll have to wing it."

"We can do that," Brand said. "Come on. Let's go find the guy who tried to steal money from us."

The SS *Vaitarna* was known in popular legend as the *Vijli*, the Gujarati word for electricity.

It was one of the first steamships tricked out with powered lights. She was a large, three-level schooner, 170 feet long, with two masts and a huge funnel connected to compound steam engines. It'd been one of the luxury liners of the Arabian Sea, until it vanished without a trace on November 9, 1888.

Naval authorities believed it sank in a cyclone. As we approached the ramp that led to the main deck, I ran my senses from bow to stern. I saw ghostly, black-and-white waves smash across the railings. A woman in a white dress tumbled past me, snatched by hurricane-force winds. Sheets of gray water sawed at the masts, and one of the fore cabins was on fire.

Almost eight hundred souls sank with the *Vijli*, including thirteen wedding parties and a whole mess of teenagers headed to Mumbai for college examinations. In the years after its disappearance, it became known as the Titanic of Gujarat, a local folklore.

Newlyweds and university students? Their moment of elation upended into a horrible death? It's no wonder they called this brothel the *Honey Pot*. The feast of emotion that stained the decks would feed spells for generations.

I shuddered and shut down my sight.

* * *

The steamship's open, outer deck was sparsely crowded. A small bar served local moonshine. Knots of Atlanteans—almost all men—drank up an appetite before moving into the brothel itself. The electric lights were antique and ornate, the unsteady stream of power reminding me of old television static. On either side of the bar were armed bouncers; and on either side of the bouncers were beehive-shaped fountains recycling honey instead of water. I inhaled the scent of clover.

Brand and I did a quick circuit of the area. Brand checked for problems; I looked for a freckled whore. Most everyone appeared to be a guest or a guard, though.

"Stay here," Brand said. He slipped into a shadow, and then another shadow, and then he was just the faint presence of movement.

Since I didn't even know where the door or hatch to the brothel was, I went over to the railing and tried to be unobtrusive.

"No, your *other* starboard," someone laughed, but unfriendly-like, as one does when they're playing to an audience.

I looked over and saw Addam, who wasn't being unobtrusive. He was flushing under the attention of a young scion.

"I asked where the main door was," Addam said to me as I walked up to them. "It seems I'm unfamiliar with ship terms." His *R*'s were sharp and Russian, which meant he was irritated or embarrassed.

"That's port," the scion drawled. He lifted a finger without actually pointing. "Starboard is there. It would be my pleasure to show you, if you'd like. I haven't seen you here before, have I?"

"Haven't you?" I said, drawing his attention. "I guess you haven't worked here long, then."

The young customer's leer went brittle for just a moment, then flowed back into *tsk*ing speculation. "Such provocation."

Two other scions stepped up to the man's back, anticipating confrontation.

It made me tired just to observe this posturing. All three were as young and stupid as a thousand other scions from wealthier houses. They were dressed in some new fashion that wasted sigil spells—the larger veins on their face and neck pulsed with colorful, glowing tracery.

"This isn't happening," Brand said, appearing behind all of us. "We're not starting the night with stupid shit. Everyone goes their own way."

"Oh, but *you*, you're familiar," the scion breathed, as if Brand hadn't just startled him. "I've seen you here. Not many humans leave the shore, you know. And you've brought *toys* this time." He was smart enough to only run his fingers in the direction of Brand's knives.

The bouncers at the bar watched this unfold, too still for actual stillness. I remembered Brand saying they didn't put up with trouble.

"Look," I said. "I get it. You're rich. You're bored. You're *edgy*. But we really don't have time for this. Maybe I can buy you a drink and send you on your way?"

The scion stared at me, while his friends stared at him, waiting for the wind to blow. The young man seemed indolent, but I'd known a lot of scions who used their uselessness like a mask. So as the half-seconds ticked by, I underestimated him less and less, and tried to pretend I wasn't checking him out for sigils.

"A human with sharp, sharp toys," the young man finally said. "You're a Companion. I hadn't realized that before. Which is a shame. I have such particular feelings about Companions."

"I'm so fucking pleased to hear that, but I'm not on the menu." Brand leaned to the left, pointedly staring at the bouncers to get their attention. "You ready to invite Lord Saint Nicholas in?" He indicated Addam with a thumb.

Addam made a sound of surprise at being named so openly. But the guards jumped to attention, and the scion trio glanced at each other, recognizing Addam's family name. Arcana court trumps greater house trumps lesser house in pretty much every card game. Inside thirty seconds, we were being shown through an enlarged hatch to the inside of the *Honey Pot*.

"I hadn't realized the plan was to gain entry by announcing my court,"

Addam said carefully, as we walked down a short corridor decorated with a lot of red velvet.

"Sorry about that," Brand said. "Next time I'll totally compromise Rune instead."

Addam gave the back of Brand's head a small, rueful smile.

"Sorry," I said.

"It is not a concern," he replied, but I got a small smile too.

Ahead of us, a warm, sulfur light spilled onto the hardwood floors. I could hear music and glassware, and the air was sweet and smoky.

Brand held up a hand, stopping us. "Smoke. Addam?"

Addam touched a platinum sigil fitted into his decorative leather belt, one of a half dozen matched set. The sigil was an exact match to one of my own—which made sense, because my disc had come from Quinn.

I felt the release of the spell. Addam reached out and touched our bare skin—Brand's neck and my cheek. I felt magic film my mouth and nostrils, and I started breathing a few heartbeats after realizing I'd stopped. No drugged or ambient smoke would bother us while the spell lasted. We'd planned on this because of the matches we'd found in Layne's bedroom.

Thus protected, we walked into the *Honey Pot*'s skintight menagerie.

About a half dozen of the ship's original staterooms had been gutted to create a large, open space. Customers and casual drinkers circulated between five different bars, which were elegant things made from black walnut and brass fixtures. Overhead, a domed ceiling of thick glass showed a blurred starscape.

The noise wasn't what I would have expected from a full room. Less like a bar, more like a polite, high-end department store. And beneath even that hum was a quieter one. The owners weren't conspicuous about it, but there were hints of sigil magic if you knew where to look—a spell to give the lights an amber glow; a spell to turn tobacco smoke into alpine mist.

The shape of the room was a clamshell, fanning away from a narrow, raised stage. Half-naked men and women walked across the platform in a never-ending loop that tried to be more artful than a conveyor belt.

A half-fae worker came up to us. He or she was thin and androgynous, and dressed in sleeveless white samite.

They held a hand to me in greeting—less a clasp than a touch. Their skin felt like actual rose petals. Then they ran their eyes up and down Brand's holster. "My, my. This is new. How well can you use that big . . . knife?"

"We need some information," he said, a little uncomfortably. I realized, then and there, that this fae was not a stranger to Brand.

"Let's find a corner, and I'll tell you anything," they promised.

"Okay, you need to dial it down," Brand said. "I'm on duty. This isn't a pleasure call."

I didn't react. I was very sure I didn't react.

Brand continued. "We're looking for someone who works here. He's not in trouble. We just need to talk to him. Tall with freckles?"

"Sounds delicious. But naming names is above my paygrade. Ask the dream sprites over there. They always know what's going on. You can tip me now."

Brand said, "Addam."

"Alright," I said in frustration, as Addam nodded at Brand and fished into his pocket for a tip. Addam pulled out a crisp fifty instead of a wrinkled ten or twenty. I tried to say something more, but Brand wheeled us off toward a bar in the corner.

"Addam's not our ATM," I hissed.

"We're already out a thousand dollars tonight. And no, I never fucked that faery. Tailor is just a waiter."

"I didn't—"

"Stay focused," he said, changing the subject.

Addam stood a step or two behind us, pretending to be uninterested. But when Brand moved ahead to grab a seat at the bar, Addam put his hand on my shoulder and squeezed. I wasn't sure if it was compassion or a friendly suggestion to stop acting pissy, but I appreciated the gesture.

So I tried to put my mood aside, again, and focus on the dream sprites.

Three of them were tending the smallest corner bar. They were the size of large GI Joe dolls, and flew around with hyper-caffeinated efficiency. They were an unusual staffing choice for the sedate surroundings, which probably accounted for the thin crowd in this corner of the room. With the exception of an enormous redheaded man who was all but destroying the fussy stool he was perched on, we had the seats to ourselves.

"We have many potent specials today," the tallest of the three dream sprites intoned in a high-pitched voice. "We would like to make you a margarita rimmed with salt distilled from a Malaysian tidal wave."

There was nothing potent about salt from a tidal wave. That was just tourist trap shit.

Brand said, "Three beers. Bottled. I'll take the caps off."

"We would like to tell you about our draft beer. We have a very special microbrew on tap that—"

Brand sat down on one of the free stools and leaned forward, just a little, so that he was making eye contact with the hovering creature. Then he looked down at a tasteful menu on the bar, and tapped a finger over one of the bottled beers.

"We will gladly provide this beverage," another dream sprite piped, and darted out of sight.

The two remaining dream sprites chittered at each other in fae. I didn't speak it myself, but it was a pretty language, full of rolling vowels, no contractions, no hard consonants. I took a seat next to Brand and said to them, "Do you mind if I ask you something?"

"Oh, yes, we would like you to ask us something," one of them agreed, bobbing over.

"I'm looking for a friend who I heard works here. Blond? Lots of freckles?"

The little man opened his mouth. Before he could speak, the second sprite—a woman—bumped him into a lower orbit, taking his place. Her nostrils flared as she inhaled deeply. "We would like to provide you with this *new knowledge*," she said.

Fae are creatures of etiquette. They would never accuse someone of lying. Whatever special senses this dream sprite had, she'd just found a polite way of calling me on my bullshit, and had spotted opportunity in it.

I cleared my throat. "I think the gentleman in question would be pleased to see us."

The woman inhaled through her nose again. Her smile widened. "We are happy to know the *very private* gentleman in question."

"Fine," I sighed. I pulled out my own wallet, which was not thick with crisp bills. I tried to put a self-conscious shoulder between Addam and the five battered twenties, but he defeated the attempt by standing behind me and resting his chin on my head.

"We are pleased to not need this very generous tip," the fae said, and hovered up so that her eyes were level with mine. "Customers take much delight in our *other skills*. We would be happy to share one of your dreams in exchange for such help."

"Would you," I said to her, slowly.

I turned to Addam and Brand and said, "Leave us."

Brand opened his mouth, and I looked at him, and whatever he saw in that look made him get off the stool and drag Addam to a respectable distance.

I turned my head back to face the fae, who was much less certain than she'd been a moment ago. The male dream sprite was hovering below her, reaching up to tug anxiously on her belt.

"Do you know what I am?" I asked her softly.

She wasn't so small that I couldn't see her swallow.

"I know your kind better than you suspect," I said. "I know that if I agree to *share* a dream, you'll be able to rifle my mind as I sleep."

"We do not *steal*, we only *share*," she insisted in a high whine. "*Share.*"

"You want to share one of my dreams? Mine? Go ahead and taste them. I know you can."

Her eyes flicked to my forehead, and then back to me. I leaned close to her, a low bow.

"Go ahead," I whispered.

She darted over and placed a weightless finger above my brow. And as she did, I thought about my dreams. I shoved them forward like water through a firehose. I thought about horrors that never aged; and images that never dulled; and sounds that never faded into echoes.

The little sprite screamed and flew backwards. She mouthed the word *Arcana* with shaking lips as blisters rose on her finger. She turned orange. Not her actual pallor—just the flickering reflection of my burning eyes, as my Atlantean Aspect flared to life.

"I am what remains of the Sun Throne," I said, "and I do not *share* dreams or memories. You may thank me for the mercy."

"We are now pleased to recognize Lord Sun!" the male dream sprite said, all but throwing the woman behind him. He bobbed in front of me, shielding his eyes against my power. "We are pleased to offer beer and smiles and directions to Kellum Greenwater!"

Atlantean Aspects are difficult to describe.

A particularly powerful magic user can look different—distorted— when strong emotion or magic is upon them. My eyes used to glow orange, but lately I've had a distressing tendency to catch fire.

It gets even more dramatic the higher you go up the food chain. Arcana—real, ruling Arcana—are the closest things to gods on this planet. They *require* fearsome Aspects—it's a survival mechanism, like a predator's coloring or the ruff of a wolf. There are stories of Arcana becoming burning bushes, scorpions, and F5 funnel clouds. My father became a pillar of light so bright that it left an afterimage for hours. Addam's mother had dangled from the ceiling like a spider.

Many scions of the newest generation don't have Aspects. A lot of academics cite this as evidence that the Atlantean race is in decline. I have always disagreed.

Just because most scions don't turn into jabberwockies or lightning bolts when they're pissed doesn't make them weaker; it just makes them children of a different world. Blending in has become *their* survival mechanism.

The apologetic male sprite herded us out of the common room, toward a stairway at the end of a hallway. The corridor was richly appointed, but it was still a ship, and soft carpets only went so far in masking the raw utility of planks and hull.

I wanted to ask the sprite more questions, but his fellow bartender—the woman who'd pissed me off—buzzed up to us. She had something in her arms.

"We are very *sorry*," she said. "This is a cherished gift to say how sorry *we* are. It is—" And here she said a word that sounded vaguely French. She held out her arms to me. In them was a button.

"A magic button?" I asked.

"It is *chord-dee-roy*," she said with great reverence.

I took it from her by carefully pinching two fingers together. She bobbed up, released of the weight; sketched a midair bow; and flew away. The male sprite that had led us upstairs pointed excitedly to a metal hatch at the end of the corridor, burbled his own goodbye, and chased the woman back downstairs.

I looked down at the corduroy-covered button, then looked up at Brand. "Don't go pressing my buttons," I told him.

He walked ahead to scout the hatch.

"That was a little funny," I said to Addam.

"Of course it was," he said. He gave the hatch ahead an uncertain look. "It would make sense for one of us to remain in the corridor and watch for trouble. You and Brandon are more skilled at the type of discussion you need to have with this Kellum Greenwater. I will remain outside."

"You think we're going to beat him up, don't you?"

"No. I think you both have very clever minds for asking questions. Now go do as much. I'll watch your backside."

He meant what he said, because I felt his eyes on my ass as I walked down the hall to join Brand, which made me feel a little better about life in general.

"Addam's going to stay and watch the hall," I said. "So keep any objections buttoned up." I held up the corduroy button.

"We don't do puns," he said.

"Is that a hot button issue with you?"

Brand pounded on the door, twice, with the heel of his hand. He didn't wait for a response. He turned the handle and pushed into the room, turned sideways so that he minimized himself as a target.

The room was empty. Almost empty. Through a closed door in the corner, we heard a shower running.

I put a finger on the side of a cup of tea, which had been placed on an elegant cherrywood bureau. "Still warm," I murmured.

"We'll give him a minute," Brand said. He began a circuit of the room, looking for any weapons or alarm systems.

I did my own tour of the stateroom. It was small and filled with lots of padding. Padded cushions, padded quilts, a padded leather headboard. The color scheme was a tasteful gray and sage. The only thing that screamed *brothel* was the collection of condoms on the nightstand. They were piled in a ceramic bowl like Halloween candy. I picked up one that had anemone-like whiskers drawn on the packaging, and held it up to the light.

The shower stopped.

Brand and I stayed on alert the full two minutes until the door handle moved. A tall, heavily freckled blond came into the room in a silk kimono, rubbing moisturizer into his neck.

"Company," he said, coming to a complete, surprised stop. He kept his hands where they were, fingers slightly splayed, projecting a nonthreatening stance.

"We're not here to hurt you," I said. "But we do need to talk to you. You're Kellum Greenwater? Sherman's kin?"

"Cousin, yes," Kellum said. The reply ran over his teeth like a sigh. "Please. Make yourselves comfortable. I was about to have tea?"

There could have been a dozen different reasons for his relative calm, but calm's hard to fake when you're unable to protect yourself, which had me on guard. So I opened my senses, and felt for magic.

He was Atlantean. I could tell that much. He had gifts. His magic—the way it felt—reminded me of seeing something through a magnifying glass, and of breathing deeply in a thick fog. I recognized the metaphor. It was my brain's way of interpreting air and water magic.

"No, thank you," I said, after a fractional delay.

Kellum moved to a vanity area in the corner, where he began to clean the lotion off his hands with a soft cloth. His robe fluttered around him with great affect. There was a skill to that, to sliding the sleeves of silk up and down your forearms, creating the illusion of wind and slow motion. It was not the skill of a low-end whore.

"Sherman," Kellum said, and smiled at nothing in particular. He unpinned his hair, which he'd kept dry in the shower. "How far has he fallen this time? Rock bottom seems to get further and further away with each stumble."

"Do you know where he is?" Brand asked.

"Will you tell me why you want him?" Kellum returned.

"Because he'll lead us to Layne Dawncreek," Brand said, which made me blink, because it was rather bloody blunt.

"Layne . . . Sherman and Layne are friends. You're trying to find where Layne lives?"

"We know where he lives," Brand said. "He ran away. He's missing."

Kellum sat down in the chair at his vanity table and crossed his long legs. The silk bathrobe parted over a thigh as dense with freckles as his face.

He gave me a slight but warm smile. "You're very quiet. For what it's worth, nothing breaks my heart half as much as a beautiful man with a bad haircut."

"I have a bad haircut?" I said, a little defensively.

"I cut my own hair. Why not let me cut yours?"

Brand said, "We've got time."

"We do not," I said sharply.

Brand looked at Kellum, looked at me, looked back at Kellum. "Right. We have more questions."

"Of course, dear. Why don't you tell me what Sherman has done now. You're here to help Layne?"

Brand said, "It's the best way to save Max from——"

I slapped my hands together, funneling a bit of willpower into a cantrip so that the clap boomed like thunder. Brand's mouth hung open; Kellum's eyes widened.

"Understand this," I said. "I have every sympathy for you and your kind. It must not be easy living in a city with such an inbred distrust of psionics. I know it's why you're hunted."

"You know of my kind," Kellum said, slowly, biding time.

"You're a merman. And you must be very old, because young ones aren't nearly as subtle as you, which is why so few make it to maturity. As I said, I am not without sympathy. But make no mistake, if you do not release your hold on my Companion, I will burn your vocal cords to ash."

And with that, the merman's subsonic spell dropped into silence, and the buzzing in the back of my brain stopped.

I saw him more clearly now, especially his eyes. They were the heavy black of deep-sea pressure.

"You mind-fucked me," Brand growled.

"You entered my room without invitation, dressed like a thug," the merman said.

Brand laughed—though it really wasn't a laugh—and clapped his own hands together. "That was *awesome*. Do that again. That sly, Hollywood, high-priced-whore look. Maybe toss your hair while you do it."

Kellum rose to his feet, but kept his hands where we could see them. "I've seen you here before. You stay in the safe parts of the ship. You're a tourist, not a member. That's not an insult, by the way. I could tell you stories of the real citizens of these docks. I could tell you stories about what they have taught me. Do you know the perfect position to put your lips before they're duct-taped shut? Slightly agape and rolled inwards, so you can relax them a bit without losing skin. Do you know how to keep whip marks from scarring? Blue kelp and powdered vitamin D, mixed into a paste—though you'll always need to keep out of direct sunlight, to preserve the myth."

"I know about duct tape and scars," I said quietly.

Kellum swiveled his gaze between us. "Then cut me some bloody slack. We all wear different types of armor, to make it through the day and put food on the table. I won't ding your armor if you don't ding mine."

Brand held his gaze for a long ten seconds. Finally, he dipped his chin, a sign of truce if not approval. The confrontation washed out of the moment.

Kellum gave a long sigh and sat down again. "Let's start over. And so. My name is Kellum Greenwater, of the Jade Tide School."

"Rune and Brandon Saint John," I said.

Kellum smiled. "Saint John. I see. I thought it might be something like that."

"We got off on the wrong foot," I said, "but if it matters to you at all, we're the good guys here. You know Layne Dawncreek?"

"Yes. We've meet twice—no, three times. The last time I saw him, I tried to convince him to keep his distance from Sherman. My cousin isn't a bad person, but he tends to fall in the path of bad men. Layne is . . . Well. There's time yet for him to find his way. You said he ran away?"

"He did. We believe Sherman has information that will help us find him. Can you tell me about your cousin? And where he is?"

"He worked here briefly, but was let go. I almost lost my position as well, since I'd vouched for him when he was hired. He's a cousin on my paternal side—he's not from my school."

Merfolk bred in maternal lines and lived in packs—in schools. The males were sterile. Psionics aside, the female's need for human sperm had always marked them as outcasts. In the modern world, at least they'd stopped eating the donors.

Kellum continued. "His father—my uncle on my father's side—was a vassal of a lesser house. My uncle fell on hard times, eventually, and Sherman . . . Sherman is a very pretty young man."

"What court did the lesser house belong to?" I asked, and knew the answer even as he said, "Lord Hanged Man."

It may have not been as simple as a piece falling into place—but at least there were more pieces on the board to make sense from.

Kellum grimaced. "Nothing I could do kept Sherman clear of them for long."

"Do you know where Sherman is now?" Brand asked.

"I'll write down the name of the bar. You'll need to find it yourself—I've never gone that deep into the docks. I'm not sure how much sense he'll make, either. He's into the Agonies."

"The Agonies?" I asked.

"It's a new class of drugs," Brand said. "I've heard of them. They're fucking brutal."

"Yes," Kellum said. "They are." He looked down at his lap, at his folded hands. "You aren't surprised that I mentioned the Hanged Man."

"Kellum," I said, but not unkindly. "You don't want to ask questions about that."

"I suppose I don't. But if Layne's fallen in with the Gallows—then I fear he's already lost."

Back on the docks outside the *Honey Pot*, we took a second to get our bearings. Addam and Brand put their heads together to talk about the layout of the deeper areas. I dialed Corinne for research.

We'd set it up in advance. Corinne was standing by to pluck whatever information she could off the Internet. She listened to me explain we needed intel on the brothel Sherman was now working in—the SS

Waratah—and then ended the conversation much like Brand would: by hanging up on me.

I went back to Addam and Brand. Brand was saying, "I've heard they even have the *Marie Celeste* down there, about a mile out. You Atlanteans are pretty fucking good at stealing human history right out from under their noses."

"What do you see in this place?" I asked Brand, a little too abruptly, and before I could stop myself.

Brand gave me a look. Addam seemed interested in either my question or why I asked it. I made a sound—more growl than sigh—and said, "Forget it. We—"

My phone rang. The Dawncreeks. I answered it, expecting Corinne, but someone was whispering on the other end.

"Is this Corbie?" I said.

"Shhh," he said. "I'm in the closet."

"Why are you in the closet?"

"I didn't want anyone to hear me. It's important."

"Okay," I said slowly.

He said, "Did you tell anyone where I hid my candy?"

I closed my eyes and massaged the skin between them. "I did not, no."

"Oh good," he whispered, and hung up.

I put the phone back in my pocket. "Corbie just wanted to chat," I explained.

Brand said, "Let's head out. We can ask people for directions on the way. Corinne will call when she knows more."

"Perhaps I could speak with the guards on the *Vijli* first," Addam said. "They may know where this *Chained Rock* is berthed." That was the name of the bar on the *Waratah*.

While Addam retracted his steps toward the *Honey Pot*, Brand stared at me. He looked uncomfortable. "Thank you," he finally said. "For making me shut my mouth back there."

"Where? With Kellum?" I said. "Not many people can resist a mer-man's siren song. It's not your fault."

"I didn't even know the bar had a merman. I should have known."

"Why? Because you go there a lot?"

"I don't——" He glared at me. It's possible my question had a little too much bite in it. "It's not like I've got a fucking punch card or something for the docks. I don't come here that often. And I definitely don't go into the sketchy areas."

"You don't need to explain."

"Apparently I fucking do. It's just . . . Places like this, people leave each other alone. It's not like being at normal bars. You're not expected to get chatty with people."

"That makes total sense," I said. "You come here to take a break from being chatty."

I smiled into his glare, which he turned into an eye roll, which meant we were okay for now.

Addam came back with no useful information at all. We took a vote and decided to head toward an area called mid-dock, which was the last crowded section of the docks before it splintered off into a dozen different, specialized paths—each one flying their own unique freak flag.

As we walked, we moved further from the neat order of city utili-ties. There was no power grid this far out—any bar with electricity had a generator or magic. And there were no lampposts, either. People walked around with whale oil lanterns, glow sticks, cell phone lights. The sheer variety of small lighting sources created a bizarre competition of shadow and motion.

And overlaying all of this—darting through the corners of my vision—were ghost images of death and destruction. Phantom icebergs, hill-sized tentacles, tidal waves that reached up and blurred the moon.

My phone rang. I answered it. Corinne spent five minutes info-dumping as much as she could about the *Waratah*, which was academically interesting, but not overly helpful. Brand tugged on my sleeve and told me to ask her if she'd gone into the chat rooms and looked at visitor comments. There was a lot of meat in unfiltered user comments, which rarely turned up in search engines. Corinne heard Brand asking, and said, "No, I just sat on my fat ass and read the Wikipedia entry. Do you want to teach me to suck eggs while you're at it?" She hung up.

Mid-dock was an immense wooden platform surrounded by weathered railings. It looked like a triage area, or a soup kitchen, or a drug den—or all three.

To my left was a naked derelict pulling ants out of his pubic hair. When he saw me flinch, he grinned and yelled, "It's easier to drink from the *side* of a skull than the *eye sockets*."

To my right, a woman with arachnid in her bloodline was pacing back and forth. Thin strands of web stretched from her footsteps. She had a sunburn and bad dye job.

None of these people looked like they had information, or at least not enough to justify the challenge of a conversation.

"There," Addam murmured, and pointed.

I looked in that direction and saw some sort of priest or healer in gray-green robes. He was holding a woman's wrists in both hands, trying to keep her from scratching at bleeding wounds on her face. She was staring into the priest's eyes with a look of unreliable sanity, saying, loudly, "She comes. You know that she comes. *It's time.*"

"You're hurting yourself, Irehne," he said quietly, as we came up behind them. "You must rest. Will you let me help you rest?"

"Will you wake me when my time comes?" she asked.

"Of course," he promised.

As she nodded, he let go of one of her hands and touched the center of her forehead. But her agreement was a lie. Her hand sprang up as soon as it was free. She managed to dig her nails into the injury before his magic overcame her, and she collapsed in a magical sleep.

The priest arranged her on a reed pallet, and kindly pulled greasy hair from her bloody forehead. He pulled a clean tissue out of his pocket and dabbed at the wound on her face.

"Who hurt her?" I asked.

The priest looked at me and blinked. After a half-second he shook his head, and really saw me. "My lord," he said. Not specific recognition; just a general sense that I was from the landed class.

"The woman," I said. "Did someone hurt her?"

"Oh. No. That would be easier to handle. She's addicted to the Agonies."

Kellum said his cousin used them. A new type of drug, Brand had mentioned. "I've heard that's a problem on the docks," I said.

The priest wiped his hands on his robe and stood up. "Irehne is fond of Itch. The worst of the Agonies, if you ask me. It localizes the high in one part of your body, and you release it in bursts by scratching. It overrides any sense of restraint. Most people break skin in minutes, and in a place like this, infection is almost guaranteed."

"It's kindly of you to help her," I said.

"Ach, no. I'm only doing my part. Might I ask for a donation, my lord? I mean no offense."

"Of course not. I mean yes—I have some money on me. I wish it were more." I started to pull out my wallet, but Addam was already there two more creaseless fifties. He ignored my look, which was just as well, because I didn't have time to feed my growing guilt at relying on his superior funding.

"Could you help us with some directions?" I asked as the priest bowed over the donation and murmured a blessing. "We're looking for a . . . contact. He works in a bar called the *Chained Rock* on the *Waratah*."

A flash of disapproval was quickly swallowed, as the man busied himself with hiding the donation in his robes.

"Not a very nice bar?" I guessed.

"Not very, my lord. Safer than most, for what it's worth. For the customers at least. It's five-square that way." I wasn't sure what a square was—maybe a block? But the direction was unmistakable.

"We're unfamiliar with these parts of the docks," I said, and looked him right in the eyes as I said it. "And we're not likely to approve what we're about to see. Could you tell us what to expect?"

He held my gaze, and finally nodded. "The *Chained Rock* is frequented by men and women who like to . . . leave marks on their purchases. I've frequently tended to a lot of their employees. If your contact works there, then he hasn't worked there for long. No one works there for long, I'm afraid."

"Fucking awesome," Brand whispered behind me.

We took our leave, heading in the direction the priest had indicated. The areas past mid-dock—lit by tar-headed torches, and hurricane lamps, and shabby light cantrips—grew increasingly derelict. I peered over the railing and saw sea foam over dark water. Something moved just below the surface, too dexterous to be a fish.

We tightened our formation, and walked in silence.

The SS *Waratah* was a five-hundred-foot cargo steamship from the turn of the last century.

It had sailed a route between Europe, Australia, and Africa until July of 1909, when it vanished without a trace on its way to Cape Town. There had been no weather anomalies in the area, no reports of piracy. Two hundred and ten souls were simply lost without a shred of evidence.

The most advanced theory about its disappearance was that it was struck by a rogue wave—a killer wall of water that could reach seventy feet in height. The broken remains would have been washed toward Antarctica or lost at sea. Indeed, in my otherly vision, I saw three meters of gray ice locking the prow of the ship to a desolate, craggy landscape.

I blinked away the ghosts and saw what the *Waratah* had become today.

The *Chained Rock*, the name of the *Waratah*'s brothel, was a play on words.

The owners had built a nest—a prison—for an ocean roc. The once-beautiful beast was tied down with cold iron chains, its links inlaid with coral and obsidian runes. In open water, an ocean roc was a master of elemental magic: it could fly as fast as hurricane winds, and create tsunamis with its wing beats. I'd heard there were only a few left in the wild, which was what made this captivity so appalling.

The creature's wings—in their glory as wide as redwood branches—were now rotting and bald. Christmas lights had been threaded through the rips in the membrane.

There were a hundred metaphors in the abasement, and few that spoke well about the type of men or women who would permit them.

The light inside the nearly empty brothel was too dim for a safe entrance. I used it as an opportunity to assert my power.

With a whisper and an exaggeratedly casual gesture, I manifested three separate light cantrips and sent them circling above my head. The average scion had enough concentration to do just one parlor trick like that; juggling several like a circus act required a sigil spell from most.

I let Brand watch my back, and waited to be approached by the person in charge.

My bored eyes flicked among the small, uneasy crowd. At a table nearby, a woman with a vacant smile burned holes in a plastic water bottle with a cigarette. She batted lashes over bloodshot eyes, inviting me over. A device covered her palm and fingers, like a filigreed glove. It was made to look like ornamentation, but it wasn't. The filigree would slide sharp metal blades under her own fingernails when commanded by the master device it was slaved to. It was a tool of torture, to keep her controlled and biddable. I hadn't thought my impression of this place could go lower, but it'd just dug another six feet down.

I thought of Max, and what we needed to do to keep him safe, and let my distaste simmer.

A man burst from the back room and rushed up to me, smiling

broadly. He hadn't brushed his teeth in so long that the calcified plaque looked like a coral reef. The thick bracelet on his wrist, I saw, was made of silver filigree.

"Is this your place," I asked, though when I was acting like an asshole scion I made it a point to speak in periods and not question marks.

"I manage it, my—"

"I've heard of it," I said.

"You honor us, truly—that is most excellent. I would be happy to prepare the very best of accommodations for you. Will you be walking through the red door or the blue door?"

I gave him a hint of eyebrow, and let him read into it.

"As you may know, we pride ourselves on providing the safest atmosphere for our customers. The red door will provide you with an employee most skilled at *permitting* your . . . personal expressions. The blue door will provide you with an employee skilled at *providing* those expressions, with all sensible precautions and controls, of course."

I stared toward the doors. A young man lingered by the blue one, staring in my general direction with intent focus. He was not a man, just shaped as such. He licked his lips with a tongue made of salt.

"Where," I asked, "is Sherman."

"Sherman?" the manager asked, stuttering on the S. He flicked his eyes behind me, where the bouncers stood—and then, just as quickly, in another direction, which was where Brand stood. Brand's expression would have made it clear that the bouncers would not be allowed to interfere with whatever happened next.

And all of the sudden, I was bored with acting bored.

"Fuck it," I said, tiredly. "I've seen *enough* of the Green Docks. I will not stretch this night a single minute past what I still need from it. So I am going to ask you questions. And you are going to answer them. Challenge me, and I send this ship to the ocean floor. Do you understand?"

"My lord . . . we . . . this is . . ."

"This is what? You what? You have patrons who would scare me? You have armed men who would stop me? Is that a challenge?"

"No, my lord," he whispered.

"What do you even have to gain from it?" I asked. I half-turned and pointed behind me. "Do you have any idea how much it must have cost to trap an ocean roc? This place pulls in far more money than they put into the décor." I dragged my eyes from his scuffed shoes to his bad dental work. "Or its staff. Protecting it from me isn't worth your life. Give me that." I pointed at his wrist.

"My lord?" The man touched the slave bracelet. "T-this, my lord?"

"Yes. Give me that."

The brothel manager did the math in his head, his gaze snapping between Brand's knives, and Addam's and my sigils. He unhooked the device and handed it to me.

"Now put on the bracelet that woman is wearing," I said.

His mouth opened and closed and opened.

"*Put it on.* You will wear it, while I'm here, as a hostage of your good will. Put it on, keep it on, and tell me where Sherman is."

Two minutes later we were on our way through the red door.

If I'd interpreted things right, the tastes of the establishment ran from beatings to being beaten. Sherman, behind the red door, was the latter. Which meant I wasn't sure what sort of condition we'd find him in this late in the evening.

As we walked down a dirty, planked hallway, Brand nodded at the bracelet I cradled in my hand. "You can work that?"

"Probably not. I was just being an asshole."

He grunted. He could appreciate that.

I said, "I want to try something different with Sherman. It's getting late—I didn't realize we'd waste so much time just walking. Let me be the bad cop—I have an idea to make this go quick."

"And does this mean Brand will be playing good cop?" Addam asked, and did a very good job at hiding his smile. Brand gave him a hard stare.

"That's the door," I said. "Just follow my lead."

It was unlocked. I opened it without fanfare. The room on the other side was barely functional, with a bed, a single chest, and a basin of water on a scuffed nightstand. Two dead flies skimmed the surface. The only thing of any personality in the berth was stale, cheap incense, and a crystal geode on the chest.

A young man kneeled by the chest. He wore a leather suit riddled with dozens of complicated zippers. The material was expensive, and the design so useless that it must have been highly fashionable, but it had been inexpertly patched in several areas.

The young man was occupied with cigarettes—or rather the threadbare assembly of them. About eight or nine already-smoked butts were lined on a napkin, and he was cutting them open with a razor blade. He'd painstakingly salvaged the unburned tobacco into a small pile, which he was now shaking into rolling paper.

There were other things I took in, in the split second before anyone spoke. On a table in the corner was a bottle of calamine lotion, rubbing alcohol, and cheap, off-brand Band-Aids. The sort of thing I'd imagine would keep this Itch from killing you quickly. Sherman might have been a drug addict who was four shaky walls away from street trade, but he was smart about it. I could use that.

The young man blinked at us, a deer in headlights. Brand, good cop, took a pack of cigarettes from a pocket and laid it before Sherman. It looked suspiciously like the last half-smoked pack I'd hidden in the rafters of my bedroom.

"Sweet of you," the young man said. "But I wasn't expecting clients." He pulled a cigarette from the pack and lit it. His lips were so dry and chapped they left pieces of skin on the filter.

"We're not clients," I said. "We need information. You will provide it."

"Information?" he said. He was high. His mouth worked around the word for a second before he spoke it, like a badly dubbed foreign film.

I could work with that, too.

He tried speaking again. "This is about Corinne Dawncreek, isn't it?"

"This is about the money you took from her, and the information you failed to provide. This is about Layne. This is about my time, and my effort, which I hold in very high regard, and which has been exceedingly squandered in this miserable place. You may think you have nothing else to lose, Sherman, but if you give me a reason, I will prove you wrong."

"No worries," he said, and jerked a ribbon of smoke at me. "No problems."

"You're right, I have no problems. I never do. I have great big holes where problems used to stand."

"Okay okay okay yes yes yes," he said. "Point made. Properly scary. Do I know you? You look familiar. What do I call you?"

I fed the smallest bit of Aspect into my eyes. Orange light fell crooked on his face, creating shadows from his broken-vein nose.

He swallowed, and lowered his eyes into another drag off the cigarette. "Ask your questions."

"What do you know about Layne Dawncreek's disappearance?"

"I didn't. Know, I mean. I do now, because Corinne told me. I haven't seen Layne in weeks."

"You're lying."

"I'm not. Or I don't think I am. It seems like weeks. We had a falling out. He was messing up. I have my own mess-ups—I don't have room in my life for his, too."

"That's another lie," I said, and let the impatience brighten my eyes. "I think you were very much involved in his mess-ups."

"Sherman," Brand said, and while he couldn't quite manage gentle, he compensated by speaking quietly. "Let's start at the beginning. How did you meet Layne?"

His lips worked around the words, then he shrugged, like he'd run out of any reason to stall. "Have you heard about the parties?"

"What parties?" Brand asked.

"The parties. In the . . . in *his* court. Do you know who *he* is?"

"I think we do," Brand said. "Don't worry—we don't like saying his name either."

"How do the parties and . . . *he* connect?" I asked impatiently.

"He has people, and his people like parties with bright, young things. That's how Layne and I met—at a fancy party with a *very* small RSVP list."

"Do you know where Layne is right now?" I asked.

Sherman paid attention to his cigarette for a moment. People use hesitations as cover when they're about to lie, which doesn't work so well when you're high and clumsy. Sherman may have realized that, because he sighed, tiredly. "I told you. I didn't even know he was missing."

"There's more you're not saying," I said, and orange light licked out with the words. Sherman's eyes dilated and he pressed back away from me. "Tell me what the Hanged Man did with Layne."

"You shouldn't say his name," Sherman stammered.

"He should never have said mine. When did the Hanged Man learn about Layne's magic?"

Bull's-eye. A damned bull's-eye. I saw it on his face.

"So you know about Layne's necromancy, too," I said. "You know that's why Layne caught the Hanged Man's attention."

Sherman closed his eyes and nodded. "Layne was invited to the parties. That's where we met. The . . . Huh-Hang . . . *He* attended one—he doesn't often. He'd always been interested in Kevan's magic—Layne's da had this weird type of death magic. And he, the lord, was interested if it ran in family lines. And it did. And . . . And there's nothing more. What more do you need to know? When that . . . when *he* becomes fascinated with you, you end up mounted on Styrofoam with pins in your wings. Layne screwed up. He got *noticed*. Where people go once they vanish inside the Gallows, I don't know, because I'm not stupid enough to *want* to know. I'm certainly not stupid enough to follow."

My phone buzzed. I ignored it. It buzzed again, and again, and again.

I pulled it out and looked at it. It said: "Read this." Then: "Read this." Then: "Read this." And finally, "Show him the stone right now."

They were all from Quinn.

I took the wardstone out of my pocket—the ward key we'd found hidden at the Dawncreeks. I went over and held it between Sherman's eyes—literally, uncomfortably, inches in front of his eyes. The loss of personal space was almost as startling as the object, because he scrambled to the other side of the room.

"You'd be insane to go there!" he hiss-yelled. "They'll catch you, and they'll make you talk, and they'll know you've talked to *me*. I'm dead."

"Where is *there*," I said.

"No. Absolutely fecking not. I'm out of here." He grabbed the crystal geode off the table and tossed it on the bed, then opened a drawer filled with T-shirts and jeans.

"You're going to tell me where this leads to," I said.

"There's nothing you can do to me that's worse than what *he* can. I've told you what I can. Go away. You can't get blood from a stone."

"Of course not," Brand said, and I could tell by the tone that he'd given up on good cop. "That's stupid. You get blood from people." He pulled out his knives.

"Brandon," Addam said softly. "There are other—"

"Sherman, I need you to listen to me very closely," I said, and softly, in a tone of voice that got all the attention in the room. "I know you think there's nothing I can do to you. You work past the red door, don't you? You're used to pain? What you need to understand is that if you don't tell me what I need to know, I'm going to bring something much worse than pain down on your life."

I picked up the bottle of calamine lotion. Rotated it in my hands. "I haven't met many drug users who treat their addiction with such care. It's obviously very important to you."

"You want to take my stash? Fine. There's a hole in the bottom of the crystal. Take it."

"You're not worried. Because you can find more, yes? You can find other drugs? It won't matter. They won't work for you ever again."

Sherman stopped, a wad of clothing in his arms. He gave me a confused look.

I held out an arm. My sabre was curled in its wristguard form. I fed enough willpower into it so that fat, garnet sparks drifted to the ground. "I can make it so that you're never high again. I can make it so that no drug, no alcohol, no substance in the world will work on you. I can make it so that you never feel the euphoria. You never feel the rush. You never *escape*."

The clothes fell from his arms, one ratty T-shirt after another. His face first froze in shock, and then slowly tightened into fear.

My sabre, of course, could do no such thing. Not that that mattered. The show of power is more important than power itself, nine times out of eight.

"Tell me what I need to know," I said, "or I will trap you in the sober remains of your pathetic life. Tell me now."

"It gets you past the portal. Or into the portal. The pocket dimension."

"Which is?"

"The place where the parties were held."

"Where is the pocket dimension anchored?" I said, because they almost always were.

"The . . . *he* . . . The Gallows has a ship. There's a ship at the end of the Green Docks."

"Which ship, Sherman?"

He closed his eyes and started shaking. "If they know that I know, I'll never be safe again."

The sparks coming out of my sabre began to hiss and leave scorch marks on the wooden floor. Sherman jerked. He said, "A battleship. They always blindfold us—they never let us see it, but . . . After enough times . . . You learn things. There's a battleship. An American battleship. It's hidden behind spells. The spells confuse you. I'm not even sure where on the ship they take me—I couldn't even tell you if it's up or down. But there's a portal on it that leads to a pocket dimension. That's where Layne met . . . him. That's where I last saw Layne."

"Is it guarded?" Brand asked.

"I don't know. I think so, but there aren't many. There's a caretaker, too. An old man. The spells are meant to confuse you, I told you—I don't know more."

"What's the name of the ship?" I asked.

"The USS *Declaration.*"

I heard Addam suck in a breath, and flicked him a surprised look. Whatever shocked him about that name immediately thawed into confusion, and then a sort of anger or grimness that was probably the most startling thing I'd seen yet from Addam. He shook his head at me: *Later.*

"The ship is at the end of the Green Docks?" I said.

"Yes," Sherman said. "The northern piers. As far as you can go."

"Is there a party tonight?"

"I doubt it. Not sure. I haven't been invited back—not since Layne became . . . special. But they only met on a full moon, the entire time I've known of them. That's weeks away, isn't it?"

I glanced at Brand, who didn't seem very happy with what I was absolutely, positively thinking. There was a lot of swearing in our near future, because we were going to this battleship.

Brand and I were at the door when I realized Addam hadn't followed. I turned around to see him handing Sherman a card.

"Call this number tomorrow," Addam said. "They'll provide a safe location, food, and a small supply of drugs. You can wean yourself off them, if you're committed. But you must not stay here. You've become a liability to very dangerous people. One that they cannot comfortably ignore."

Brand and I exchanged a look, which we ended before Addam registered it.

* * *

We left the *Chained Rock*. I threw the slave device on the ground at the manager's feet as I passed him. The only thing I regretted as we headed down the plank outside was the ocean roc. I couldn't free it, not until I figured out who owned it, and how much shit I'd be in for interfering. I filed it on a very discrete "to-do" list in the back of my brain.

"You've heard of this *Declaration*," Brand said to Addam.

"I have. More than that, I suppose. Do you remember that trip Quinn and I took a month ago? We invited you, but you were busy. Quinn wanted to visit America, and he picked North Carolina. While we were there, he insisted we tour the USS *North Carolina* every day. It's a battleship—a museum now."

"You have got to be fucking kidding me," Brand said, already seeing where this was going.

I felt the next few questions pulse in my head like migraines. I'd hoped we were done with surprises like this from Quinn.

"The *Declaration* is the sister ship of the *North Carolina* and the *Washington*," Addam said distractedly. "There were only three of its type made. The *Declaration* was lost at sea not long after it launched, on its way to Asia during World War II." His frown tightened into a look of extreme displeasure. "Quinn didn't provide any context when we visited it. He didn't mention it was important."

"Brand, call Corinne, and have her email as much as she can on this ship and how it allegedly sank," I said. "Addam, get Quinn on the phone. Let's find out what he knows before we get there."

"Please tell me we're not going," Brand said, more than halfway resigned. He'd want to retreat and do research first, so we knew what we were walking into.

"Think about it," I said. "We've caused a scene. We need to assume the Hanged Man or Jirvan may learn we've been here. Sherman said the ship isn't used outside the full moon—and I think he was telling the truth. This is a good plan."

"Is it?" he demanded. "Is it a good plan? Maybe we should write it down. Here, I'll give you a crayon."

"Brand," I said. "We're out of time. There is no more time. With the formal notification period over, the Gallows can move on Max."

He made an unhappy sound, but pulled out his phone to get in touch with Corinne.

THE BATTLESHIP

Between Corinne, her email dumps to our phone, and Addam, we were able to get some quick information.

The *North Carolina*, the *Washington*, and the *Declaration* had been built from the same military blueprint. They were commissioned in the 1930s, back when Germany's nationalistic rumblings mustered into tank tracks and ammunition assembly lines. With Japan also poised to enter the mess, the USA realized it needed to sharpen the edge of its naval superiority.

The *Declaration*, like its siblings, represented a technological leap in ocean warfare. It was a floating fortress—able to withstand an atomic blast; armed with guns that could flatten harborages; staffed with the best veteran officers and newly enlisted men of its generation. The ship single-handedly rewrote the narrative on what it meant to be an American sailor.

It sailed out of the oil slicks of Pearl Harbor in the fall of 1942, passing the Marshall Islands in good time. Before it reached Midway, though, it sank in a typhoon. The wreckage was never recovered, and there were no survivors.

And that? That stank of Atlantis. It stank of altered memories, trans-location, and the sort of general mind-fucking we got away with before we went to war with humans in the 1960s and, beaten, limped to Nantucket as a consolation prize.

Addam said, and not happily, "Quinn is not answering. It is very unlike him."

I thought about that, thought about Quinn, and pulled out my phone. I texted: *"I'll send Addam and Brand back home, and go onto the ship myself."*

Three seconds later my phone practically vibrated out of my hand.

Quinn didn't even wait for the hello. "You never do that!" he gasped. "Don't do that!"

"Let's chat," I said.

"I'm busy?"

He sounded out of breath. "What are you doing?" I asked.

There was a long stretch of him trying to muffle his panting. Then he said, "Max threw me down the stairway. All the way down. We're looking for ice now."

I heard angry, outraged dialog in the background.

"Max threw you all the way down a tight, narrow, spiral staircase?" I asked.

"Did I ever tell you that sometimes you live in a palace and the stairway is made of pink marble?"

"Quinn Saint Nicholas, you were told to stay at Half House. Max was told to stay at Half House. If I find you're not at Half House, there will be war."

Addam stared hard at me.

"I am not outside," Quinn said, a little too carefully. "And we never get in trouble, even though there's almost always a tidal wave or a fire if I look deep-deep-deep enough, but there's no tidal wave or fire here, so that really says something about how safe we are."

Addam was going to have a fucking cow. I rubbed my forehead with my free hand and said, "Why did you go to the USS *North Carolina* with Addam?"

"Why did . . . But . . ." He sounded genuinely confused. "You should know about the battleship now. Is this a trick question?"

"I know about the battleship, but I don't know why you went there with Addam, and why you didn't tell me earlier, and what you still haven't told me."

"I don't know *nearly* as much as you think. There's a battleship in front of you. You have to go through it. But it's . . . cloudy. It's in fog—it's been locked in fog for years and years and years. It's not a good place. I don't like you being there."

"Max, please promise me you are not on the Green Docks," I said.

"Please promise me you have no intention of even stepping on the Green Docks."

"Oh, I can do that. That's easy. I promise."

I thought about what I had said, and realized Addam was better at Quinn's wordplay.

Then I heard Max, in the background, say, "You're sitting on the knife," and Quinn hung up.

"I am very, very unhappy," Addam said, which was a feat, because his lips were pressed together so tightly they were nearly a vacuum seal. And I hadn't even mentioned the knife yet.

"What did he say? Are they not at Half House?" Brand asked. "Who threw who down a stairway?"

"In no particular order, Quinn was bullshitting to cover up the fact that he and Max are on the move. Quinn promised that he won't step on the Green Docks."

"Did he promise you he was not near or at the Green Docks?" Addam asked.

I thought back.

Addam closed his eyes. "He's nearby."

"Then why didn't he tell us earlier he'd be nearby?" Brand asked. "Why didn't he give us a heads-up? Do you know what I could have done with more time? I could have pulled blueprints. Tidal patterns. Fucking satellite photos."

"It's most difficult to explain," Addam said, looking more than a little frustrated at having to defend Quinn. "His ability . . . Imagine it like this. Days before an actual moment—before this moment—there are a million possibilities. Hours before the actual moment, there are hundreds. But the closer he gets to where we are now, there are very few options, which is why he acts so impulsively. I strongly doubt Quinn planned this move until now."

Part of me said, *Let it go.* This wasn't the time or place. But, unfortunately, the part of me that puzzles out tactful approaches usually works slower than my mouth.

"Addam . . . I'm not so sure that's a good assumption." I didn't realize until just now how much I wasn't looking forward to this conversation, or how much I'd been deliberately putting it off. "He's not a child anymore. Or at least, he doesn't have the powers of a child anymore. I think he puts more into motion than you suspect. I think he makes judgment calls."

"Judgment calls," Addam said. The words were cool. "You make my brother sound somewhat diabolical."

"That's not what I mean. He has a good heart. But I wouldn't rule out he made a conscious decision *not* to tell us about the battleship."

"But the medication . . ." Addam tried to say, but his heart wasn't in it.

"He must be outgrowing it," I said. "Or his powers are stronger than we thought." Or, I added to myself, they always had been, and he'd neglected to tell us.

Brand had pulled out his phone and was scowling at it, thumbs dancing across the screen.

"Texting Max?" I said, glad for a diversion. Brand grunted. "The phone still trying to autocorrect all your fucks?" He spared me a glare, which matched Addam's glare, because Addam was not ready to let this go.

I sighed. "Look. We can talk about this later. Let's just try to finish what we need to do, and then find Quinn and Max. If they're interested in the Green Docks, they can come back later with Brand. He'll give them a guided tour."

Brand's thumbs froze. I felt our bond slam shut for three full seconds before he opened it back up to an even, blank emotion.

"I didn't mean anything by that," I said carefully.

"I think you did," he said.

"I didn't. I know you come here. And I know you don't come out this far—to places that are out this far on the docks. I don't *care*, Brand."

"You don't care. That's better?" he asked.

"Do you want me to care?" I asked, and the first flickers of my own anger rose. "Do you want me to forbid it? Do you want me to bloody chaperone you? What do you want? Just tell me. I can't say anything right today."

"Then don't say anything," he snapped, stepping right up into my space. "We're on the job. This isn't the goddamn time or place for you to keep bringing up goddamn Oprah moments. How about we just get our fucking heads in the game. If it makes you feel better, I'll start a list for later about all the things you can't say right."

"Maybe we should both stop saying things——" I started to yell.

I felt a surge of magic, then I was in the air, turning around in a slow-moving somersault. I heard swearing next to me and saw that Brand was also floating and disabled.

Addam stared up at us, hand raised, a sigil spell blurring the outline of his fingers. I saw—in rotating, Ferris wheel glimpses—a hard expression on his face.

"The hell," I said.

"Addam," Brand said, only he was suddenly very calm, and his diction very precise. "Put us down now. You've left Rune exposed."

Addam lowered his hand, and we bumped onto the planks.

"Be silent and listen to me," he told us in a quiet, intense voice.

"Addam——" I started to say.

He bowled right past my objection. "I have never, in all my life, met two people who understand each other better. I have never met two people who protect each other better, who stand so closely against the horrors the world throws at them. I have never been so jealous about the relationship between two friends. And I say this as someone who has a remarkably close relationship with his own brother."

"Addam——"

"You will *listen to me*," he said angrily to Brand. He turned on me. "You. How can you not see what Brand is feeling? There is nothing more in this world that could possibly upset him more than your judgment. This is one of the few—one of the very *few*—things he does without you, and your reaction to it has scared him. Your brotherhood defines him, as it does you, and the loss of your respect would be most brutal."

"But I . . ."

"And you," he said, turning on Brand. "You know, more than anyone, that Rune refuses to see those things he does not wish to see. You have made it your very *purpose* seeing those things for him, and protecting him from himself. How can you not understand what this place must mean to him, even if he refuses to see? This is a place that trades flesh. It is a place that, the deeper you walk into it, disregards any polite fiction of consent and conscience. How can you not understand how that must trigger him?"

"That's . . ." I felt all my emotion drain into bafflement. "That's not what I'm thinking. I'm not . . ."

Oh, shit.

I looked at my feet, and thought, *Oh, shit.*

"Rune," Brand whispered hoarsely. I looked up, and saw that his face had gone ashen. "Oh Rune. Oh fuck me Rune, oh, God."

"I'm n-not . . ." I stammered. "I wasn't thinking . . ."

He was so upset that he couldn't control our bond. He couldn't control what he was thinking, and I couldn't control what I was sensing. I could tell that he was terrified that I would think—that by him coming here, without me—he was somehow condoning the violence that had happened to me.

I shot forward and grabbed him by the head, hands like a vise. "*No,*" I said. "*NO.*"

"I let you come here, and I didn't even tell you what to expect," he whispered. His blue eyes swam with tears. "I didn't think . . . It didn't even occur to me . . ."

It was like he was in shock. Nothing I said would matter. So I used the one tool left between us—the one that always cut both ways. I pulled our Companion bond open and let my emotion sing through it. It was not something I could do often, but when it worked, it was an emotion so complicated and layered it was nearly a soliloquy. It expressed the concept of *Companion.* It said *brother.* It said *ally.* It was nearly the type of connection that existed between *tallas.*

And then there was no space between us as Brand crushed me in a hug. He moved so quickly that my muscle memory almost performed a counter-attack. I finally relaxed, and buried my face against his shoulder, and let the world turn around us.

"We don't fight," he said fiercely. "*We don't fight.*"

"We don't fight," I said back.

After another few seconds, we parted, though our hands slipped to a wrist hold, still connecting us. There was another few seconds of that, of that satisfaction, then Brand cut a glance at Addam.

"He looks pretty fucking smug," Brand said after a moment.

Addam blinked.

"You know," I said, "we haven't even talked about that stunt he pulled at the *Chained Roc*. Giving Sherman help. Sherman was a bad person. He stole from Corinne."

"It's like Addam is judging us," Brand said.

"We help plenty of people who deserve our help," I said. "Sherman didn't deserve our help."

"I know," Brand said. "What the fuck is up with that shit?"

Addam sighed. "I would have you remember that you went easy on him, too. You never even demanded the thousand dollars back."

Brand and I exchanged a look. I was reassured both that he'd forgotten about that too and that Addam thought I wasn't above turning that young man upside down and shaking our livelihood out of him.

I squeezed Brand's wrists one last time before letting go. "And if you stop coming here because you think I disapprove, I swear to the gods, I will organize a fucking car pool."

"Whatever," he said. He ran his forearm across his eyes. "Okay. Let's get this done."

The docks grew narrow and sparse, the further north we went. The water on either side of us was not clean. It was black and oily, filled with trash and body-shaped flotsam. In its final stretch, as a gray mist thickened in front of us, we passed a quarter mile of floating debris. The debris was barely recognizable as ships. They'd been burned to the waterline—either the site of an attack or, possibly, a sign of the Hanged Man protecting his own special real estate.

Finally we came to . . . I wasn't sure how to describe it. A barrier, of sorts, though more mental than physical. It affected each of us differently. I simply recognized it; Brand and Addam were influenced by it. They both stopped and looked behind them, as if ready to turn and retreat, without even questioning the impulse.

It was not so easy to mess with my mind, though.

Filling my limited collection of sigils for a field action was always a bit of a gamble. I had eight slots that allowed the potential for thousands of spells, everything from aggressive and defensive magics to stealth and psionics. I did my best to balance the load for all occasions, sometimes with more success than others.

I pressed my fingers against my thigh. Under my pants was a round sigil threaded through a leather strap. I connected with the spell—taking a second or two longer than direct touch would have allowed—and released it.

A sensation not unlike carbonated soda hissed and sizzled across my senses, and then I had Clarity.

"Don't move," I told Addam, who had begun to walk in the other direction. "You're being influenced. The ship is behind mental wards."

"Shouldn't we go back to shore?" Brand asked, haltingly, fighting the words.

I held out my hands toward them and extended the protection of my spell. The magic washed over them in stops and starts, leaving them blinking, facial muscles twitching. Brand ground his palms into his eyes, and stared around him with fresh acuity.

"Motherfucker," he pronounced.

"I'm glad I thought to bring a spell like this," I said, crossing my arms over my chest and staring at the mist in front of us. It was a backup plan, in the event Addam's Antitoxin spell failed. "I knew we'd be encountering ghosts. But not something quite like this."

I took a few steps forward and drew the toe of my boot across splintered, rough planks. It was like dragging a finger through a cloud—insubstantial but real, with a sort of damp resistance. In that approximation I felt the basis for the magic: water. The spell was anchored to wards powered by the churn of the surrounding ocean.

Magic is metaphor, and I knew the metaphor that would work best. It would come with a cost, though. I had seven spells left and was loathe to waste any more outside battle. But I needed what was in my gold ring. I needed Fire.

I swiped a thumb across the ring, sending a hot flush shivering through my muscles. I gathered Fire into Clarity, and pushed it out like a needle of flame.

The result was both physical and dramatic. Magnesium-bright threads webbed the air in front of me, burning into the magic protecting the battleship. I kept my focus tight and narrow—not to shatter the barrier but to burrow through it, to make a mouse hole slip of an entrance: something easily overlooked and easily repaired, to cover our trail.

I felt my spells break through into whatever lay ahead of us. Pulling the magic back into me—while still affording Brand and Addam a circle of Clarity—I studied the wisps of smoke in the air.

"Come on," I said quietly, and stepped forward in a straight line. The tunnel I'd made wasn't entirely physical, but I felt the tug of resistance along my head, making the hair on my neck stand up.

The grayness around me thinned and I emerged onto a clean, swept dock.

And before me was the battleship.

Six stories of painted metal; a monstrosity of hull and antennae, with massive guns jutting from it like bone spurs. I knew it would be big, but this was . . . It was a floating city. It filled up so much space that the stern and bow were lost in the haze of distance. The sheer scale was so large that the idea of searching it blew fuses in my brain.

"Rivers below," Addam swore. "How?" He said it like there were several paragraphs of subtext squeezed into the single word. How would we find what we need? How did it get here? How does the world not know the Hanged Man has it? How did he come to own it?

"How did this just . . . just fucking *vanish* from human history?" Brand said. "A country doesn't just misplace something this huge. This isn't spare change in a fucking sofa cushion." His gaze sharpened, somewhat hungrily. "And look at the size of those *guns*."

I had an image of Brand chiseling away at bolts with a screwdriver, which only got clearer when he added, "How much do you think they weigh?"

"I am very uncomfortable with that question," I said.

"Ninety-six tons," Addam said.

Both Brand and I stared at him.

"Okay," I said slowly.

"Quinn . . ." Addam pressed his lips together angrily. "I know many details of this ship."

"That's a good thing," Brand said.

"I am beginning to see the layers of his subterfuge. He told me he wanted to do an essay on the *North Carolina.* For his tutor. He encouraged us to use an Eidetic Memory spell, so we would remember details, and so I could help him afterwards. At the time, it was very logical. He made it sound very spontaneous and . . . logical." He closed his eyes. "Oh, Quinn. Quinn, what have you been playing at?"

"So you know the layout," Brand said. "You can help us get around."

"If the layout is the same as the *North Carolina*, yes. And since Quinn arranged that visit, I would suspect the layout is, indeed, similar." His voice was so thick with accent I almost missed a couple of the words.

"Look," Brand said. "He may have gone about it wrong, but he's done a good thing for us. Depending on how wrong things go—and trust you fucking me, they'll go wrong—he may have given us information we need to get out in one piece."

Addam, after a chilly moment, dipped his chin.

I went back to the question Brand had raised, before he got distracted by the idea of sticking a ninety-ton gun in his back pocket. "Addam, you said this ship was lost at sea, right?"

"Not long after it launched. In the 1940s, on its way to the Pacific theater during the humans' World War II."

"Define *lost*," Brand said.

"It sank in a storm, somewhere between Pearl Harbor and Asia. There were no survivors. Nothing remained—no record, even, of the exact location it sank, though many people have looked for it since."

I stared up the metal gangplank. Everything in eyesight was clean, though old. Spots of rust had turned stretches of metal into brittle lace. The deck was even—the ship did not list. "It doesn't look like something that was translocated from the ocean floor," I said. "How big a deal was the disappearance of this ship?"

"Very big."

"And somehow it wound up here," I said, and in the back of my head, I felt the first green shoots of a plan poking through the soil.

And then a ghost ran through me.

"Bloody *HELL*," I shouted as my heart skipped a beat.

Brand pulled a knife, and Addam had his hand on his sword, but neither saw the handsome young man stop on the gangplank, holding his hat to his head in an invisible wind.

The ghost looked back over his shoulder with a terrified expression, seeing something through me that scared the shit out of him. He wiped the side of his hand over his gray and white forehead, and continued running up the gangplank.

"Rune," Brand snapped. "What is it?"

"Ghost. One hell of a ghost memory. I didn't even need to draw on my willpower to see it." Curious, I looked up, raking my gaze across the visible deck ahead of us. I saw monochrome flickers as the past slid through the present, jetsam on an invisible stream.

I'd extended Clarity to Addam and Brand, but had left myself uncovered. Experimentally, I stretched the spell back over me as well, and watched the staticky flickers vanish.

"Can it hurt us?" Brand asked.

"No. They're just imprints. Memories. I've covered you and Addam with my Clarity spell, but I'm going to keep it off me. I may be able to learn something."

He didn't look too pleased with that. "How long are we planning to be here?"

"Not long. We don't have a choice. The Clarity spell won't last longer than an hour, maybe ninety minutes—less if there's anything mentally aggressive on board."

"And the longer we stay, the greater the chance of detection," Addam added. "I agree: we must move quickly."

The gangplank was wide enough for cargo, and made of metal covered in a rough surface, the better to keep footing. The ghost memories popped and faded like camera flashes ahead of me. I narrowed my gaze, to avoid being overwhelmed. It was unusually difficult. Ghost memories were normally not so forceful—they almost never affected me when I wasn't trying to see them.

The main ship deck was covered in teak wood. Before I could take in more of my immediate surroundings, two ghosts shimmered into view against the casing of an enormous, two-story gun. They had their hands cupped around cigarettes. A storm splattered gray raindrops across their bowed faces.

"We better find a bar of soap before we go back below deck," one of them said. The cigarette, shielded from the rain, was pooling smoke against his palm. "If they find out we copped a Lucky, they'll keelhaul us."

"We're fine," the other said. "Not like there are gonna be bandits flying in this weather, right? Dunno why they bothered shutting off the smoking lamp tonight." The man—nearly a boy—stiffened. He craned his neck forward and squinted. "Is that Pretty Boy?"

"Who the heck you calling pretty?" the other cough-laughed.

"No. Pretty Boy. Over there. You know him."

"Oh yeah. He's weird."

They faded away. I turned and looked in the direction they'd been staring. Above me, the sky began flashing between past and present—yellow stars; a gray and white storm; yellow stars.

About twenty or thirty feet away, standing in a metal archway that sheltered a stairway to the deck above us, was the same man I'd seen running up the gangplank. He was, indeed, a very pretty man. His hands were curled around the thick metal edges of the hatch. Even in grayscale, I could see how his fingers were white with the pressure of his squeeze.

I moved closer to him—and saw a look of horror appear on his face. He stared past me at the sky. I heard a soft thump as something settled behind me, and I swear to gods, I felt breath on the back of my neck.

"You promised you'd let me go," the boy stammered, just as I was about to turn. "You promised you wouldn't come after me."

"If it eases your mind," a man whispered, "I shall hunt you last."

A hand latched itself to my shoulder. The past vanished as Brand shook me out of it.

"I don't like this," he growled.

I stared shakily at the bright constellations above me. The clouds were gone. I said, "The memories are so damned strong. They shouldn't be this vivid."

"It's creepy as fuck watching you sleepwalk into walls. We need you here, Rune."

"I'm learning things. This is important. I can hear *conversations*. That shouldn't happen. It's almost as if . . ." I trailed off.

Brand growled again and squeezed my shoulder.

"It's almost as if they're reinforced," I said. "As if the memories have been anchored in place."

I blinked and looked around me—at the real around-me. The gangplank took us near the stern of the ship. It was covered in guns. I barely had the vocabulary to describe the sheer variety in them—massive main guns with four gigantic barrels, three times the width of Half House; smaller gun mounts at the side of the ship; large machine gun–like installations so big that the shooter sat in a metal seat that swiveled around like a videogame cockpit. It seemed a very American thing to do, putting the gangplank here, among all these weapons: to welcome visitors by asserting how badly they could be fucked up when they stopped being welcome.

Many of the guns were twisted, the blackened stumps so freshly destroyed I could almost smell the sulfur and cordite. That was not natural. No rust or age—they were preserved in the moment of their destruction. It stank of stasis magic, but worse. Stronger. Stronger than any Stasis spell I've seen.

I couldn't think of many good reasons to freeze parts of a scene like this—a drop of death preserved in amber. While heightened emotion created fuel for magic, you didn't need to go to lengths like this to create the fuel. It would have happened naturally, without mucking with the imbued memories.

Addam went over and kicked at rotting canvas. "This covers the main guns, normally. Protects them from saltwater erosion. When the guns are used, they blow the covers off with compressed air."

Brand made the connection immediately. "The guns were uncovered. Which means they were used. And they didn't have time to tidy the fuck up afterwards. And over there—see. Something blasted the hell out of the antiaircraft guns."

I turned in a circle. The amount of deck on the stern was large and relatively open, maybe half the length of a soccer field. A clear area nearest the tip was scorched black, the teak charred to flake.

The present blinked gray, and I watched as the storm-swept deck filled with panicked men racing around. On the now uncharred stern was a very small plane, barely bigger than a car. A pilot was scrambling into the seat, while a team undid the plane's tethers.

I heard the whistle of a huge weapon, and then a fantastic explosion of light filled the sky. Not an attack—the ship had fired flares. In the sharp relief of their resulting light, the plane took off. It moved like a catapulted toy.

Gunfire. Behind me. The ghost of bullets and screams.

I turned and saw pinpoints of light against the mid-deck tower.

There was another whistle—but a different sound. Not human guns. Magic. A surge of magic, shaped like a comet, launching itself from the tower.

It collided with the catapulted plane, which exploded in a huge fireball.

I closed my eyes and shook myself into the present. Brand's hand was back on my shoulder.

"What are you seeing?" he demanded.

"An attack. There used to be a plane there. There was fighting on the tower—that tower there—and when the plane took off, someone used Fire to destroy it."

"Was it the Hanged Man?" Addam asked.

"Maybe? But there's no storm."

"The storm where they said the ship sank?" Addam asked, confused.

"Yes. The sky is clear. They launched flares, and I could see stars. But I saw a scene earlier where the Hanged Man landed on the ship in a storm—or at least I think it was the Hanged Man. Which means whatever happened did not happen quickly. Not if a storm came and went."

"Look at the deck," Brand said. He pointed to the ruined guns, and the charred area where the plane had been, and the wide area around us. "Parts of it are swept. Are there any wards that would keep it this clean?"

"Some of the damage is frozen in a type of freaky strong stasis magic. And there could be wards to prevent much of the corrosion and rusting. But wards that keep a deck swept?" I shook my head.

"So we may not be alone," Addam summarized.

"Let's go back that way," I said. "To that tower."

"That's where navigation will be," Addam said. "And the captain's sea quarters. It's called the signal tower. It would make sense for the portal we're looking for to be there—it has the best view."

"Yeah, because real bad guys love fucking exposing themselves in penthouses for the view," Brand said. "That's a myth. I'll bet every cent Rune has that we're going to wind up in the fucking basement."

We backtracked the way we came, and climbed to the next deck. It was smaller than the one below us, but still the length of a city block.

High up, against the bulkhead of the signal tower, were fresh, colorful flags, preserved against age. They flapped in the sea breeze.

Addam pointed. "Those are the captain's quarters. At sea, he would have slept in a room by navigation, but he would have used this larger space for meetings and office work. It may be worth our time to look there."

Brand went over to the metal door. Hatch? I think they called it a hatch. The hatch looked like it would open directly into the cabin. But the handle wouldn't move. "No rust," he said, running his finger along it. "I think this is a personal record for us. We went five whole minutes without breaking things. Rune, make us a door."

"Allow me," Addam said instead, touching one of his sigils. I saw how he snuck a look at me and Brand before focusing on the lock. Whatever the spell was, it surrounded the locking mechanism in a semitransparent bubble of light. The light flashed bright for a second, and bits of metal spat and bounced off its interior, quickly turning to red dust, which burned away in fat embers. When Addam released the spell, there was a clear hole where the lock used to be.

"Something I've been toying with," Addam said. "My boyfriend, I've come to learn, is not very impressed with flowers or candy."

"That's so fucking cute," Brand said. "You're impressing him with a new stealing spell." He scratched his chin as Addam tried to hide a pleased smile. "I wonder what would happen if you stuck the spell on someone's face." Addam stopped smiling.

I pushed open the door, which now swung free. The room on the other side wasn't large, but it was nicely decorated. A thick oak table was bolted to the floor. Scissors, brushes, and bottles of black ink were scattered across the place settings.

I put a finger on a piece of paper. It was a handwritten letter, riddled with dark blots that completely obscured whole lines or phrases.

Addam and Brand flickered away, and the past settled over me.

Six men were sitting around the table, sifting through mail. One of the men had a chaplain's collar. A light lunch was laid out before them—mostly fruits and salad, nothing hot. A good choice in tropical heat.

One of the officers said, "Why'd the Old Man ask us to meet in here? Is something wrong?"

Another man came through the door, snapping everyone to attention, which he waved off. He had a piece of damp paper in his hand. Even through the ghost memory I smelled the antiseptic sting of mimeograph ink. "Plan of the day," the man said, and put the paper down.

He dropped heavily into a seat and tugged cigarettes out of his breast pocket. Only when he was sucking his first lungful did the other officers pull out their own cigarettes and light up.

"Captain coming, Exec?" one of them asked. "Why'd he want to see us?"

The exec tapped his cigarette against an ashtray bolted to the table. "One of the MAAs reported in. Strange fucking stuff. I think the heat's getting to people."

"Strange stuff?" the chaplain repeated.

"One of the enlisted men had to be sedated. Ran through his berth last night screaming about a monster. And one of the engineering team says a couple of their guys haven't reported in. That's why the Old Man wanted us here."

Everyone stopped what they were doing. They exchanged looks with each other, and then waited, through an exhale of smoke, for the exec to say more.

"What does that mean?" the chaplain finally asked. "Haven't reported in?"

The memory faded out, back to the present, back to Brand's fingers on my forearm. I said, "They were looking into disappearances. People have gone missing. Let's go further up the tower. You said the control room is here?"

"Navigation," Addam corrected.

We went back onto the deck and found a steep metal stairway to the next level. Even two flights up, the signal tower still loomed several stories above us. It was capped with antennae and searchlights, all of them outsized and ancient, from an era before everything shrank to pocket-sized.

"Any chance you brought your fancy drone with you?" I asked Brand. "Might save us a climb."

"Fuck off," Brand said, which meant he hadn't thought about it and was pissed at himself.

It would needle him if I didn't drop it. So I said, gleefully, "What about those headsets? You must have thought to bring those sweet expensive headsets with you."

I grinned at his look, and grabbed the metal railings of the narrow stairway to swing myself up a step.

On the next level, an open door in the bulkhead led inside the structure proper. I stepped over the hatch's high rim into a cramped metal hallway with three narrow doors.

"Sea quarters," Addam said. "When the ship is at sea, the captain and the navigator sleep next to navigation."

I didn't need a gut instinct to guess bad things had happened in this tower. Whatever the Hanged Man had done, he would not have left the bridge untouched. Tactically, it would have been one of his first targets if he was looking to disable any sort of leadership or resistance.

The door to the captain's quarters was literally a door—or at least a door set into a metal hatch. Through a glass pane, I saw a space no larger than a closet. It held a bureau, a single twin bed, and floor space that would only have fit the three of us if we'd stood in a group hug. A pack of unfiltered Camel cigarettes sat on the bureau, which had a raised rim on the top to keep items from skittering off.

I opened the door—and the grayscale past yawned around me.

A balding man was squeezed into a corner of the bed, his face pressed into the bulkhead. Metal rivets had left indentations on his cheek. The nails on his left hand were torn away, and the brown paint on the bed's metal frame had scratches.

"We need to get below!" a voice barked behind me. "The master-at-arms has a plan to free the marines. It's our only chance. *You need to move, sir!*"

"This is a dream," the captain stuttered. "It's a dream."

"Fine," the voice said, resigned, and I recognized it as the exec. "Stay. But we're going to fight back."

The door banged shut, and I was back in the present.

"What are you seeing, Rune?" Addam asked.

I didn't answer directly—I just said what I was thinking. "So the Hanged Man landed on the ship in a storm. Or at least, he revealed himself during the storm. He was after someone. A young man called Pretty Boy. In that room below, the captain's cabin, they said people were starting to go missing. But right now—here—something has already happened. They said there were people ready to fight down below."

I turned in a slow circle, and walked over to an adjacent door. On the other side was some sort of conference room. Huge, unspooled maps covered a six-foot-wide table.

I looked back toward the hatch we'd entered through, at the midnight stars sparkling off the higher elevation. "We're going the wrong way," I said. "This is . . . it's a story. The Hanged Man has preserved the story, like a trophy, and whatever happened in the end, it happened below, not here. He'd have wanted the story to last as long as possible—he would have enjoyed having people have to walk through all of it."

"Like I said, the basement," Brand said, and spat.

I walked back through the hatch, into a spray of salt air. There were stairs on both my left and right, and, right in front of me, a tiny platform fitted with something that resembled a chest-high fire hydrant, with two metal globes attached to arm struts.

"Magnetic compass," Addam said, seeing my interest.

It was catching my attention: less like a twenty-dollar bill fluttering on the ground, and more like a too-slick stone in a flooded river you were attempting to cross. There was something important in front of me. Something I needed to see.

Swallowing, I walked up to the compass. It was closer to the *something*, but the pull was tracking . . .

Upwards.

"What are those structures?" I asked.

Addam grimaced at the knowledge that came easily. "Those platforms are Sky I, Sky II, Sky III, and Sky IV. They helped coordinate fire, especially against aircraft."

"Beautiful view from up there," I murmured. "Addam, can you use TK to lift me up?"

"No," Brand said.

"Just the one right there. I'll stay in eyesight. I think I need to see something up there."

"If you remove your Clarity spell from me, I could do it," Addam offered.

"I think I need to do this. I've always had a knack for sensing magic. Even without Clarity shielding you, I'm not sure you'd see what I'm seeing. Brand? Please?"

He gave me a long look. Then he bent over, pulled up his pants leg, and removed a gun from a holster.

I sucked in a breath. The use of guns was sharply, sharply regulated in New Atlantis—mainly because it would have evened the playing field in a magical firefight, and scions liked to be the only ones with an unfair advantage. "We didn't get a pistol dispensation for this trip."

"Do you want to have this conversation?" he asked. "We can have this conversation. Go ahead and have this conversation with me, Rune."

"Do you at least have a—" I started to say, before he pulled a silencer from one of his ammo pockets and began attaching it to the gun.

"Stay in my line of sight so I can cover you," he said.

Addam touched one of the sigils on his belt. His hands began to waver, and he held them out, palms up, like an offering. The magic jumped to me, and for a half-second all of my internal organs felt like they were floating as the spell stabilized.

"Up I go," I said, and used the Telekinesis—TK—to lift myself off the ground. It wasn't pretty—I flopped a bit, like one of those dancing dashboard figures. But Telekinesis was more versatile than Levitation, and could be used aggressively as well, which was why Addam preferred it.

I rose through the windy salt air to one of the metal catwalks at the top of the Sky Tower. As I approached it, the power of barely restrained memories surrounded me.

I lifted myself above the platform railing, past it, and then down to the metal walkway. The moment I made contact, the past washed over me again, but with a scope that staggered me.

My entire field of vision—the entire stretch of deck at the rear of the ship—was filled with bright gray afternoon.

Two stories down, men sunbathed on the teak planks, or sprawled in the shade of gun mounts. There were over a hundred of them—dozens and dozens of kids barely old enough to buy alcohol, even in the American rules of that era. The juxtaposition of their ease on this ship, on this massive weapon of war was . . . surreal. Awful. I'd heard once that warships used teak wood because it absorbed heat, sound, and shrapnel. They were tanning on top of military logic, the same planks they'd bleed on.

This was a curated memory. A powerful, powerful curated memory. To do something like this? To tie off a single memory and share it with others? In such astonishing detail? I could smell coconut tanning oil.

It was only as I started looking around that I saw the man.

On another sky platform in front of me, off to the side. He wore black trousers and a black shirt. A huge silk cape rushed around him, fastened over one shoulder. It should have looked ridiculous, but it didn't; it should have seemed anachronistic, but it wasn't. It was the perfect fit for a modern-day nightmare.

I was pretty sure I was looking at the Hanged Man.

Even more strangely, he was not from my present, but nor did he have the gray coloring of the distant past. I felt time—the actual current of time—grow thin and stretched as our moments of observation overlapped.

As I tried to pull myself back to the present, the Hanged Man stiffened. He slightly—just slightly—turned his head to the side. I caught a hint of a strong chin, and a thin, sharp nose.

He raised a hand, and the ghost of a spell streamed outwards. The world shuddered and flooded with color—the gray afternoon bled into a blue sky and a burning yellow sun.

He said, "I feel you."

I squeezed my eyes shut and called on my willpower to resist the pull. I was stronger than this. I was my father's son. I was heir to a throne of the Arcanum, and I would not be any memory's slave.

The Hanged Man said, louder, "Look at how you flutter. Like a match flame held behind rice paper. I can almost see your outline! *When* are you, little flame? Are you enjoying my great act?"

It was at that point that Brand slapped the shit out of me.

I put a hand against my stinging cheek and blinked at fake stars and real stars and the sound of waves. I was still on the Sky Tower, and it looked like Brand and Addam had levitated to reach me.

"Did you even try pinching me first?" I asked. "Even once?"

"You seemed agitated," Addam said behind Brand, and he looked like he wanted to slap the hell out of something too. "I do not think this is healthy, Rune."

"No, it isn't. It really isn't." I licked dry lips. "But I'm learning some things."

Like why the Stasis spells were so strong. I hadn't caught on, at first, because it was a type of magic no one had experience with. It was forbidden.

It was on a very, very short list of magic that would get you killed in New Atlantis. No one—Arcana or otherwise—was allowed to interfere with time.

And yet here was time magic. Bolstering the Stasis spells on the ship. Preserving this theater.

"What are we learning?" Brand demanded. "The Hanged Man killed lots and lots of people. The end. What do we get out of knowing that?"

"I need to see just how many people he killed. I need to see everything the Hanged Man did here."

"Why?" Brand demanded again, in genuine exasperation.

"Because there are limits to what even an Arcana can do without consequence. And understanding how close he came to those limits is knowledge. And knowledge informs tactics." That was one of Brand's favorite lines.

"Let's get back down," Brand said, ignoring me. "We're exposed up here."

Addam used Telekinesis to float all three of us off the platform and back down to the magnetic compass.

"We should leave," Brand said, once we had our footing. "You know that, right?"

"We need to at least try to find the portal. If we can't do it within the hour, yes, we'll leave. I promise. I just need to see more. I need to understand what happened."

Brand bit down hard on his teeth and glared at me, then threw his arms up in the air. "I am fucking *mad* at you again!"

So I said the one thing I knew would calm him down. It was one of the dirtiest tricks we played on each other, and it always worked.

I admitted I needed help.

"Can I hold your arm while we walk?" I said. "It'll keep me grounded. Don't worry, not your knife arm."

Brand watched my face sullenly. "As if I throw better with one hand than the other." But he looked a little mollified, and held out an arm to me.

BELOW DECK

As we went back to one of the lower decks, Addam said, "I would feel better if you told us what you are seeing *as* you are seeing them."

"Up there? I saw sunbathers. Men sunbathing."

"That's why you froze up for five minutes?" Brand demanded. "You are fucking shameless."

"*And* I saw . . . Well, I saw Lord Hanged Man," I said. "He was watching the sunbathers. It looked . . . It looked like he was in a different time than both me and the sunbathers. I think . . . I think he comes back and watches these memories a lot. He called it his great act. And that says something."

"Wait a fucking second," Brand said. "You saw Lord Hanged Man? Does that mean he saw you?"

"It was a ghost memory," I said.

"You said that it means something, that he comes and watches these memories. What does it mean?" Addam asked.

"I don't know yet. But . . ." I trailed off. "Consequences. I need to get a better understanding of what happened here, and then we need to consider the consequences. Let's go downstairs."

Addam said he knew the way to a hatch that led to the galleys, which he explained were the main ship kitchens.

On the way to the below-deck hatch, I saw more flickers of ghost memories. I saw sailors repairing cargo nets. I saw sailors dying their hats in a bucket of blue dye. I saw sailors smoking, and laughing, and living under the heavy regard of a tropical sun. And the closer we drew to the entry point to the lower decks, the darker the memories got. People running. Shouting. I think I saw someone roll across the deck on fire, but the image came and went like an eye blink.

A ghost sprinted through me. He was running up to the exec, who shimmered ahead. The ghost said, "Bedsprings are down, sir. Techs say they can't be repaired. We're blind."

"Then we punch every direction at once," the exec spat. "Let's get the bird in the fucking air first."

It was night again—or at least a darker shade of gray. The two men went over to a group gathered around a gun. The gun was big enough that the person firing it was secured in harness netting.

"Light it up," the exec shouted.

The man with the most colored bars on his chest turned to the team and barked, "*I Division! Find us an enemy!*"

The gun shot a round into the sky. Flares attached to parachutes exploded to life in the sky above me, turning night into day. Smoke rose—thick enough that the men started using hand signals to coordinate through their coughing.

The next thing I knew, the huge guns on the side of the ship were blasting a salvo. The force of their trajectory was so powerful that the entire ship seemed to move sideways—an optical illusion as the rounds actually flattened the ocean waves.

Brand's fingers pressed into a cluster of nerves at my neck. I shook myself back into the present, to his worried expression.

"They didn't know what was happening," I said. "They didn't know where the threat was coming from. He toyed with them. He made this last."

"Anything else?" Brand asked.

"Yes. Apparently you really do swear like a sailor."

I stepped on something that crunched, and looked down to see a spinal column. My humor drained. The skeleton was in pieces, trailing from an overturned whaleboat. Rotting flags, life jackets, and first aid supplies spattered the ground.

"Let's go downstairs," I said, subdued.

Brand sighed and made an *after-fucking-you* gesture.

* * *

None of the steep stairways on the ship were easily transversed. The floor of one level was right in front of you as you descended, more or less at forehead height. There were no rounded corners or padding—walk into it, and you were catching a metal edge in your skull.

The level below us buzzed with energy. Not just the ghost memories, but actual stored power, the type you found in traumatized ruins. I manifested two light cantrips, then sent them across the room, chasing away ambush points.

I turned in a slow circle at a hatch door and saw a long series of compartments running along the side of the ship. Kitchen galleys, mess areas, and further along something that almost looked like a concourse.

I'd have expected to hear creaking or groaning, or the rattling of old pipes. But the ship was as silent as the end of the world.

In the corner of that first room was an open chapel. A wooden altar; two rows of easily storable and collapsible benches; a podium draped with a purple cloth, and the blue and white stars of America. On the altar was a two-sided cross, which could be reversed for different Christian services. The side facing me showed the Jesus, a hanged man of a much different temperament.

I felt the edge of a ghost memory vibrating in front of the altar. I tapped Brand's forearm and then wrapped my fingers around it.

I relaxed into the grayness. The handsome young man—Pretty Boy— was on his knees in front of the cross, on a painted metal floor that had the unforgiving feel of concrete. Another man squatted beside him. He said, "You're cracking up, buddy boy."

"I'm not," Pretty Boy whispered. "You'll see. People are already missing, aren't they?"

"Probably sleeping off some of that moonshine crap one of the zilches snuck aboard. Exec is crapping exclamation points over it."

Pretty Boy peeled his eyes off the altar and gave his friend a small, sad smile.

"Hey-o, I know what'll make you feel better," his friend said, with a glance over his shoulder. "I stole some twelve-hour liberty chits off port watch. We can use them when we reach the islands."

"We won't reach the islands."

"Yeah? God tell you that?"

Pretty Boy looked back at the altar, at its reversible metal cross. "That's the problem." His eyes glazed over with tears. "How can I believe in one god, now that I know there are twenty-two of them?"

The memory faded away.

"Let's walk through these rooms," I suggested.

The mess hall with the chapel was separated from kitchen galleys by a metal grill painted in white. The first room was unmistakably a bakery, holding a dough mixer that was twice the size of a water barrel. There were also racks of canned goods with old-fashioned labels like Victrypac Dark Sweet Cherries, and a row of petrified black discs that may have once been fresh pies.

The next two galleys were separated by bulkhead doors that could be sealed in the event of an emergency. Broken, rusted tables. A caged storage area filled with the dried remains of rotted lettuce and a gnarled, old forest of spudded potatoes. The occasional bone. On one table, perfectly preserved with that unholy blend of stasis and time magic, was a pristine game of dominoes.

"What's that open space ahead of us?" I asked, pointing. The air in that direction vibrated, heavy with memory.

"Stores," Addam said. "Quite literally—a recreation area where sailors could congregate and buy things. I think there are other . . . amenities? I cannot think of the word. Practical shops, such as barbers and cobblers."

"Like a village square," I said. Magic was always heavy in places like that, which was designed around basic human appetites.

The floor on the other side sloped up, sharply enough that I felt the change in my ankles. There were collapsible tables here as well—some upright with brittle playing cards on their surface; some overturned and eaten to rust fibers. Grilled shop fronts lined every wall. They weren't stores the way I expected—just counters, where only the clerk had access to the merchandise.

The world flashed gray. Ahead of me, across the room, a sailor in a dark jacket was shooting a flamethrower. Without color, the flame was as bright as a magnesium flare.

The entire image vanished a second after it appeared. "Shit," I whispered. "They must have been scared witless to be using a flamethrower."

"What?" Brand said.

I shook my head and continued. Old pieces of mail crunched under my feet as I moved across the room. An ice-cream machine was surrounded by vats of calcified powdered milk. Behind more grillwork were rows of unfiltered cigarettes.

"Damnit," Brand said. "This place is making my skin—"

The past tore across me. Brand and Addam were gone and I was swimming in static gray that quickly settled into clear, grayscale memory.

I walked through the past—across the empty rec room, the fallen mail and playing cards, now clean and new, and a batch of ice cream melting across the floor.

I didn't have to see a single twitch of movement to know I wasn't alone, though. The area stank of fear and sweat, and if I listened closely, I could hear the low breathing of men, just shy of hyperventilation.

They were hiding all around me. Terrified. And I knew I'd been right—that the Hanged Man had grown tired of picking off the crew one by one. By this point in the story, the main focus had gone from the slow stalk of a predator to the frantic scattering of the prey.

"We can lock ourselves in the gedunk!" a black man hissed, tripping into the room. A white man ran after him. Shock had turned the white man's complexion to a shiny transparency. He had one arm pressed against his stomach, and the wrist ended in a bloody stump.

The black man began ramming key after key into a grated door. On the other side was a counter lined with bottles of bright, colored syrup.

I heard a clatter behind the mailroom counter. I went over and looked through the glass pane of a small door. Inside, a sailor had knocked over a typewriter. He'd piled chairs and a tipped cabinet next to a waist-high black safe, a makeshift barrier. Then he froze, and looked through a mail slot, in the direction of the soda fountain where the other men were trying to hide.

I heard a horrible scream from that direction—the ripping shriek of someone who was being irreparably damaged—consonants rising and falling with the force of the violence being done to him.

I did not look. I did not risk being drawn that close to that memory— or worse, drawn to another observer of them, from another time like my own.

The mailroom clerk opened the huge safe with shaking fingers. He pulled bags and stacks of paper from the inside, along with two removable shelves. Then he climbed inside, weeping, and shut the door behind him.

"Gods*damnit!*" I yelled as Brand took about an inch of flesh off my love handles.

"I pinched," he said angrily.

"It's been several minutes, Rune," Addam said. "What are you seeing?"

"People running and hiding. Him pursuing them. This is sick."

I was still standing in front of the door to the mailroom. The glass was now cloudy and caked with grime. Through it, the old black safe was still shut. I knew what I'd find if I opened it.

If that was the end of the story, how horrible must the middle have been? How bad had it been if suffocating yourself in a safe was preferable to even taking a chance at surviving?

"I'm not even sure where to go next. There are ghost memories everywhere."

"Let's go right," Brand said, watching my face. "We can check down there."

I took a few steps and Brand said, "Wait! Look down."

"Tripwire?" I breathed.

"No. Look at your shoes, and imagine that someone drew an L and R on them. Now ask yourself if you just turned to the fucking R."

I gave him a dirty look. "Yes, I'm distracted, point made. But I still need to see this."

So I took my other right. The open concourse of kitchens and shops immediately narrowed into a single iron hallway. A brass sign above a hatch told me that I was entering a supply department, though the plaque was too clouded with age to make out the specific division headings.

"What's up here?" Brand whispered to Addam, taking point.

"Tailors. Barbers. Cobblers. Laundry and print shops below us. There are stairs to engine rooms two levels down, as well, but I seem to remember that this is largely a dead end."

Brand held up a hand. He flicked two fingers toward one of my light cantrips, then flicked them toward the ground. I followed the direction, and lowered my light cantrips so they floated an inch above the join between floor and bulkhead.

I saw what Brand had already seen. The sweeping here was imprecise: but along the edges, in the caked dust, you could see partial footprints.

Brand knelt. "Bare feet." He pointed at another partial imprint. "Boots. Same size. Not a high traffic area." He rose from his squat and took point again.

The narrow corridor opened into a cul-de-sac. A metal stairway led down, and the landing around the stairway had hatches, doors, and wired cages. It stank of old oil and burned metal, probably from the engines below.

"What is that?" I asked, not entirely easily, while pointing to a door in front of me.

Addam's eyes reflected the pale yellow of my rising light cantrip. "That compartment? The barber shop, I believe."

"We're not going in there," I said. I felt the emanations from the room, and it didn't take much creativity to picture what a serial killer would have done with scissors, swivel chairs, and razors. I swallowed and said,

"I'm not feeling portal magic anywhere around here. I'm just sensing dark murdery shit."

"Let's go back down the other side of this deck," Brand said.

"Okay," I said. "But I want to make absolutely sure we're on the same page. Are you saying we *should* have gone left and not right?"

Just before Brand could tell me to fuck off, Addam froze and turned his head sharply. "Do you smell that?" he whispered.

"All I smell is old engine oil," I said, but Brand bullied past me and started sniffing like a bloodhound.

"Sweat," he said, softly, and looked down the stairwell. "How about that." He palmed a knife, turned sideways, and began to descend the steep stairs in a prowl.

I followed him. At the bottom, I called my lights to me, and sent them spiraling toward another dead end. Smudged bronzed signs announced a laundry compartment and a print shop, and something called a lucky bag. I could smell what they did, now; an underlying stench of unwashed body.

Brand had pulled out a penlight and was shining it along the floor, looking for scuff marks and disturbances in the dust. He seemed very interested in the shortened corridor leading to the lucky bag.

"What's that? What's a lucky bag?" he asked Addam, who was climbing down the stairs behind us.

"A bit like a lost and found. Allow me." He swiped a finger over one of the sigils on his belt, and sent his own light cantrip bobbing in front of his face. His hands whistled with moving air for a second, then he did something I couldn't follow—until a brilliant spotlight knifed through the air in front of him and hit Brand squarely in the eyes. Brand dropped both of his hands to his side, each with a knife, and lowered his head—the portrait of an assassin frozen in the moment before heavy swearing.

"What did you just do?" I asked cheerfully.

"Sorry about that . . . Somewhat stronger than I expected," he said. "I used an Air spell to create a lens, and then used a cantrip as a light source. You have inspired me to be creative with my spells."

"Nice one," I said, and meant it. "Shine it in there."

Brand glared at Addam, and put his back to the light, taking the lead.

The lucky bag was a closet-sized space with a wire door. I'm not sure what it would have looked like on a working battleship, but here, someone had turned it into a nest. Three rotting mattress were stacked in a corner, as well as a pitiful pile of ragged shirts and pants.

"Whatever lives here wears clothes," I murmured. "That's encouraging."

Brand said, "There's a glass of water by the mattress. This isn't abandoned. Maybe Sherman was right about a caretaker. Let's head back."

We backtracked to the recreation area, this time taking the hatch along the other side of the ship from the way we'd entered. The string of compartments started with a cleared mess hall, and then a second mess area, and then a third and large space.

"What's ahead of us?" I asked Addam.

"Berths. And the surgical suites. Across from . . . some sort of soldier compartment? Special naval soldiers?"

"Marines," I murmured. And I thought: *Ah.* "That's where the portal is. That's where it is. The exec was joining a plan to free the marines. And surgical suites . . . have instruments. For after. When the resistance failed. Trust me, that's the last place I want to look, but . . . It would have been a godsdamn candy shop for the Hanged Man. We need to go there."

I almost tripped over a bowling ball that was sitting in the hatch door, only the bowling ball was really a skull, which was a pretty grim omen for what we'd likely see in front of us.

Brand said, "Rune, send your cantrips—" But I already had them moving ahead.

Brand holstered his knives and drew the gun from his ankle holster. He approached the door at a crouch, kicking the skull so that it vaulted ahead and clattered against a far metal bulkhead. He waited for it to startle any potential ambush, then, satisfied, slipped into the room while bringing his gun in a semicircle, from wall to wall.

"*Shit,*" Brand said again, with feeling. Then, reluctantly, "Clear."

I walked into the clean, dry remains of a slaughter.

About a dozen rows of benches were facing a film screen. The ground was littered with skeletons—most of them relatively whole, excepting gouge marks on the bones below necks, biceps, faces, thighs. Stasis magic had preserved the bones in a bleached, cinematic whiteness.

I felt the past tremble. Before I could drown in it, I pulled Clarity around me like a Kevlar shroud.

"I'm guessing this is where he got tired of the ambushes," I said heavily. "This is the middle part of the story."

When we were well clear of that compartment, I pulled Clarity off me again, keeping it on Brand and Addam to preserve its duration for as long as possible.

The sleeping berths started in the next room. Rows of mattresses were slung from the ceiling by metal chains. The beds were frozen in time, their surfaces surprisingly springy, still smelling like detergent and cheap soap. One of them had bloodstains faded to a rust color.

On the other side were shower areas, and past that another corridor. Before we could step into it, though, a clank echoed toward us, brutal and loud in the stillness.

We stood there, frozen, for six minutes. I knew without counting it'd be that long—Brand always waited six minutes, never five.

When the sound didn't repeat itself, I whispered, "It's late, and we're overthinking this. We're just one deck below open air. We are not trapped—there is no bulkhead that can keep me from making an exit. So let's move out. Let them hear us come."

I strode past them, into the corridor. Brand didn't waste energy arguing. He kept his gun pointed at the ceiling, one hand on his opposing wrist to protect his aim, and followed.

I had no doubt this was the path to the portal. I felt the odd flicker of its magic in the distance, not unlike a desert mirage. And the educated hunch was backed by swept floors; by the stasis-fresh walls; by the way the edges of my vision trembled with history.

The paint on the walls went from dark tan to olive green. The corridor opened into a platform with a descending stairwell. Brand flashed his penlight down, but my own attention was drawn forward, at the next series of compartments.

"Look there," Addam said, coming up to my side. He stared, with me, at the large slabs of bulkhead lying across the floor, revealing the skeletal structure of the walls. One compartment was completely peeled open, showing a room filled with an old-fashioned diving suit fallen to the ground—complete with a round Jules Verne helmet and a sealed, astronaut-thick suit.

"Brand," I said quietly. "Let me hold onto you. I may be able to get a sense of where the portal is anchored. We're close. I can tell."

"The marine quarters are there—on the right," Addam offered as Brand looked around us unhappily. "The medical suite is on the left."

"Brand, please," I said again, only I was halfway through lowering my defenses as I asked, because I wanted to see what was in front of us.

As the past seeped across my vision in gray and white flickers, I felt the weight of my Companion settle against my side.

There was a ghostly group of men in front of me, all with guns, all in active wartime gear. They were lined in a barricade formation. They faced away from me, and before them—opposite my own position at the rear—was the one called Pretty Boy.

"You need to listen to me," he said in a broken voice. "He is *hunting us.*"

"Son, stand aside," the exec said.

"*Listen to me!*" Pretty Boy yelled. "You don't understand—he said he would let me go, but he didn't, he followed me, because no one ever tells him no. He is *angry* and when he's through we will all be *gone.* There are people like him, *things* like him, and they do not ever reveal themselves. That's why he won't let us go. Don't you understand?"

"Son, I will say three things, and I will say them with minimal fucking patience," the exec barked. "One, what you are saying *will* get you court-martialed. Two, if I hear one more word about monsters, I will lose my shit. And three, we are being attacked by an enemy, and we are prepared for this, because we are the US Navy, and we stand on American steel, armed with American firepower, ready and willing to put American bullets in some un-American fucking heads."

One of the soldiers in the back row—nearly in front of me—shifted his weight. His shirt came untucked, enough to see the knife tear above the right kidney. The tear was bloodstained, but the skin beneath it was corpse white.

The man pulled a hemp rope from under his collar. Even across the gulf of time, I recognized it as a mass sigil, felt the ripples of its power.

Pretty Boy blinked, spotted what I had spotted, and screamed.

The rivets on the wall began to pop out of place. They split in half, and the halves fluttered into wings, spitting paint flake to the ground. Animated into massive beetles with pincers like fork tines, the rivets flew at the men, targeting soft, exposed tissue.

I raised a hand and bore down hard with my willpower. The world stuttered—I felt the weight of the frozen memories. I lifted my other hand, and, just short of calling my Aspect, focused. My power cut through the noise of the ghost images, and banished the past.

"This was their last stand," I said hoarsely. "Let's check the surgical suites and the marine compartment."

"Can I borrow that first?" Brand asked, pointing to Addam's sword.

Addam was, kind of fairly, taken aback. "You want to . . . use this? For what?"

"I'm sorry—I mean, may I please have the fucking sword?"

Addam handed Brand his sword. The moment it was settled in his hand, Brand whipped around and put the point at the jugular of the old-fashioned diving suit on the ground.

He said, "Nod your head if you understand that I have a blade at your neck." And I nearly jumped out of my skin when the diving suit nodded.

"It's a smart hiding spot," Brand said, "but you fidget. Are you the caretaker of the ship?"

"Yes," a muffled voice responded slowly. "I'm not armed."

"Take off the helmet," Brand said. He handed the sword back to Addam, and trained his gun on the prone figure.

The bulky arms rose to tug at the round helmet. What emerged was a wizened old face, gaunt and pale, creased with wrinkles.

I said, softly, "Well now. We should make introductions. I don't know your real name: your shipmates only called you Pretty Boy."

When you lived in a society where people's apparent age shifted over decades—both forward and back—you gained a knack for identifying the basic facial features that remain unchanged. I saw the ghost of a beautiful young man in the shape of those cheekbones and those wide, faded eyes.

"He was the start of it," I told Addam and Brand, without breaking eye contact with Pretty Boy. "The Hanged Man followed him onto this ship."

"It wasn't my fault," Pretty Boy rasped, in the cracked tones of one who rarely spoke.

"It was not," I said. "I know. We're not going to hurt you or blame you."

"But will you kill me?" he asked. Water formed at the corners of his eyes; one drop ran over and through deep wrinkles. "Please? I can't do it myself."

"We don't have time to question him," Brand said. "Let's take him and go—we're running out of time, and he'll have information."

"I can't leave the ship," Pretty Boy said. "He . . ." Pretty Boy waved a clumsy, sealed hand at his head.

"You're under a geas," I guessed. "A compulsion."

Pretty Boy nodded.

"And maybe even some wards which keep you alive," I murmured. His age wasn't impossible—not with modern human medicine—but it didn't seem like he'd have had access to that. His life was being prolonged, if not reversed, by magic. And since rejuvenation magic only worked on humans who were bonded to an Atlantean, that meant something darker had been done to make this happen. Something that involved a transfer of life, usually from an unwilling donor.

"Clarity is still running," I told Brand. "We have some time. Addam, can you find a chair for . . . Pretty Boy?"

"My name is John," Pretty Boy whispered, looking from my face to Brand's, to Addam's.

"Addam, please find a chair for John. Brand, would you please help him out of the suit? He won't hurt us."

Addam and Brand gave me room to handle this, and did as I asked. Addam found a stool in the surgical suite; Brand undid the locks and clasps of the diving suit. Underneath, John was dressed in a once-pristine soldier's uniform that had dissolved thread by thread over the years.

"My name is Rune Saint John," I said, once John was hunched in his chair. "Do you know what that means?"

John paled. "Saint . . . They're all saints."

"You mean the Arcana families. We started using saint names at the start of the 1900s. It's just for show. Trust me, we're not saints."

John nodded. "And you're like tarot cards."

"Well," I said. "We came first. Better to say that tarot cards are loosely based on us. John, I am the Sun."

John began to shake. Tears shook loose, pooling along his nose. "You're one of the cards. Like him."

"I am nothing like him," I said.

"If you're not like him . . . Are you good? Will you kill me?"

Addam made a sound. "Can we find a way to help, Rune? Can we break the geas and take him with us?"

"Not easily. Not quickly. But eventually? Yes." I looked at John. "How patient can you be, John?"

Now his fear seemed to crumble under another emotion. Something like hope. "I have not left this ship in over seventy-five years. And it hasn't driven me insane yet."

"Does the geas prevent you from answering questions?"

"Not . . . exactly. But I can't say anything that would harm . . . him. But I could—" His face twisted in pain. He started breathing rapidly. He held up a hand when I moved closer to him, and repeated, in a very slow and clear voice, "I can't *say* anything that would harm him."

"Paper and pen," Brand snapped, because we'd been in situations like this before, and knew the potential loopholes. He began patting down his ammo pockets. He had a small miniature golf pencil in one pocket—sharpened to a stiletto point—and Addam had a receipt in his wallet.

"If you read what I write, it may harm him," John said once Brand had stuffed the writing utensils in his hand. "I will need to fight you."

"Yes or no questions, and he'll draw a big *N* or *Y*," Brand said. "Watch the movement of his hand. Don't look over his shoulder."

John gave Brand a surprised look.

I took a breath. "John, do you hate the Hanged Man?"

His hand on the paper lifted and dipped, a clear but shaky *Y*. I did not try to look at the paper and risk sparking the geas.

"Have we set off any alarms on this ship?" I asked. A single pencil motion—an *N*. "Will you be forced to tell him that we were here, excepting being asked a direct question from him?" An *N*. "If I promise to try to help you, will you try to keep our presence a secret?" A *Y*.

Addam took a knee in front of the elderly man. He said, "I do not think it would harm Lord Hanged Man if you were to tell us about yourself. And we are very . . . moved by your situation. No one should be compelled by magic. It is an outrageous abuse of my people's gifts. Can you tell us your story, John?"

John stared at the pencil in his hand for a long minute, and cleared his throat. His first words were spoken brokenly, nearly a flinch against expected pain. "I was a sailor."

When nothing happened to him, he went on. "I was a sailor aboard the USS *Declaration*, in the war. I joined the crew in New York many, many years ago. I thought . . . it would save me. I thought it would take me away from *him*."

"So you already knew him by that point," I said.

"I was in an alley. In New York. The year before I enlisted. It was late, and I was very drunk, and men tried to rob and kill me. And then he was there. He swooped down from a roof, and he stopped the robbers. They had knives but . . . But he saved me." He closed his eyes and licked dry lips. "He fell in love with me. Or . . . he said he did. He told me secrets. He told me about a secret world. He said he loved me, and would take me there. And I was lost in him, because he . . ."

He shook his head helplessly. "He was endless. He was a walking god."

"He is no god," I said.

John's eyes flickered to mine, and he gave me a cracked smile. He had had no dental care over the years, and his teeth were the gray of dead nerves. "I didn't know that, at first. And even with what I know now about you and your kind, I would still call that a lie.

"Still, I loved him, in the beginning, but even then I knew he had this . . . darkness inside him. After all, I saw what he did to those men who had robbed me. But over the next six months . . . I saw other things. And it scared me. I told him I wanted to leave. I begged him to let me leave."

John began to shake. He tightened his hand around the pencil, crumpling the receipt. "I will never forget his smile when he agreed. He says, yes, John, you can leave. Yes, John, you can walk out that door. Yes, you can join your friends on the ship and you can sail away. But . . . it was a trick, wasn't it? He never said he wouldn't follow. He never said he'd let me go. No one tells him no. *No one.* He gave me just enough of an escape to make it exciting to hunt."

"The history books say this ship sank in a storm," I told him. "That didn't happen, did it?"

John started to speak, then flinched in agony, gritting his teeth together. His breathing quickened again.

"We know what happened on the ship," Brand said quickly. "Don't ask about it."

I changed tracks. "We've been told there's a portal on this ship—the entrance to a secret room or realm. Are you aware of it?"

John went back to his paper. The receipt was covered in overlapping letters now, like a big squiggle—and I turned my eyes away from it, watching just the motion of the writing. He'd traced a *Y*.

"Do you know where the portal entrance is?" I asked. Another *Y*.

Brand said, "We've promised you that we'll try to help. It may not happen today, but it will happen, because I'm pretty fucking sure that at the end of this only the Hanged Man or we will be standing. Do you believe that I'm being sincere?"

Y.

"Okay, I'm going to trust you," Brand said. "With a very important piece of information. That'll be like collateral, right? Against our promise to come back and help you."

I took over, understanding where Brand was leading. "John, do you know Layne Dawncreek?"

A quick look of surprise. Then: *Y*.

"Is he alive?" I asked.

John didn't know how to answer that.

Brand said, "Is Layne Dawncreek in the portal room?"

A sharp, immediate *N*.

"Is there anything in the portal room that would lead us to Layne Dawncreek?" Brand asked.

Another hesitation. John looked between us. And then something seemed to occur to him. He gave the paper and pencil an almost surprised look, and smiled. "Can I ask *you* questions?" he said. "After all, it may help . . . him if I knew more. It would not harm him, if I knew more."

"Go on then," Brand said.

"Are you here for Layne? Is that why you've come here?"

I exchanged a look with Brand before answering. If Lord Hanged Man knew we were looking for Layne, he'd piece together we were using the investigation as a Trojan horse to help Max. We'd lose an element of surprise.

I could live with that.

"Layne Dawncreek has run away from home," I said. "We believe he's vanished into the Hanged Man's court. His guardian has asked us to find Layne, and bring him home safely. From everything I know about the Hanged Man—from everything *you* know about the Hanged Man—I think you'll agree it won't be easy. He won't give Layne back. Which means we'll need to take him. You understand what it means, when I say I'm the Sun, right?"

"A card. You're a card. The sun card."

"That is my court. If I face the Hanged Man over Layne, it will be like . . . like a war. When courts face off against each other, it rarely ends peacefully. As Brand said, only one of us will be left standing. But as scary as the Hanged Man is, you would do well to bet on me, John. I will be in a position to help you later."

He breathed out a long, fetid breath. He nodded.

Then he started writing on the receipt. In a minute, he'd run out of room, so Addam and Brand fished out every piece of paper they had on them, and he continued his story on a grocery shopping list, a movie ticket stub, an ATM receipt.

When he was done, his hand went slack, and the pencil dropped and clattered against a fallen bulkhead. He said, "It would hurt so much if this paper was taken from me. I would have to fight back, to protect it. And it may trigger alarms on the ship, magical alarms, and the guards may come. Perhaps if—"

Brand pinched a vein on the back of John's head. John stiffened; his eyelids dropped; and in less than a half minute he was sagging in the chair. The last thing he said was: "They'll be coming soon."

Brand took the papers from his arthritic fingers and handed them to me.

I flipped through quickly, handing each piece to Addam and Brand as I read it. At the end, I swallowed, my spit sour with anxiety.

"This could mean a lot of things, but none of them good," I said.

"We should go," Brand said. "We've learned what we can."

"There's a stairway up there." Addam pointed.

My pocket vibrated. I pulled my phone out, saw Quinn's number, hit the speakerphone. "Quickly," I told him.

"Um. Okay. We may have sort of borrowed a boat, but Max is a very very bad driver. He forgets the battleship is there because of the can't-see-anything spells the Hanged Man set, and keeps driving into it, which can't be very good for this boat that we, um, borrowed."

From behind us, back the way we'd come, I heard a loud wailing noise.

"Quinn," Addam said. "Quinn, do you know what type of guards this ship has?"

"Something very bad," Quinn said, "only I don't know what."

Then Max yelped in the background of the phone call. "Holy shit, I think there's something in front of us!" It was followed by a wooden thunk. Quinn fumbled his phone, which went dead.

"We're moving," Brand said, and set the pace.

EDGEMERE

Back at Addam's condo, for a handful of stolen minutes, I ignored the world.

Ignored my anger at Max and Quinn, who had definitely stolen a boat. Ignored what I'd learned on the battleship. Ignored the fact we were closing in on a serial killer. Ignored the uncomfortable commute back to Addam's home, where no one was much in the mood to talk to each other.

Brand had ordered Max and Quinn into Quinn's bedroom. They'd argued they weren't children. Brand went into the kitchen, grabbed a handful of dry rice, and threw it onto Quinn's carpet. Then he said they had to pick up every grain, or he'd beat the shit out of them like the adults they were.

Now Brand was in the kitchen ordering breakfast. We had called Corinne, and asked her to bring the kids to Addam's condo. There were reasons for that, which were tied up into the Very Big Conversation we all needed to have.

But again, I was ignoring that. For just a handful of minutes.

I was in Addam's bedroom, where my boyfriend was striding back and forth in a mood.

I stood in the corner and tried to figure out what to say. I wasn't very good with talks like this. Making battle plans against the Hanged Man? Slice of pie. Emotions? I was nearly in hives.

But one of the things I'd learned in the last couple months was that I couldn't take Addam for granted. His feelings were more resilient than any man I'd ever met, but he'd reached a breaking point. He was facing a real issue with Quinn, and it was eating at him.

Since we didn't have time for a long conversation, I settled on another approach.

A few seconds later, he came to a dead stop in the middle of his pacing. He stared at me and said, "Hero. You appear to be taking your shirt off."

I dropped my shirt on the ground. This usually shut me up when he did it to me.

"You are attempting to manage me," he said, and his accent was back, which meant he was either very amused or very upset. "The difference is, when I do this to you, I do not plant my feet in battle formation."

I looked down. I'd shifted my left leg forward and turned sideways, to minimize targetable body space. "Shit," I said.

He came over to me. Slowly, he leaned forward, and brushed his lips on my forehead. "You are sweet," he murmured.

"Do . . ." I took a breath. "Do you want to talk about this?"

"I suppose I am being quite surly, aren't I?"

"You're not being surly enough by half. I can't even imagine what's going on in your head."

He shrugged, not meeting my eyes. "My brother is growing up."

"No," I said, and wouldn't leave it at that. "Your son is growing up. Don't trivialize this. You raised him, Addam. You once knew him better than anyone in the world—but kids grow up, and they learn their own things, and then they have their own secrets. This must suck."

He went over to the bed and fell against the mattress, sliding back at the same instant so that he could recline against the pillows. Like every motion Addam made, it was beautiful and fluid and left me grasping awkwardly behind him. I crawled onto the bed and self-consciously adjusted my position next to him.

He scooted down low, and I followed, so that our eyes were even.

He said, "Everyone has always called my brother slow. They never understood him. Never understood his potential. For his middle grade science fair? He created a miniature castle replica—with real, miniature wards. Real wards. Barely twelve, and he'd created a freshness ward the size of a pin head. One of the bullies in his class tried to knock the castle down—and his hand caught on fire. Quinn had put a tiny defense ward on the battlements." Addam shook his head at the memory, and smiled. "His . . . gifts have been a part of his life always. And I've also seen how quick and smart he is. But now I'm seeing these two parts of him coming together—a prophet using his quick, smart mind."

"He's growing up. You're right."

"So why should I be surprised? That his powers are maturing? Should I be upset by it? That seems rather ungenerous."

I stared at Addam for a long minute. I needed to get this right. Only it was hard to concentrate, because he had a perfect five o'clock shadow.

"You are staring at my chin," Addam commented.

"It's a nice chin. And I'm trying to think of the best way to say this. Because, yes, Quinn's powers are growing. I'd thought the medicine he'd been taking was muting his abilities, but . . . Well. We'll need to look into that. But yes, his powers are growing, and we should respect that, not ignore it. His type of ability is too dangerous to be left to develop on its own. Maybe instead of medication he just needs training."

"I feel like there is another *but* coming."

"There is. You can't make excuses for him. What he did? What Max did? They are not ready to operate like that without guidance. They will get killed. I can already hear you finding ways to forgive him—you always forgive him. He's Quinn. He's very forgivable. But this time, there needs to be consequences. They need boundaries."

"It appears that we are both parents of a sort, then," he decided after a moment of thinking. "Perhaps we will consult Brand on the punishment. I expect he is very good at arranging such things."

I smiled and kissed him, because it seemed like a good moment to do that. That went on for a while, and I forgot what else I was thinking about. It did occur to me that I hadn't kissed many people like this in my life. Hollywood got it all wrong. Kissing is sort of loud and sloppy. The movies really dumb down those side effects.

Addam's hands strayed after a while. I was okay with it, but my body wasn't, because I froze the moment his fingers went below my waist.

He very carefully drew his hands back to my upper arms.

But the moment had chilled. I looked down at the pillow instead of his eyes, and pulled back. It was a nice pillow. It even had some drool stains, which made Addam a bit more approachable.

"Rune," he said softly. "Please don't."

"Fuck," I hissed. "Fuck fuck fuck my life."

"Please. Don't."

"Don't what? Don't apologize? How can I not? You deserve more than—"

He reached out and poked me hard in the chest. I was so surprised that I just blinked.

"Brand did that to me," Addam said. "In the Westlands, at my family compound. When I tried to blame myself for what Ashton caused. Brand poked me and said that I didn't do *this*. That *this* was done to me. Rune, what happened to you . . . It was done to you. You did not cause it. I think the world of you for how you've handled it. I truly do."

I closed my eyes, not mollified in the slightest.

He kissed my eyelids. "Know this, then: I am where I want to be. Right now, I am where I want to be, and it makes me very, very happy."

"Out of curiosity, what made you happiest? Searching a ghost ship? Pissing off one of the oldest and most dangerous Arcana? Trying to figure out how to punish your kid for stealing a boat? You are very easily pleased, Saint Nicholas."

"No. I'm rather not."

"It doesn't . . ." Don't say it. Don't say it. Don't say it. I grimaced. "We've been together three months. It doesn't bother you, how slow I'm taking this? We've . . . been close. But not . . . as close as we could be."

He watched my lips, and my eyes, and a spot in the middle of my forehead. His half-smile—the one he did with a corner of his mouth—never wavered. "Would you have fallen for me if we'd just met at an event? At a party? Instead of fighting a lich? If you'd passed me on the street, would you have looked twice?"

"Does it matter?" I asked.

"Only because I asked," he said.

And he was right. I had one of those weird moments of insight that felt a little like déjà vu. It mattered because he asked. Addam gave many everyday things in my life meaning, just because he commented on them, like fighting and granola and light switches.

"I would never have thought I'd be lucky enough to have the chance to fall for you," I said honestly.

"I look forward to you understanding, then, how I feel. And I repeat, again, that I am exactly where I want to be, ghost ships and all."

Someone pounded on the bedroom door. Brand shouted, "Wrap it the fuck up! There are children on the way!"

I leaned my face against Addam and smiled into his cheek.

A month ago, Addam had formally moved out of Justice Seat, the ancestral home of Lady Justice's court. He now lived full-time with Quinn in his condo in Edgemere, which had been built in a rehabilitated and deconsecrated church. As part of his permanent relocation, he'd bought the second condo on his floor—something, apparently, that rich people did—and knocked out the wall between them. He had the entire top half of a gargantuan stained glass window to himself, sharing the bottom half with the two units below him.

I knew the relocation was his way of coping with the fallout that had followed his recent kidnapping. He'd lost a sister and two friends—two business partners. The third business partner, Geoffrey, was in the process of being bought out. So the condo move was Addam's way of restoring some of those empty holes.

Now that he lived in a space without a small battalion of estate servants, he'd become obsessed with cleaning products. Last week he'd brought over his first vacuum cleaner to Half House to show it off. He'd actually demonstrated it and asked me if I wanted to try.

I liked my boyfriend.

When he and I emerged from his bedroom suite, Brand was walking around the living room with his smart phone, on which he'd opened the calculator app. Periodically he'd stop in front of something, make a sound in his throat, research it on his phone, then add a number to his running total.

Addam and I watched in silence for a minute or two until Brand pointed to a pile he'd gathered. A tin of caviar, a pen, a watch, and a razor. He said, "That's Half House."

"Half House is worth more than that," I said.

Brand pointed again at the pile. "That razor? Zafirro Iridium."

"I do not know what that means," I said, and gave Addam a side glance, whose cheeks went red.

"It's made from fucking meteors," Brand said. "It could survive being dunked in molten lava. The blades are made from *sapphire*." He pointed again emphatically. "Half House."

"We must not leave him alone again," Addam murmured. "And that razor is meant to become an heirloom. To be passed down through generations."

"So what you're saying is the fucking T-shirt reads *I plan for generations* and not *Rich scion with credit card?*"

"Breakfast," I said, clapping my hands. "You ordered, right?"

"Yeah. Corinne and the kids should be here any minute. Max and Quinn are still sulking and picking up rice. I think Quinn is trying to cheat with Telekinesis."

"Are you sure about calling in that security team?" I asked Addam.

Earlier, Addam had offered to send a Justice security team to Corinne's house, to sweep for bugs or other magical listening devices. The deeper the investigation got, the less secure their residence would be. This would at least buy us a little peace of mind.

"The team had an opening in their schedule," Addam said. "It is only a small favor."

"Your mom won't get pissed?" Brand asked.

"Possibly. But then, I do not entirely care," Addam said. He hadn't completely forgiven his mother yet for her . . . absence? Or at least her unwillingness to intervene in recent events. When Addam had gone missing, it had been Lord Tower who'd hired me to find Addam. Addam's own mother believed in letting her children survive their own battles. Now she was down to one child at home, Addam's oldest brother, Christian.

I changed the subject. "Brand, we decided you get to punish Max and Quinn."

"Did we? Is that how this fucking works now?" Brand asked. "Because if it does, I'm coming into the bedroom with you next time. I'll bring a magazine."

"It is only somewhat a joke," Addam said. "We must discuss Quinn and Max's actions at some point. But not now. There are more pressing urgencies."

So Addam and I went to set the table for guests. Brand fetched Quinn and Max from the bedroom and told them to clean the living room. Max glared at everyone and pointedly dumped a handful of dirty rice back into its original box. Quinn ran around the living room with a dust rag, wide-eyed and pale. He'd never really had Addam angry with him before. You'd think a prophet who saw probabilities would've been prepared for this.

In due time, Addam buzzed in the delivery man, who arrived at the same time as Corinne, Anna, and Corbie Dawncreek. Corbie ran into the room ahead of everyone. When he saw a crowd of strange people, his mouth opened in a tiny 0. He turned and sprinted back out the door.

"Kids, take off your shoes," Corrine said from behind the delivery person, and ushered Corbie and Anna inside.

Her unnaturally lined face was tight with anxiety. When her eyes latched onto mine, I gave her a nod that could mean anything. Addam stepped forward with an outstretched hand. "My name is Addam. It is very good to meet you."

Corbie kicked off his sneakers and stared around him with full-moon eyes. "Fancy fancy," he whispered in his hoarse little voice. "Is there a pool?"

"Corbie," Corinne said patiently.

"We bought much food," Addam told everyone, and raised a hand to the dining area on the other side of the living room. "Please. It's been a long night. Let's eat before we talk, yes?"

While Addam paid for the meal, the kids descended on the table, Max and Quinn included. Max was seventeen years old and growing, and was adept at balancing both an unending appetite and a grudge.

Corinne came close to me when everyone was out of immediate earshot. "Layne?" she whispered.

"We have leads," I said back. "We'll talk soon, I promise."

Quinn, playing the role of the penitent brother to the hilt, unpacked the meal. Brand had ordered a massive spread of eggs and breads—scrambled, omelets, sunny-side up. Addam kept the chatter going as we dug in. The weirdness that accompanied eating a meal with virtual strangers slowly faded. Even Max seemed to forget he was sulking.

"Did you see ghost ships?" Corbie asked me excitedly.

"We saw many ghost ships," I confirmed.

"Were there skeleton pirates? Did the skeleton pirate have a parrot? Was the parrot a skeleton too?"

"No skeleton pirates," I said.

"Did you see the giant squid?" Quinn asked, in his own excited voice. When I just stared at him, he shrugged. "Sometimes you did. That was always a good story."

I said, "No giant squid. And we didn't have a fight near boats either, Quinn."

Quinn stared at his eggs for a few seconds, long enough to have Corinne narrowing her eyes at the strange statement. Then Quinn shook his head like a wet dog and said, "Not yet."

Addam put down his fork and knife with a plastic click. Metal utensils would have been more dramatic, but Quinn still flinched like he'd been yelled at.

Now Corinne was really giving us a strange look.

Anna, who'd been alternating her sharp, smart glance between her plate and the people talking, said, "Aunt Corinne researched a battleship for you."

"We've talked about eavesdropping," Corinne said.

"We've talked about paying attention, too," Anna said. Undeterred, she continued. "The *Declaration*."

Brand stared at her. "She did research for us, yeah."

Anna said, "It sank."

"That's what they say."

Anna was quiet for another minute while the adults exchanged looks and Corbie drew a parrot in his ketchup. I knew the gears were still turning in her head, but even so, what she said next made my breath catch. She said, "Won't the people who run America get really mad if they found out?"

"Yes, Anna," I said quietly. Because I'd been very, very aware of the same thing. "I imagine they would."

Soon after, the food was done, and there was no more stalling. No more pretending that this was a social call.

The first thing I did was to remove Anna and Corbie from the discussion. I said, "Corbie, there's a pool in the building. Maybe Quinn and Max will show you and Anna?"

While Corbie bounced around making hoarse dolphin sounds of joy, Anna glared at me, and Max looked upset.

She said, "I should be able to stay," which was more or less the exact same thing Max said, while Quinn, still playing the apologetic sibling, was halfway out the door with Corbie.

"You want to be a badass?" Brand asked Anna. "Part of being a good badass is knowing that sometimes you need to take no for an answer."

"This is all my fault," Max insisted. "And you said you'd let me help!"

"Help how?" I asked, while Corinne said, "How is this your fault?" Which made me even angrier, because Corinne wasn't aware that we were helping her in order to achieve two ends. I turned on Max, and made sure the look I gave him was shared with Quinn, who was standing just outside the front door. I felt the dull burn behind my eyes: my Aspect, wanting to flare. "Help how?" I repeated. "Abandoning the safety of Half House? Stealing a *boat?* Driving that stolen boat to the shielded property of one of the city's most dangerous men? How are you helping, Max?"

"Quinn said there were guards, and the guards almost always attacked you! We were giving you an exit strategy!"

I stepped right up into his face and said, "I *am always* the exit strategy. To think I needed to be saved is an insult. To put yourself at risk, with everything we're doing to save you, is an insult."

"But . . . Rune, please. You were seventeen the first time the Tower let you do a mission," he argued. "How am I different?"

"I was seventeen," I agreed with Max. "My court had fallen. I had lost my father's tools of war. I had only as much protection as the Tower chose to extend. I had no *options.* You do."

"My court has fallen! I have no sigils! How are we different? Because of what happened when your court fell? Do you have any idea what *I* lived through? Do you have any idea what my uncle—" Max choked off, his brain catching up with his tongue. I saw the exact moment his anger broke into despair.

He turned around and ran out the door. Anna decided she was done protesting too, and hurried after them.

As Addam shut the door, I looked at the ground and tried to figure out what the hell to do next. The picked bones of the breakfast spread caught my eyes, and out of nowhere I thought: Max used to eat scrambled eggs, and now he eats them the same way that Brand and I do.

"How is this his fault?" Corinne said sharply.

Brand didn't just rip the Band-Aid; he excised the skin around it with a sharp knife. "Before Max became our ward, he was promised to the Hanged Man. For marriage. We can't go after the Hanged Man directly. You're our way in. That doesn't mean we're not doing everything we can for Layne."

"I never said otherwise, boy," she bristled. "And I've been around enough Arcana to know they have plans behind their plans behind their plans. I just thought *this* one was different." She didn't even spare me a look.

"He is different," Addam said.

"Corinne . . . I'm in a corner. I need a way into the Hanged Man's orbit. That doesn't mean Layne isn't a priority. It doesn't mean . . . What it became, when I realized . . ." I held my arms out, frustrated. "You're my people."

She stared at me, and I stared back at her, and if she continued to be angry she buried it deep behind a neutral expression. Not unlike my own Companion, when he was furious with me.

"Tell me what you learned," she said.

It took a solid half hour to recount everything. Corinne stopped me frequently with questions. They were good questions, too. Again: not unlike my Companion.

At the very last, we got to the note that John had written on the back of the scraps of paper:

They did not know Layne would run away. I heard one say, "What a waste. We can't keep him now." And another say, "At least he'll feed the bottom line." Haven't seen or heard since.

Corinne read the note three times, and by the end, her fingers were shaking.

"We can't jump to conclusions," Brand said. "You know that. We do the work, we follow the leads, and we don't make assumptions."

"They're going to kill him. That's what this means."

Brand leaned forward in his chair, low, so that he was looking up at her eyes. "Think. It maybe doesn't. Maybe they're just moving him to another location? Or putting him into captivity?"

She put the papers down on the table and drew her fingers into a fist. She gave Brand a tight nod.

Addam stirred. "Rune, you saw things on that ship that Brand and I did not. What did you learn?"

"Some questions we need to ask, from people who may have answers," I hedged.

"Rune," Brand said, a little pissed, because he knew I was hedging.

"Consequences," I said. "What the Hanged Man did on that ship? It had consequences. That's what we'll find out."

"And that helps us?" Brand asked. "It happened over seventy years ago."

"It did, but something on this scale . . . Addam, you said yourself the sinking of the *Declaration* was infamous. It sank in a storm during a human world war. More than a thousand lives were lost. No wreckage found. No *survivors*—at least that the human world knows of. You cannot cover something like that up without help, and that sort of help would have consequences. The Arcanum had to have known. They had to have helped clean up the mess. That's *vital* to our own plans."

I stood up and began pacing. "Think of it. This all happened at least twenty years before the Atlantean World War. Atlantis was still a secret. Did you know they had an entire branch of government devoted to keeping the homeland hidden? And I'm not just talking about the illusions that shrouded it from sight—I'm talking about disinformation campaigns, and fucking with people's memories, and hiding bodies in graves so deep you'd have to crack the planet open to find them again."

"He's right," Corinne said. "I was there. I remember."

"So you're saying there was a cover-up," Brand said.

"I think that's what we'll find out."

"And that fucking means something," Brand prompted, now irritably, because this was about politics, and it was one of the few areas where he tended to trail me in putting the pieces together.

"It does. It corrects a bad assumption I made. I've always thought the Hanged Man's court was reclusive because that was its nature. I thought the Hanged Man had refused to join the modern world—like other Arcana courts that never adapted to the Unsettlement. Right? Sort of the opposite of Arcana like Lord Tower or Lord Chariot, who created empires and fortunes, who embrace the new era. Hell, Lord Chariot is listed on human *stock exchanges*. But other courts just . . . retreated. I thought the Hanged Man was one of them. But what if it wasn't his choice?"

"He retreated as punishment? He was made to retreat?" Addam guessed.

"I think we're going to find out that the attack on the *Declaration* was impulsive. And that he paid a very, very heavy price in the aftermath. I think we're going to find out that the reason his court is so small and reclusive is because working with the Arcanum to cover up the attacks was insanely costly. That it cost him money. And favors. And freedom. And—"

"Allies," Addam whispered. He met my eyes, and understood. He'd grown up with a mother like Lady Justice, after all. "We know that he's not popular. But this . . . it means he made enemies. It means you may have more allies than you thought."

"I can't take on the Hanged Man alone," I said. "Not matter how small his court is, it's a hell of a lot bigger than the people sitting in this room. I need *allies*."

It was at that exact moment that my phone began to make the beeeeeep-beeeeeep-beeeeeep sound of a dump truck backing up.

I looked at the screen and immediately shot Brand a dirty look, to accuse him of messing with my ringtones again. And he gave Max's empty chair a defensive look, to accuse him. And I gave him another dirty look, to say that Max had picked up that prank from Brand, so it was still Brand's fault. And Brand gave me a final look, which was like him shrugging and saying, *but admit it, the ringtone fits.*

I answered the phone before it could go to voicemail.

I said, "Hello, Lord Tower."

"I've sent a car," Lord Tower said. "You'll join me for breakfast."

LORD TOWER

I have no idea how many times Lord Tower has rejuvenated, though I have reason to ballpark his age at well over four centuries.

As long as I've known him, he's appeared as a man just shy of middle age. He has Spanish features, a swimmer's build, the hands of a classical pianist. I had a crush on him once, long before I'd been trained to look behind all the masks that a person could or would wear.

Lord Tower came to power when the Emperor and Empress still ruled the homeland, in the era before the Atlantean World War. He was their spy and interrogator—the spider of a web that stretched between every court and major house. When the war left the homeland a biological wasteland, he'd adapted with an almost ruthless efficiency. He moved his torture tools to the basement; turned his interrogation chamber into a sunroom; and became a business magnate.

In a city of bull's-eyes that narrowed, circle by circle by circle, to the true center of power, Lord Tower stood at the heart of the Arcanum, the collective body of ruling Arcana. He was the head of the Dagger Throne, and had been my patron since the fall of my court.

While I liked to think I'd evened the scales by taking on assignments he trusted no one else with, nothing would erase the fact that, once, I'd woke in a hospital bed, nearly dead from torture, and survived the aftermath only with his protection.

He'd saved me. He'd saved Brand. He'd given me shelter until I was strong enough to clear my own tiny space in the world.

I'd spent the last twenty years being careful to never put myself in a position where I'd be set against his wishes. Because the thing about spiders? They hated when anything fucked with their webs.

* * *

The limousine hissed over wet, gray-glass streets. The sun was a smudge of rose and indigo on the horizon, filtered through storm clouds.

Before I left, we'd made quick plans. Addam would coordinate the efforts of the team sweeping the Dawncreek house for wards, traps, or listening devices. Brand would stay with the kids and Corinne at Addam's condo. We'd all meet there later to discuss our next move.

Corinne had gone quiet the moment she knew where I was headed. Even more curiously, she'd asked if I was going to meet with Lord Tower *and Mayan.* Mayan was the Tower's Companion—though he operated in a much, much different capacity than Brand did with me. Mayan ran the Tower's massive security enterprise; so the two were rarely joined at the hip. How Corinne knew him, I wasn't sure.

The limousine came to a gliding perch by a freshly painted curb. I peeked out the window and saw the awning of a restaurant called *Rivers.* I'd never eaten there myself. My credit score was too low for the loan I'd need to afford it.

I got out of the car's bulletproof backseat, making an effort to sweep my attention in a full 360—not forgetting to look up and down, thank you very much, Brand.

At this hour, even the early commuters were sparse. One of the nightclubs across the street had just closed, and a rare Assyrian sphinx was sweeping glitter into the gutter, proving yet again that commerce will always trump the gravitas of old mythology.

Rivers sat on Nazaca Road, which was built over one of the world's thickest ley lines. The pavement hummed under my feet as I crossed to the restaurant doors, which swept open at my approach.

My sense of blue-collar superiority lasted about half a second after I walked through the next set of doors.

I couldn't help it. It was just that damn interesting.

Fixed translocation portals were scattered at either end of nine or ten sunken waterways, which crossed a dining room the size of a warehouse. Each canal held water that flowed from portals leading from, and then back into, a famous river from the larger world. Venetian bridges crossed the channels, with translocation plaques providing details on the living geography.

There were few diners at that hour, and the Tower had a table in the very back. I was led over three bridges, crossing from the blackwater mirror of the Amazon valley's Rio Negro to the glacier-fed Blue River of Greenland. In a deep Scottish river, the last I crossed, I watched as a coal-black horse raced along the bottom with the arm bones of a skeleton tangled in its mane.

"Fancy fancy," I said.

The Tower looked up from his phone. The surface of it steamed; not from his breath but from whatever wards and spells had been worked into the plastic mold. He disconnected the call and said, "Rune."

I sat down and scooted my chair up to the table.

"Quite an exciting evening you had," he said, unfolding his napkin.

"It was," I agreed, without batting a damn eyelash. "Just out of curiosity, how did I rank on the report this morning? Still at 157, or have I moved up in the rolls?"

The Tower paused in the act of smoothing the napkin. He smiled. "That was a remarkably well-informed statement."

Point to me. Every morning, Lord Tower reviewed a report on the whereabouts of over 150 people in the world whom he had a vested interest in keeping track of. I'd caught Mayan preparing it once.

"I almost never get to surprise you," I said happily.

"Not often, no—though you didn't quite stick the landing. If you hadn't felt the need to show off the exact numbers, I wouldn't have been able to pinpoint when you learned of it. There haven't been 157 names on that list in over twelve years."

He lifted a hand without turning, and a waiter darted in. "Zavier, we'll have the omelet."

"Excellent, Lord Tower. Today's recipe is—"

"With the yartsa gunbu. Maybe a little cheese. Chef's choice. And another pot of this excellent tea, along with some orange Italian sodas."

"The . . . yartsa gunbu?" the waiter said, swallowing. "Of course, my lord. Right away, my lord."

When he was gone, I pointed. "I saw that look on his face."

"It's a mushroom. Very expensive, but there's a farm that grows it locally."

"I should probably mention up front that Brand asked me to confirm, in writing if possible, that you were picking up the tab."

"My treat, of course," Lord Tower said.

"Excellent. How does Corinne know Mayan?"

Lord Tower's smile didn't cool—it rarely did, with me—but it sharpened. "Mayan helped train her. Mayan trained many Companions for the Sun Throne—like Brand."

"Oh, don't *even* let Brand hear you say that. He considers himself fully formed when he started sparring with Mayan."

"There's quite a bit of reciprocity that happens when Companions are trained. It was one of the arrangements I had with your father."

"Did you know Kevan Dawncreek?"

"I did, actually. Not well."

"Did you know his son is missing?"

"Did you know his son was missing before you needed a reason to wedge your way into the Hanged Man's court?"

I felt my nostrils flare, but kept my tongue, because he was right. "I know now," I said.

"I am aware, and I appreciate how that must weigh on you," he said, and not insincerely. "But my intent was to point out the real issue at play here. Your ward's well-being."

"Yes."

Lord Tower held my stare. If the silence was bait, I didn't take it. I inhaled, slowly. I smelled food and riverbeds: mud and spice, with the slight aftertaste of human pollution.

"Have I ever asked you a favor?" Lord Tower said.

In my head, I imagined Brand saying, *Only all the fucking time.*

Lord Tower raised a hand, reading my expression. "No. Not work. Not compensation. A favor, from me."

"He wants Matthias," I said. "Don't ask me to back down."

"There are ways to delay. There are stalling tactics. I will help you myself."

"What good will stalling do? Do you honestly think you can change the Hanged Man's mind? Do you . . . do you even *know* what he's done? Did you know about the battleship?" I saw it on his face. "Of course you did."

"He has paid for that mistake for decades," Lord Tower said. "I made sure of it, if that makes you think better of me."

"It would if you hadn't just called what happened a mistake. Have you even been on that ship?"

"I have not. And it's not the issue before us. The Hanged Man is being . . . managed," Lord Tower said. "Within the Arcanum—among those who fight to keep this city from eating its own tail—is a small group concerned about the Hanged Man's interests. So we harry his businesses. We disrupt his holdings. We keep his attention divided between distractions, to dampen his appetite for worse things. We will corner him into making an unrecoverable error. This will happen."

"Max—"

"Can be protected. The marital pact can be challenged. And the issue of the Hanged Man will resolve itself before the challenge even needs to be addressed."

"And Layne Dawncreek?" I asked.

"Cannot be your concern. You do not have that luxury. You know this. There are real, living, present dangers to people already under your protection, and you risk them if you try to save both young men. I'm sorry, Rune. I know you want otherwise."

"I can't just give up. Not anymore."

"You cannot take on the Hanged Man. And you have no reason yet to move against him. No proof to ground your accusation. No protocol to protect yourself against retaliation."

"The Dawncreeks were once my people."

"And they're worth risking yourself? And Brand and Max? What about Addam and Quinn, Rune."

"That's a low blow," I said.

Two waiters glided to the table, heads lowered. One deposited a basket of fresh, honeyed rolls; the other the tea and flavored soda water. They glided away without waiting for thanks.

Lord Tower rearranged his cutlery, an oddly fidgety gesture from him. "I remember a day. It was . . . perhaps six months after Quinn was born. Addam appeared at my door with Quinn, wrapped in a blanket, nestled in Addam's backpack. Quite literally: a backpack. He'd turned it around so that it rested against his chest. He told me that his mother was not arranging a ceremony for Quinn, like she had with Christian, Ella, and himself. He asked me if I would be Quinn's godfather, as I had been godfather to him."

Addam had told me stories before. Not this one, but others. His mother hadn't been interested in assuming direct oversight of the sickly baby that Quinn had been. Addam had filled the gap from the start, as fantastically unprepared as he'd been at his own young age.

Lord Tower said, "I have people too."

I stared down at the lazy bubbling of my Italian soda, as carbonation flipped the ice cubes in circles.

"I'm sorry," I finally said.

Lord Tower gave me a long, pained look. "That's disappointing."

"What if I get more proof? If I find something tangible? I could approach the Arcanum then. I need to move quickly. Layne has been missing too long. The Hanged Man is past the point of protocol with Max—he is actively pursuing him. I need to move *quickly*."

"Wherever Layne Dawncreek is, if he's even alive, is deep in the Hanged Man's court. You will trigger consequences by invading it."

"I'm not just talking about Layne. There's more proof than that, isn't there?"

"Proof of . . .?"

I played the one card I had up my sleeve. "Aren't you concerned that the Hanged Man has been using time magic?"

The Tower kept his face blank, but the emotion behind it became unsettling and dangerous, like a vague whiff of burning plastic from an electrical outlet.

"Be very, very careful, Rune," he whispered.

"So you really haven't been on the ship."

We locked gazes until my eyes burned. Thankfully, the waiter showed up a minute later with two steaming plates. Fluffy, folded omelets were topped with what appeared to be cheese and worms.

"Thank you," I said politely, until they'd withdrawn. Then, "Not even if it was the last plate of food in a zombie apocalypse."

The tension frayed, as if I hadn't just accused an Arcana of forbidden magic. The corners of Lord Tower's mouth twitched. "Try them."

"Those do not look like mushrooms."

Lord Tower picked up a fork and turned one of the long, thin, pinkish mushrooms in a circle. "I wasn't sure I was going to explain what they are. But since you asked . . . Outside the island, in the human world, you would need to farm these at an elevation of over thirty-five hundred feet. Himalayans. Fortunately, there's a local farm. Owned by Lord Hanged Man, interestingly enough."

"The Hanged Man grows mushrooms."

"As I've said, we've pushed him to a rather perilous state of finances. Still, the farm is quite fascinating, for what it's worth. It feeds some very expensive menus."

Lord Tower picked up his knife and said, "Let's enjoy our meal."

* * *

As I headed out of the restaurant an hour later, my thoughts were spinning. Conversations with Lord Tower had a tendency of doing that. Nothing was ever straightforward. He didn't so much drop breadcrumbs of knowledge as he scattered handfuls of thumbtacks. It was a careful and slow task to pick your way through them, avoiding the sharp bits while at the same time discerning the pattern.

I know he was telling me things—I just needed to pick apart the warning from the knowledge.

In the foyer, as I waited for the car to arrive at the curb, I was distracted by my buzzing phone. I looked at the screen and saw Quinn's name.

"You never call to say hello," I answered. "Not even once. What bomb are you about to drop on me?"

Quinn said, "You should stop by the pool on your way back to the condo."

"My earlier question stands."

In a quiet voice, he said, "You need to see something I did not see until now. Something I didn't expect."

And damned if those words didn't send a shiver up my spine.

You'd think in a building with only six residential units that it'd be difficult to get lost. No so. It took me an embarrassingly long time to find the pool, which turned out to be on the roof and not the basement. That said, in a pinch I could now locate exercise equipment, mops, and underground garages.

The pool area was in an atrium, thick with warm, chemically clean steam. Huge panes of glass overhead were speckled with raindrops, looking out on a churning gray sky. The pool was Olympic-deep, if not wide. Most of the space was given over to expensive patio furniture.

Corbie was in the hot tub, hanging to the edge while kicking his feet behind him. He laughed hysterically at something his sister was doing on the wooden planks that surrounded the tub. Max, watching them, blocked my view.

Quinn was at the door, either having waited for me or because he knew I was about to walk in.

"When you say *unexpected*," I said, "do you mean most of the time it's unexpected? Sometimes it's unexpected?"

He chewed his bottom lip. "I see more now, but I didn't before, not until she made the drawing. It's like when you watch a movie, and you think it's a drama, but then everyone laughs like it's a comedy."

"What does that mean, Quinn?"

He gave me an oddly straightforward look. "I think this story is about something else entirely. You should go check on them."

I walked over to the hot tub. They must have been swimming in the pool earlier, because water was splashed everywhere. My boots left chlorine footprints as I approached.

Max saw me first. He looked up, a puzzled expression turning into a smile, and then back into a puzzled expression, then went back to staring down at Anna.

Anna looked up and blushed, something between pride and embarrassment.

Dancing along the rim of the hot tub was a tiny blue doll. Or at least that was my first impression. Because what I was seeing? It was one of those things that my intellect needed to absorb in stages. First it was a doll. Then it was a plastic figure. Then I thought, how did the Dawncreeks afford an enchanted plastic action figure? Those were actually somewhat expensive. And then the other shoe dropped.

It was not a doll, a figurine, or something they'd purchased over the counter. What I saw—what I now witnessed—was a tiny creature given three dimensions by very recent, and very present, magic. It had started its life as a crayon drawing. Its paper home was under its tiny dancing feet. Its skin was the waxy shine of a cadet blue Crayola.

It was a gargoyle. A sentient spirit pulled from a physical outline—

drawings, murals, charcoal sketches. I opened my inner eye to the magic around me, and saw the vaguest wisp of willpower that tied Anna to the miniscule monster.

Whatever expression was on my face made Anna's flush deepen. The magic crumbled, and the gargoyle dissolved into fat blue flakes.

Corbie made a sound of disappointment, which immediately became delighted giggles as he got distracted by a hot tub's air jet.

"Rune?" Max asked, squinting at me.

"Max, stay with the kids. I need to talk to Brand."

"Is everything okay?"

"Please, Max." I took a few steps back, turned, walked back to Quinn. "You were right to call. Stay with them."

I didn't even pretend to be casual about it. I turned in a slow circle, and searched out every camera. A building as expensive as this would have cameras everywhere for security. Possibly even onsite officers. I would need to find out.

I pulled out my phone, but didn't bother calling Brand. I could already sense his approach. He was alarmed at my shock—he knew I wasn't in danger, but he knew something was wrong. He was moving fast.

I called Addam. Before he got the word *hello* out of his mouth, I said, "Are you still in your condo?"

"No. I'm a few minutes away from the Dawncreeks. Is something wrong?"

"I need you to have every minute of video surveillance from the pool area found and destroyed, for the entire day."

"Has something happened?" Addam asked, startled. "Are the children fine? Is Quinn okay?"

"Everyone is okay. Addam, I need this done immediately. Please."

"It will be done. Can you say anything?"

"Later. In person. I have to go."

I hung up as Brand stalked through the doorway. He hadn't pulled out his knives, but he'd put on his chest harness. His eyes sought mine, then a quick surveillance of the area. When he was done, he said, "Tell me."

"Not here." I touched his arm, urging him out the door. He didn't want to leave the pool area—I could tell he was confused. The bond wasn't precise enough to convey where the danger was. But he trusted my direction.

In the hallway, after watching me check for cameras, he said, "Did something happen with Lord Tower? What's going on?"

"Not Lord Tower. But Quinn told me to stop by. He said there was something I needed to see. Anna . . ." I turned around and looked through the glass door to the pool area. Condensation obscured everything, but I could make out the huddled figures of the children. "She summoned a gargoyle."

"Like the ones we've fought before?"

"No. Yes. Sort of. It was tiny. She summoned it from a crayon drawing. To make Corbie laugh. She's twelve years old. She should not be able to do that at twelve years old. I couldn't."

"Is this one of those times I'm supposed to stroke your ego? You did plenty of cool shit when you were twelve."

I shook my head. "You don't understand. I couldn't do that *now*."

Brand froze.

I said, "Not without a sigil. Not without hours and hours meditating over a sigil in a sanctum."

Brand's eyes tracked back to the foggy door, just like mine did. He knew I was upset. He knew I'd just said something big. But he hadn't put the pieces together yet. How could he? I barely understood the magnitude of this myself.

"So you're saying she's powerful?" Brand asked haltingly.

Because I needed him to understand, I said, "She's a principality at the very least."

Now his jaw dropped. "A principality? Like Ciaran?"

"A principality is just an Arcana without a throne, Brand. Do you understand what I'm saying?"

Brand's mouth softened as he tried to work out more words. He settled on:

"Fuck."

Brand and I dragged a big patio chair to the other side of the pool. Since we were going to wipe the video surveillance, it seemed the safest spot to have this talk. We'd been there long enough that my shirt and pants were damp, and hung on my frame like a heavier cut of cloth.

We squeezed into the chair, side by side. It'd make it easier to talk in a low voice. Also, really, it was a comfortable position, ingrained since childhood. That was how we'd learned about the world: squeezed side by side, murmuring questions in each other's ears.

I tried not to stare at Anna, but it was difficult.

After a minute or two of silence, Brand said, "How bad is this?"

"It's not her power that's the problem. It's her circumstance. If she were a member of an established court? We'd be drinking champagne. I have no court, though. Her family is being pursued by the Hanged Man. She is too young to defend herself, and I don't know if I can, either." I rubbed my forehead. "If her powers were known, she would be targeted. Coveted. The best of us would try to recruit her. The worst would try to own her. And those are just the political scenarios. There are a lot of other creatures who don't give a damn about rules. Brand, she is in so much danger. Everything has changed. Everything."

Brand did not want to say what he was about to say. But he said it anyway. "You are my responsibility. Max and Queenie are my responsibility. Are we . . ."

I stared at Anna again. "Power like that doesn't appear out of nowhere. It may skip generations—but there's always a common denominator. And her line lies in the Sun Throne. We'd match in a blood test."

"The *fuck?* You may be related?"

"Distantly. Maybe many branches removed. I'm almost sure. But either way . . . She's our people. If things had happened differently? If my father and the court had survived? She would have been our responsibility, too. I don't think we can turn our back on this."

Brand slammed back in the chair. "A year ago, my biggest fucking worry was keeping you from hitting the snooze alarm ten times. How did we get here? People never liked us before."

"Simpler days," I agreed.

"Did you take the armored car back?" he asked me, because that was the sort of thing he worried about.

"Yes."

"Where did you eat? He paid for it, right?"

"Yes," I sighed.

"Did you check for listening devices? Are you sure he didn't bug you?"

"He only does that to you, because he thinks you're amusing when you're mad. He doesn't play those reindeer games with me."

Brand said, "There's always a fucking first with him." And then, as if he was hesitant to even find out, "What did he want?"

"He knows what we're up to. I don't think he'll intervene—I've made him curious—but he's not happy. He says the Hanged Man is a known problem, and wants us to let the Arcanum handle it. That'd be fine for Max, but not Layne. And maybe not Anna."

We were interrupted then as the poolroom door opened. A man in a burgundy uniform and shoulder cloak came in. He slashed a glance across the room, spotted Brand and me, and double-stepped over.

"Lord Sun," he said. "I report to Lord Addam Saint Nicholas. He had me secure all video footage from this area for the entire day. I took the liberty of sequestering footage of the entire floor, if that's acceptable. It's on this." He handed me a small flash drive.

"Nicely done," I said, slipping it into my pocket. I'd burn it later.

The man bowed, exchanged a professionally curt nod with Brand, and left.

"Smart move," Brand said, nodding at my pocket. I tried not to react, because he didn't like it when I preened, but he was so sparse with compliments that it was hard not to at least smile. He rolled his eyes. "Now tell me everything Lord Tower said."

So I did. After the years we'd spent doing assignments like this, you got the hang for reconstructing conversations word for word. I omitted only a few details—like the bit about the time magic. Lord Tower was right. I needed to be very, very careful about an accusation like that unless I was ready to use the proof I had.

When I got to the part about the omelet, I said, "Did we know the Hanged Man grows mushrooms?"

Brand creased his forehead. "Yes? A farm, I think. He doesn't have many businesses."

"By design, apparently. What is a yartsa gunbu? The Tower made me eat one. Rich people make no sense."

Brand whipped out his phone and opened a browser. He pulled a face. "You ate something called a ghost caterpillar mushroom?"

"I did not!"

"You so fucking did. It grows out of the head of an actual caterpillar. And . . ." Brand's face fell. "Well, shit. It sells for like two thousand an ounce. Did you bring any leftovers home? We could sell them on Craigslist. Dude, you ate something that grew out of a caterpillar's fucking head."

"People are messed up," I said in disgust. "Who even thought to eat that in the first place? There are better things to feed—"

Pieces slammed together.

My teeth clicked shut.

Words and phrases flashed apart and then together. *He'll feed the bottom line.* A farm. Mushrooms and their organic food. Lord Tower scattering thumbtack clues in my path.

"Brand," I said softly. "Feed the bottom line. What else do mushrooms grow out of? We need to find this farm. Now."

SATHORN UNIQUE

"Insane," Addam said. "That is *insane.*"

"It's *important*," Quinn argued.

"As is what Rune, Brand, and I will attempt. As is your life. As is Max's life. Nowhere, in all these levels of importance, would I place the need for your presence on the Hanged Man's property."

Brand and I sat on Addam's sofa. We followed the confrontation with the mute turning of our heads. Our go-bags were at our feet, ready for our approaching departure.

"It's really, really important," Quinn said. "And I don't know why. I just know that it helps if I'm there when you need me."

"We are more than capable of locating Layne Dawncreek. It requires magic, not prophecy."

"That's not what I *mean!*" Quinn said in growing frustration. "And I'm not saying that I need to go into the building with you right away. If we all showed up at once, the unicorn might attack, which would be really bad. But when you're done with that—"

Brand's hand shot up. He said, "Unicorn."

I added, "Fight?"

"It feels like a unicorn," Quinn said, and then made another helpless sound of exasperation. "Addam, you know I can go where I want. I can always tell where cameras are. Or when guards are looking. You know I can. Why don't you trust me?"

"This is not about trust. You are—"

"A child?" he shot back.

"Inexperienced," he stressed. "You are not combat-prepared."

"I hate this!" Quinn said. "There's got to be a better time than this—this—this—this space of time between when I'm your brother, and when I'm a freak, and when I'm useful."

Addam bore down on Quinn so hard that Quinn almost fell backwards on his ass. He grabbed Quinn's shoulders and dragged their faces together. "Not even you," he said in a low, angry voice. "Not even you may call yourself that."

"So then I'm useful! I'm your useful brother!"

"Wouldn't it be smarter if someone else drove the car?" Max suggested. For once, he wasn't just leaping into the conversation; he actually looked a little frightened to raise his voice. "It seems stupid to park it a few blocks away. What if you need it quickly? I know how to drive. I even looked at the map. I found a good alley we can wait in."

"So you can be our getaway driver," Brand said reasonably, which should have clued Max in right there.

"Yes!" Max said.

"Cool," Brand said. "How many one-way streets are there in a ten-block radius? Where are the traffic lights? Which corners have traffic cameras? Is there any construction going on right now—what did the Public Works Department website say, when you checked it out?"

Max gamely pulled out his phone, as if this was a test he had any hope of passing.

"Three, every intersection except the corner of Magness and Glacius, and they're tearing up the sidewalk in front of the Convention Center," Corinne said, walking into the living room. "This conversation is tiresome. It makes no sense to ignore a prophet; and you promised to let the fae boy help. I'll accompany them."

"Corinne," I started to say, carefully.

"They *have my son*," she hissed. She tightened a strap on her chest harness. The hilt of a long, curved sword rose horizontally above her left shoulder. "It's bad enough you made us waste the daylight hours, but this is intolerable. And now that I know you have as much to lose as I do, I feel comfortable saying that you need to get your shit together."

"Quinn and I have some ideas," Max said hurriedly. "About the building. We heard Brand talking about it, so we did some research."

Around lunchtime, Brand had finally identified the location of the mushroom farm: we'd be searching a skyscraper in downtown New Atlantis. It seemed a hell of a place to build a farm, but the research was conclusive. So we'd spent the hours until then waiting for dusk, meditating over sigil spells, and catching a few hours of sleep.

Corbie and Anna were safe for the moment. Addam had sent them, in Queenie's care, to the Enclave. They would be protected at the beach resort by many, many guards along with Addam's aunt Diana, who owed us a favor. Only Brand knew what we'd learned about Anna—I hadn't even confided in Corinne yet. That was a problem for tomorrow.

"What research?" Brand asked.

Max and Quinn exchanged eager looks. Max spoke first. "We researched all the expensive restaurants in town, and all the reviews on them, and all the user comments. We found a few references to two other mushrooms grown by the Gallows—truffles and mandrake's mother. And then we thought, well, right there, you have three different environments altogether. Truffles are grown in European forests. The ghost caterpillar mushrooms are grown at high altitudes. Mandrake's mother is grown in deserts. So . . ."

"So we think the building has been refitted with biospheres," Quinn said. "And it makes so much sense because I *see* thin air and dry sand and oak trees, and how can you get all that in a single building?"

Brand and I looked at each other, mutely wondering how much biospheres—and their unknown terrain—would fuck with our preparation.

"Rune," Quinn said in a plaintive tone. "I really think I need to be nearby."

Everyone stared at me, including Addam, who didn't look like a man who thought he was about to get overruled. "Well, first, allow me to take this opportunity to genuinely thank you, Quinn, for forcing me to negotiate your presence in a possible firefight. This will absolutely deepen my bond with Addam."

Addam's face hardened. Now *that* was the face of someone who knew he was being overruled. "You think they should go."

"Addam . . . A prophet just told us he thinks he'll be needed. That's not something we can ignore. Not in New Atlantis, not in the kind of lives we lead, not in any story in the history of the world. Even if the prophet is Quinn. But—"

"Fine," Addam said. He picked up his own duffle bag and walked out the front door.

I swore under my breath and started after him at the same exact second that Quinn did. I stared at him. He sat down again.

I caught up to Addam in the private hallway outside the condo. He'd stopped in front of a window, and was shredding the frond of a potted fern, waiting for me to catch up.

"I need to tell you something," I said. "Something that will really make you angry at me. And afterwards, if you want to pull out of this—and take Quinn with you—I'll support it."

Addam went still, not sure what to make of that. He stared at me and waited.

I took a deep breath. "Lord Tower gave me an out. He said he could buy time to save Max. He said he could help me stall the Hanged Man, long enough to make the issue of a marital contract irrelevant. All I have to do is forget about Layne Dawncreek."

Addam's nostrils flared. "Lord Tower said that."

"He cares about you. He cares what happens to us. He thinks there are limits to how many people I can protect."

"You said *you*," Addam repeated, warily. "Lord Tower mentioned me specifically? Quinn?

"Your accent just got very Russian."

"I do not appreciate being used for guilt, especially when a boy's life is at stake. It is monstrous to think we would abandon Layne. To turn our back on Corinne? On her children? It is monstrous. It is not an option worth considering."

"But . . . I shouldn't be dragging you into my messes. This isn't your problem. You're a scion of the Crusader Throne—I am creating complications for you and your family."

Anger—genuine, real anger—sparked in his eyes. "I call you *hero*, Rune, but you do not own the concept. This young man is in danger. I am a scion, as you said. A scion of *Justice*. I have a duty here too."

I opened my mouth to say something, then snapped it shut. I was smart enough to know there was no good response. Especially when dealing with someone like Addam, who was painfully noble, and lived in the world that should be, not the world that actually was.

And Addam read every single one of these thoughts on my face.

"There are situations where I find your arrogance massively endearing, Rune," Addam said.

He left the *but* unspoken, turned, and slammed into the stairwell that led to the parking garage. I went back into the apartment. I pointed at Max, Quinn, and Corinne. "I am pissed at *you*. I am pissed at *you*. I am pissed at *you*. There was a better way to handle this."

"But we're going?" Max asked.

"Yes," I said.

"This is what's going to happen," Brand added. "You will drop us off and drive a mile away. You will sit in a public parking lot, with lots of light and people, with your hands in your fucking laps. If and when we need you, we'll call. Quinn, if you *feel* you need to come after us, you'll tell Corinne, and she'll make a judgment call. We're burning night, people. Let's fucking move."

Translocation magic and teleportation magic are fraternal twins: closely related, but not identical.

Teleportation is a smaller type of magic—like the portals that Lord Chariot operates that provide easy access from the island to the rest of the world, or allows rivers to magically appear and vanish in a restaurant.

Translocation magic is more practical for the enormous, hulking expenditure of moving entire buildings across the planet. It actually relies on the motion of the planet itself to ease the burden of casting. Imagine two global-sized abacuses, laid perpendicular to each other, with thousands upon thousands of rows each. You can slide the clay balls up and down—the longitude; and sideways—the latitude. The movement up and down would be powered by the talent of dozens of spell-casters, unified in a Greater Work. But the sideways motion, across the face of the world, relies on the turning of the actual planet. That's why it could take up to twenty-four hours to bring a building from *there* to *here*.

Studying translocation history, especially the ruins that were brought to the resettled island of Nantucket, was a hobby of mine. Yet for all that, I'd known little about the Sathorn Unique Tower before researching it today.

Sathorn Unique was one of the most recent acquisitions, from the end of the last millennium. It wasn't open to the masses—and truth be told I hadn't even known the Gallows owned it. It appeared to be their only translocation on record, which was unusual for an Arcana court.

I knew Sathorn Unique came from Bangkok, and had been abandoned with the Asian market collapse in the late 1990s. It had started its life as a forty-seven-story residential skyscraper, targeted for a very rich clientele. The architecture had both modern and Greek influences—unattractively at odds with each other, in my opinion. It bulged with columns, balconies, and railings, narrowing in increasingly smaller square-footage to the smallest floor of all: the roof.

It had been built on a graveyard. Bangkok had nicknamed it *the ghost tower.*

It was there we would find the mushroom farm. Which made sense, because our luck pretty much kept us from anything named after rainbows and puppy paws.

"A goddamn minivan," Brand muttered, and not for the first time, as Corinne drove the six of us in the Dawncreeks' wheezing car toward Sathorn Unique.

"It draws less attention than a town car," Corinne said through gritted teeth.

"Sure, look at all the fucking soccer moms casing joints after dark," he said.

I held up a *shush* hand as the corner of the building approached. I dropped the control I kept over my senses, letting them ripple outward. "Damn," I whispered, as my magic scraped over a thick lace of wards. "It's locked down. He's put a lot of work into the building's defenses."

"Let's get closer," Brand said. "Do you think you can drill through the wards? Like you did on the battleship?"

I shrugged, saying nothing as Corinne drove two blocks past the building.

We were on the edge of the skyscraper district of New Atlantis. The crowds were thin, mostly random couples and small groups dressed for the nearby restaurants and nightclubs. Corinne found us a quiet side street, barely the width of an alley, and shifted into park.

"Give me a second," I said. "Corinne, can we talk outside?"

She left the motor running and stepped out. I had to climb over Addam, who was still mad, but not so mad he didn't offer me his arm for support. I eventually stumbled through the sliding door onto the pavement, and joined Corinne on the other side of the car.

"I'm not going to like this, am I?" she asked.

"I have no plausible defense if I'm caught. I open us to retaliation."

"You're trying to find my boy, who may be *buried in there*," she seethed.

"Your boy. Now I need you to make him *my* boy."

Whatever she expected, it wasn't that.

"Layne has not reached his age of majority," I said. "You can swear him into my service. That means if I'm caught, I'll have a defense. Not much of one—and it may not keep the Hanged Man from coming after me directly—but at least it means I'm not entirely unprovoked."

"What does . . . what does this mean, exactly? Swearing him into your service?"

"It means that you trust me."

She ran her hand along her leather holster, fingering the worn bits. After a few moments, she nodded.

"I need you to say it," I told her.

"As the legal guardian of Layne Dawncreek, I swear him into your service."

"I accept his service. Harm to him is harm to me." And I felt the small frisson of magic, as the universe recognized the vow. Not much of a defense, no. But something.

The passenger side window rolled down. Brand hauled himself through the opening and peered above the roof of the car. "What did you just do?" he demanded.

"Nothing."

Brand tapped his head, because he'd felt it through our bond.

"What needed to be done," I amended.

"I've grocery shopped with you," he said. "I know exactly how you convince yourself you *need* things." But he pulled back into the car and rolled up the window.

In due order, Addam and Brand disembarked, and Corinne returned to the driver's seat. Quinn and Max glanced at us through the back seat, their eyes a little wide around the edges.

Addam paused, then went over to the sliding door and leaned in to say something to Quinn. Quinn's eyes filled with tears a half-second before he launched into his brother's arms.

Brand and I decided to give them a moment. I tapped my knuckles against the glass in front of Max's face, wondering if we were supposed to have a heartfelt moment too. I ended up giving him a thumbs-up.

"What about that research they did on the mushrooms," Brand murmured as we headed to the cross street.

"I *know*," I whispered back. "I didn't want to brag in front of Addam. Maybe we really do need to start training them."

"You've had worse ideas," Brand said.

"I've had *many* worse ideas," I agreed.

Addam joined us with a curt nod. We took a backstreet toward Sathorn Unique, away from the busier main street. As we approached the building's cornerstone, I felt the wards surrounding it inch across my skin like curious gnats.

"Keep walking and stay alert," Brand said in an undertone. "Head to the alley on the other side."

I kept the building in my peripheral. The first floor was sealed stone. No windows. A metal door as thick as a bank vault. I wanted to look up—toward the higher floors—but it would have been too obvious.

We rounded the far corner, into an alley that ran between Sathorn Unique and its neighbor. It was swept clean, empty except for a fire hydrant and two dumpsters.

"*Rune*," Brand barked in a whisper. "Three-sixty."

Which meant I wasn't looking up or down, something he constantly needled me about. The ground was unbroken asphalt, so I looked up, and saw a man in black observing us from the fire escape of the adjacent building.

The man, spotted, walked down the metal stairs slowly and without making a sound.

Mayan was tall, and impeccably dressed in a black suit, with brown hair tied back by braids. He had the Tower's dark complexion, though while the Tower veered toward Spanish ancestry, Mayan's people had roots in North Africa.

"Quick spot," he told Brand, finally, walking up to us. "You haven't forgotten everything I've taught you. That's something, I suppose, even if you keep letting your scion walk into situations like this."

Brand said, "Give me a fucking break. Like you *let* the Tower do anything. He says jump and you build a fucking bridge."

"I never let it get to the point where I need to influence him. I just keep it from happening in the first place."

"Okay," I said, and stepped between them. "Mayan, why are you here?"

"Because he thinks he knows you better than you know yourself, and he doesn't. You forced his hand, and now he's changing plans on the fly, and I don't think those plans will work. They will backfire, and he will need to step in. Do you have any idea what it will cost Lord Tower if he supports you?"

"I didn't ask for his support."

"You never ask, but you're a liar if you're telling me you don't expect it."

It was honest enough to have me clicking my mouth shut. But as Brand started to muscle around me to get at Mayan, Mayan abruptly held up a hand, as if in apology, and rubbed at his eyelids. "Sorry. I'm just as mad at him as you. He just had to be so clever, feeding you those mushrooms, didn't he?"

"But he *did* give me that clue. I'm not entirely sure this isn't what he wants."

"He knew all along, even before breakfast, that you'd blunder forward regardless of what he said. So now he's trying to lead you in a new, narrow direction where you learn what you need to; get caught; and are taken off the game board. Bonus points when he swoops in and saves you from jail. Only I'm not convinced the Hanged Man will put you in jail. I think he'll pin you right to the game board and force Lord Tower to make a wholly unexpected move."

"Layne Dawncreek doesn't have time for games."

A muscle moved in Mayan's cheek. "Chances are the boy is dead. You know that."

"Do you know what we're going to find in there?" Brand demanded. "What aren't you sharing?"

"Lots of things. Mostly the parts I don't want screwed up. Is there anything I can say that will keep you out of this building? Until we're ready to move on it?"

"No," I said.

Mayan pulled an item from his pocket, and handed it to me.

I saw a plain brass ring in my palm. It nearly vibrated with magic.

"He's keyed that sigil to you," Mayan said. "Use the spell."

I locked gazes with him. And knew that if I couldn't trust Lord Tower or his people, I was fucked.

I swiped my thumb across the surface of the ring. The stored spell flooded out, twining up my arms, wrapping around my torso, sending tendrils down my legs—and then again, and again, and again, and again—a mummy's wrap, a continuing roll of magic.

"Extend it to them," Mayan ordered.

"This is a mass sigil," I gasped. The power kept flooding me, pouring from the million-dollar artifact in a never-ending stream. I reached out and grabbed Brand's arm, transferring the flood to him; and when I sensed Brand fully wrapped by the spell, took Addam by the hand.

"You have two hours. It will get you past wards, but won't physically hide you from guards or guardians. Destroy anyone or anything you come across. Do not allow word back to the Hanged Man that you were here, or that Lord Tower helped you."

When the three of us were sealed, I handed the mass sigil back to Mayan. My fingers shook, and I nearly dropped the ring. I'd had rare opportunities to use mass sigils in my life, and the experience was a knife's edge balance between heady and frightening.

"It wasn't as easy to arrange this as it seems, and I called in a lot of favors with the Tower," Mayan told me. "You need to understand how dangerous this is. You are playing a political game with a creature older than politics. His civility is only a veneer. He is toying with you."

"I know," I said. "But that doesn't change that I need to go inside and find Layne."

"And what else will you find? And what will that discovery set in motion?" Mayan grimaced and pocketed the mass sigil. "You owe me, Brand."

Mayan walked out of the alley, while Brand stared after him, upset on a level I wasn't entirely sure about.

"It works," Addam said. He'd gone over to the building, and was running a hand across the molded cement. "I feel the defensive spells parting around my touch."

"Let's try the door," Brand said, pulling lock picks from a pouch on his ammo belt. "Can you sense anything on the door except for the wards?"

"Nothing," I said. I felt only the same sensation Addam had: the rippling, slick evasiveness of whatever spells defended the building. No traps.

It took Brand less than a minute to open the lock. The door opened on oiled hinges.

"Addam," I said as we stepped onto dank, pitch-black stone. "You stored Night Vision?"

I felt a sigil spell activate. Addam sent the magic over us, and the darkness began to lighten with staticky shades of tan and sepia, balancing into a daybreak gray.

We got our first look at the inside of the building.

"Shit," Brand said. "Are we in the basement?"

"No. This is the first floor." I stepped forward and stared at the sight before us. Huge concrete pillars supported a ceiling at least two stories high. The floor was an expanse of cement covering a city block. The air smelled like leaf mold and dirt, and was very humid.

"Our floor plans are useless," Brand said in a resigned voice. "This is a complete redesign."

"Look there," Addam said. He'd pulled out his sword, and now aimed it to a far corner of the room.

My boot heels clicked as we walked in that direction, and the clicks echoed. We drew closer to a series of cylinders, larger than industrial water heaters. Brand pulled a penlight from his vest to augment our enhanced vision. He played a dusty beam across glass panels.

Addam read a label affixed to one. "Nitrogen." He moved down the line. "Carbon. Fresh water—with base and alkaline filters. These are biosphere ingredients, aren't they?"

"Raw materials," I said.

Brand played the penlight upwards, to the huge tubes and pipes leading to the floor above us. "There's a ladder behind us, in the corner. Up we go."

"Would it make sense to attempt your Tracking spell?" Addam asked me.

"It would," I agreed, and patted my pockets until I remembered where I'd slid the swath of canvas.

I'd had Corinne bring a pair of Layne's sneakers to Addam's condo. With her permission, I'd cut a large square from one. In the movies they always fed a coat or sweater to bloodhounds. For me, nothing worked better than shoes, especially from someone who didn't have many of them, and wore whatever pair they owned to tatters.

I concentrated on my thigh circlet next, the one I wore threaded through a leather band. The released magic left me light-headed for a moment—stretched thin, as if my atoms were scattering like marbles—until it balanced. I squeezed the sliced piece of canvas and concentrated.

"Anything?" Brand asked.

I looked down. Looked around me. Looked up. No telltale violet traces. "No. But . . . up. Nearby. Up."

We headed to the ladder.

"Rivers," Addam whispered in awe.

Brand said nothing. He'd unholstered his gun, and had it pointed to the ground as he turned in his own circle.

The biosphere was lifelike. Bigger than lifelike. It was surreal. Everything above the ladder's trapdoor skewed to gigantism—the trees, the size of their leaves, the atmosphere. I could not even see the ceiling. Nine stories above our head, the air simply ended in its own weather system, a low-hanging cloud bank. Whatever passed as a sun in the biosphere burned dully behind the mist.

It was a European forest on steroids. It was crazy enough that—in a single unsettling moment—I almost wondered if it was us that had shrunk, and the forest remained normal.

"You can see the walls at least," Addam noted. They were covered in moss. We stood at the western end, by the alley we'd arrived in.

"And my Tracking spell is showing something that way," I added. "Let's follow the wall back to the front of the building."

"You follow, I scout," Brand said. "Try not to step on every fucking twig." He took off at a quick walk, stepping first with his heel, and then peeling his foot onto—and off—every step.

"Are you still mad at me?" I asked Addam, as Brand vanished behind a stand of giant oak trees.

"We will survive a single fight, Hero."

"So the fight is over?"

"I am not mad at you. Because I am not sure you're wrong. And I am not sure I'm right. This is a very bad time for this talk, Rune."

"People keep saying that to me."

Addam bent toward me and said in my ear, "We will discuss how fights are supposed to end, between such as you and I. Later, and in private."

He walked off in the direction of Brand. Sweat popped out along my hairline. His voice sounded very Russian then. I wasn't sure if I was supposed to feel sexy or threatened. But my heart was racing.

I caught up with him, and both of us caught up with Brand. I only stepped on three twigs, though each of them made a sound like a finger snap.

The air was rich with the scent of wet earth, heavy with mineral and chemical nutrients. The season was set at autumn. The foliage was different from Nantucket's blaze of New England colors—the oversized trees here were mostly shades of orange—but no less beautiful for it.

"This is a simulacrum of Italy," Addam said. "Piedmont region. You mentioned the Hanged Man farmed truffles?"

"Truffles cost a lot of money," I said, remembering that much from watching *The Smurfs* when I was a kid.

"The price goes up exponentially the larger the whole mushroom. That must be why everything here is on a large scale. You can do that with a biosphere. He would make well over ten thousand American dollars for a mushroom over two pounds."

"Have you eaten ghost caterpillar mushrooms?" Brand accused.

"I know you well enough to avoid questions asked in that tone of voice," Addam said. "Rune will simply say *scion* and scoff. You will say *fucking scion* and roll your eyes."

Brand rolled his eyes anyway.

"There," I whispered, and pointed. A flagstone path led from the northern wall to the apparent center of the massive atrium. The flagstones, from my perspective, were streaked with glowing, violet patterns that alternated between footprints and drag marks. "The signal is strong. That's good. Layne has been taken through here within the last day or two, maybe? They go that way."

As we walked, Brand ejected one cartridge from his gun, chose another, and slapped it into the stock. He was wearing his special ammo holster, lined with gun cartridges marked with different chalk symbols.

He aimed the gun upwards and pulled the trigger. There was a barely audible, pneumatic *hsss*, but no powder flash. He pulled out his phone, opened an app, and grunted. "About eleven stories."

"That makes sense," I said. "Quinn and Max said there would be at least three different biospheres."

"I wonder if they are all human habitats?" Addam asked. "There were some rather . . . odd types of fungi in Atlantis. Not unlike those in the Westlands."

"That means they're going to try to fucking eat us," Brand said. "Heads up. Look ahead."

I spotted glass through the foliage, which reflected the dull, fake sunshine. We made our way toward it until the outline of a round glass room came into focus. Through the window, I saw racks of clothing and gear, including helmets with mosquito netting, fur coats, and thin, blouse-like lab coats made of wicking material.

The flagstone path led to a sliding door. There was a heavy concentration of violet images here, including clear fingerprints along the rim. Layne had been taken past that door.

Calling on my willpower, I gathered the Tracking spell in my mind and pumped it with more energy. The violet path flared brighter: splotches appeared inside the glass room, and trailed upwards into thin air, vanishing into the mist.

"This is an elevator," I said in surprise. "It's an elevator."

Addam pressed a button by the side of the door, and a panel slid open with a sci-fi *whoosh*.

"How good is your Tracking spell?" Brand asked. "We don't have time to search every floor—or jungle or swamp or whatever the hell is above us."

"I should be able to tell the exit point where Layne left the elevator."

Brand walked into the elevator, and we followed. The lift controls were in the exact center of the glass room, like the bridge of a ship. Brass tubes and glass-faced dials gave it a decidedly steampunk vibe, which was puffed-up artifice, because the spell-work powering the elevator was as basic as mass levitation.

I pulled a lever toward me, and the elevator grinded like I was stripping the gears of a stick shift. I reversed the direction, and the elevator shuddered again, but with the buoyancy of ascension.

We began to rise.

We passed into the cloudbank at about the ninth story, which turned out to be a thinner layer than I'd expected. In a moment we'd breached it, and were close to a cement ceiling. It was dominated by a burning glass orb filled with the energy of nuclear fusion. We shielded our eyes against it as, above us, an aperture opened like an iris.

The elevator slid upwards into the space between floors. It was about two stories in height, and filled with the same sort of cylinders and pipework we'd seen in the basement level. The violet streaks of Layne's passing continued upwards, so I didn't slow our ascent.

Another hole spun open above us, and we passed into the second biosphere.

Even in the sterile air-conditioning, the raw force of desert heat pressed in on us. This biosphere was a wasteland—a blistering furnace of land where the distant walls shimmered with mirage heat. The terrain was studded with sand dunes and rocks, and interspersed with stands of spiny trees fighting for survival among the inhospitality.

"Please tell me Layne isn't out there," Brand said.

Above us were three glass suns. It was almost impossible to make out the purple tracers through the furious brightness, so I had to close my eyes and feel the trail with other senses.

"He isn't. Up," I finally said.

"Small fucking favors," Brand sighed.

We rose toward the scorching suns. Shielding our eyes wasn't enough by then—we had to throw our arms around our heads and hope the elevator was smart enough to carry us through the next hatch. I felt it when we passed into the next machinery level. Darkness pulled across our faces like ice on a sunburn.

I blinked away sundogs. The purple trail was back, and rose above our heads, so I didn't slow the elevator.

Until the elevator slowed itself.

"What's happening?" Brand asked.

"I don't know. I didn't touch anything."

The lights dimmed. We heard a gas-like hiss. Our Night Vision readjusted to the darkness. I hovered a hand above one of my sigils, ready to blast our way through one of the glass walls.

"Not gas," Addam murmured from a bank of equipment in a corner of the room. "I believe . . . I know this. Lord Chariot has a deep-sea vessel that uses something similar. We're pressurizing."

The hissing stopped, and the ceiling iris opened. We ascended through a layer of metal—much thicker than the flooring between the last two biospheres. For the briefest of moments I heard the crash of water against the roof of the elevator, and then we were completely submerged.

"I can't see anything," Brand swore.

"Night Vision requires some light," Addam said. "This biosphere mimics the deep places in our oceans."

"Tell me this isn't the stupidest thing I've ever let you do," Brand said to me.

"You should feel free to use the *I* voice sometimes. Like, *I* was the first person to step on the elevator."

"Whatever," Brand said. "Are we stopping here? I don't want to stop here."

"Don't worry. Still up."

Brand swore under his breath, a grateful sound. The elevator rose at least five more stories, then there was a *chunk* as we came abreast of another structure. Reflexively, I pulled the elevator to a stop, and whispered a light cantrip.

We had docked with a small facility, a clear glass room not unlike the elevator itself. It contained diving suits embroidered with runes and rows of special tools. There was a short hallway attached to the facility that may have been an airlock, because attached to the other end was a small submarine. An actual bloody submarine, big enough for four people.

"I thought you said Lord Tower and other Arcana forced the Hanged Man into *reduced circumstances*," Brand said.

"He did."

"If this is what the Tower calls poor, we need to invite him over to Half House for a fucking sleepover. He can sleep on the floor, between the broken washing machine and the milk crates I use for shelves." Brand came over and pulled the lever for me, sending us toward the next ceiling. As it had below, the elevator ground to a halt before connecting with the aperture. There was another hiss of gas as the pressurization rebalanced us to sea level.

The next biosphere was a murky swamp so choked with massive, steaming megaflora that it brushed the glass walls, leaving sticky trails of sap. "Still up," I said, as we rose toward a six-story canopy.

"There can't be more than one biosphere left," Addam said. "The building was under sixty floors, yes?"

"There was a dome structure on the roof, too," Brand added. He shook his head. "We need to start looking in the last place more often."

"But don't the villains rarely make their lair in penthouses?" Addam asked, too innocently to completely hide the little needle.

Brand cut a dirty look at Addam as we passed into another machinery level. Above it, the ceiling yawned open to a strange blue sky—more like a child's watercolor version of a summer day than actual atmosphere.

"Here!" I said sharply, and pulled on the lever. The elevator ignored my command for a second, as it sought alignment with the floor of the biosphere.

Around us was a grassy slope surrounded by that fake blue sky. A single false sun was a marble-sized dot above us. The purple Tracking spell left the elevator, thick and fresh, into the rough grass outside.

"Cold," Addam said, touching the wall of the elevator. "This would be the biosphere for the ghost caterpillar mushrooms. High altitude."

"Fuck me," Brand said, squeezing his eyes closed. "I didn't even think—we'll be at a disadvantage. Oxygen levels."

"The Tracking spell is a straight shot up that slope," I said. "I think there's a building there. The Hanged Man's people would be just as much at a physical disadvantage as we would—I bet that building has better air."

I went over to the door and pressed the button. It hissed into its recessed slot, and cold air tripped over itself in a rush to freeze the tip of my nose.

The fake mountaintop was desolate—just scrubby grass and trees; false blue sky; distant, cool sunlight. The deep breath I took felt like I was inhaling through a straw. It barely filled my lungs.

Brand was facing the other direction. He said, "Fucking unicorn my ass."

I turned and saw . . . not a unicorn. Grazing at the bottom of the slope was a creature not unlike a fur-covered castle siege engine with a massive, sharp tusk jutting from its head. The tusk alone was the size of a small automobile.

"What is it?" Addam breathed.

"I'm fairly sure it's a dinosaur," I said. I decided, since it was a uniquely new sentence in the history of all my sentences, to repeat, "It's a dinosaur."

"Did we know dinosaurs still exist?" Brand asked.

"Only the ones with magic. Unless . . . Maybe it was summoned? Or it could be a—"

Brand's pocket began vibrating. He pulled out his phone, glanced at the screen, and swiped a thumb over the speaker button. "Corinne," he said.

"We're coming up," she said. "There's—"

"No," Addam insisted immediately. "Do not go through the biospheres. You are not warded with spells like we are."

"There's a private elevator in the corner. Quinn says we'll be okay if we take it. It goes straight to the roof, and he says he thinks Layne is there. You need to be careful, though—you're being st—"

A flurry of sparks shot out of the phone. Brand tossed it away just as actual flames licked up the side of it. Thin smoke and the stench of burning plastic hung in the air.

"Defensive or offensive?" Brand demanded, looking at me. Shorthand for whether we'd blundered into a defense ward, or whether something or someone had us in its crosshairs.

"Don't know," I said, doing a 360. "We're being *stuh*. *Stuh?* What do you think she was saying?"

"I do not want Quinn and Max in this building," Addam said anxiously. "We must call them back."

I started to reach into my pocket for my phone. The air above me swirled with thick smoke, and I was lifted off the ground. Coarse, wiry arms pinched my own arms to my side. The world flashed dark and then light, striated with a vibrancy that felt like it was supposed to be color, a rainbow on an old black-and-white television set.

The arms let me go. I crashed back onto grass—not the sparse mountain covering, but a rich, carpet-like lawn. I rolled onto my back while shaking my sabre loose. It transformed into hilt shape so fast that the metal burned dully in my palms.

Nothing.

The Night Vision was gone—I was far enough away from Addam that the source of the spell had snapped loose.

I scrambled to my feet, swinging my sabre in a W-shape, trying to catch all the cardinal points. All I could see was the lawn beneath me, and a crown of stars that stretched from horizon to heaven. They were slightly blurred—a hairline refraction that made me think of a Shield spell. Brand had mentioned a dome on the rooftop.

I whispered a new light cantrip, and sent the single ball of light spinning away at enough of a distance to minimize the target it presented. I counted out thirty *Mississippis*, then made the light cantrip fly around in a wide circle. Its path drew shapes out of shadows, revealing a marble pavilion to my extreme left.

"At ease, Brand, at ease," I whispered, feeling his panic through our bond. It wasn't telepathy, but if he calmed down enough he'd know I wasn't in immediate danger. I stood there like that for just a minute, taking measured breaths, until I felt our Companion bond go frosty with Brand's resolve. He and Addam would come after me.

Since having a roof over my head would reduce points of ambush, I moved toward it. The pavilion was a solid twenty feet in diameter, with walls that alternated between open windows and stone wall space. Paintings, encased in plastic, hung at eye level.

I summoned a second light cantrip, gliding it across wicker furniture, a potted plant, thin tapestry serving as a floor covering.

The encased paintings looked like a child's finger paints, only the red-brown brushstrokes were bodily fluids, not paint. It was called plague art.

Viral imagery done in blood, shit, pus, and semen. A plaque at the bottom of one read *Ebola*, a second said *Marburg*.

The pulverized pebbles in the potted plant were not decorative stone, either; they were bone. I was certain the rug was woven from human hair.

This, then, would be the Hanged Man's personal space.

I heard a snap of displaced air—the sound of large, beating wings—followed by a soft susurrating glide.

For a moment, my brain whirred like a slot machine, until *magic* aligned with *physical form* and *prehistoric familiars* formed a winning, clattering combination.

I stalked back into the open, gathering the two light cantrips and sending them spinning above my head. I whispered a few more cantrips, and created lenses of air that I set in the air around me. Then I slowly leaned my head back until I was staring into the stars.

At the edge—by the hazy refraction of the force field—I spotted something large and hovering.

"You're just the pet monster of a monster," I said. "Too scared to take me on directly. You think you're boxing me in a corner? I've lived in corners since I was fifteen years old."

I gathered my light cantrips while summoning two more, and then lined all four with the lenses. Addam's little trick, fattened with my own magical ability. The resulting effect sent searchlights in four separate directions, an expanding nova, clear and white.

The creature flying at the apex of the invisible dome was older than sentience, which is probably why it had a penchant for prehistoric guardians. Raw magic ran through its veins, with a special affinity for air. It was humanoid, but covered in brown fur. Its wings were thick and fleshy, covered with sable like the arm membranes of gliding rodents.

"I haven't seen an ifrit in a dog's age," I said. "You must have messed up pretty bad to be accepting the commands of someone like the Hanged Man."

The ifrit chittered and hissed at me. It glided out of sight, ducking behind a structure to the north of the lawn. I lowered my eyes to follow its progress, which is when I felt the tug of magic in the back of my brain. The Tracking spell.

I looked at the lawn and saw a torrent of violet lines—a tangled skein of running footsteps, and short staggers, and drag marks. And in the center of all that purple, I saw . . .

"Oh," I said, but softly, less a gasp than a gut punch.

I waved away the bright lenslights and stretched Shield over me—it'd buy me seconds if the ifrit attacked. I sent the light cantrips ahead, lighting up the path between me and the body I now saw lying on the lawn.

I walked toward it. It was probably the most peaceful minute of the night. Cool autumn air; a sky jammed with stars; half a football field's worth of grass as thick as moss.

But each stepped robbed me of denial, until finally I was staring down at the ruined body of Layne Dawncreek.

His clothes were shredded. He had red, swollen gash marks on his face. A rusty stain on his shirt hinted at a horrific chest wound. His hair was greasy and clumped with dirt and grass. He smelled like vomit and shit.

I looked over my shoulder, at the railing of the pavilion. I imagined the Hanged Man watching as Layne was harried across the lawn by summoned beasts.

Behind me, something chimed—the sanitized sound of department stores and office buildings. The darkness parted as a recessed elevator opened in the wall. Brand was the first one off, gun pointed down. His eyes unerringly found mine. He led the group to me, which now included the boys and Corinne.

"Brand, no," I called out. "You should stay there. Keep everyone there."

But Corinne was staring at the ground past me. She did not stop walking.

Brand whispered something to Addam and the others, and they maintained a distance. I met Corinne before she could get too close, but adrenaline had turned her strides into steel. She pushed past me and kept her eyes fixed on the body.

"There's an ifrit in the vicinity," I told her.

She nodded, but didn't hear me.

"We need to leave soon," I added. "I wish we didn't have to rush, but we do."

"I won't leave him," she said hoarsely.

She wouldn't, and I wouldn't make her, even though removing the body was more or less a shot across the Hanged Man's bow. It would reveal we'd been here.

"Okay," I said, and walked back to Brand and Addam.

"What attacked you, and is it dead?" Brand asked immediately.

"Ifrit. Ancient creatures—they've been around for millions of years. It won't attack when it's outnumbered. Probably. I don't know what sorts of commands have been laid on it. Max, why did you and Quinn come upstairs?"

Quinn was staring toward Corinne, who was kneeling by the crumbled form. He gave no sense at having heard me.

Max reached up and nudged Quinn. "I started asking him questions about the unicorn, because it seemed stupid that you'd fight one. When you ask the right questions, it makes his visions sharper. So we Googled the details and there's something called a Siberian unicorn. It's, like, extinct. Then Quinn—Quinn!"

Blood had started pouring from Quinn's nose. It bubbled over his breath, created stripes on his chin. But when a panicking Addam reached up to Heal him, Quinn shook his head and pushed away unsteadily.

He touched a disc on his belt and released a spell. His burgundy eyes—so much like Addam's—flashed with light.

"What have you done?" Addam asked. "Quinn, I do not like this."

"It's an Eidetic spell. I need to remember this. I . . . see him," he whispered, and turned in drunken circle. "I see all of them. This is an . . . an abattoir. A compost pile. Food for his fancies below. *I see them*. Broken lines. Apple pies and Sunday football, and then nothing. A love for poetry, and then nothing. Fastest runner on his academy track team, and then nothing. Red hair and blue eyes; a mole on his right cheek; pink beads in her pony tail; a badly healed foot that hurt in the rain; and then nothing, all nothing, dozens and dozens of lifelines that break off *into nothing!*"

"Brother, this is not good for you," Addam said desperately. "Why must you remember all this?"

"Because Rune will know what to do with it, when the time comes, and it's coming soon. But . . . wait. Not there." He pointed to Corinne.

"Not what? What's there?" I asked.

"Two lifelines. Neither is broken."

For a second I stared at him dumbly, and then I was sprinting back across the lawn to Corinne's side. I threw myself to my knees, startling her stone-like vigil. I pressed my hands against the dried blood on Layne's wrist, but couldn't feel a pulse. I started to look for one on his neck, but it didn't matter, because the moment I touched his flesh I felt the heat of the infected skin.

Infected.

"Immolation magic," I whispered. "Corinne, he's not dead. Layne's not dead. He's burning off the infection to keep himself alive. We need to get him to the hospital immediately. Brand!"

"I heard," he said, coming up behind me. "Addam, help me pick him up."

I almost missed it—the shushing displacement of air. I ripped the Shield off my body and projected it above our heads like a buttress, just as the ifrit came at us with clawed hands outstretched. I had leverage this time. The monster slammed into my Shield like a hammer against rock. It shrieked in pain and pushed off, trying to retreat.

Brand aimed his gun and fired. The bullet caught the retreating creature in its fleshy wing. It veered off course and fell at an angle, thudding into the lawn about seventy feet away. It scrambled onto all fours, lifted its furry head, and shrieked at the sky.

The magic force shield above us trembled and broke. The ifrit leapt into the sky and soared off the building.

I figured it out. "It may be under a compulsion—fight if you can, flee and give alarm otherwise," I said quickly, because that's what I would have done. "It's going back to the Hanged Man."

Brand tried to sight it with his gun, but the creature had already glided below the edge of the skyscraper.

"It only has limited teleportation," I said. "I can catch it." No one else could do this. I had at entire suite of spells ready for just something like this. I looked at Brand and said, "I can do this."

"Yeah," Brand asked, swallowing his own unease, which vibrated along our bond. Concern. Trust. So much trust. He said, "You trained for this, right? It can't always be me in the spotlight killing everything. Slacker."

I coiled my sabre back into a wristguard, and zipped up my leather jacket. It had impact wards that would keep me from crushing myself. The boots had to go, though—they wouldn't help me on slippery surfaces. I ripped them off.

Then I touched my ankh. I touched my white gold ring. I touched my emerald ring, and my platinum disc, and focused on the thin gold chain around my angle.

The release of so many spells at once caused me to sink three inches into the turf. Magic whipped my bangs across my forehead, made the blood pop in my ears. My feet burned as the small bones and tendons in them thickened and toughened.

Through the roar of magic, I saw that Addam's lips were moving. Max looked terrified. Brand just stared.

I turned, ran a few feet, and leapt.

The Jump spell carried me in a soaring arc off the building.

There were always consequences with magic. *Always.*

Did you want super-speed? Or super-strength? Fine. But in the absence of ancillary spells, you'd end up ripping muscles away from your bone with the first punch; or blister and shred your skin with the friction caused by breaking the sound barrier.

So you needed spells to supplement spells. Spells to toughen your skin, fortify your bones, protect your tendons and ligaments—a spiral of cause and effect that required a lot of practice.

I had practiced moves like this—something I called urban stealth. Brand made sure I had.

I had Air and Fire. Shield and Jump. I had spells to protect my skin and skeletal structure. Everything I needed to leap between buildings like the little god I was supposed to be.

The Jump magic was not flight or levitation—it was a wild and uncontrolled burst of movement tainted by the omnipresent requirement to *land*.

The first leap took me in a massive, block-long arc off the building. At the peak of my trajectory, I spotted the ifrit, wobbling on a wounded wing.

A slanted copper roof loomed ahead of me, its penny shine long gone green with verdigris. I screamed a challenge into the roaring wind, hit the slant at a run, and felt magic absorb all impact. I kept running along the rough, weathered surface, and flung myself into the air.

The running start tripled my arc. I soared over a street, the world beneath me a neon river. The ifrit was just ahead, resting on elevator housing, a small cement square bare of anything else except a tall brass weathervane.

I threw Shield in front of me. The invisible panel dragged at the air and altered my descent. In a sequence as quick as instinct, I grabbed the weathervane and swung my knees into the back of the ifrit. I felt the barest brush of coarse fur along my pants legs, and then the impact sent the monster tumbling off the edge of the platform. It had time to throw its wing into the air current—not enough to soar, just enough to keep it from slamming into a penthouse patio beneath us.

I swung counterclockwise around the weathervane, which bent but didn't break. I pumped my foot off the ground and leapt, throwing Shield above my head, now shaped as a hard parachute.

The patio was filled with people in tuxes, gowns, and Celtic masks. The ifrit had landed against a bar, its clawed hands digging into the surface, sending bottles of liquor shattering to the tiled ground. People had just started screaming when I landed in a crouch.

There were a million nasty moves I could make to end this fight now, none that favored a panicked crowd.

"Find cover!" I shouted. "Now! *NOW!*"

The ifrit backed away from the bar and threw its hands wide. *Oh, no, you fucking don't.* Behind it was a towering decoration of fronds and dry reeds. I reached out with Fire and made the straw-like material burst into flame. The edges of the small conflagration licked the ifrit's fur and caught fire.

One of the scions on the roof took advantage of the creature's thrashing to make a bum rush with a short sword. The scion's mask was an intricate whorl of green ink. I'm not sure which of us was more stupid—him for ignoring me, or me for more or less warning the ifrit that I cared what happened to a crowd. The anonymous scion found his first and only sword thrust dodged. The ifrit grabbed the man's tux collar in a clawed grip and tossed him off the edge of the roof. Then the creature crouched and sprang straight upward, using his wings to glide away.

I was at the edge of the roof a heartbeat later, pulling Air magic around me like a coiled whip. I spotted the scion—already one story down, heading toward a distant alley floor—and lashed out with hurricane winds. Dozens of windows shattered in the building directly across from me. The scion was tossed through one, carried by my blast. I heard him scream as he raked along the glass. A violent rescue, and hopefully he was smart enough to store Healing spells in his sigils.

I turned, ran a few feet in the direction of the ifrit's glide, and jumped. He was already on the far side of another adjoining building. Its roof was lower than the penthouse. I hit its gravel-strewn surface at a run. The sharp stones were barely a pressure against my toughened soles.

I jumped again and flew over another main road. A truck-sized video marquis, scrolling movie names, passed under me. I landed on the roof of a skyscraper mall. No open patios, at least—no people to tie my hands.

The ifrit had crashed into a candy cane–shaped air duct. I'd burned a bald patch on the wing that Brand had shot. It didn't have many flights left. I saw the exact moment it decided to turn on me and hold its ground.

An air vent blew the smell of fresh popcorn at me. I felt the low rumble of Hollywood gunfire through the cement slabs under my feet.

Ifrits are creatures of air, elementally opposed to water. Lightning sparked on its clawed hands as it prepared to send a bolt of electricity toward me.

I called on my Aspect. Fire erupted along my arms, fluttered up my chest. My fingernails burned like coals as I reached up and let the lightning burst against my fist. The white stream of energy deepened to amber, and became a massive tongue of flame.

The creature shrieked as its hands began to burn.

"I'm the Day Prince, ifrit," I said, striding to it. My Aspect carbonized my footprints. "I'm the last of the Sun Throne, and you would do well to respect my mercy. Yield."

The ifrit's scream became a broken, hurt chitter. It lashed out with a current of wind. The Air wrapped around my arm at the same second I sliced it apart with the edge of my Shield. I turned the monster's tactic back on it, sending a spiral of my own Air to latch onto its thin ankle. I whipped the ifrit off its feet and sent it slamming onto the stone roof.

"Come on," I said. "You haven't lived millions of years to die on the roof of a bloody mall. I will not offer you clemency again. *Yield.*"

It drew itself to its bony knees and screamed. Power burst from it like a cyclone. I threw my Shield in front of me and dropped to one knee for leverage. The cyclone broke, and when it had cleared, I saw that the ifrit had leapt into the air.

It was too wounded to fly. Too weak to teleport. It sunk fast toward a low, rooftop garden across an alley separating buildings.

I ran and jumped after it. My Aspect fanned the air behind me with a roaring crackle, extinguishing itself.

The ifrit tried to meet me in the garden with claws outstretched, but I threw a burst of Air underneath me and did a backwards somersault, landing roughly on the edge of a fountain several yards away.

With a quick glance, I mapped the terrain: fountain, hedges, flowering bushes, a water tower that likely held rainwater. I half-stepped, half-jumped off the rim of the fountain, as if to dodge behind the water tower.

The creature was already upon me when I landed. Its talons raked the edge of the Shield I'd thrown up.

I brushed a finger along my gold ring, aimed my arm upwards, and unleashed Exodus.

Once, the gold ring had contained a version of Exodus that I'd reinforced for years. I'd used it in a cathedral and took the building down around me. Months later, the new version was weak, but more than enough to hit the underside of the water tower like dynamite.

Metal sheered free. Seven hundred gallows of stagnant rainwater flooded down. My Shield left me anchored, while the ifrit—who had few natural protections against water—was washed toward and over the side of the roof.

I ran to the edge and jumped, using Shield and Air to slow my fall. A burst of Air at the dirty asphalt, one story off the ground, bled off all remaining momentum.

Trash and debris spiraled away from me as I landed. I saw that the ifrit had broken its spine on a dumpster. It lay on dirty newspaper. Its claws scrabbled for purchase, but its legs did not move.

I transmuted my sabre from wristguard to sword hilt, and built a glowing garnet blade. Fat, red sparks fell down from the forged metal, onto the ifrit's terrified face.

"I'm so sorry," I said.

NEW SAINTS HOSPITAL

New Saints Hospital, the largest hospital on the island, had been translocated from North Brother Island off the coast of New York.

Built in 1868, the former Riverside Hospital spent much of its existence as quarantine for the mentally ill and contagious. Riverside had been the site of the 1904 *General Slocum* disaster, in which eleven hundred souls had been lost as the ship burned and foundered on the shore of North Brother.

It had also been the final home of the infamous Typhoid Mary, an Irish immigrant and asymptomatic carrier of the typhoid pathogen. Her death count had been relatively tame, from modern perspectives, but her spread of illness among New York's elite was the stuff of tabloid legend.

Psychic residue is a potent, tangible source of power. And power isn't good or bad, just like one body of water can't be wetter than another. Healers are just as able to plug into the remains of tragedies as death ritualists are.

It went a long way to explaining why we're a city stitched together from asylums, hospitals, temples, and palaces.

I bounded across the rooftops of New Atlantis, turning a twenty-minute car ride into a full-throated straight line that barely cost me ten minutes.

A rooftop entrance at the hospital took me down a stairwell to the first floor. I cancelled the spells on my way, all except for the one that toughened my skin and kept me from tearing up my feet, now covered in tattered socks. As the Jump magic drained, I spent a few wistful seconds remembering the sensation of soaring through midnight lights.

My phone regained cell phone reception as I entered the first-floor lobby. I was halfway through dialing Brand when I spotted them in the general waiting room. They'd staked out a corner to themselves, protected by an invisible boundary formed by Brand's glare.

Anna Dawncreek was braiding his hair.

They hadn't noticed me, so I paused in the stairwell door and relished the image. I honestly hadn't thought the night could get stranger.

I spent a few seconds trying to find the camera on my phone. Without even turning to face me, Brand raised his voice and said, "Allow me to explain why that'd be a mistake."

I put the phone back in my pocket. Hopefully Max had been quick enough to get a snapshot. He and Quinn were huddled on a padded bench. I also spotted Addam, Corbie, Queenie, and Diana Saint Nicholas, Addam's aunt, who had been roped into babysitting duty. The only one missing was Corinne.

"Do you need a scrunchie?" I asked Anna. "I'd like to volunteer to pick out a scrunchie for his pony tail."

"It's a *war braid*," Anna said in outrage. "He needs to keep his hair out of his eyes during a fight."

"Maybe we can find a scrunchie with little daggers and guns on it," I said.

Diana was giving me the sort of look I deserved, because, hospital. My humor drained. I said, "Layne?"

Brand's eyes—and Addam's too—were sweeping me from crown to feet, looking for damage. "I'm okay," I said. "How's Layne?"

"With the healers," Brand said. He flicked a glance at Anna, who sat down in her chair and stopped messing with his hair. "Corinne is watching him. Addam put in a call to his security team—they're going to head here as soon as they're done sweeping the Dawncreek's house. You?"

I cast a quick look around me, then said, quietly, "It's been handled. I've bought us some time. But sooner or later, *he'll* figure out we . . . took something from his building."

Queenie rushed over with my boots and a fresh pair of socks. I have no idea how she'd found fresh socks, but it was Queenie, and I'm fairly certain there was an entire pantry-sized dimension in her purse.

I put my boots back on, drumming the heels into place. There were many things we needed to talk about, but I didn't want to spend an entire conversation evading nouns for the sake of eavesdroppers. "Why are you here?" I asked Brand.

"Where should we be?" Addam asked. "The hospital is well protected."

"I know, but Arcana have their own private waiting room. Don't they know who you are?" I asked Brand.

"Why the hell would I want that?" Brand said.

"Because the Arcana waiting room is a more easily protected space," I said, thinking of its soft sofas, plump cushions, and free coffee service.

I went over to the nurse's center on the other side of the room. There were two men and one woman, and the woman's name badge had the word "supervisor" on it. "Excuse me," I said.

"Yes, my lord."

"I'd like an update on—" I bit off the sentence. I wasn't entirely sure Layne had been admitted under his real name. It was the sort of detail Brand wouldn't have overlooked. "I'd like an update on a patient, but first, please escort my party to the Arcana's waiting room."

"Oh . . . I see. My lord. I'll need to . . . check. The room is normally reserved for members of the Arcanum."

"When you say *my lord*, are you being polite and generic, or do you know who I am?"

"Of course, Lord Sun."

I was heir to my father's throne, and, someday, I was nominally guaranteed a spot on the Arcanum. But words like *heir* and *nominally* didn't have the same ring as *rich enough to own heavily guarded compounds*. And I was not in the mood to split that hair. It had been too long a night, and there were too many problems bearing down on us.

"Do as I say," I told her.

"I'll make a call to my supervisor of c-course, Lord Sun."

"Don't make a call. Provide an escort. Now."

I felt a presence appear at my shoulder. Felt the closeness of the

Companion bond. "Cut her some slack, Lord Sun," Brand said. "I'm kind of impressed she has the balls to say no. Doesn't she know you have the Tower on speed dial? Let's call him. Hey, ma'am, what's your name?"

The woman slapped her clipboard over her nametag. "Jonah, please escort Lord Sun and his party to the third floor. Lord Sun, I'll have the third-floor supervisor provide you with any updates you require."

I stomped back over to Addam. Brand was a half-step behind me, breathing the word, "Easy."

"Mayan is right. We do use the Tower as an excuse. We need to stop name-dropping him like that." I squeezed my eyes shut and grimaced, and took a breath. So much for Superhero Rune jumping from skyscraper to skyscraper. "Forget it. We need to talk, and we need privacy."

The private waiting room on the third floor was empty, and covered by a thick carpet. The sofas and chairs, the artwork, the lighting—like a fancy living room doused in sterile, antibacterial cleaning solution.

Aunt Diana and Queenie corralled the kids in a corner. It was late enough—or early enough—to have all of them drowsing. Addam, Brand, and I, fighting our own sort of exhaustion, huddled in another corner of the room.

"How much time do you think we have?" Brand asked.

"I don't know," I said, draining the last drop from my coffee cup. "Maybe not much. But even a few hours will make a difference right now. Layne needs medical attention, and we need to set guards on him. Move him, if possible."

"My team should be here within the next two or three hours," Addam said. "They're almost done searching the Dawncreeks' residence."

"Have they found anything?" I asked.

Addam frowned. "Yes. Several wards. Most likely eavesdropping devices, but we can't rule out anything more malicious."

"So we need to operate as if the Hanged Man knows everything we discussed there," I said in a resigned tone.

"He'll know we went to the Green Docks," Brand pointed out.

"The ship," Addam added. "While we were at the Green Docks, we had Corinne researching the *Declaration.* If they're tracking her computer use, or even overheard her phone call to Rune, they'll suspect we were there. They'll know about Sherman. They'll know you found that ward-stone that Layne hid."

"What's our exposure?" Brand asked. "How much trouble are we in for breaking into the biospheres or the ship?"

I leaned back into the embroidered chair cushion. The spells that had provided my skin and muscles with extra endurance had finally burned out, and what wasn't cramping and knotted was sore and tender.

"We found Layne," I finally said. "And we can testify where we found him, even if he's not awake to testify himself. Custodial interference trumps breaking and entering. We just need to air our grievance to the right audience."

"I don't like the sound of that," Brand said.

"It was always heading in that direction. I can't take on the Hanged Man directly. I need the Arcanum on my side."

"Will they take sides?" Brand asked.

"That's the question, isn't it? I have . . . thoughts. But I need more information. I need data points. I need Ciaran."

Ciaran was a principality I'd made deals with in the past. He knew something about everything, and while the information always had a crippling price tag, he'd never disappointed. On top of that, he'd gone out of his way to help us during the Rurik episode. I'd counted on him to have my back, and that meant something in a city where most people wore a target on theirs.

"Ciaran," Brand said. "Shit."

"Why *shit?* We like Ciaran now. Don't we?"

"He's dramatic," Brand said. "He fucking bleeds glitter."

"He helped us out a lot recently. And he likes Quinn."

On the other side of the room, Quinn was yawning and blinking awake from a nap. He heard me mention his name, beamed, and trotted over to make sure he wasn't missing anything interesting.

"Quinn," I said. "We can trust Ciaran, can't we?"

"Oh, yes. Almost always. Except for those times he's your archenemy, but when he is, his hair is always combed, which I don't really understand, except that it's properly scary, but he doesn't *really* comb his hair now, so I think you can trust him."

"Translate," Brand ordered Addam.

"Yes," Addam said. "We can trust him."

"So I need to see Ciaran," I decided.

"We're going to Spain?" Quinn said excitedly. "I love Spain!"

I sighed into my palms and massaged my gritty eyes. "Do you mean that sometimes he's in Spain, or most of the times he's in Spain?"

"No. He's really-really in Spain. He sent me a postcard."

"I am displeased," I said. "And I'm not going to Spain."

Quinn pulled out his phone and started texting. "I'll see if I can reach him. Oh! Maybe he's already bought me a box of Miguelitos! He said he would buy me some on his way home, Addam!"

"Perhaps focus, Quinn?" Addam asked in that patient and amused voice he usually used with Quinn, which was a nice change, though hopefully he hadn't forgotten what I said about needing to punish the boys.

Addam and Quinn moved off to the side. I watched them, while Brand watched me. When his regard became too heavy, I sighed at him. "I would like a Miguelito right now. It sounds like a tasty baked good. Speaking of baked goods, I like your man bun."

"You're exhausted," he said. "Are your sigils empty?"

"Yes."

He closed his eyes. "Even Exodus?"

"Yes. But I only blew one thing up. Well, two. Or maybe a few dozen if you count each window separately. Wait. Do we count people damage? Hopefully the scion had a healing sigil on him."

"Any chance the people to draw up the damage bills don't know it's you who ran amuck?"

"First of all, I was running *after* the creature running amuck. And second, I'm not sure who noticed me, because all the people at the party were wearing masks."

"Forget I asked."

"Can I ask you a question?" I said.

"Yes, I count people damage as a problem."

"No. About Mayan."

Brand's face closed down. I don't think it was a specific reaction, more just a default setting.

"Mayan mentioned *our* plans," I said. "And you didn't look very happy about that."

"I don't have any plans with Mayan."

"I know. But I can't stop thinking about the *our*. Whenever he and the Tower are up to something, it's never *our* plans, it's *his* plans. Mayan never talks about the Tower like a *we*—their relationship isn't wired that way. So it makes me wonder who *we* is, in this case."

Brand's face remained shuttered.

"Is this a bad subject?" I asked.

"He . . ." Brand's lips finally broke from a flat line, as if he'd tasted lemons. "Companions . . . talk. We're connected. I think Mayan is making plans with other Companions, and he didn't tell me about it, so don't fucking ask."

"I always thought you were joking whenever you mention a Companion guild."

"I am. But . . . Rune. Do . . ."

He trailed off, which more or less cemented my interest in the subject. "Brand?"

"Do you have any idea what it would do to me if you were hurt?"

"Like . . . physically? The bond?"

"No, Rune, not *like physically*. Physically I'd have a lot less fucking migraines. I'm saying what it would mean if I, as a Companion, lost my scion. Companions aren't supposed to lose their scion. We stand in front. We take the bullet. To outlive your scion is . . . awful. Can we fucking change the subject?"

A light flickered in the back of my head, and warmed to a steady glow. "Corinne lost Kevan. Corinne was trained by Mayan. Mayan takes Kevan's murder personally."

Brand hesitated, and nodded. "I don't think the Tower is the only one who wants to see the Hanged Man go down."

"But . . ." Now I was the one trailing off into ellipses. I'd never had to have a talk like this with Brand before. I didn't think there was anything he kept from me. "It's good to know this, Brand. This is useful."

"How is it useful? Mayan's already made it clear he's not dealing me into this hand."

We were interrupted by Quinn, who rejoined us with a huge smile. "He'll talk to you."

"I need to see him, Quinn. I don't trust phones for this sort of talk. How far is he from a portal?"

"Not far. But he'll see you *now*."

Brand started to ask Addam to translate again, but Addam held up a hand. "Dreamwalking. Ciaran can dreamwalk, remember? I can't imagine a more private way to have a conversation. It's a good idea, Rune. You just need to be asleep."

"I can't fall asleep," I said. "I just had coffee and jumped across tall buildings. I'm freaking wired. Do you have any sigil spells that may help?"

Brand pulled his gun out of his holster, removed a cartridge from his belt, and slapped it into place. He aimed the gun at my leg and shot me.

"What the hell, Brand!" I shouted. I looked down at the blue, feathered end of a dart. "You did that *really* quickly. It's like you've been waiting for the chance."

Brand smiled.

His smile went screwy, like a melted crayon drawing, and then the entire world was melting too. Dark edges flowed to a pinpoint, which snuffed altogether.

In that peculiar way that dreams work, I became aware of myself halfway through a story with no beginning.

There was a cold room carved from pale, peach marble. A giant map was etched on the ground, and lined up next to it were knee-high metal figures, not unlike the pawns of a chessboard.

There was a woman. She was, if not beautiful, at least arresting. She had brown hair and a faint overbite, and her eyes simmered with power.

"Where does the throne go, Matthias?" she asked.

The boy looked up, worrying on his knuckle with a gap-toothed frown. He stumbled over to one of the metal figurines and picked it up.

The woman clapped her hands together three times, a sharp and angry sound. "*Not* like that! Use your cantrips, Matthias."

"I can't," he said. "They just tip over."

"Because you are not trying hard enough."

"I am trying! But cantrips don't work like that. They're small things."

"There are no small magics, only small minds, only small willpower. The meanest cantrip, in the hands of an Arcana, can work miracles."

"I'm not an Arcana," the boy whispered, scared.

"And you never will be if you do not *try*," she said, and slapped her hands together again for emphasis.

The scene dissolved into darkness. The darkness pulsed, and grew bright in reverse. There was now sand under me. A foaming surf washed up to the edge of my boots. Slowly—brain cell by brain cell—true consciousness returned.

"Apologies," Ciaran said. He was standing next to me. "I overshot. Your ward must be nearby, sleeping. Such sad dreams he has."

"That was Lady Lovers," I said slowly. "She thought Max had Arcana potential?"

"Once. They had great hopes for him. His magic, sadly, never manifested."

"People are more than their magic," I said, an edge to my voice.

"As you say," Ciaran apologized, but grinned.

Principalities were sort of a freelance Arcana—all the power, without a formal court. Ciaran had been around for centuries, and had the smooth, plasticky skin caused by numerous rejuvenations at Lady Priestess's rejuvenation center. He had blue hair, lips the color of a murder scene, and eyes that moved with sunlit ripples. He said, "Hello, Sun."

"Thanks for speaking with me."

"Indeed. Rumor says you're taking on the Hanged Man. Chew carefully before you swallow, my friend. That's quite a big bite."

"He's after Max."

Ciaran stared at me a long moment, then sighed at the sea before us. The water was unfamiliar, and filled with red and blue blossoms. Something from his head and experiences; not mine.

"We don't have much time," Ciaran said. "It's difficult, doing this."

"I have questions. I need your help. We can settle the tab later, if that's okay."

Ciaran laughed. "Oh we must be friends, if you'd write a blank check like that. Or your feet must be very close to the fire. Go on, then. Tick tock. Let's see if I can provide you with some pieces for your puzzle."

If he expected me to meander into the conversation, he was wrong. I already knew what the puzzle looked like, and I already had my pieces—I just needed to know how to place them.

"Okay," I said. "Which Arcana does the Hanged Man have alliances with? Which Arcana have significant grievances with the Hanged Man? Which houses have provided the Hanged Man with marital alliances? What do you know of those marriages? Which Arcana are known to be good parents, and currently have minor children? Which Arcana have Companions, and which of those Arcana have a particularly close bond with their Companion? Which Arcana have taken a position on unconditional punishment for the use of forbidden magic? Which Arcana have vital investments in the human world?"

Ciaran opened his mouth.

"What do you know of his powers?" I said, bowling ahead. "Have you ever known him to engage in a duel? How did he win?"

Ciaran raised an eyebrow at me. I nodded that I was done, for now.

"Such questions, Sun. They're bursting with information. It's nearly a full exchange—I'll be quite busy filing all these little tidbits away."

"Maybe, but as far as tidbits go, these will have a short shelf life. There aren't many ways this thing between the Hanged Man and me can end."

Ciaran bent down and plucked a flower from the surf. I can't remember ever smelling things in dreams before—I'm not sure I was actually smelling anything now—it was more like my brain told me I was smelling honeysuckle and salt.

"The Hanged Man," Ciaran said. "You haven't met him yet."

"Not exactly. Glimpses."

"It wasn't a question. You have not met him, because if you had, you wouldn't ask about his powers. He's not one to hide his light under a bushel. He wears his Aspect constantly. He assumes the appearance of death injuries. He has chronic blood poisoning, and his veins stand out like ugly red scratches. He reeks of power. You will not best him in a duel."

I didn't say anything.

"He wears his Aspect constantly," Ciaran repeated. "Do you have any idea how difficult that is? How long can you burn, when your Aspect is upon you? Rune, while it's true that the Hanged Man surrounds himself with very few helper bees, you won't take him one-on-one in a duel."

"If it comes to a duel, I won't be alone," I said. "That's the entire point of this conversation. It's why I need the answers to those questions."

"Brilliant," Ciaran said. "Let's begin."

My eyes opened, which was more or less where movement began and ended. Whatever Brand had doped me with had cut my wiring. My limbs sagged into plump sofa cushions, refusing to budge at my half-hearted instruction. I decided to enjoy the painlessness while it lasted.

Brand and Addam were talking animatedly on the other side of the room. Everyone except Corbie appeared to be asleep. Corbie had found some toy cars and stuffed dinosaurs somewhere, and was happily moving them around the carpet. He was at peace: his brother had been found, and the rest was just adult stuff.

He made one of the dinosaurs pick up a car with its mouth. He made munching sounds. Then he lowered his voice and walked the second dinosaur over. "That's wrong, Barry! Don't do that! You need to shake the car first. If it squeaks, it means it has a creamy center."

I laughed, which was sort of a movement, and seemed to signal to my body that it was okay to jumpstart my nervous system.

Brand came over and knelt by the sofa. "I've got a shot that'll purge your system," he said.

"I bet you do, you freak. If that gun clears its holster, it will be war."

I groaned and sat up. My head was still stuffed with fresh cotton, which smoothed the edges of my ruthless thoughts. I was okay with that, too, if just for a little while. There were so many dominoes to set up. It made me tired just to think about it.

"Give me a few minutes," I said, as Addam came over. "I'll catch you up, but I need to do something first."

I pulled out my phone, found what I needed, and started typing.

Brand and Addam stayed quiet, but kept exchanging glances.

After a few minutes I growled at the screen.

"You're making me nervous," Brand said. "Is this going to be like that time you opened the Home app and unlocked our front doors?"

"No. I just hate these self-righteous squiggly red lines. Why not just fix the spelling mistake? Why program mockery?"

"Rune," Addam said. "We are being very patient, and would like to know if you spoke with Ciaran."

"I did. And I think I have an idea." I put my phone away. "Addam, it's fairly well understood that the Moral Certainties owe me a few favors, right?"

The Moral Certainties was the common name for the alliance between Lady Justice, Lord Strength, Lady Tolerance, and the Hermit. They had all figured heavily in the events of the summer.

"You do not need to call in a favor. I have offered help."

"What I'm trying to say is that it's plausible that I called in those favors for the assistance your security team is providing. It means the use of your guards doesn't have the impression of an alliance."

"And an open alliance with me is a bad thing," Addam said, his Russian accent rising to ice the T's and D's.

"For you, maybe. Not me. Knowing you is one of the best parts of my life. But where I'm going, your mother may not want you to follow. That's a boundary I need to respect."

It was an oddly unguarded response, and he understood that, because his anger flowed into surprise.

"I know what I have to do," I told both of them. "And it's important, at this point, to . . . play it close to the vest."

"Uh-huh," Brand said.

"Just for a while," I said.

Brand stared for a few beats. "I've got this idea in my head. You saying, 'Golly, look at this lovely cliff. What a pretty view. Oh no! I accidentally pushed you off it!'"

"Sort of, only I'll make sure we stick the landing."

Brand closed his eyes. He kept his thoughts to himself, but in his brain, I had no doubt he was filling the swear jar like it was a slot machine.

A woman ran into the room. Her hair was slipping out of a blue surgical cap. "Your lady friend just pulled a knife on the doctor!"

I gave a quick look at Corbie, who had dropped his dinosaur with wide eyes. Queenie was shaking herself awake next to a sleeping Diana. She said, "I'll watch them!"

Adrenaline burned away the last bit of drugged fogginess as Brand,

Addam, and I sprinted through the hallway. The nurse barely kept the lead as she led us through a sterile maze of corridors and doors. She swiped a card in front of the trauma unit. As soon as it swung open, we didn't need her anymore, because Corinne's shouts were cutting through the air.

She stood in front of Layne's bed in a recovery suite, legs braced, combat knife in hand. A doctor had squeezed himself into a corner, trying to defuse the situation by waving his hands around helplessly.

"Corinne," I said, clear and calm.

"They're trying to use antibiotics on him," she said.

"Corinne, lower your weapon."

"They—"

"He is *mine* to protect," I snapped. "He is sworn to *me* now. Disarm!"

Corinne let her hand fall. In the middle of her unnaturally aged face, her eyes were clear and white and filling with tears.

I faced the doctor. "You are unaware of the boy's abilities."

"My lord?"

"Immolation. A very particular form of necromancy. You are apparently unaware of it."

"N-no, my lord, it's in his chart. But it was my medical opinion that—"

"Your medical opinion? You are an expert on this necromantic discipline? That's very impressive. It's so rare."

"Not an expert, Lord Sun, but—"

"But what? The boy lived this long by feeding off his infection. He will continue to grow stronger, at an accelerated rate, by feeding off those infections. I'm surprised Corinne didn't instruct you to limit your attention to the care of his wounds, and not the infection."

"The surgeon who operated on him did just that. But now that he is in recovery—"

"Now what?" He opened his mouth to speak again, so I slashed the air with my hand, startling him. "I've had to cut you off three times now. There won't be a fourth."

The healer's mouth snapped shut.

"Treat the injuries," I said. "Stop the bleeding. Respect his native magics. Am I clear?"

He nodded.

"Leave us."

He scrambled out the room's glass ICU doors.

Corinne waited all of three seconds before fixing her glower on me.

"If you challenge my authority in the presence of others, you weaken me," I said. "You jeopardize my ability to protect your children. You were a Companion long enough to understand that."

Her glower broke into tics. She wiped at her eyes and turned her back to me, staring down at the thin, pale body on the hospital bed.

I went around to the other side and looked at Layne. He had been very beautiful in the photographs that Corinne had showed me, but it was a different person in this bed. His magic may have saved him, but it was a Pyrrhic victory. His skin hung on wasted muscles. His fingernails were yellow with jaundice.

"Has he regained consciousness yet?" I asked gently.

Corinne shook her head.

"There is no better care in the city. Between their efforts, and his abilities, he will survive. He'll survive, Corinne."

"What happens when the Hanged Man comes after him?" she asked on a shaking inhale.

I didn't insult her with bravado. I took the time to word my response carefully. "There's always the chance that Layne knows something unexpected—something that may implicate the Hanged Man in other crimes. But, more likely, the threat Layne poses involves the manner of his injuries. Since we found Layne at Sathorn Unique, the Hanged Man is already culpable. It would be exceptionally risky for the Hanged Man to strike against Layne now, for so little benefit."

"Plus," Brand said. "Rune's done everything he can to make himself the target. It's one of his favorite fucking moves."

Addam put a hand near Corinne's arm, close without actually touching. "It has been a very long night. Let's find some food. Rune and Brand will stay with Layne."

"I can't leave," she said, shaking her head. A single tear scattered down her cheek.

"Just for a little while. The children need to see you. Corbie was awake when the nurse came for us."

"Oh, gods," Corinne said, and laughed into her palm. "There's a good chance he's already running through the hallway, kicking orderlies in the shin and shouting my name. Okay. Okay, just for a few minutes."

On her way out the door, she hesitated and looked at me. She didn't say anything. She didn't need to. It lay between us on the hospital bed. I nodded at her, she nodded back, and Addam escorted her away.

Brand and I stood watch over Layne. Or at least that was the plan. I took one of the chairs, sat down, and the next thing I knew Brand was shaking my shoulder.

I rubbed my eyes. "You let me fall asleep."

"You're exhausted."

"I know. Someone shot me with a tranquilizer."

"You need to fucking let that go," Brand said.

"Admit you enjoyed it. Just a little."

"You act like wanting to shoot you is a secret. I've practically painted murals of it on my wall. It's the closest I can think of to an off switch when you're about to do something fucking stupid. And we don't have time for this: one of the hospital people wants to talk to you."

My eyes moved to the bed. Layne lay there, unmoving. None of the monitors were making bad sounds. My eyes tracked the door, where a man stood just past the threshold, massaging his hands nervously.

I got up without groaning, and went over to him.

The man had a shock of carrot-colored hair, and a shiny, pale face that reminded me of shock victims. "Lord Sun," he stammered.

"What's wrong?"

"We have an expert. On immolation magic? We've consulted him, and I'm afraid . . . My lord, I'm afraid I have very bad news. I'm so sorry. Our expert thought you might want a briefing, before we speak with the immediate family. I'm sorry."

That was the thing about dominoes. A change in wind could knock them over before you'd barely set up a single line. I closed my eyes, rubbed them again, and nodded at him. "Brand," I said. "Will you watch Layne? Is Addam's team here yet?"

"Most of them are en route," Brand said. In a lower voice, he added, "We'll need to decide if Layne stays here, or if we move him. He's been admitted under an alias, but the hospital staff has his real identification. It's not secure."

"Okay. I'll let you know what I find out."

I followed the man—doctor or administrator, I'm not sure which—through the older wing of New Saints, the parts original to North Brother Island. Images—echoes of the deep psychic residue—flickered in and out of my vision. Until the battleship, New Saints had been one of the few places where that happened unprompted.

"Is there anything you can tell me?" I asked, as the man walked obliviously through a ghostly woman with a frazzled mop of hair and an armful of laundry.

"I cannot, my lord. I only know that they've learned something about the boy's condition, and you'll need to make a . . . difficult decision."

The translucent ripples thickened as we approached an elevator. A handful of ghosts—burn victims; corseted nurses; men in old-fashioned straitjackets—stared plaintively at the doors. If I remembered correctly, the elevator led to the higher floors of a recent hospital addition, beyond the hallowed ground of the original floor plan.

Inside, the man put a key into the panel, and took us directly to the fifth floor. A long corridor of modern offices ended in a closed door. The air smelled like expensive wood and fresh paint. All of the offices were closed;

I glanced at my watch and saw that we were advancing on dawn. It was a small thing, but I looked forward to morning, when the oblivious daytime crowds would at least offer the illusion of normalcy.

The man gestured to the door at the end of the corridor, bowed deeply, and backtracked at a nervous pace just half a second short of a jog.

Without knocking, I entered the room.

A man stood at the window, framed by a graying sky filled with vanishing stars. We were facing the western side of the city, where the vertical skyscraper lines collapsed into a horizontal sprawl of residential neighborhoods.

I saw the man's face first as a reflection: elegant Asian features, marred by deep, fresh, festering claw marks.

"Hello, little brother," Lord Hanged Man said, and turned to face me.

THE HANGED MAN

Ciaran had warned me, but the difference was still startling, like the gap between a photo of fire and its actual heat.

The Hanged Man wore the face of a handsome dead man, its body brutalized by something like an animal attack. Beneath the graphic gouged wounds, his lips were bloodless.

He studied my discomfort and gave me a pale, septic smile.

I closed my eyes and lowered my head, drawing my thoughts into me. The very worst thing that could happen—the thing that would end me—would be triggered by panic. *Brand.* My panic, through our bond, would be a red and blistering emotion. Brand would feel it and run to my defense, and the Hanged Man would kill him. So instead I thought of the aftermath. I thought of Brand killed, leaving me alone forever. The grief of that was white and cold, and covered the bond between us in a slick layer of ice. He would think I was getting bad news. He already knew as much.

When I opened my eyes, the Hanged Man had tilted his head to the side, studying me. "What was that?"

"Something a man like you would never, ever understand," I said softly.

The Hanged Man smoothed the front of his shirt and stepped away from the window. He wore black. A black silk shirt, a black over-the-shoulder cape, black trousers. It was a sharp contrast to the raw wounds on his face, and the blood poisoning that darkened the veins along his neck.

"You'll want to keep this pleasant, Rune Sun," the Hanged Man said. "I'm the aggrieved party, after all. You owe me an ifrit."

"It's not a great loss. He did an awful job at burying all those bodies for you."

The torn, mauled lips stretched into a wider smile. "You have no idea what you saw."

246

"I know exactly what I saw."

He laughed. A dribble of gelatinous blood escaped a cut on his chin, which he dabbed. "Oh, child. You are so young. I forget what that's like—that shiny, freshly scrubbed sense of entitlement and self-righteousness."

"Lord Hanged Man," I said patiently. Very patiently. Very formally. The tightrope in front of me was made of razor wire. "You and I both know I have what I need to make cause against you. Abandon all efforts against me and mine, and this will go away."

"It's refreshing to see that your attackers left you with your balls. The news reports from the night your throne fell were rather vague on that score. Maybe you'll have what it takes to be an Arcana after all."

Now I smiled at him.

He stared for a few moments, then shook his head. "I've walked this earth for centuries, little brother. Let me share one of the greatest lessons you would learn, if you have the opportunity to live as long. The morality of killing is situational. It is a human fabrication. Nations, for instance, kill all the time. All through history. For wounded pride. For oil reserves. For a half mile of dirt. They and their kings look at their people—who don't know luxury, or decent medical care, or consistent food supply—and say, 'An offense to me is an offense to you.' Not unlike what you just said. And then the people scramble onto the chessboard and die like pawns. They take the bullets and cannon-fire and sword blades, all to satisfy the scratched egos of their leaders. So why pick a fight with me, Rune Sun? What do you care about the bodies I've buried? Is it really in the best interest of your people?"

The tightrope snapped. I couldn't help myself. I said, "Are you fucking serious?"

He folded his hands along the back of a conference room chair. "I am."

"For the love of gods. This is the reason I avoid most scions and Arcana. Nothing is straightforward with you. It's exhausting. It's fucking *exhausting* trying to determine what your point is. I mean, what? What is your real lesson here? Do you want me to think you're nuanced? Com-

247

plicated? Like me? You're not. You're a bad man. And I care about the bodies you've buried or may ever bury because *two of them are mine.* I'm not making this offer again. Desist all attention on me and mine, and I'll desist my attention on you."

"I promise you, Rune. I won't focus on you for long. I have wedding plans to make, after all."

At that moment, the gray morning tripped into dawn. Orange light, sliding from an unseen sunrise, colored the room. The Hanged Man's dark eyes began to glow, and he tilted his head back in relish.

The voice that came from him was different—brittle and hard. He said, "I fought my brother over a woman, and he buried me in the snow." The Hanged Man's injuries smoothed into unmarked copper skin, and then the skin paled into the bluish tint of a frozen man.

Power pulsed from his body—the drumming presence of an Atlantean Aspect at full force.

He smiled at my unsettled expression. "You see now. I am not something you have faced before. Do you have any idea how much stronger I am? Who are you, to threaten me with consequences? Greater men and women have tried."

"I think we're done. This will get us nowhere."

I turned to leave, heart pounding, and the Hanged Man lifted a hand. The wood paneling—of the door behind me, of the wall it was attached too—cracked and split. Vines sprouted and wove a web, covered in thorns as large as carpenter nails.

"Come here first," he whispered. "Come see this."

My sigils were empty. I could call on my Aspect, or transmute my sabre. I did not think I would win in a fair fight, though; and I had very few ways of cheating.

He laughed at my stubborn stillness. "When I'm ready to hurt you, you'll know. Peace, little brother. Come see this." He went to the window and tapped on the glass.

I moved closer, my legs stiff and cramping.

The Hanged Man pursed his frostbitten lips and breathed on the glass. The surface fogged with thin arteries of ice. He wiped a perfect circle with the side of his hand and said, "Look. Right there. A step to your right, maybe? The angle is everything."

I did as he said, and stared through the circle he made. I don't know what I was supposed to see: we faced many blocks of residential areas, near the northwest of town.

As I watched, a pinpoint of yellow flared. An explosion.

"Such a dangerous world we live in," the Hanged Man said. "Thank goodness the Dawncreeks are here with you. That's their neighborhood, I believe. Do they have issues with gas leaks, perhaps?"

No. My brain had trouble catching and holding a thought, a stuttering car engine. *No. No no no no.*

"As I said, thank goodness they're here with you," the Hanged Man said.

I stared at his cold, smug smile. He didn't know. He couldn't know, or he wouldn't have done something so phenomenally stupid. Something so phenomenally aggressive against another court.

"They are," I said. Addam. His men. *Oh, Addam, I brought you into this.*

I wanted to hurt the Hanged Man. I wanted him to know how closely he had veered to a black hole, how far he was past the point where he could ever return. "There's one thing I can't stop thinking about," I whispered.

"Which is?"

"Did you ever find the sailor who hid in the mailroom safe? Or did he suffocate in there? You should check, the next time you time-walk back to masturbate over the ship's slaughter."

Lord Hanged Man's frozen lips curled in a slow smile. "Perhaps . . . Perhaps I'm ready to hurt you after all."

I had a half-second's notice. He didn't touch the noose around his neck; but I felt the magic release from it. The power of the mass sigil surrounded me like a vise.

I couldn't move. I couldn't even blink. My mind was locked inside a mess of dead-ended nerve impulses.

"The body is a miracle," Lord Hanged Man said. "Its ability to operate on a conscious and unconscious level is nothing short of divine. Have you ever stopped to think how much it does without explicit command? You don't tell your heart to beat, nor your eyes to blink. And *breathing*. Imagine if it were an entirely deliberate choice. An action entirely dependent on conscious thought."

He touched my Adam's apple with an ice-cold finger and drew the finger up to my chin.

He stepped back, and as he did, the paralysis broke. "This is a formal act of aggression," I said breathlessly. "You need to understand that—"

Spots danced in front of my face. The black spots of a nearing faint. I wasn't breathing. Panicked, I opened my mouth and took a long, noisy breath.

I drew on that calm I'd used earlier—that arctic certainty that I'd lose everything if I gave in to panic. So I added facts together. I *could* breathe. But it was no longer an involuntary response. I just needed to remember to breathe.

The Hanged Man clapped his hands together. "What fun. I am going to make you eat your fingernails next."

"I'm not sure you'll want to do that," I said, to the soundtrack of my fast pulse. *Breathe.* I made myself breathe. "Not until I show you something."

I reached into my pocket. The Hanged Man tensed only until he saw my phone. He watched, amused, as I tapped a few buttons. Then I put my phone back in my pocket. And breathed. *Remember to breathe.* I took a low, steady breath.

After a few more moments of polite smiling, he said, "You were planning to show me something?"

"No. I lied." *Breathe.* "You're just like every old Arcana I know, completely oblivious at how dangerous technology can be. I was just stalling for time while I hit send on an email I drafted a few hours ago."

"An email," he repeated.

"Yes. To every Arcana I know. Every Arcana I have contact information for. Every Arcana who owes me a favor; every Arcana who has supported me in the past. I've requested an immediate forum to present claims against you. I also mentioned that, if they're receiving this email, it means I've sent it in your presence, or the presence of men I suspect are in your employ. I don't want there to be any confusion if something were to happen to me."

The Hanged Man went still. Not so much shock—he was too slick for that. Just the stillness of a very old Atlantean who momentarily forgot the need to mimic the movement of normal people.

"You're bluffing," he said.

"Am I? My boyfriend is second in line to the Crusader Throne. You've just killed his men, by the way. He had a team at the Dawncreeks' house." *Breathe.* Breathe and enjoy the look of surprise on his pallid face. "The Moral Certainties already owe me a favor, and the Hermit has stated publicly that he's in my debt. The Sun Throne was once a power bloc with the Celestials. And Lord Tower? Well. He and I have a long-standing arrangement."

My pocket started to buzz. As, actually, did his.

Now I smiled. Spots danced in front of my face again, and I remembered to breathe. "Looks like someone's trying to reach us."

"Let them accuse me," he hissed. "They'll never find your body."

My pocket stopped buzzing. But his? His started buzzing again.

He pulled a sleek phone out of his robes, and eyed the screen. His face went back to that inhuman stillness.

"Do I look like that?" I asked. "When I read a text message from the Tower? Let me guess. He's warning you he'll be calling me shortly, and he'll expect that I'll answer."

"Little brother," he said. "When this is over and done with, I will plant daisies in your skull."

Shadows dashed across the room, creating a sphere of darkness around Lord Hanged Man. As he vanished into it, he continued to stare, so that those dead eyes were the last I saw of him.

Alone, I sagged. I yanked a chair away from the conference room table and collapsed into it. My skin prickled with the pins and needles of shock.

I gave myself only a few seconds, focusing on my stalled breathing. What would it take to counter a curse from a mass sigil? I pulled my phone out of my pocket and dialed Brand.

"Hey," he answered. "What did they—"

"Zeta protocols," I told him.

He took barely a half-second to rearrange his entire life. "Home or hole?"

"Hole up here for now, then we'll head home in force."

"Chapel," he decided. "First floor. Interior room. Nearby access to a stairwell. God fucking damnit, Rune."

"I'll tell you more when I get there. Gather everyone. We're at war with the Hanged Man. And—gods, Brand." Spots. Faintness. *Breathe.* "The Dawncreek house has been destroyed. Keep it quiet, but tell Addam. Find out if . . . any of his men . . ."

"I want you here," Brand said, and this was when his urgency cracked into worry.

"I'm on my way."

I ignored the Tower's call, because I was in the middle of using my sabre's garnet blade to burn away the vines. If I was being honest with myself, I was also trying to keep from hyperventilating, because the curse hadn't lessened. What would happen if I panicked and passed out? If I couldn't tell my body to inhale, would I . . .

I needed to get back to Brand. I needed the others.

When I'd destroyed what was left of the conference room door, I dialed the Tower back. He answered by saying, "Good day," to which I immediately responded, "Good day yourself." It was a sign and counter-sign code we'd established years ago, for use in situations where free will might have been compromised.

"Rune," he sighed.

"I didn't have a choice," I said, starting down the hallway toward the elevator. I transformed my sabre back into a wristguard. The warm metal tightened against my flesh.

"You had abundant choices," he said. "That was the entire point of breakfast the other day. I provided you with options."

"He ambushed me, not the other way around. He forced my hand."

There was a pause. A hesitation. Then, "Rune, what happened? Are you hurt?"

I didn't feel like admitting I'd let the Hanged Man get the jump on me. "Just my pride," I lied, then told my body to breathe.

"And the meeting of the Arcanum you called?"

"I have a plan," I said.

"A child with a stick of dynamite may have a plan, too. It doesn't make it a wise plan."

I stopped walking, my finger an inch from the elevator button. I counted out a few *Mississippis* in my head. "I deserve better," I finally said. "You trained me better."

He sighed again. "Apologies. I am just . . . concerned with what you've set in motion."

I pressed the elevator button. "Have you gone to the ship yet?"

He didn't reply.

"You have," I said, confident. "It's not the sort of thing you'd leave to anyone else. I know you well enough for that. You saw what I saw, didn't you? What he's turned that ship into? The patches where time—"

I think at that point Lord Tower may have tried cutting me off, because there were some conversations you didn't have over a cell phone, no matter how secure Lord Tower's connections generally were. But I didn't hear him, because I'd forgotten to breathe, and everything went wobbly.

Next thing I knew, I was on my knees in a moving elevator, trying to will oxygen into my body.

Through a darkening tunnel, I heard Lord Tower calling my name.

I may have been hyperventilating; or maybe the Hanged Man was reaching out through whatever spell he laid on me; but there was not enough air in the world to keep me conscious.

I felt a spell tear into me, like a stiletto sliding into my brain. The magic grabbed onto my thoughts—grabbed onto my Companion bond—and shot out along the connection that linked me to Brand. I heard Lord Tower shout, *"FIND HIM NOW, BRANDON! BRING AID TO HIM NOW!"*

Then everything was black.

Then everything hurt.

Then it felt like my bones were cracking.

Then I *knew* my bones were cracking. I felt a rib splinter as a mouth breathed into mine. I gasped and pushed the weight off my body. I was in another hallway. Curious ghosts were gathered around me, and Brand was giving me CPR. In the background, Anna Dawncreek shouted about glass. I didn't understand any of it.

"Tell me what happened," Brand begged. "Rune!"

"He needs to break the glass!" Anna yelled.

"Anna, quiet! Go find a healer!" Brand yelled back. "Rune? Rune-gods-fucking-damnit-talk-to-me!"

"Spell," I gasped. I made myself breathe, but it was like inhaling though a crooked straw. "Curse. Can't breathe."

I struggled to an upright position. Anna was trying to get past Brand, but Brand held her off with a raised arm. He didn't see her face, but I did—I saw her eyes burning with a brilliant orange light.

Anna grabbed Brand's arm and pulled. Brand flew into the air, tossed backwards down the corridor. Anna dropped to her knees next to me and punched my chest. I tried to stop her before she drove a rib into my heart.

"Don't you see the glass?" she said. "Break the glass!"

She swung her arm and punched me again. The light from her eyes flooded the ground around me. The curse broke into glowing fault lines and *shattered*. She'd somehow managed to break a spell cast from a mass sigil. It vanished into squalls of wind that made my bangs flutter.

I took a clean, clear breath.

The light faded from Anna's eyes. She gave me a grim, satisfied look, and sagged against the hallway wall.

"I'm okay," I said as Brand scrambled back up to us.

Brand gave Anna an astonished look, and left her a lot of space as he knelt on my other side. Emotion after emotion raced across his face. So he took a second and closed his eyes. The wrinkles around his eyes deepened as he drew all his panic into cold bodyguard reflexes. "Talk to me," he said.

"The Hanged Man put a spell on me. It messed with my breathing. Anna . . . countered it. And none of this just happened. Do you understand me? None of it happened."

"But—" he started to say.

"I cannot appear weak. I cannot spare the time to convince myself to feel strong again. I just have to *be* strong." I was babbling, but there were so many layers to what was going on, and what was coming next. "Anna, nothing happened. You will speak of what happened to *no one*. Brand, zeta protocols. Now."

He grabbed my arm and hauled me to my feet. I kept the hold for just a second. Maybe two. And then I let go and stood on my own. I'd need a Healing for my ribs, but other than that, I'd felt worse.

"Everyone is in the hospital chapel," Brand said. "I was outside when Lord Tower . . . did whatever the fuck he did. No one else knows you were attacked."

"Does Addam know about . . ." I cut my eyes to Anna.

Brand nodded. "He's trying to reach his team."

I turned to Anna, who was still sagging, exhausted, on the ground. I held out my hand to her, but she stubbornly climbed upright on her own. "Am I in trouble?" she asked.

"Not even a little. But you cannot tell anyone what happened. Not yet. Please. This is so very, very important." On so many levels. So many dominoes. So many things set in motion. I didn't have time to deal with the birth of Anna Dawncreek's Atlantean Aspect. I didn't have time to consider that her Aspect—the glowing amber eyes—was what my own Aspect had been, in its early days. I didn't have time to consider that her Aspect was already, plausibly, stronger than mine. *She'd broken a curse from a mass sigil.*

"I promise," she whispered.

"The chapel is this way," Brand said, and led our little group down the corridor.

As I went, I pulled out my phone and texted the Tower the words: *I'm fine. Thank you.* (And right there was something else I didn't have time to consider. How had he taken over my Companion bond? I had the sinking suspicion that, yet again, I'd forced the Tower to reveal one of his hidden secret defenses. It was not a comfortable hand of cards to hold.)

My phone buzzed. A return text. *Secure surroundings; then contact me.* Only the Tower would take the time to use a semicolon in a text.

Brand turned us down a small tiled hallway that ended in ornate wooden doors with frosted glass panels. Diana Saint Nicholas was pacing in front of them. When she saw us, she straightened, and folded her arms across her stomach. I'd learned over the last couple months that it was her *take-no-shit* pose.

"We will talk," she said quietly, stepping toward us.

"There's no time. Let's get inside the chapel."

I tried to brush past her, but she didn't move, and I had better manners than to push her aside.

She said, "I'm sorry. Am I merely a bit player in this episode of the Rune Saint John show? Do I not have my own lines? By all means, Lord Sun, allow me to mutely step aside while you draw my nephews into further danger."

I winced, because she wasn't wrong.

"Addam has received word from the team that—" She flicked a glance behind me, at Anna. "From the team. Two are dead."

I let the guilt sink deep. Let it calcify, adding another layer to all the guilt I've accumulated over my life, all the other lives I'd had a hand in ending. "I did not know this would happen," I said. "It was not expected."

"Irrelevant. What danger are we in *now?*"

"That's what we need to evaluate. We need secure surroundings. I'll move us to—"

"*Young man,*" she said, and actually stomped a foot. "Will you *listen?* That's what I'm trying to establish. In moments, the remainder of the security team will be here. They are the victims of an attack, and are sworn to Addam, Quinn, and myself. Inside the room behind us is that boy, Layne. Is it true he's been sworn to your service?"

"I . . . Layne. Yes."

"Then those sworn to you are under attack as well. Why haven't we invoked sanctuary privileges?"

"Here? Sanctuary here?"

"New Saints is neutral ground. They have profound defenses. You may not have a seat on the Arcanum, but you're entitled to its privileges. You—we—can request sanctuary for seventy-two hours. This *is* a secure location."

I hadn't known. I took the information like the remarkable gift it was. One way or another, all of this would be over in seventy-two hours. Knowing Queenie, Max, Quinn—all of them—would be protected would free my hands.

"Will you contact the hospital administrator for me?" I asked Diana.

"I already have. He's on his way. I'll speak to him when he arrives—go inside."

I was about to tell her that she shouldn't be alone in the hallway when a group of seven men and women in dark suits and somber expressions turned the corner. They had swords on their belts, and the Crusader Throne crest on their breast pockets. Several of them had streaks of ash on their face; and one of them was bleeding.

One of them also had belts filled with platinum discs draped over her arms—the matching sigils that Justice favored. She silently handed a belt to Diana, who fastened it around her waist.

I decided Diana could stand in the hallway on her own.

I swept into the chapel with Brand and Anna. The room was small, and filled with tripping obstacles in the forms of pews and statuary. Someone had cleared an area by a non-denominational altar. Layne was there, unconscious and in bed with an IV. A scared doctor stood next to him, pinned to the wall with one of Brand's knives through the sleeve of his blue hospital scrubs.

Max and Quinn. Corbie in Queenie's lap. Addam on a phone, which he spoke into and put away upon seeing me. His complexion was ashen. *Oh Addam.* He was so far into this now that he wouldn't be able to escape its orbit. If I failed—if the dominoes fell the wrong way and something happened to him—the grief wouldn't calcify, it would crack.

"Listen closely," I said, and put aside all my uncertainty. "The Hanged Man has moved against me. On Diana's advice, I will claim sanctuary, which will afford us short-term protection within the walls of the hospital. Their defenses are formidable, and I have to believe that the Hanged Man will not risk a frontal assault. In the meantime, I've called a forum of the Arcana to air my grievances. We'll stay here until that happens."

I looked at Addam. At the deep wrinkles around his mouth and eyes, a perversion of his laugh lines. I slid my glance to Corinne. Her body was tense, prepared for an ambush; she knew something very bad had happened. She was just waiting for confirmation of it.

"There is more," I said. "I am so sorry to have to say this, but in his move against me, the Hanged Man destroyed your home. The lives of two members of the Crusader Throne were lost. I did not anticipate this move. The best I can tell you is that I will answer this affront tenfold. On my name, I will make the Hanged Man pay."

"Our house?" Anna whispered.

"But . . ." Corbie said. He squirmed around to look at Queenie. "But?"

Corinne went over and picked Corbie up. Scared, he buried himself against her neck. I could see his clothing quiver as he started to shake or cry.

"Stop saying *me* and *I*," Corinne told me. "That creature has moved against *us*."

I swallowed. "I did not mean to imply that this didn't involve you. I have promised you my protection, and I—"

"That's not what I'm saying," she said, nearly a growl. "I'm telling you that you're not alone. We're on the front line of this together."

We exchanged stares for a second, and I gave her a small smile. It didn't change the fact that I'd never been more alone in my life. It wouldn't change the fact of what I'd need to face tomorrow. But it was a nice thought.

"Addam, can we speak?" I asked.

"There's a room. There," Addam said, pointing behind him.

"Rune," Brand murmured. "You need a sanctum. We need supplies from Half House."

"Soon," I told him. "And . . . I need to talk to you. Alone. Just give me a minute?"

He stepped back, planting himself in front of the main chapel doors.

I followed Addam into a small room that was basically a large supply closet. He shut the door, his back to me, and paused for a moment.

I stared at his broad shoulders, bowed under the weight of the moment. "I am so sorry," I said, my voice finally losing all certainty.

He turned and pulled me into a full-bodied hug. I felt him along every line, every curve. It was a warm and beautiful sense of complete safety, and I enjoyed every second of the lie it offered.

After a long minute, he sighed and kissed the curve of my neck. "Hero," he said.

"I didn't know this would happen."

"Of course not. But it has. And as Corinne said, this is not something you are allowed to face without us. I would have your promise on that."

"My promise on what? That I'll drag your entire court into my fight?"

Addam pulled away until he could meet my eyes. He said, simply, "Yes."

"Have you talked with your mother?"

"I have."

"She can't be very happy about this."

"She is not. But she also understands the choice I made."

"I didn't give you much room to make any other choice, though, did I? The Hanged Man—"

He made a sound like *chha*, and waved me off. He looked around, spotted two metal chairs, and unfolded them for us. He kicked them close, so that our knees would touch when we sat down.

"Pay attention," he said closely, after we'd taken our seats. "Try not to interrupt."

"Okay."

"Such as that."

I smiled at him.

He picked up my hand, and wrapped his fingers around it. He frowned at how cold I was, and breathed warm puffs into my palm. As he rubbed my fingers, he said, "I was not speaking of the choices we have made, or must now make, regarding Lord Hanged Man. I am speaking about *us*. You insist on behaving as if I am dragged unaware into your troubles. Like a child with his eyes closed. But I am not a child, Rune Saint John. Nor are my eyes closed. I know what it means to be with you. To be honest, I'm surprised you haven't pieced it together by now."

I forgot I wasn't supposed to interrupt. "Pieced what together?"

"My brother is a prophet, Hero."

"Prophecy," I sighed. "Let me guess. Quinn's warned you that there's a really high probability that I'll keep dragging you into emergency after emergency."

"Quinn knows me better than anyone in my life. He knows what I want. He knows what I want from *existence*. I want to help people, Rune. I want my living to *matter*. I have struggled for so long to find an identity apart from my family. My work with"—and here he paused, only to make a sour face—"Ashton, Geoffrey, and Michael was a poor outlet for that. My charitable works—those were better. Those were satisfying. But I still struggled to *matter*."

"You matter," I said.

"And then one day," he continued, as if I hadn't spoken, "I was kidnapped. Thrown in a dungeon. Saved by a hero."

"And almost killed after the hero dragged you into more danger."

"And then saved the city. We saved *the city*, Rune. We did that. We stopped Rurik."

"But I'm not sure this is the same. I'm not asking you to save the city. I'm asking you to get involved in court warfare. This isn't—"

"*Hero*," he said, not loud but firm, and he squeezed my hand. "You act like this is the end of your story. I would remind you again: *my brother is a prophet*. I once asked him, not long ago, if you and I would be good together."

Addam leaned close and whispered the next bit in my ear.

"And the prophet said—while picking chewing gum off his shoe, as it were—*he hogs the covers, but most of the time he makes you very, very happy, especially when you help him save the world*."

Addam leaned away. "And so my mother accepts the choice I've made. Not to drag *my* court into the fight, because, in many ways, I have already stepped away from her. My mother understands the alliance I have made. And she will offer her support to the court that you and I are making."

He kissed me on the lips. I didn't respond, because my brain wasn't responding to anything right now.

But I didn't pull away.

And I didn't tell him he was wrong.

After I had the doctor Heal my ribs, Brand and I went to the roof.

The security of the hospital extended there, and I needed the fresh air. I needed to be alone with Brand. We sat down on a parapet, looking out at the stillness of the scarlet-skied morning.

Finally he said, "Nothing good ever happens when you say we need to talk. Either you forgot to pay the cable bill, or you're going to try to tell me you need to go tearing off on your own."

"I paid the cable bill."

"Did you notice the part where I said you're going to fucking *try* to do something on your own? Because we've been over that shit before."

I looked him straight in the eyes. "I'll need you at my side. More than ever before."

"Oh. Well fucking okay, then. What else do we need to talk about?"

"Back home, in my room, is a folder. I found it in the attic. At Sun Estate."

"Okay," he said, again, drawing it out.

"It's a file on your biological family. It has the names of your biological mother and father and brothers."

Brand stared at me. Then he said, "And?"

Now I stared back at him. "And what? I mean. This is big, right?"

Brand bristled, swinging around to face me, with such exaggerated movement that I grabbed his sleeve to keep him from falling. He said, "Is that why you've been so fucking weird the last few days?"

"It's . . . well. Yes? Sort of?"

"Rune, I've known that for *years*."

I blinked. "But . . . How did you find out?"

"Are you shitting me? The first time it even occurred to me to be curious, I just looked it up on the Internet. Back when we had fucking *dial-up*. When I was, like, *eight*. Do you have any idea how easy it is to figure that shit out?"

I gaped.

"Why are you so stupid about these things?" Brand demanded in genuine exasperation. "Why do you think it would even matter to me? I thought we dealt with this when we were kids."

"When did we deal with this?" I asked, exasperated myself.

"You were five. Remember? Your father explained to you what a Companion was, and how he'd bought me. You got all weepy and ran to me and told me you were setting me free."

"You punched me in the nose!"

"And it was dealt with. Why are we having this conversation again?"

"But . . ." I trailed off. I scratched an eyebrow. "This is a different conversation than I expected."

"Goddamnit, Rune. You always act like this is something bad that happened to me. It happened to you, too, you know. You didn't have any choice either. You didn't get a vote when a strange baby was plunked down in your crib and stole all your toys. Are you mad they did that to you?"

"Of course not!"

"Well, I'm not mad either. What is it you think I missed out on? Growing up to be a thirty-year-old American with two-point-five kids and a nine-to-five job?"

"But—"

"And that's ignoring the whole fucking fact that any parental urge I have is satisfied by dealing with you every damn day!"

It's possible too many things had happened in too short a time. There are only so many acrobatics you can do when rug after rug is ripped away. So I turned my eyebrow scratching into an eyelid rubbing, and tried to hide the fact that I may have been crying.

"Hey," he said. I felt him nudge me. "Hey. Stop it. I'm trying to say . . . I love our life. This isn't a thing to be worried about, Rune."

"It's not—" I said, and had to stop to take a breath. "It's not just that. I don't even know why I mentioned this. I tell Addam I feel like shit because I'm dragging him into this, and he says it's a choice he already made. And this . . . you . . . I don't . . ."

His hand curled on my shoulder. A fixed point against the spin of gravity.

I took another, shuddering breath. "Brand, I know what I need to do. Tomorrow. I think my plan will work, but if it doesn't, we lose everything."

"Shit. We've been friends with those odds for a long, long time."

"This is different. The more and more we get swept up into the affairs of the Arcanum, the less and less options I have." It was like a stone cracking in a dam. Words poured out, a spray of water backed with the force of a river. "I'm scared. I am so scared. There are landmines every-where, and it's not a question of finding a path through them—it's a question of how well I can protect us when I set one off."

"Hey," he said, and shook my shoulder. "Come on now."

"I don't know if I can do this. I don't know if I can be what I need to be."

"*Hey,*" he said, again, and I felt his own worry thrumming along our bond. "Look at me, damnit!"

I opened my eyes. Saw the blue of his. One of my first memories ever: those eyes, narrowed at me, right before he slapped me with a rattle.

Brand said, fiercely, in a breaking voice, "You're my boy. You can do anything. *Anything.*"

We stayed like that, and stared at each other, and I finally nodded. He put his arm around my shoulder and held me close.

We stared off the roof into dawn.

THE ARCANUM

The hospital administrator, in a fit of politically motivated charity, gave us a suite of rooms in the coma ward. I didn't complain. Coma patients were unlikely to get out of bed and hover outside our door and snitch on our plans.

Diana turned out to be frighteningly competent in emergencies. She arranged for food and napping quarters; sent a security team to Half House to retrieve weapons Brand wanted; and, most unexpectedly of all, brought in tailors and seamstresses with a rack of clothes.

Addam, Brand, and I were changing in one of the rooms, while Corbie played with plush centaur dolls on the ground.

For clothes, I'd opted on a simple, clean look. Black business slacks, a black button-down shirt. They went well with my boots, at least. Brand was struggling with a tie—*"And not another fucking word about it"*—because most Companions wore suits and ties to the Arcanum. Addam had settled on actual court clothes, which included a burgundy shirt that showed a long V of chest, along with tight gray pants. Very tight gray pants. When he bent over to pick up a boot, my jaw dropped so fast I almost dislocated it.

Brand caught me staring and mumbled, "You're fucking shameless."

"But," I said, and flicked my eyes to Addam, as if to say I wasn't wrong. Brand rolled his eyes back at me, as if to say that Addam was fucking shameless too.

On the other side of the room, Addam sighed. "You both seem to believe your spooky telepathic bond is quieter than it actually is. It is not. Do you need assistance with that tie, Brandon?"

"Fuck you," he said. He glared at us, untangled his tie, and started again. The problem was that the only knots he knew required piano wire and someone else's neck.

Quinn came into the room, clutching a piece of notebook paper. He gave me a serious look and handed it to me. I scanned the list of family names he'd written, folded the paper, and put it in my pocket. A secret ace, which I'd reveal at the right opportunity. "That's amazing work," I said quietly. "But I'm sorry you had to go through it."

"It was important," Quinn said, cutting his eyes at Addam.

"It was," I said. "Is Max ready?"

"Yes. Diana got limos. The scary ones, that can stop bullets and tornadoes."

"Just out of curiosity," I said. "Are we going to be driving through a tornado? Even some of the time?"

"Oh no," Quinn said seriously. "I don't see that. Most of the time it's quiet until later, when there's fighting and booms and icicle screams."

"Ice cream?" Corbie said, perking up.

"No. Icicle screams. I'm not quite sure what it means. It's hard to see things that happen in the Convocation building. They made it that way on purpose."

We took this prophecy in stride, because it always came down to screaming, fights, and magical booms. That's why I'd spent hours in the hospital's public sanctum, storing an arsenal of aggressive magic. It hadn't been easy—it was never easy to store spells in sigils outside your own personal sanctum—but I'd been motivated.

"But is there ice cream too?" Corbie asked doggedly.

Quinn stared at the ceiling. "Maybe?"

"While we're looking at the future," I said, "Does Brand ever let someone tie his tie for him?"

"All of you stop encouraging him," Brand said. "Quinn, when it comes to prophecy, I'll be pretty fucking happy if you just let me know when the blades are so close that they're whistling. Got it?"

"I'll try," he said.

Corinne came into the room with a cardboard tray full of coffee. I decided, right there, that I loved Corinne. She angled the tray toward me, and I descended on it like a rockslide.

"Is Layne doing okay?" I remembered to ask.

"Better," she said. "He hasn't woken up yet. But his powers are working. He's . . . feeding . . . off the infection."

I cradled the hot cup between my hands, and peered at her. "You know there's nothing bad about his powers, right? Necromancy isn't evil. There are just evil people. And he's not one of them."

Her mouth—that unsettling blend of new wrinkles against smooth skin—pursed. "It's Kevan's magic. That's what worries me, not whether it's good or evil. I saw how it made him a target."

I took a sip of my coffee, swishing it around my mouth under the potentially inaccurate biological assumption that my saliva ducts would inject the caffeine directly into my bloodstream. I needed to have a talk with Corinne soon about Anna. She thought Layne was the biggest thing to worry about? Wait until she learned Anna—who'd fallen into an exhausted sleep in the chair by Layne's bedside—had the power of a principality.

Corinne was still speaking. " . . . which is the most ironic thing."

"Sorry, what is?"

"That the magic that fascinated the Hanged Man in Layne is what's actually keeping Layne alive, and making him a threat to the Hanged Man."

I dropped my coffee. Straight up dropped it.

I retreated into my brain, putting pieces together. I was barely aware of the activity around me—Brand's alarm, Addam's confusion, Corinne keeping Corbie from running his stuffed animal through hot coffee puddles.

"I know how to kill him," I whispered.

I blinked and came back to myself.

Corinne cut her eyes toward Corbie, whose own eyes had gone wide. Was there a murder jar? I shouldn't be talking about killing people in front of children.

I hurried over to Quinn. "Do you see a mass sigil filled with healing magic in my future?"

Max and Anna came into the room behind me. Corinne put a hand on their arms and kept them to the fringes. She'd been a Companion. She knew enough to let moments like this play out.

"Quinn," I said again. "Do you see anything like that? Me with a Healing spell?"

"Why a Healing spell?" Addam asked. "Rune, what is this?"

"His Aspect. It's his own magic. I . . . can't explain. I need to think it through. Quinn? A Healing spell?"

"I can't . . . it's hard to see. The Convocation makes everything fuzzy, and I'm . . . It's . . ."

"Think," I said anxiously. "It's important."

"Don't ask like that," Max said from across the room. When everyone turned to stare, he blushed. "It's those stupid drugs. The ones that don't work. The ones that just make him sick all the time and make everything blurry." And for just a second, Max shot a quick, dirty look at Addam, whose face went slack with shock.

"All the time?" Addam said. "Quinn? They make you feel ill all the time?"

"Max!" Quinn shouted. "You promised!"

"Don't use that tone with me, Quinn Saint Nicholas," Max said. "You threw up in my new loafers. Addam needs to know. And that's not even important right now. You need to do like we practiced. Rune is talking about a big Healing spell. Is Brand proud? Or is he rolling his eyes?"

"Is Brand *what?*" Brand demanded.

"The stupid drugs make it harder to make associations," Max said, "but it's easier if he ties it to things that are really, really important. He watches everything you and Rune do. He may not understand what he's seeing, but he always seems to remember what makes you happy, and what doesn't make you happy."

There was a lot happening right now. I tried to shelve everything except what I needed to survive the next few hours. I looked at Quinn, who was giving Addam a mournful look. "Quinn?"

"Brand's not rolling his eyes," Quinn whispered. "He wants to crack a joke because you're puffed up and clever, but he doesn't, because you *were* clever. That happens now. It's suddenly . . . there. It happens now. You're going to try something."

I turned to Brand. "We need to find Diana. I need another favor."

"Are you going to explain whatever this is about?" he asked.

"Do you trust me?"

"You're playing that card an awful lot. And, see, that's never what you mean when you say that. What you mean is, will I follow you through the great big fucking mess you're about to make." And then, to my surprise, he smiled. "Stop fucking asking."

Atlantis is, on the surface, bicameral. The general populace elects people to serve the Convocation, which passes rules and codes and regulations, which presents the perfect mimicry of representative democracy.

But at the heart of all power in the city is the Arcanum—the collective body of Arcana.

The Arcanum uses its power sparingly. They allow the passage of laws they have no intention of following; they allow elections and appointments of everyday Atlanteans in much the way they're amused by parades and beauty pageants. But at the end of the day, when it comes to the future of our people, their whispers are reality.

At that time of the morning, the public levels of the Convocation building were a frenzy of bureaucracy. As my party wound its way to the more private layers of government, we passed a constant throng of people and groups looking to press their agendas. I paid attention only haphazardly, as a way of distracting me from the audience ahead.

More interesting was watching Quinn's face as certain things were said. He appeared politely interested in the colorful madness and dance-like movements of some adherents of the Revelry, Lord Fool's court. He smiled as a group of Lady World's people came by with flower pots sprouting poinsettias in fast-forward motion.

But Quinn grew quiet as a were-panther and were-wolf snarled at each other, while hints of their animal forms morphed across their bodies in their spitting rage. The schism between shape-shifting cats and wolves was getting a lot of attention in the press.

And his smile faltered altogether as we passed a group of people with picket signs, arguing for the release of Juror Waylan, a Convocation representative recently arrested on corruption charges.

I tucked those details away. They weren't part of Today; they just had the faint stench of the sort of Tomorrow you got by hanging around a prophet.

The daylight pandemonium thinned as we approached a set of marble stairs padded in inch-thick red carpeting. Members of the guarda stood at the foot, bristling with weapons and attitude.

I held up a hand, and my friends stopped behind me: Brand, Max, Addam, and Quinn. We'd left the others at the hospital under Corinne and Diana's aggressive protection.

"You seem to be in my way," I told the guards pleasantly. "Your name?"

"Anaïca, my lord. I'm a lieutenant guarda captain for the Convocation." The woman had three yellow eyes—two on her face, and one tattooed to her wrist. She smelled strongly of plain, clean soap.

"Hello, Anaïca. I will pass now."

"I'm sorry, Lord Sun, but the Arcanum meets," she said, still unruffled. "Sitting members only, I've been told. We can find you a private suite to wait."

"Wait," I said, tasting the word.

Brand said, "Get the fuck out of our way, or I will literally kick you so hard that your descendants will have a birthmark in the shape of a bruise."

Addam put a hand on Brand's shoulder—which earned him a furious look—so Addam turned it into a pat. He said to the woman, who was just smiling at Brand, "Lord Sun is the reason the Arcanum meets."

That finally gave her a little pause. She frowned at me and said, "I'm sorry, Lord Sun, we received word from the Arcanum that they had other matters to deliberate before your audience."

"Did you," I said. Someone was trying to stick a finger in the middle of my domino chain. "But now—right now, in this very moment—you're receiving word, from me, that you should move aside. Which order will you follow, I wonder."

"My lord, I—"

"Good *grief!*" Ciaran said, sweeping down the stairway. There was a sealed garment bag across one arm. The startled guards turned to face him as he said to me, "Put a little gas in it. We're about to get started. Oh, hello, Anaïca. Love the new tattoo."

"I, that is, we were told—" she said, finally disoriented.

Ciaran pushed the garment bag into the crook of his arm, turned over his hand, and offered the guarda his wrist. A gleaming silver ward burned there, reddening the skin around it. A spark of magic enclosed in a circle: the symbol of the Hex Throne.

"I'm about the Magician's business," Ciaran said airily. "No time to turn you into frogs and newts, dearies. Sun?"

And it was that easy. We all trudged past the line of bowing guards, up the carpeted stairs.

We kept our silence—well, I kept my silence, while Ciaran filled the void with some aimless, non-specific chatter—until we had a measure of privacy in the cold, undecorated marble hallway above us.

"Not sure where to start, Ciaran," I said finally. "But thank you. I thought you were staying in Spain?"

"I was, but I kept having such *dreams* of you, Sun, even after we spoke. And I'm not talking about the ones with the pearl strands and hockey stick. No, these were more like true-seeings. I think the next few hours will be *most* entertaining."

We unabashedly paused to size each other up. Ciaran was wearing a rather conservative outfit, a blue and crimson three-piece affair that tug-of-warred between a business suit and runway fashion. His blue hair was perfectly styled, and he'd added a crescent of earrings to one ear. Light rippled across his eyes, a rolling sheen of magic.

Ciaran was less complimentary. "Bars and banks, Rune," he said. "What are you wearing? You smell like Velcro and polyester blend. Do try harder."

"It's simple and elegant," I said defensively. "And not fussy. I hate fussy clothing. Fussy clothing looks ridiculous on people after they're done gutting monsters or crawling through sewers."

"Yes, well, perhaps you can save your fun to-do list for later. This is the *Arcanum.*" He smiled behind me. "Sweetness."

Quinn squeezed between Brand and me and threw himself at Ciaran. "You tricked me!" he said. "I didn't know you'd be here."

"We're very good poker players, you and I," Ciaran said, and ruffled Quinn's cowlick, which sprang back up. "And look at all of you! It seems you've emptied the entire tree house for this field trip."

Addam shook his hand. Brand gave a gruff nod. Max tried to give a gruff nod, too, but it came off as nervous. Max was never sure where he stood with anyone outside our immediate circle.

I broke up the greetings. "Lord Magician marked you," I said. "That's new."

"Lord Magician did *not* mark me. He owes me favors, not the other way around. This allows me access to the festivities. And his symbol matches my jewelry."

I changed subjects. "Do you think the Hanged Man is trying to block my access?" I asked.

"Delay it, at best. He'll be putting worms in people's ears, no doubt. We'll need to hurry after we deal with your clothing."

"Please don't tell me you expect me to wear whatever is in that garment bag."

"It's rude to turn down presents. But first," he said, and reached up to touch the sleeve of my shirt. The rippling light in his eyes flared white.

Ciaran operated as a principality—a very powerful, freelance Arcana, of sorts—with an affinity for dreams and wild magic. I've known his powers to have an unpredictable effect on reality. I've seen him change wood to brass; plaid to paisley; and the color of a theater usher's eyes, in one extremely uncomfortable situation. But I've never known him to be able to do it *deliberately.*

The colors of my shirt and pants shifted—a shimmer of colors that didn't so much brighten as shift into different, shadowy colors. Moments later my pants were a deep garnet color. My shirt was a blackish umber.

They were the color of my father's throne.

"Oh," I said. "This isn't bad."

And then the second wave of magic hit. The pants dug into my balls, the cloth made some tearing sound as it slithered and tightened under my armpits. "Godsdamnit," I said, realizing I was now wearing official court pants, as tight as Addam's.

"Don't you get stroppy with me," Ciaran said. "I've already thought ahead. Can't have you holding your hands in front of your crotch all day." He unzipped the garment bag and pulled out a cape.

It was less the sort of thing a superhero would wear; more a Roman centurion. The colors mixed crimson and coal. The symbol of Sun Throne—a flare of fire in a closed circle—was sewn on the breast.

"Oh," I said again, as he fastened it around my neck. I think the chain was solid gold.

"Does it have pockets for weapons?" Brand asked.

"This isn't our first rodeo together," Ciaran tskked. "I just wish I had time to do something with that hair. Most people don't grow bangs just so they have something to tug on, Sun."

The cape went over one shoulder and under the other. Addam smoothed the shirt of the bare shoulder, and smiled at me.

Ciaran tapped a cigarette out of a silver case and began field stripping it. Permission to smoke in the Convocation was directly proportionate to your ability to defend your smoking instrument. "Come children," Ciaran said, lighting the tip with a purple zippo. He waved us and his smoke down the hallway. "We still need to yield our weapons."

Brand tensed next to me. This was one of the things about my plan that bothered him most. I saw it more as a mutual deterrent. No one was allowed weapons or sigils in the inner chambers, including those people who were set to use them against me.

Ciaran led us to the weapons checkpoint, where a series of cubicles was shielded for privacy. Ciaran and Addam went first. Max hesitated a second to whisper, "I like your hair," and then ducked into the third booth.

There was only one booth left. I nodded at Brand, who shook his head *no* and looked at Quinn. I gave him my *please* look. He bit down on a scowl and went into the booth.

As soon as Quinn and I were alone, all of the oxygen escaped me in a long, slow hiss, and I gave my nerves a moment to clamor. The closer I got to the Arcanum, the less room I had to maneuver. This was happening. This was really happening.

"Do you know what I'm going to do?" I asked Quinn quietly.

He stared at me for a long, long moment. Direct questions like that made him unhappy. They were a clear admission that he always knew more than he let on. But he and I had done this dance before. In some ways, I understood him even better than Addam. I knew what it was like to stack the deck too.

"Yes," Quinn said. "Mostly. But there's still time to zig instead of zag."

"Quinn, tell me this. When you look ahead . . . Most of the time . . . It doesn't get better, does it? The bad guys only get scarier, don't they? The risks only get higher, don't they?"

"You know they do."

I nodded to myself, and swallowed. "Then what needs to happen isn't just about the Hanged Man. It's about whoever is standing behind the Hanged Man. And whoever is standing behind them, and them, and them. There is no peace in my future, is there?"

274

Quinn gave me a sad look, and then shoved himself into a hug.

"So there's really no zigging, is there," I whispered. "Are you sure you want to go inside with me? It was stupid of me not to have asked you earlier. I shouldn't assume. You should decide on your own if you want to plant yourself as my ally."

"I've decided more times than you can imagine," he said. "Even that time when Max was my archenemy. It's always more interesting following you. And you'll always need me."

Since I would, I accepted his friendship for what it meant, and hugged him back.

The privacy booths were meant for one person, but Brand was my Companion, and I wanted him at my side.

I stepped in behind him as the Convocation guard was sorting through what appeared to be every weapon Brand owned. He was giving the woman his most innocent expression.

"And this?" she said, holding up a tube.

"My eczema cream," he said.

She set it in a pile opposite the knives, darts, and gun cartridges.

"And this?" she said, holding up a zipped leather booklet.

"My diary," he said.

She unzipped it, saw paper, and shrugged.

Since he was human, he didn't get the magical dampening bracelet that was soon fastened on my wrist. I yielded all eight of my sigils. In anticipation of it, I'd already unfastened the gold anklet chain, as well as the metal circle threaded through the leather band I usually tied around my thigh. I saw the woman's eyes linger on the circle in puzzled surprise, though she was far too disciplined to comment on it. Not every sigil was shaped like a ring or pendant. Beggars couldn't be choosers, especially when it came to magic cock rings.

The dampening bracelet wasn't as thorough as a null zone. It'd keep me from calling on sigil spells and cantrips, but my bloodline had deeper magic. Still, my breath stuttered a bit as I put the last sigil—my mother's cameo necklace—in the bombproof container.

"We will return these when you leave the Arcanum's private floor," the woman said, in the even tones of repetition. "While they remain in our custody, they will be protected with our lives."

"Thank you," I said, as she stepped aside to let us through the other door of the privacy cubicle.

On my way out, I murmured, "Eczema cream and a diary. Which one explodes?"

"That's an awful thing to say," Brand told me, still maintaining his innocent face. "You're always making hurtful accusations. This is why I need a diary."

"You know, there are some rules you really need to follow."

He blew a raspberry at me.

The others were waiting for us. Quinn, whose sigils were all strung along a single belt and thus easily yielded, was close behind.

"Ready Freddy, are we?" Ciaran said, clapping his hands. "Let's hurry. I want some of the popcorn before the butter gets cold."

The hallway before us was simple and bare, but mined from the most expensive marble in the world. Magic had played along the architecture, smoothing the seams and rounding the angles. It made me think, not quite comfortably, about the throat of a great stone beast.

"The Iconsgison is just ahead," Ciaran murmured. "Are we entering with you right away?"

"You *want* to enter with me?" I asked.

"Quite so."

"Ciaran," I said. "You'll be making a statement. You know that, right?"

"So serious," he said, straightening his sleeves. "I'd think you'd be grateful. There are those in that room who owe me favors. It might come in handy."

"I have no doubt. And it would be an honor to have you at my side, if you're sure."

"Who needs a safe and comfortable life? Onwards, Saint John."

We were barely a dozen yards from the door to the Arcanum's meeting room when the next obstacle arose.

The antechamber entrance—two immense wooden doors, gilded in gold, as tall as a river troll—opened, and Jirvan exited with two armored guards. Lord Hanged Man's scarred seneschal stopped. I'd wondered when I'd be seeing him again.

"There's nothing you need to say that I need to hear now," I told him. "Step aside."

"Lord Hanged Man has requested an ad hoc item for the agenda," Jirvan said. "The Arcanum will remain in closed session until he's done."

"That does sound like something he might want to do," I agreed. "But it would require a vote, and given the reason we're here today, I don't imagine he'll get it. How about we duck in and see?"

"I have my instructions," Jirvan said.

"I thought your instructions were to bring Max to the Hanged Man?" I waved my hand at my ward. "Here he is."

Jirvan stared at me, his eyes clear and white in the mess of burn scars. His expression seemed largely resigned.

"I'm sorry," Jirvan said quietly. "I have new directives. Please, Lord Sun. This morning could go very, very, very badly. It's not too late."

"I believe it is."

"I see." Jirvan looked at the guards. "Lord Hanged Man wishes a private moment with his fellow Arcana. You have your orders."

Ciaran swept forward and touched the sleeves of both guards. Their clothing—shirts, scale mail, trousers—turned to solid bronze. They slammed to the ground with a clank.

"Mind your manners, love," Ciaran said.

Jirvan looked past him, at me. "The Hanged Man looks most vulnerable only when his teeth are at your throat. Please think this through, Lord Sun."

It was a startling admission, and didn't seem to be in the best interests of Lord Hanged Man. If I had more time, I'd stop and listen; but the clock was about to run out.

We walked past him. Brand took three steps ahead of me—not-exactly-accidentally kicking one of the guards in the head—to open the door.

We entered the Iconsgison, the twenty-two-sided audience chamber of the Arcanum.

The chamber was made from jade and sapphire—a planet's priceless treasure of gemstone, magically smoothed into tiles. It had a domed roof of solid marble, and twenty-two platforms, filled with real people or flickering projections. Not every Arcana had been on the island when the call went out for the assembly. Others, though local, found that a virtual presence was enough to sate their curiosity.

The Lovers pedestal remained empty, as it likely had since the raid that dismantled their court. For all I knew, the chamber would be renamed if the twenty-second number was lessened forever. It had happened before. They'd once numbered twenty-three, before the Hourglass Throne—the court of Time—was erased from history. Time magic was a sore point, which I would gratefully be pressing on soon.

The pedestals for the Empress and Emperor were empty, as they'd been since the Atlantean War. The Emperor's court had remained sealed and unfilled since his death, and the Empress was long, long estranged from our refugee city on Nantucket.

But the Magician was there, along with Lady World, Lord Chariot, and Lady Death. Lord Tower had a seat to the right hand of Lord Judgment, the current head of the Arcanum.

The power bloc known as the Moral Certainties was there: Lady Justice, Lady Tolerance, Lord Strength, and the Hermit. I'd co-opted two of their sons, currently standing behind me, and been intimately involved in the deaths of two others and the exile of another. That said, I'd also saved them from a fatal loss of reputation—after four children in their direct lines broke Arcanum law—and they owed me.

The Celestials—another power bloc, once led by my father—had a space on the left side of the room. Lady Moon was a renowned recluse. Her projection wasn't even human, just a simulacrum of a moon in a circle shining from behind a silvery cloud bank. And, of course, Lord Star wasn't here. How could he be? He was known as the Anchorite, and had been bricked in an underground vault for a very long time.

Lady Priestess, the head of the Papess Throne, was there, robed in white. She stood by the grinning figure of the motley Fool.

The Hierophant was there in person. I'd accidentally taken advantage of guest privileges in his Westlands compound a few months back. His generosity had been retroactively approved, along with an oblique warning to keep my mouth shut about what I'd seen in the manor house.

Lord Wheel—the Wheel of Fortune—was a glowing pair of playing dice. He'd been drinking his way through the backroads of America for years now; I'd never actually met him in person. Lord Devil was also a projection. The flickering image showed him in his animal form, a massive tiger slouched in shadows.

And then there was the Hanged Man. In a bitter twist of coincidence, his pedestal was next to the seat for the Sun Throne, empty since my father's death.

These were the Arcana of New Atlantis. The men and women whose mercurial and violent attentions maintained what remained of the Atlantean race.

And there I was, about to pull their unwavering focus on me.

"I object," Lord Hanged Man said calmly. "We have not finished voting on my motion."

Lord Judgment raised a hand. He was the aging quarterback of the bunch. Stupidly good-looking jaw, bronzed Native American skin, muscles just going to paunch, a lifetime devoted to making his own rules. His staff of office—a six-foot monstrosity—was in his hand.

"I haven't said I'd bring your motion to the floor," he replied. "And I won't. This nonsense ends now." He angled his hand into a point. At me. "This is a very unwise gambit, Lord Sun. I do not appreciate your man-handling my agenda."

"Matters overcame diplomacy," I said with a little bow. "When you hear me out, I'm sure you'll understand."

"Is it necessary that I understand? This is a private grievance between Gallows and Sun."

"It began that way," I admitted.

"And now?" he said.

"And now we discuss a threat to our people."

"Outrageous," Lord Hanged Man said. "Brothers and sisters, this is an affront. He's young and untested and unworthy of our time. He's using you as a shield against his own well-deserved peril."

His Aspect pushed at me—all carrion and frost. He regarded me with dead eyes in a dead, frozen face.

I smiled at him, like I would any dog whose bark and bite I had sized up.

"Gods' teeth," Lady Death sighed. "Just tell us what this is about." A tall black woman with shoulder-length braids, she wore a sharp business suit in burgundy and smoke. Not too much older than me, she was the youngest of the Arcana. She'd assumed her throne when her mother, the Dowager Lady Death, was wounded during the Atlantean War.

Seeing the Hanged Man glaring at her, Lady Death waved a hand. "Stop with all the posturing. Go on, Lord Sun. And keep it simple. Too many adjectives and adverbs, and I'll start chucking water balloons at you."

"Fair enough," I said, and gave her a bow.

"Little Brother," Lady Justice said, and fixed her sharp gaze on me. My heart skipped at that, because it was a good sign. She'd called me brother before; an early sign of respect. "You've been dragging my son through all sorts of adventures recently."

"I have, Lady Justice."

"It's his decision, of course. My headstrong boy." Her gaze filtered behind me and, for just a second, I saw an unexpected twitch of muscle. "Boys. My headstrong boys."

Addam had once told me that she treated Quinn like an afterthought. I turned my head in time to see Quinn give his mother a happy wave, which said everything about him, and, maybe, everything about her.

But I needed her and the Moral Certainties on my side.

"I will hear him out," Lady Justice said to the rest of the room. Her stare lingered on the Hanged Man. "He is young, you're right. But he's hardly untested. We've all read the red-pages."

I didn't know what red-pages were, but a few other Arcana made murmurs of accord, including Lord Judgment.

Lord Tower, though, just stared at me. A cat on a ledge, waiting to spot the entirety of the game spread out beneath him so he knew what to pounce on.

"Then we'll hear him speak," Lord Judgment said. "He's a child of the Arcanum. He's entitled to a voice. Lord Sun, are you seeking redress in a grievance against the Hanged Man?"

"No," I said.

"Beg pardon?" Lord Judgment said.

"As I mentioned, matters have grown beyond diplomacy. There is a threat to my island. I have the same responsibility to New Atlantis that all of you do."

"I don't . . ." Lord Judgment gave Lord Tower a quick look, who continued to just stare. "I'm not sure I follow."

I took a thin breath.

There weren't many moments like this in a person's life.

Most of the time, change fell on you like a load of bricks. You didn't see it coming. You didn't plan for it. You didn't have an actual awareness of the moment as you tumbled and slammed through it.

But sometimes?

Sometimes you were the one that stood with your hand on the lever.

Sometimes you were the one that stepped off the cliff, or walked in front of the gunfire, or pulled the pin from the grenade.

"I asked you here to bear witness," I said.

And across the room, Lord Tower straightened in his chair.

"From this moment forward," I said, "I would have it be known that I have claimed my father's throne."

And as my pulse doubled—like quick sharp finger clicks—I said the words my father had once said:

"In thought and deed, in mind and heart, I claim what is mine by law and legacy. Let it be known that from this moment forward, I am, as I was always meant to be, the voice and the will of the Sun Throne. I am Arcana. I am Arcanum. I am the Sun of Atlantis."

Lord Tower rose to his feet. He stared at me and mouthed my name, shaking his head.

I took three steps to the center of the room, away from my friends. Away from Addam. Away from Brand, whose stunned amazement was racing along our bond.

In a building warded against spells and cantrips; and despite the bracelet against my wrist that barred most of my abilities; I drew on my deepest magic. I called on my Aspect.

Flames burst from me. They raced from my eyes, down my face; swept along my arms; fanned across the jade floor in a plume of solar yellow. The world became my silhouette.

I repeated, loudly, "I am Arcana. I am Arcanum. I am the Sun of Atlantis."

Our most potent vows happened in threes.

I turned in a slow circle. Saw upraised arms, against my light. Saw shocked expressions. Saw the Fool doubled over in uproarious laugher.

I saw Quinn pressing into Addam's arms, both their eyes reflecting my flames.

Saw Max with both hands over his mouth.

Saw Ciaran dip his chin, eyes to the floor.

Saw Brand. And I saw Brand. And I saw Brand.

I shouted, "I am Arcana. I am Arcanum. *I am the Sun of Atlantis!*"

My vow pulsed through the chamber in a roar of magic.

The fires died, leaving the Iconsgison in utter, thorough silence.

Into that silence, I added, "And as a member of this body, I officially petition for a raid on Lord Hanged Man and his holdings."

LORD SUN

"Clear the room!" Lord Judgment shouted into the unrest. "We move into closed session *now!*"

Most of the Arcana subsided, though the mad Fool still shook with laughter. He must have had handfuls of spare change in his pockets; his delight sent metallic clinks across the room.

Addam was the first to come up to me. His eyes were glassy with either shock or sun-blindness. "You are either crafty or impulsive, Hero. But either way, I did just tell you we would make a court. Good luck. We shall be close by. I'm going to kiss you now."

I opened my mouth, but wasn't sure what to say.

"Arcana do not hesitate," Addam whispered against my lips, and kissed me.

Then he tugged on Quinn's sleeve to pull him away. Quinn stayed long enough to whisper, "It's so loud. I can't hear what happens. We shouldn't have given up our sigils."

The last bit raised goosebumps on my arms.

Max still had his hands over his mouth. "You'll be fine now," I promised him.

"You did this for me," he said through his fingers.

"Of course I did. I protect my family. Stay close to Brand, until we're home. Watch your surroundings."

He nodded. Brand, who had come to stand by Max, murmured something to him. Max hurried after Addam and Quinn.

Ciaran didn't look like he was about to go anywhere, but he did step away to give my Companion and me a private moment.

I gave Brand a guilty look. "How much trouble am I in?"

"I don't know. Do I get a raise?"

I barked a surprised laugh. "Do I? We split everything fifty-fifty."

"Fine. Can I get in writing that we'll always split everything fifty-fifty when you become a god?"

"Brand."

"Rune," he said, mimicking my tone. He bumped my shoulder, enough to show he cared, but with a little extra to leave a bruise. After all, I had kept him in the dark.

"Go ahead now," he whispered. "Show them who you are."

Then Brand was gone too.

"Ciaran," Lord Judgment said. "You'll need to leave."

"I don't believe I will," Ciaran said cheerfully. "I have material evidence to present. I've explained it all to Lord Magician."

"And I'll explain it to the Arcanum as appropriate," Lord Magician said stiffly. He was, like so many other wealthy male Atlanteans, handsome and tall. His good looks were as predictable as the mint toys that a collector kept sealed in their original packaging.

"We did talk about this," Ciaran reminded Lord Magician. He smiled in apology as he said it, but there were teeth in the look he gave the Magician.

Lord Magician lowered his face as a flush crept up his neck. "Fine. He should stay. He knows things."

"It's not unprecedented," Lady Justice offered. "Principalities have been welcome in our session before."

"Then so be it," Lord Judgment said impatiently. "We are now in closed session."

The avatar of the Devil—the massive tiger—rumbled. It rose and stretched, furred muscles rising along its back like ocean tides.

Lady Death laughed. "What he said. Let's get this show started, yes?"

The Hanged Man tapped a thin finger on the arm of his chair. "I'll admit, it was a pretty declaration. But a slow child could say the same words. It doesn't make it binding, and it certainly doesn't make it enforceable. He has no court; he has no seat of authority; and his sigils are the equivalent of beggar rags. Aside from that, the lack of Arcana Majeure—"

"Lord Hanged Man!" Judgment said in a surprisingly loud, sharp voice. "You will guard your words, or this will become an entirely different discussion."

Ciaran cleared his throat. He was enjoying himself entirely too much. He was all but grabbing my cloak and waving it behind me to ratchet his sense of spectacle. He said, "My most august colleagues. That is why I wished to remain. I do believe Lord Sun has already stumbled on that particular secret, even if he doesn't have the full grasp of what it is." Ciaran gave the room a red-lipped smile. "Rune has used the Arcana Majeure."

The whispering in the room rose as Ciaran added, "I was there when it happened. I will provide witness."

I had no idea what was happening—or, no, I had an idea, I just didn't understand the actual words. The Arcana Majeure? I'd never heard of it.

And yet . . . In my head I saw churning clouds ripped apart to reveal a blistering blue sky. It was a leap of intuition, helped by the memory of Quinn's scared voice. He'd once said, about that moment, *It was the most important thing in the world.*

"We monitor such things," Lord Judgment said. "We would have known if he'd shown the ability. Unless . . ." His eyes roved to Lord Tower.

The Tower took a tired breath, and made everyone wait as he exhaled it. "Unless," he admitted, "I employed resources to obscure the fact."

"It's true then?" Lord Judgment said.

Lord Tower nodded. "In the Westlands. The incident with the lich. Rune used the Arcana Majeure to break that weather spell."

At least three distinct questions itched up my throat, but I kept my lips clamped shut. I needed to listen. I needed to listen very, very closely.

"I see," Lord Judgment said, but his disapproval was lost in Lord Chariot's own rising voice, who said, "That was poorly done."

Lord Chariot, a short man with a line that stretched back before modern Asian countries, stared at Lord Tower. He repeated, when the Tower remained silent, "Lord Tower, that was poorly done. We have agreements. This knowledge would have been of vital interest to this body at the time you learned it. I am immensely disappointed."

Lord Tower raised his gaze and stared at Lord Chariot. Lord Chariot finally broke and aimed his bluster elsewhere. And even then, Lord Tower continued to stare, for another long moment, until the Chariot—arguably the richest person on the face of the earth—was fidgeting.

"And so," Ciaran said into the uncomfortable moment, "Rune *is* one of you. He has passed the threshold that marks Arcana and Principalities. Let's not whip this conversation in circles, when there are better things to discuss."

"He is *not* one of us," the Hanged Man objected. "Amongst each other, if not the city at large, we stand on ceremony. Raw skill doesn't translate to the right to take a seat amongst us. There are formalities to be attended. This talk of a raid—of him taking a seat—is intolerable."

Lady Priestess stirred for the first time. In a wispy voice, she said, "He learned a Soul Bind spell from me." She blinked at everyone else, as if the point should be obvious. "A very advanced magic. Have you used it yet, Lord Sun?"

"I have," I said. "Recently, in fact. Against a go-ryo, on my—" *My father's estate,* I was about to say. Not anymore. No longer my father's throne; my father's pedestal; my father's compound. I said, "On my estate."

"Your ruined estate," Lord Strength said, which earned him a cool look from Lady Justice. I was very reminded of the fact that I'd killed his son Ashton, and in doing so, saved his court from probable ruin. There was no predicting his thoughts on that, even though I knew he and Ashton hadn't been close. "Let's speak plainly. The Sun Estate is uninhabitable. It's one of the most haunted plots of land on the island, excepting Farstryke. You can't live there. Your only home is a house barely larger than this room. How do you expect to survive as a court? How do you expect to *defend* your court?"

"Though . . ." Lady World said. "That Aspect. There hasn't been a burning man since . . . Well, since Rune's father. You all saw what I saw. If

I'm not wrong, it's mixed with bless-fire. His Aspect isn't simply a manifestation—it has utility. Very rare."

"Enough," Lord Tower said, as the Hanged Man began to object again. "Rune is Arcana. It's done, and we all know it. Take your seat, brother."

Shivers raised the hair along the back of my neck. With as little self-consciousness as I could manage, I walked over to the chair my father had once sat in.

I sat down. The world didn't shift on its axis. The ground didn't rumble. Though I did have to go the bathroom very badly.

Next to me, I felt quiet, cold hatred pouring off the Hanged Man. I smiled at him, and glanced over at Lady Death, who was on my other side. She was scratching what looked like a mosquito bite on her ankle, which seemed like something I would do. She needed a Brand in her life. I could already hear it. *You can literally heal bullet wounds, but you're going to sit there and fucking annoy me.*

She stopped scratching and gave me an aggrieved sigh. "Now there's nowhere to toss my jacket. You better be a good neighbor."

"We shall have order," Lord Judgment said. "Let's return to the matter before us."

"And the matter before us," Lord Tower said, "is Lord Sun's request to destroy another court. It's his claim to defend."

He looked straight at me as he spoke. I didn't need a cartoon thought bubble to explain it. He was telling me I'd forced his hand, and now I'd well and fucking truly play through it on my own.

"We will not vote on a raid," Lord Hanged Man said. "I will not abide."

"I wouldn't expect a vote," I said. "A formal hearing will need to be scheduled. But I'm entitled to present statements of fact to justify that hearing. Isn't that right?"

Lord Wheel's ivory dice laughed. "In other words," he said in an American drawl, "he's allowed his shot across the bow." The dice shimmered and stretched, into a virtual representation of a carrot-haired man.

He was thin to the point of sickly, with needle marks along his arms, and underwear-model cheekbones you could shape diamonds with.

Lord Hierophant stirred. "I want to hear what he has to say. Please do stop objecting, Lord Hanged Man. You'll have a chance to refute."

"I won't sit in silence and listen to lies," the Hanged Man said, and for the first time, his anger didn't have the glossy polish of rehearsed remarks. His composure was cracking.

"Why not?" Lady Justice asked. "Why wouldn't you? Slander would only help your cause. Let him lie and dig holes beneath his feet, if you're so certain he has nothing honest to say. Lord Sun. It is time. *Speak.*"

I took a few shallow breaths, hiding my nervousness as a pause. Before Lord Judgment could prod me, I stood up.

"Lord Strength is right. I don't have a compound. My own sigil collection is limited. Ragtag, you might say. But for all that, I am New Atlantis. I am a child of our reduced circumstances. Here, in this room, we shouldn't deceive ourselves. We lost the war. We live on the sufferance of humanity, which outnumbers us in the billions. In the *billions*. Without a single spell, without a single magical weapon of war, they could crush us simply with their growing mass."

I turned and swept a look along the semicircle. "Our sigils are a lost art. We fight amongst each other. Our most powerful beasts lie dormant. The dragons of Atlantis sleep—and that is an uncomfortably accurate metaphor."

"More pretty words," Lord Hanged Man said. "Please do continue. Tell us how weak we are."

"That's just the problem," I said. I smiled at him, and ignored my heartbeat. I didn't have the room yet. I had their attention; but I didn't have them. So I pointed. "That. Right there. That mind-set. It's not a question of power—it's a question of adaption. Yes, I have a limited collection of sigils, but I am not weak. I have learned to operate within my restraints. And yes, we live on the sufferance of humanity. Which is why it's vital we find a way to share the planet with them. Lord Tower and Lord

Chariot have found a way. Their economic interests are tied closely to the human world. And they have *flourished*. Lord Wheel lives in America. Lord Magician operates portals in six out of seven continents. They, too, have *flourished*. They have *adapted*. But you have not. You, Lord Hanged Man, jeopardize New Atlantis."

"Is this concerning a grievance against the Sun Throne," Lord Strength asked, "or are you accusing the Hanged Man of larger acts against our interests?"

"Both. It certainly started as a grievance. One of the most distasteful parts of his character tried to find root in my court."

"This is——" Lord Hanged Man started to say.

"You are a pedophile."

I turned to face him, and heard the unrest of the crowd as they reacted to the word. "You interfere with minors. You interfered with one of my retainers, a fifteen-year-old by the name of Layne Dawncreek, and left him dying in a shallow grave. You seek now to marry my seventeen-year-old ward against his wishes."

"It is a marital alliance brokered by his grandmother, and there is nothing untoward about that," Lord Hanged Man said loudly.

"He is a minor, and you seek to possess him against his wishes. There is *everything* untoward about that."

Across the room, the Priestess shifted in her chair. She was a mother to over three dozen children. In an age of diminishing fertility, her court had always overflowed with offspring.

"And it's not enough that you interfered with Layne Dawncreek," I said. "You decimated his family to obtain him. You left his twelve-year-old sister with hideous facial burns. Harmed a boy who was barely three years old at the time. And you killed the Atlantean scion of a bonded Companion. I have a Companion, Lord Hanged Man. It is one of our most ancient traditions. Do you have any idea what it does to the Companion, when her scion dies? Do you have any idea what you've done to Corinne Dawncreek?"

"It's a walking death," someone whispered. The virtual image of Lady Moon, who had married her own Companion, flickered.

"But, as Lord Strength said, those are just my personal grievances," I said to the room. "I'm quite capable of handling them on my own. The fact remains that these disgusting acts drew me into the Hanged Man's orbit, where I learned of the real threat to this city. He has gone unchecked for too long. The punishments he's faced have been too lax. He has grown indulgent and impulsive, and his sick hobbies will put this entire island at odds with the human world."

"And how is that?" the Hanged Man said. "What armies do I have? How, *exactly*, am I threat to humanity?"

"There it is again," I said, with another finger point in his direction. "That utter lack of understanding about how things work in the modern era. You don't start a war with armies anymore. You start wars with head-lines. How do you think the human world will react when they learn of the USS *Declaration*?"

"That matter has been addressed," Lord Judgment said. "Decades ago. He has made reparations."

"He hasn't, because it's still happening. I've been there. I've seen that sick playground."

"You trespassed," Lord Hanged Man said bluntly.

"I did. If I hadn't, I would never have seen what a threat that ship has become to the autonomy of New Atlantis. If people know what you do on that ship, it would cause global outrage. We would drown in the consequence. America would turn on us. The pacts that gave us this land? Nantucket? Gone. Over. They would turn on us in a heartbeat."

"How so?" Lord Wheel asked sharply. He loved America—he'd trav-elled it for decades. He greatly enjoyed the freedom of his visa.

"He abases the dead. He has their remains arranged in theater. The trauma done to every soul on that ship has never settled—they are still damaged to this day." I flicked a look to Lady Death and Lady Priestess, both who had very strong feelings about the well-being of souls. "The entire Arcanum could devote six months to that ship, and we'd barely raise enough Soul Binds to drive half the ghosts to rest. I'm not even sure a Soul Bind would work. He has frozen their grief. He preserves the moment of their death in stasis."

I moved on quickly; I'd circle back to it soon enough. "It's not unlike the abattoir in that skyscraper of yours, Lord Hanged Man. That mushroom farm."

"More trespassing," the Hanged Man said, though his voice was now a soft whisper.

"More trespassing," I agreed. "And more headlines. You sell those mushrooms to the city. To the human world. What would happen, if they learned you fertilize the soil with corpses? It's one step short of cannibalism. It is an atrocity. You preyed on the weaker houses in the city to fuel an *atrocity*."

I turned back to the room while pulling a piece of paper out of my pocket. The one Quinn had given me. I'd asked him to return to the moment on the skyscraper roof, to remember the broken lifelines he'd been forced to see. I read, "Howell. Lambarti. Rusknokov. Quincy, Brushmane, Zimbata, Ionic. Dozens more. *Dozens more!* Were they all your brides and grooms?" I looked at the Hierophant, the Hermit, and the Fool. They were among the weaker Arcana, more prone to sell distant kin into marriage as a way to shore up their power base. I'd read names from their courts. Lesser houses that had, over the years, permitted marital arrangements with the Gallows.

"Is this true?" Lord Hierophant said.

"Zebulon," the Hermit said. "Cousins of cousins . . . I remember one. He married her."

"His brides and grooms always vanish," I said. "Haven't you ever wondered where they went?"

"They are removed from the public eye, safe in the Westlands!" Lord Hanged Man shouted. "How dare you bring my marriages into this! This is not decorum. These are not things we speak of in this room!"

"That would be a mistake, and I'll gladly see it put to a vote. Headlines, Lord Hanged Man. You beg for headlines."

"I will kill you," he said. "Raid me. Raid me, Rune Sun. I will kill you."

"Will you?" I said. "Or will you just bring me to the point of death, and put my suffering in stasis? You are very good with that blend of stasis and time magic. You like returning to the moments of your depravity again and again."

"What is this?" Lord Judgment said sharply. "What did you say?"

"Do you remember me?" I asked. I walked to the edge of the pedestal. One toe-length away from the Hanged Man's own circle. "Once, in the past, you saw me on your ship, and tried to pull me through time. As an amusement. Don't you remember? *Like a match flame held behind rice paper.* Have you figured out yet that it was me?"

As surprise and uncertainty flickered across the Hanged Man's face, Lord Judgment leapt to his feet. "*What is this?* I will not repeat myself again."

I looked at Lord Tower. He regarded this appeal stonily, and said, "This is new information. I learned of it barely a day or so ago. I am investigating it."

"What does that mean?" Lord Judgment said. He spun and faced the Hanged Man, and banged the staff of office against the ground. "Have you used time magic?"

"A parlor trick at most," Lord Hanged Man insisted.

"That is a lie," I said. "The ship is littered with items that retain not only their form prior to the application of stasis magic, but their smells. You can smell the cordite, and burning rubber. Even physical properties like the glow of melting metal. Normal stasis spells do not work like that, not unless they're doctored with other magical disciplines. He's using time magic, and he is very good at it."

"It has harmed no one!" Lord Hanged Man roared.

"How long?" Lord Judgment said in horror. He looked at the Tower, and something passed between them.

Judgment looked like he was about to say something else, but stopped himself. Once again, I knew I was missing the real language of the discussion; I was only getting an impression of a larger issue.

Lord Judgment said, visibly upset, "No. Not here. This discussion will not happen here. We will hear Lord Sun on the matter of a raid tonight. Sunset. We will continue this discussion at sunset in the true Arcanum, where our privacy is assured. All Arcana will be there in person."

"This is insane. I require more time to answer these half-truths and misdirections," Lord Hanged Man protested.

"You will not get it," Lord Judgment said. "You will be there, or I will find you myself."

"In a room of killers, you would cast stones at me?" the Hanged Man said. The barest hint of a flush rose under his dead-man Aspect. "This hypocrisy will not go unanswered. You . . ." He looked at me. "You actually think you'll win."

All my aces had been played. I didn't need to circle around my rage anymore—not around my anger at the jeopardy Max had been in; the loss that the Dawncreeks had been exposed to; the deaths of those poor sailors.

So I said, "Yes. I will win. Because you're ready to fall. I have as big an ego as the next guy—don't get me wrong. I'd love to think it all came down to my skill and power—that I forced my way onto your ship, and up to the top of your skyscraper. But the truth is that your defenses are lax. You've been allowed to operate unchallenged for so long that you're not even taking the most basic precautions against intrusion. Defense shields around the ship with an elemental weakness? One ifrit and its pet dinosaur? You've grown fat and lazy, like a fly outside the swatting distance of the horse's tail. Taking you down won't require a feat of brilliance. It'll be as easy as sticking out my foot and watching you crash over it as you pace around giving your mastermind oration."

I pitched my voice low, for his ears only. "And think on this. I know a lot of prophets. I am hip-fucking-deep in prophecies about my future. Are you? Are there any prophecies about your future?"

"Oh, child," he whispered. He got to his feet and went to the edge of his own pedestal, so that barely an arm's length separated us. "Oh, child," he repeated. His breath left imaginary traces of death on my skin, like ashes from a house fire.

"Go ahead," I said. "Take a swing. Take two. It. Won't. Matter."

Judgment slapped his hands together in an angry clap. "Sunset. This meeting is adjourned. *Now.*"

"I'll discuss the logistics with Rune," Lord Tower said.

He stood up and brushed his hands along the lap of his trousers.

"Let's talk, little brother," the Tower said.

He led Ciaran and me through the door we'd entered. Brand and the others were in the hall, and they'd been joined by Mayan. Brand and Mayan were in spitting range of each other, having a low, furious conversation.

Lord Tower lifted his palm to a blank wall. The marble melted and spiraled into a round opening, showing another room beyond. He stepped over the threshold without seeing that we would follow.

"You're not going to keep calling me brother, are you?" I asked, hurrying behind him. "It makes me feel funny."

His shoulders squared, but he didn't reply.

The new room was a waiting area—strictly utilitarian, but built from the best materials. When we'd all crossed into it, he held up his palm again, and the doorway resealed.

"Rune," he said, his voice as blank as I'd ever heard it. "There are certain things you heard in that room that made no sense to you. Certain . . . proper nouns. You will assume it's not safe to speak of them, until we have a private moment."

"But what *happened?*" Max asked. "Can't you tell us that?"

"Oh, he was very dashing," Ciaran said. "Though he made poor use of the cape."

"Did you fight?" Brand said. "Your adrenaline kept spiking. Are you hurt?"

"That would make you happy?" Mayan asked. "Having your scion fight while you sat outside the door?"

"I didn't fucking *know!*" Brand shouted, and it had the sense of a middle-of-the-argument line. "He walked in there with his own plan!"

"You should know him well enough to predict these things!" Mayan shouted back.

"You're no one to fucking talk. The Tower's hand is so far up your ass that he probably can draw your knives for you!"

The Tower—who'd started pouring a finger of amber liquid from a decanter—put down his glass with a single, loud click. "That will be enough."

Mayan's nostrils flared, but he kept his mouth closed.

"May I expect better of you?" Lord Tower asked, staring at his Companion.

"Of course, Lord Tower. Apologies."

"Then please watch the Hanged Man."

Mayan gave a tight bow—barely a nod—as the Tower unsealed the room long enough to let Mayan out.

The Tower settled his gaze on Brand. "May I expect better of you, as well? We are in a serious moment, Brandon."

"Of course it's serious. You're not in pajamas, and you put on some fucking shoes."

"Oh gods," I whispered, and smothered my face in my hands. "I need a drink too. Brand? Please?"

"It's all right, Rune," the Tower said. "It couldn't have been easy for Brand. Mayan doesn't like to wait outside either. But, Brand, perhaps I should point out that the threat has not ended, which means I require you to *do your fucking job.*"

I pried apart my fingers to look, because I'm not sure I'd ever heard the Tower drop an F-bomb.

That didn't pass by Brand either. I'm not sure there was even a word for the expression on his face, both alarmed and alarming.

Addam cleared his throat. "I would like to know what happened, godfather."

The Tower continued to stare at Brand, then picked up his drink again. "It was much of what you'd have expected. Rune presented evidence against the Hanged Man. Rune intends to make a bid to form a raiding party."

"And will there be one?" Addam asked.

"In the normal way of things, the Hanged Man would have had a chance to refute the evidence. There are exceptions, of course. The raid that took down Lady Lovers was authorized *in absentia*. But then again, we had a two-thirds majority. Her presence was never needed. I'm not sure Rune will start with that support." Lord Tower paused, and nodded at Matthias. "Apologies, if the memories unsettle."

"They don't," Max said. "My grandmother tried to sell me. What do you mean *would have had?* Why won't the Hanged Man defend himself?"

"Oh, trust me, he will defend himself. But this will not end in a council session. He will retaliate soon." He poured another drink, and handed it to me.

I sipped so deeply my jaw clicked. Whiskey. It burned like cheap gasoline for all of three seconds, and warmed to gold and honey. I coughed and said, "Maybe Lord Judgment will issue raid approval *in absentia*. He can do that. I think he wants to do that. You saw him. He nearly had a heart attack when I mentioned time—"

And that's when Lord Tower's calm pretense evaporated.

He slammed his drink down and said, "Even the fact you'd say such a thing out loud demonstrates how fantastically unprepared for this you are! I just *warned you*."

"You're right—fine—but I am *not* unprepared," I said angrily. "I've trained—"

"This is not about your talent. It's not about your brain. It's not about your capability. It's about *what you do not know*. Do you think it's as simple as Lord Judgment being offended at the use of forbidden magic? Do you think his sense of rules so fragile? Has it occurred to you that there are reasons certain magic has been forbidden? There are doorways which must remain closed. *You do not know.*"

In the tension that followed, Quinn said, "Does he need to?"

"Quinn," Addam murmured.

"No, Addam," Quinn said. "I'm right. Well, I mean, right *now* this second I'm right. None of this is important *now*. All that matters *now* is stopping the Hanged Man. He's going to try to hurt us. It's going to happen. I can feel it already happening."

"He will try," the Tower agreed.

Quinn searched his face for some sort of understanding, then let loose a frustrated sound. "You're acting like you're going to make a plan. But everything is screaming. Everyone is screaming. It's already too late." Quinn rubbed at his nose. "Now there's just fighting, and you're one step behind instead of two steps ahead because you're focusing on the wrong thing."

"Quinn Saint Nicholas," Lord Tower said in a low voice. "We have had this conversation. Do not spin prophecies around me."

"Then don't spin plans around *me*," Quinn said, in the most clear and lucid voice I'd ever heard from him. "There are bigger things at stake than hurt feelings. I don't see ocean waves the size of skyscrapers around *you*—I see them around *him*. Wake up and pay better attention. You've waited so long for this moment to arrive—for the beginning to really start—that you don't realize you're in peril of driving right through it."

He sneezed and blinked. A trickle of blood ran from one nostril.

He smudged it along the side of his hand, and gave us a worried look.

I tried to kill the tension by turning to Lord Tower and saying, "So I suppose this means you're going to fall in line?"

Lord Tower gave me a blank look for a moment, and then, thankfully, the corner of his lips twitched. "Little Brother," he said.

"You know I had a crush on you when I was younger, right?" I said. "Can you see why that's creeping me out?"

Lord Tower's phone chimed, interrupting us. He pulled it from his breast pocket, read the screen.

Then he flung a hand at the door, which spiraled open. Mayan was in the room in a second. Lord Tower said, "Where?"

"Nearby."

"What is it?" I asked.

"Fatalities reported," Mayan said. "Assailant unknown. We're not secure."

Quinn said, "I see screaming icicles."

ENDGAME, PART I

Brand pulled the diary out of a jacket pocket, ripped it in half, and dislodged a thin ceramic throwing knife from the lining in the spine. Mayan had produced a secret weapon of his own—an extendable baton.

We hustled out of the room. The door to the Arcanum's chamber was open, and Lord Judgment had spilled from it with a small group of Arcana. I spotted Lady World, Lady Death, and Lord Hierophant.

Judgment lifted his staff of office and banged it against the stone floor. He barked the word, "*Seal!*", and magic flowed along the stone corridor. The sensation was familiar—I'd done something similar to Addam's family home in the Westlands.

"Which levels did you seal off?" Lord Tower asked.

"Our floor and the main boundary."

"So we're in here with whatever is killing people?" I heard Max ask nervously from behind me.

"No, child," Lady World said. "We are Arcana. *They* are in here with *us.*"

"Nevertheless," Lord Tower said, "We need intelligence on what, exactly, has happened. Mayan and Brandon, take point."

Mayan and Brand exchanged a look. I've never known them to decide on the color of the sky without fighting, but they wordlessly came to an agreement. Mayan took the lead, while Brand faded to the rear.

Mayan led us down the hallway, toward the checkpoints that separated the Arcanum's floor from the main Convocation building. We saw the bodies almost immediately—scattered along the hard stone in front of the privacy booths where we yielded our weapons and sigils.

Lord Judgment started toward the fallen guards, but Lord Tower held up a hand. "Preserve the scene, for the moment," he said. "Mayan. Brandon." He hesitated a second, and added. "Rune."

I took the compliment with just a blink or two. Mayan, Brand, and I walked forward, cautiously, stopping within a foot of the first body. I wish the dampening bracelet was gone; I would have been able to uncoil my sabre, at least.

"This makes no sense," Mayan was the first to say.

"We need to get closer," Brand said.

We walked between the bodies, careful not to disturb anything evidentiary. The rest of the group shifted to the spot where we'd just been standing.

There were a total of eight dead men and women. Some with fatal wounds. Some dead but unmarked. Some lay in blood spatter patterns; others had just fallen dead where they stood. One dead woman still had a dagger in her hand. Its blade was sunk into the neck of a creature with shriveled brown skin. The flesh was tight over muscle and dehydrated fat, with the exception of plump cheeks. It looked like those apple dolls human children made, an uneasy blend of rot and cute appeal.

"It's a banshee," I said. "Godsdamnit, a banshee was on the loose. It must have been an old one. Banshee screams usually wouldn't kill this many."

Mayan said, "Blade scores on the creature. They attacked it."

Brand knelt down. "Look at the pattern. It took a lot of hits. Some of the wounds are bleeding more than others—meaning its heart pumped a while before it died. Why didn't the banshee scream the first time it was hit?"

"That's a very good question," Mayan murmured approvingly.

I felt a prickle of . . . something . . . and the hairs on my arm lifted. Looking around me, I saw only three possible exits. The weapons checkpoint ended in a magical barrier that shimmered like liquid nitrogen. Wisps of magic curled off its surface. That would be the shield Lord Judgment had set.

The hallway continued in the other direction. And there was also an alcove, where I caught a glimpse of a metal door.

The shadows in the alcove shifted. Spidery fingers crept along the corner of the archway, pulling a shriveled, grayish face into the light.

"Banshee," I whispered. "My four."

Three things happened at once.

Lady Death shouted, *"NO!"*

Brand whipped toward my four o'clock position and cocked the ceramic knife.

I grabbed Brand's sleeve on an instinct I couldn't even properly explain.

Brand would likely have taken the monster in the throat, but my disruption sank the knife into its chest, close to where a human heart would be.

"Heal it!" Lady Death shouted. "We need to heal it *NOW!*"

Insight exploded in the back of my brain. I scrambled over to the dead banshee on the ground and peeled back its eyelid. There was no iris—just a single dark pupil. "Winter banshee," I whispered. "It's a winter banshee." In the wake of shock came fear. "Addam, the kids, get the kids out of here now!"

"Our sigils are locked up," Lord Hierophant said. "If I had them, I could heal—"

Magic flared. Lady World had thrown back her head, and was floating off the ground. Magical runes made of living green moss rose to the surface of her skin, and a crown of rosemary needles appeared on her forehead. A pale, honeyed light washed from her in an unnaturally slow wave. As the light seeped over me, all pain disappeared. My trick shoulder. My knee—from where I banged it throwing myself to the ground. All gone.

With her Atlantean Aspect upon her, Lady World floated to the fallen banshee. She lowered to its side, touched its chest, and poured magic into him.

"It's bloody difficult with these damnable bracelets on," she panted. "But I've stabilized it."

"What's a winter banshee?" Addam said. He had Quinn's sleeve in one hand and Max's in another, ready to run.

"A race thought to be dead or secured underground," Ciaran said. "Too dangerous to walk the streets. Its cry is much stronger than the average banshee, but it only screams as a death curse. If it had died, we'd be dead now."

"*Oh*," Quinn said. "Icicle screams. That wasn't very helpful of me at all, was it?"

Brand gave me a horrified look. "I didn't know. I thought—"

"Brand," Mayan said, loudly but not sharply. "I would have done the same. Focus now. What do you see?"

Brand blinked away his emotion and settled into his bodyguard mode. He stared at the banshee lying quietly under Lady World's ministrations. "It's not struggling. It's not attacking."

"These are old, old creatures of the Bone Hollows," Lady Death said, referring to her court. "I thought I'd imprisoned the last of them when I took over from my mother. They are barely sentient, and used as puppets. Controlled at short range. We'll find someone nearby with a wand made from elephant ivory. It will have runes inscribed with melted rubies, glowing red."

"It's a delaying tactic," Lord Tower murmured. "Lord Hanged Man is keeping us pinned down, for some reason."

"We shouldn't make assumptions yet," the Hierophant said. "Let's focus on the matter before us. If we regain our sigils, the creatures will pose no harm to us."

"But they'll pose a threat to bystanders," Lord Judgment said. "Gods. What am I thinking?"

He banged his staff of office on the ground again. The tip of the staff rippled as humming waves of sound radiated outwards. When he spoke next, his voice came from the very walls of the building.

"*This is Lord Judgment. The building is locked down while members of the Arcanum handle a grave threat. There are creatures on the premise that look much like banshees. Do not attack. Do not interfere. They are dangerous only at the moment of their death. I repeat again, do not attack, at risk of death. Allow us to handle the emergency.*"

He tapped the staff again. "I'm going to release the shield on our floor, so we can seek out any other creatures in the building and keep them contained until we recover our sigils."

As he issued the command with his staff, I saw a flash of movement in the corner of my eyes. I turned to see Mayan grab an axe from the waistband of a dead guard. He was rushing toward Lady World. On the ground beneath her wide-eyed surprise, the banshee was raking its ragged, desiccated fingernails across its jugular. Mayan swung his arm back, and slammed the axe blade across the creature's throat. Its head rolled free.

Lady World looked like she was about to slap the literal life out of Mayan. Lady Death stepped forward with both hands raised. "Peace, sister. It was about to self-terminate. I think Lord Tower is right—it has instructions to keep us pinned in place. It didn't react until we made plans to move past it. Rudimentary, but effective."

"Are we so sure this is the Hanged Man?" Lord Hierophant asked.

"We'll know when we find the control device," Lady Death said. "And whoever is using it."

"We need our sigils," I said. "We need to get these bracelets off."

"Agreed. We should split up," Lord Judgment said. "One group finds a way into the armory to secure our sigils, another group tries to locate the person controlling the banshees."

I practically heard Brand roll his eyes. In situations like this, he didn't hear, "Let's split up. It will be a tactical advantage." What he heard was, "Let's split up. The sorority girls take the ramshackle hut on the edge of the property; the frat boys take the overgrown graveyard."

Brand muttered, "What makes it even more fun is Rune's wearing a red shirt."

Mayan actually cracked a smile at this. He shook blood off the axe and stood up. "Lord Tower, I can't allow you to split up until you have your sigils. None of you have any abilities to call on, outside your Aspect, due to the bracelets. That needs to be our first priority."

"I . . . may be able to assist," Lord Hierophant said. "I have a certain . . . practiced influence over control devices. I could remove the bracelets from two, perhaps three of us, though it would leave me insensible afterwards."

"Could you," Lord Judgment said, and gave the Hierophant a steady look. "I wasn't aware you wore the bracelet as a choice."

"It's a difficult endeavor," Lord Hierophant said stiffly. "And as I said, it leaves me vulnerable."

I wasn't surprised in the least that Lord Hierophant was good with control devices. He had a terra-cotta soldier hidden in his Westlands compound, a golem strong enough to tear buildings apart with its bare hands. Being able to control it was a requirement of ownership. But I'd promised I wouldn't speak about that to anyone, so I threw him some cover. "It's a solid offer. I vote we take him up on it."

"Lady World and Lady Death are disciples," Lord Tower added. Some Atlanteans, rather than invest their training in sigil magic, practiced grueling, lifelong magical disciplines. They were able to manifest limited and specific abilities without sigils. Lady World was an adept at nature magic; and Lady Death was the strongest frost mage in existence. "Remove the bracelets from them, and Rune."

"Me?" I said, before I could help myself.

"I've watched you take on groups of armed men with nothing more than a light cantrip. You can handle yourself without sigils, and you'll be able to use your sabre."

"Oh," I said. Was that the second time he'd complimented me? I wasn't sure how I felt about the Tower deferring to me. Did Quinn break him?

"Then we move on the armory," Judgment said. "It's behind that metal door. Can you take it down with frost magic?"

Lady Death stepped over the banshee's head and stared at the door. "I can make it brittle. We'll need to ram it."

Brand cleared his throat. "I may be able to help with that. I . . . forgot . . . I had some plastique on me."

"Brandon," Lord Tower sighed.

"I brought some accidentally as well," Mayan said in solidarity with Brand.

"We will be rethinking our weapons policies," Judgment said, but wiggled his staff at the Hierophant.

Lord Hierophant called on his Aspect—a surge of elemental earth magic that turned his skin to marbled quartz, while his eyes leaked magma tears. He rotated his hands in a complex gesture, and the bracelet snapped from Lady World's wrist.

The pressure of his Aspect increased, and my breathing became labored.

The bracelet snapped from Lady Death's wrist and my wrist at the same time. Lord Hierophant's Aspect vanished and he began to sag. Brand, probably thinking being helpful would eclipse the fact that he'd smuggled explosives into the Arcanum, offered his shoulder, which Lord Hierophant grasped. Brand led him over to a padded bench not far down the hallway.

"Addam," I said. "Can you take Max and Quinn back to the Icons-gison? If there are banshees there, find another empty room."

"But I can help!" Quinn said.

"Not until the banshees are accounted for. I can't fight and worry about you, not with creatures like this about." I looked at Addam, whose jaw was set mulishly. "Please. Please, Addam. I need to know our kids are safe."

Max, who was about to add his own complaints to the mix, went quiet. He stared at me, then tugged on Quinn's sleeve, nodding.

"They will be safe," Addam promised me, and led them back the way we'd come.

Mayan and Brand produced their contraband—Mayan from a hidden compartment in his boot heel, Brand from the tube of eczema cream. Lady Death, free of the bracelet's dampening power, touched the metal door and sent waves of frost magic into it. The metal squealed and made brittle cracking noises. Waves of glittering fog rose off it. When she was done, Brand and Mayan traced thin lines of explosives around the hinges.

"Did you bring a fuse?" Mayan murmured.

"Disguised as shoelaces. But they're short," Brand murmured back.

"I've got this," I said. "Everyone move."

The group retreated to a safe distance. I shook my sabre off my wrist and aimed the hilt. The first shot made a blackened dent against a hinge. The second shot struck true, and an explosion of magnesium-bright light was immediately followed by a sheering sonic boom. The metal door toppled into the hallway.

"Take point," Mayan told Brand. "You're better in ambushes."

"Roger."

"Because you *lead* him into ambushes so often," Mayan added, just in case Brand thought he was being too friendly.

"Fucking roger," Brand said again.

I came up to his side, and we led the group into the armory suite.

A single hallway, decorated in gray carpet and modern florescent light fixtures, led about thirty feet into the building, ending in closed double doors.

The carpet was crowded with bodies.

None of the neat, unmarked deaths of banshee screams. This had been a fight. All of the bodies wore guarda uniforms, but Brand was quick to point out the differences.

"Frayed collar on that one. Sewn tear on that sleeve. Those buttons are square, not round like the other guarda uniforms."

"Lord Hanged Man's men?" I guessed, though it really wasn't much of a question. I knelt by one body in a false uniform, and pushed aside the collar of the shirt. There was a brass torc around his neck that emanated a nasty, slippery magic. "Control collars." They reminded me of the master-slave devices I'd seen in the Green Docks. Horrible devices to force people to act against their survival instinct.

"The Hanged Man infiltrated the Convocation's guarda ranks," Lord Judgment said behind us. It was a casual tone, and not at all unlike the one the Tower used when he ordered an execution.

Ciaran said, "Well, that's that. It's all over but for the tears and bandages."

"What is he hoping to accomplish?" Lady World wondered. "Why delay us? Is he running to ground?"

"He'll have a bolt-hole," Lady Death said. She had not relinquished her hold on her frost magic. Tendrils of fog twined about her fingers and drifted into the air. She added, "We all do."

"He does," Lord Tower said. "A compound in the arctic circle. Very remote. Impossible to take by stealth. It will be a costly nuisance to dig him out."

"Lord Sun," Judgment said. "Under the emergency powers granted to me as head of the Arcanum, I approve your request to mount a raid on the Gallows."

"The Gaia Throne will join," Lady World said.

"As will the Dagger Throne," Lord Tower added. "And I am reasonably convinced the Chariot will attend us."

"The Bone Hollows makes bid as well," Lady Death said.

"I think I heard the Hierophant say something rather enthusiastic outside," Ciaran announced from the back. "And I'd wager the Magician would hate to be left out. What fun. You'll certainly need to rename the Iconsgison after this."

"Stay on task," Mayan said. "Brand, move us forward."

We hadn't gone more than ten steps when the double doors at the end of the hallway burst open. Six men with guns, two rows deep and three abreast, rushed forward, firing.

A blast of wind pushed the bullets off course, a furious gale that shoved me from behind, courtesy of Lady World. Lady Death threw up a shield—a rocky wall of ice that shivered under the gunfire. The bullets didn't pierce, but cracks sent chips of ice flying at us like broken glass.

"Judgment is down," Mayan barked. "Get *low, people!*"

I ducked down and turned to look at the Ladies Death and World. "Can either of you see in the dark?"

"I can," Lady World said.

"I'll take the lights, Lady Death drops the wall, you hit with precision." A drop of blood raced down my cheek and over my lip. I'd taken damage from the ice barrier. "Ready?"

Lady World whispered something, and her eyes rolled with a faint green light. "Ready."

"Shield down," Lady Death said.

The barrier cracked and exploded outward. I fired my sabre at the light fixtures overhead. The room went dark in quick stages. Before the last chunk of ice from the barrier hit the ground, Lady World sent another gale of wind howling down the hallway, turning the shards into grenade shrapnel.

All six armed guards went down. Lady World sent veins of luminous moss racing along the walls, bathing us in a dull light. Mayan and Brand whisked down the corridor, using weapons from dead guards to take out the survivors.

"Save one!" Lord Tower barked, just as Mayan cut the throat of the last threat. Mayan looked ahead of him, into whatever room was on the other side of the double doors. He said, "We have one. He's holding a pretty white wand."

I took a second to look back, to see how badly Lord Judgment was hurt. He was propped against the wall, still conscious, a hand pressed over his bleeding shoulder. He saw my look and said, "Get our sigils. Retrieve the control device. Lead your raid, Lord Sun."

I straightened and walked down the hallway, stepping over bodies. The remaining eddies of wind magic made my cloak flutter, which I was sure pleased Ciaran.

The room on the other side was a security center. Large, and filled with banks of monitors and computer stations.

Sitting in a swivel chair, an ivory wand glowing red in his lap, was Jirvan.

"If I do anything against the interests of Lord Hanged Man, the device on my neck will release a fast-acting poison," he said calmly. "I can tell you that much."

Others gathered in the room behind me. I expected the Tower to step in, but, when I glanced at him, he only waited. Lady Death caught this and grinned, saying, "I'm not the baby of the family anymore! Very well. Dance for us, Rune."

I walked over to Jirvan, pulled up another swivel chair, and sat down. "You have my leave to act within the parameters of the device. Don't answer any questions, or perform any action, that would cause the poison's release."

Jirvan swallowed. He nodded.

"I am not blind to the fact that you tried to warn me earlier," I said. "I do not believe you want to be here. I do not believe you wanted matters to come to this. I know what it's like to be left with no choices."

"Thank you, Lord Sun," he said.

"But matters have come to a head. We need the information you can offer. Are you able to tell me anything about the device around your neck?"

He paused, then shook his head *no*.

"Does the torc have more than a single charge?"

The scarred muscles on Jirvan's neck twitched. With a scared expression, he closed his eyes and shook his head no. When nothing happened, he sighed, and opened his eyes again.

"If you were in a position to help us, would you?" I asked. "Are you worth saving, Jirvan?"

He licked his lips and said, "I walk with a limp, because I use a prosthetic. Imagine, if you will, a man who uses a prosthetic because he had displeased his master. Imagine a master who believes in grotesque responses to displeasure, as a way of making his feelings known, and serving as examples to others. Imagine a man whose leg was removed, and cooked, and served at dinner. Imagine a man who knows the taste of his own burned flesh. Would a man like that want to be saved?"

"What would happen if we try to retrieve our sigils? They'll be around here somewhere."

"I do believe that would be against my instructions," Jirvan said.

I swiveled my chair to face the people behind me. "Lady World, is your Aspect strong enough to slow the spread of poison? Or do you have any nature magic that would help?"

"Yes. Though I'd want the use of a healing sigil as quickly as possible."

"Our sigils?" I asked Lord Judgment, who'd been brought into the room.

"Past the vault door, there." He glanced at a heavy metal door in a corner of the room. "I have an override code."

"If you use the code—" Jirvan started, but I put a hand on his arm.

"Do you know the layout of the vault, Lord Judgment? Where our sigils are exactly stored?"

"Arcana have their own shelf," Lord Judgment said. His breathing had deepened, nearly to a pant. "The shelf is partitioned with court logos."

"Please share the code with Mayan. Brand, be ready, I'll need my ankh. Lady World, if you'll be ready, once the poison releases?" I turned back to Jirvan. "This is your only chance."

He nodded.

Sometimes things happen exactly as planned. Sometimes the universe throws you a meaty scrap of good luck. Mayan opened the vault. Brand dove into it. Jirvan stiffened as he made no move to stop us, thus releasing the poison. Lady World's Aspect flooded the room in healing light. I sat there, enjoying the narcotic warmth of her proximity, as she put her hands on Jirvan and fought the spread of death.

Brand rushed over to me with my ankh. I closed my fingers around it and released the stored Healing. I put my palm on Jirvan's scarred cheek and sent hot magic into his body. I felt the corruption of the poison boil and curdle, making Jirvan scream, because nothing about magic was painless, even the helpful kind. When I finally withdrew, I left a hand-shaped sunburn on his skin, but he was alive.

With shaking fingers, Jirvan undid the clasp on the back of the torc and threw it across the room. He said, "I hope you end him."

I leaned toward him, close enough to have him squirm. "Answer every question I ask, perform every order I issue, as quickly and efficiently as you can, to prove you were worth saving. Am I clear?"

The seneschal nodded.

"Make the winter banshees stand down."

Jirvan picked up the wand, which he'd dropped while being healed. He wrapped his thin fingers around it and began to move his lips silently. After a half minute, he nodded, and handed me the wand. Lady Death neatly inserted herself in front of me and plucked the control device out of my hands.

"I've reversed all earlier commands," Jirvan said. "The remaining banshees will gather outside the armory, under instructions to hurt no one."

"Mayan," I said, "please go tell Lord Hierophant what's happened, so that he's not startled into action when the banshees arrive. Then find Addam? Thank you."

Mayan left without objection, passing Lord Judgment on the way, who seemed taken aback by the insight of the instruction. Truth be told, I'm glad it had occurred to me.

"The banshees," I said to Jirvan. "They were to delay us from pursuit?"

"Yes."

"Why did he assume we'd pursue?"

"I'm not entirely sure. He only said that your final accusation damned him, and Lord Judgment or Lord Tower would set people on him immediately. He wouldn't be allowed to operate without eyes on him."

"Is he fleeing the island?"

"Yes. But . . . there is more. This isn't the only delaying action."

"Tell me," I said, and I felt my eyes warm, the oldest hint of my Aspect ascending, from the days when my irises would start glowing with a bright amber light.

I saw that light in Jirvan's frightened gaze. "He's retreated to the battleship. It is operational. He will attempt to deactivate some of the city's safeguards and launch a shore battery. The damage will be considerable, and he'll flee into the human world in the confusion."

"Is there anything else I need to know?"

He did not want to say whatever he was about to say. Ducking his gaze from mine, he whispered, "He went for the children."

"What children?" Brand said sharply. When Jirvan hesitated, Brand swooped in, grabbed the man by the jaw, and yanked his face upwards. *"What children?"*

"Lord Hanged Man found a flash drive. It showed a recording of a video feed. I'm not entirely sure what was on it, but it made him very keen on securing Annawan and Corbitant Dawncreek."

The bottom dropped out of my stomach. I saw it there—right in front of me, like a damned flow chart. Addam's security man handing me the deleted surveillance of the pool at Addam's condo. Me putting the flash drive in my pocket. It would have been on me as I bounced across rooftops. I'd probably left it right next to the fucking ifrit's body. It would have shown the crayon gargoyle dancing between Anna and Corbie. It was likely not even clear which of them had manifested the magic.

Brand pulled out his phone. After a second he said, "Corinne's voice-mail."

"Run, Brand. Get Addam. Tell him to try Diana, or his team, anyone. Go!"

Brand bolted out the door.

"We need to move on the battleship," Judgment said. "Tower, with me. We'll see if the Hierophant is sensible yet. Lady World?"

"I have a herd of pegasi nearby," she said. "We can move quickly."

"I'll wait with Rune," Lady Death said. "I'll follow if I can, or assist elsewhere if needed."

Lord Judgment came over. He removed his hand from his shoulder injury and clapped a bloodstain on my shoulder. "Apologies for the intervention, Sun. It's still your raid, but this must be handled."

"I need to make sure the children are okay. They're under my protection." Worry pounded in staccato with Brand's footsteps, as I felt him, through our bond, running for Addam.

"Well met, then, brother." He looked behind him, at the other Arcana. "Perhaps some of you would find your own sigils, and offer me a Healing spell of my own? I've been bloody shot. And let's get these damn bracelets off too."

ENDGAME, PART II

I was used to causing mayhem and skipping out while the powers-that-be picked up the pieces. It was a modus operandi that worked well for me.

Now that I *was* the powers-that-be, I realized how much shit separated the potential momentum of a moment and the actual execution of it.

Lords Judgment, Tower, and Hierophant left for the battleship along with Lady World. Since I was waiting on word from the hospital, Lady Death and I were delegated oversight of the Convocation. We would need to find a spell-caster strong enough to take temporary ownership of the ivory wand, and give field promotions to fill new, and mortally emptied, leadership gaps in the guarda's chain of command.

Fortunately, I looked so hapless at the thought of doing that that Lady Death hurried out to administrate, leaving me to guard Jirvan. Jirvan, exhausted from the painful healing, was sound asleep, which more or less meant I was free to aggressively self-judge.

"I already messed up," I murmured.

"When?" Brand asked. He'd returned a few minutes ago, leaving Addam to contact the hospital, Max to keep ringing Lady Diana's line, and Quinn to reach Addam's security team.

"When the Arcana were all looking at me to question Jirvan," I said.

"What else were you supposed to do? It's your raid. And it's not *the Arcana*, it's *the other Arcana*. You're one of them now."

"I know, but I promised myself I wouldn't be like them. You and I are partners. We should have questioned him together. I know I missed some obvious questions."

Brand's face went neutral. "You did a very, very nice job."

"What did I miss?" I sighed.

He kept giving me that blank bodyguard face, which had always been his tell. He knew that, though, and tried to deflect. "I lost my cool when he mentioned the kids, too. It was easy to get distracted."

"If you tell me what I missed, I'll learn from my mistakes."

"Okay. *Maybe* you could have asked whether the Hanged Man had a guard contingent with him when he retreated to the ship. And maybe we could have found out if any of the houses in his court were going to rally to his side. And—and this just occurred to me—I'm not sure how he expects for a gun battery to get past city defenses. He's got to know something we don't."

I groaned. The last one was a particularly good question.

"Rune," Brand said, with an unusually serious look on his face. "We'll find the kids. This will be over soon. Beat yourself up later. Figure out the weirdness later." The expression softened, and he bumped my shoulder, this time without leaving a bruise. "*We'll* figure it out later, because *we* are still a *we*, regardless of your new country club membership."

I smiled at him. "And what about you and Mayan?" I marveled. "You were almost, like, chummy."

"That's strange? The Tower looks like he's halfway done writing the charter for your fucking fan club. Is this what it means to be on the Arcanum? People trying to get along with us?"

"I don't know. Maybe? What did you think it would be like?"

"That they'd throw money and resources at us, then leave us alone to do what we do best. But this is more like . . . teamwork. With other people. I don't really like other people."

"We're going to have problems with this," I agreed. "Maybe we should—"

Addam strode into the room. He had a stricken look on his face that bled bad news.

"Tell me," I said immediately.

"Corinne and the children are missing. Diana has already mounted a search and rescue mission. We have every reason to believe they have been taken."

"Why do they believe that?" Brand said.

"From what Diana has pieced together, Corbie had been off on his own. He must have been taken. There were signs of a . . . struggle. They may have used him as a lure to get Anna and Corinne."

"What sort of struggle?" I said.

Addam looked at me bleakly. "There was blood. And . . . teeth. Children's teeth. He must have been hit in the face." Addam saw the expression on my face and crossed to me. "He was likely just struck for compliance. There is not enough blood to signal a more serious injury. We will—"

I heard this through a dull, rising roar. My Aspect—the divine monster inside me, already fattened with today's emotion—burst forward.

I thought of blood and teeth; and a girl with a scarred face; and a dying Companion. I had brought them into this. Used them as bait. Used them as leverage to pry my way into the Hanged Man's court.

I may have lost a few seconds. The next thing I knew my chest was burning. Only it was cold, not heat. Lady Death was in front of me, and her palm, brimming with frost magic, was pressed over my shirt. The fabric glittered with rapidly melting, crusty ice.

"Are you with me, Rune?" she said.

I blinked away the orange light. The fire died. We were alone in the security room, except for the sleeping Jirvan.

She bunched her fingers in my shirt and shook me a little. "Listen to me, little brother. I'm going to teach you something I learned the hard way. Are you listening?"

Licking chapped lips, I closed my eyes and nodded.

"The fact that you can manifest an Aspect like that—one that has a physical impact on the world, not just a smoke-and-mirror reflection of your court—is a testament of raw power. There are very, very few people in the world who can do that. And the exercise of such a powerful Aspect will determine the type of court you build. If you manifest your Aspect on impulse or emotion, you will be surrounded by impulsive and emotional people. If you use it to cow your enemies, you will be surrounded by people who expect to be ruled by fear or strength, and will in turn rule others beneath them in the same way. But if you exert control—if you govern your Aspect with your will—your court will become an extension of those abilities, and not a reaction to it."

I cleared my throat and nodded again.

"Okay then. We've done as much as we can do here," she said, and brushed snow off my shirtfront. "We should operate as if these children of yours are on the battleship. I have cars waiting outside."

"There's not enough time," Quinn said from the doorway.

Lady Death and I turned toward him in unison.

Quinn flashed a guilty look over his shoulder, and back at me. "There are so few choices left. We can't reach the Tower—he's in the clouds—and when they land, they'll want to sink the ship."

The chill that swept through me was warmer than Lady Death's palm print. Even then, I almost hesitated. We very rarely acknowledged Quinn's gifts in front of others, no matter his tendency of blurting them out. We definitely didn't discuss his gift of seeing probabilities. It was a coveted ability, and would make him a target.

But there was no time for discretion.

"Are the kids on the ship?" I asked him.

Quinn did something that was half-shrug, half-nod. "You scream whenever the ship sinks. So . . . I think so. It's hard to see the specifics—just like it was before, when Max and I were there last time—there's strange energy there."

Powerful places protected by wards or hauntings had always screwed with Quinn's ability, even more so since we'd started blunting some of his abilities with medicine. I can't imagine how the presence of time magic would interact with Quinn's far-seeing.

I took a few breaths to calm myself, and quickly pulled apart what Quinn had said. The ship. I needed to keep the ship from sinking. Lord Judgment led the Arcanum. He knew the ship posed a threat to the shore. If I were him, and had to coldly calculate the best odds, I may be tempted to avoid a close-quarter fight—with potentially thousands of lives at stake—by sending the entire battleship to the floor of the ocean.

"We'll never get there quick enough driving," I said, and felt the urgency rising up my throat like a shout. "We need to find the kids before they decide it's easier to sink the *Declaration*. We need to get there now." I looked at Lady Death in desperation. "Please. Do you have any ideas?"

"Do . . ." She frowned. "Flight? Do you have Flying spells stored?"

"No."

"I don't have enough for even half of us. There's . . ." An idea lifted the muscles of her face—the way people did when surprised by a thought. And then frustration drew the muscles down into another frown.

"Please," I whispered.

"They are important to you. These children."

"They are," I said.

She waved her hand, dismissing the nimbus of frost magic, and then rubbed safely at her eyes. A disarmingly normal gesture. "This will be your birthday gift for the next sixty years. There's a fountain on the roof. Let's move there. Pick your companions."

"I need to come," Quinn said immediately.

"Must you?" Addam asked from behind him.

Quinn did a jerky twist and saw that others—Max, Brand, Addam, Ciaran, and Mayan—were crowded in the corridor outside.

"I stored four Clarity spells," Quinn said. "We'll need them."

Another detail I'd overlooked. Without some sort of spell to resist the fugue on the battleship, we'd be lost to the ghost visions. I should have warned Lord Tower—though likely he'd figured it out already, if he'd been there himself.

"And I may be able to help find the kids and Corinne quickly," Quinn added, speaking now to Addam.

"I'm getting good at helping Quinn understand his visions," Max jumped in. "This all started because of me. I want to be there. I want to help."

"You are my useful brother," Addam said to Quinn, and put a hand on the teenager's head for just a moment, smoothing the cowlick. "But you are still so young. There is so much you need to learn about situations such as this."

"This is part of that learning, Addam," Quinn said softly.

For a second I saw that lost expression on Addam's face, as he watched his brother get older before his eyes and move a little further away from where Addam was still standing.

Addam nodded.

"Then you all move out," Mayan said briskly. I hadn't even realized the Tower had left him behind—but then, he wasn't the same sort of Companion to the Tower that Brand was to me. Mayan would need a stable location to order Lord Tower's entire security unit into deployment.

Mayan looked over at Brand. "Reconsider?"

Brand paused, but shook his head. Mayan looked disappointed at that, but accepted it. "I'll make sure Jirvan is put in custody. Go. Hurry. I'll keep trying to raise Lord Tower. They won't wait long."

"Roof," Lady Death said, and pushed through the bottleneck in the doorway.

We moved in mass after her.

Brand was with me in the rear, so I whispered, "What was that with Mayan?"

"He wanted me to stay behind and organize backup with him."

"Oh," I said, surprised, and maybe a little uncomfortable.

Brand looked over at me. "You're not going to be like every other Arcana? I'm not going to be like every other Companion. I'm where I'm supposed to be."

I let it rest. I wasn't entirely sure why Mayan wanted Brand to remain behind, but, then again, this wasn't the first time in the last few days I'd misunderstood the undercurrents around Atlantis Companions.

Lady Death led us up a private stairwell to the hospital roof, where a small garden had been planted. The nature sprites tending the trees and shrubbery chittered excitedly as we burst out the door, flitting to the top branches and shedding excited sparkles of light.

Lady Death marched up to a large frothing fountain. She looked at us over her shoulder and counted. "We'll need to pair up. Odd man out gets his own steed."

"Quite unnecessary," Ciaran said. "I can move fast on my own. I'll do my best to hold Lord Judgment from a hasty decision. *Vaya con dios*, dears." He tapped a sigil on his neck—a pendant made of actual finger bones—and his suit ruffled with wind. He knelt down in a curtsy, and shot into the sky with a sonic pop. He did a wholly unnecessary figure eight above our heads, and cannonballed toward the north.

"Three steeds, then," Lady Death murmured. She shifted her gaze to me. "You better be worth these gray hairs."

She held out an arm. Her frost magic rose, forming shining rivulets of ice above the veins of her hand. The fountain's moving waters stilled. From a spot in its center, the liquid froze solid with a tremendous crack, radiating outwards, creating jagged fracture lines in the stone wall of the basin. Chips of ice flew into the air in a glittering haze.

"Come to me," she whispered. "Come to me. *Come to me!*"

This time, she used no sigil. What happened wasn't frost magic, nor a manifestation of her Aspect. I could identify no actual source of power—it was just suddenly there, blindingly bright to my inner eye, focused entirely on the solid ice before us.

The surface of the fountain splintered into spikes. Through the broken surface, creatures climbed upward. Horses of solid ice, one after the other, until three translucent beasts had clattered onto the tiled rooftop.

The horses reared, throwing their head toward the skies. The ice split like a shell, revealing white stallions shining with a pearl-colored light.

It took me a moment to realize I was looking at the ghost steeds of the Bone Hollows—creatures passed down through Lady Death's ancient bloodline. I still didn't know how she'd summoned them, though there were ideas forming in the back of my head, tied to those words I'd heard. What was the Arcana Majeure?

"Where is this battleship? In the Green Docks, I know, but where?" Lady Death asked.

"Northern point," Brand said. "Furthest ship out. Maybe a bit toward the northwest. You won't see it, though, unless you're as good as Rune at seeing weird shit. Just look for where the docks end."

"We double up," she said. "Riders with non-riders, if necessary. Mount."

The seating resolved itself with minimal muttering and bad feelings. Quinn and Addam were experienced riders, as was Lady Death. Max paired up with Quinn, and I felt it was only polite to take the spot behind Lady Death. That left Brand having to let Addam take the lead. I felt it grate along our bond, but Brand had sunk into his bodyguard mode, so you'd never tell by looking at his face.

I clambered up behind Lady Death after returning my sabre to wristguard form—with a lot of graceless flailing, but I ended up facing the right way. It had been ten years or more since I'd ridden a horse.

But this was not a horse. There was no saddle on the ghost steed, and its back gave way in a manner completely unlike real flesh.

"Trust your steed," Lady Death said. "It will find level ground. You only need to point it in the right direction, and it'll move in a straight line. Whatever you do, don't aim it at the center of the bloody earth, not unless you want to wind up as a very curious fossil a thousand years from now."

"Are you listening?" I heard Brand asked Addam.

Lady Death dug her heels into our steed, which reared. She shouted, "*Ta!*" and we leapt off the roof.

I'd thought the horse would fly. It didn't. It rocketed to the ground many, many stories beneath us. I felt the plunge in my stomach, but it was a curiously psychological sensation, the way your belly plunged when watching a roller coaster's descent on a television. We may have landed on a million mattresses, for all the impact I felt in my spine.

The other two horses went straight down, vanishing beneath the parking lot pavement. Quinn popped up almost immediately; and Addam about ten anxious seconds later.

Lady Death aimed her horse toward the north and shouted, *"Ta!"*

And we were off, leaving a glowing, phantomlike trail behind us. No living mammal could move as fast as we did. No real mammal, for that matter, had such blasé disdain for things like walls or people. We moved in a straight line, phasing through any solid object. Through buildings, speeding cars, food vendors and pedestrians; through a bank vault with gold bars stacked in pyramids; through a men's locker room, and then over the surface of an indoor lap pool. We moved so fast that I only caught the scenery in brief, fractional hesitations. In what couldn't have been more than ten minutes, skyscrapers become an industrial neighborhood. We rode through a warehouse filled with half-assembled yachts, and over a series of muddy canals. The Green Docks appeared on the horizon, a motley collection of canvas sails and rigging rising toward a bright mid-morning.

Rather than urge our party toward the boardwalk, Lady Death took us along the surface of the ocean in a wide circle. Even that was another curiously blank sensation—I saw waves break along our steed's hooves, but smelled no brine, felt no sea spray.

"There," Lady Death said, and pointed off to the left. I spotted Ciaran first, in his bright suit. He was all but sticking his finger up Lord Judgment's nose. They were gathered just outside the influence of the magical barrier that Lord Hanged Man had erected around the ship.

Lady Death took us toward that section of the boardwalk, covering the last few yards in a fantastic leap. When all four hooves were on the scuffed green planks, she reached back and took my hand in a firm grip. The ghost steed melted beneath us, bottom-up, lowering us to our own feet as it did.

Behind me, Addam's and Quinn's horses did the same. Brand caught my eye as he regained his footing and, for just a second, I saw a little bit of my own wonder reflected in his eyes.

There was no time for more, though. I was not a sightseer to this moment; I was its catalyst. It was time to take ownership of what I'd set in motion.

"Lord Sun, we can't be sure your subjects are on the ship," Lord Judgment said as I approached.

"They are not subjects—they are children. I need time to find them."

"Let me be clear. We've tried to create a barrier around the ship," he said, and the faint whiff of patronization nearly made me show my teeth. "Whatever magic Lord Hanged Man has raised to shield the vessel from our eyes is uncooperative. In the absence of raising a shield, I have no other option. We must destroy it."

"The shore is protected," Ciaran said loudly, as if he'd been arguing the same point over and over again. "Lord Magician himself worked on its wards. Gunfire from a World War II–era weapon *will not* succeed."

"That is the most obvious assumption, Ciaran," Lord Tower said, "which is why it's false. Lord Hanged Man knows something we do not. We must expect that the wards are compromised."

"I have made my decision," Lord Judgment said.

Now my lips did peel back. It was an animal instinct because, in the end, and in the beginning, and in every important middle point, we all acted from animal impulses. Dominance. Subservience. Show of strength.

This was my raid, and I would remain in control of it.

What I did next came less from a sense of confidence in myself than it did in every shattered half-truth and secret I'd learned over the last few months. Arcana, I now knew, had a power that no one had told me about. I'd just watched Lady Death summon extraordinarily potent creatures without any visible source of magic. In my own greatest need, not long ago, I'd torn the sky open.

So, with all my intent, and with all my control, I invited my Aspect to the surface.

I walked to the edge of the barrier Lord Hanged Man had raised around his ship. Days ago, I'd pierced it. Now I let fire race along my body, gathering as spheres around my hands that were so bright even I needed to close my eyelids against them. And I said to myself, *this barrier must fall*, and pushed out with all the potential to make it so. I imagined how it would have felt to have had a sigil filled with the right spell to make it happen, and that imagination, married to my willpower, became reality.

A nova's worth of light seared my eyelids, dying in seconds. When I opened them, the barrier was simply gone.

I asked my Aspect to retreat, as if it were a thinking being. And its fires died in a wind-like whoosh.

"This is my raid," I said to the people behind me, without turning. "I will find the children and their guardian, and I will hunt the Hanged Man to ground. Your help would be much appreciated."

I heard someone sigh, and Lord Judgment said, "Very well. I'm moving to the shore, to shield what I can. Lord Chariot is en route to assist me. The Tower will lead the party onto the ship."

"We should sink it," Lord Hierophant said to him. "That's what your gut is telling you."

"My gut is telling me I've been missing far too many gut impulses. Lord Sun, Lord Tower, you have little time. Go."

"We will find them," I said. "Quinn, please release your Clarity spells. Anchor one to me, and another on Lord Tower. If the situation requires us to divide our forces, the rest must keep to one of us. The ghost imagery on the ship is powerfully strong. They won't pose a threat, but the impact of them is disabling. The Clarity spell will protect you from that. Let's move."

Quinn released his spells, blanketing the crowd with each release, and yielding the control of the spells to Lord Tower and I. Brand and Addam took point, while the rest of us filed behind them. Lord Tower put a hand on my shoulder, though, and with an expression drew me to the rear of the group.

When we were apart, he said, quietly, "You will have figured out by now that you are using an ability we call the Arcana Majeure. It is a guarded secret, and there is no time to explain it. Do not rely on it, Rune. Do not trust it. Wait until we have time to talk."

"No magic is safe. If it helps me find the kids or take the Hanged Man down, I'll take the risk."

"The risk of what?" Lord Tower said, but patiently. "Damage to yourself? There is no *risk* of damage. You *are* damaging yourself every time you use it. There is a lifetime cost."

"Those kids are there because of me. I can handle the cost."

"Can Brand? Because you are injuring him too."

I stopped in my tracks. Stared at Lord Tower. My reaction was such a tangled ball of emotion that I couldn't separate the uncertainty from the anger.

"This is not something I could have told you sooner. You learn as it happens, and it's most unfortunate that it's happening now, in a living moment. Please, Rune. Do not rely on the Arcana Majeure until you understand it."

I continued walking up the gangplank. I didn't argue. It was just one more bit of weirdness to load into the bullet chamber and fire into my aching head later.

We rejoined the rear of the group. I could tell that some of the Arcana were messing about with the Clarity spell on them. Lord Hierophant, in particular, probably looked a lot like I must have, the first time one of the unnaturally cohesive ghosts ran through me.

They would also be noticing the other preserved damage—they would smell the powder of recently fired guns; see the destruction of the Hanged Man's decades-old assault fixed in the moment of delivery. Armed with my hindsight, they would already be figuring out that the stasis magic had been entwined with time magic to stage this damage.

I went through the crowd and shook the shoulder of anyone lost to the images, barking at them to re-engage the Clarity spell. I didn't like the look in Lord Hierophant's eye, in particular. If I had to, I'd lock the spell on him like a damn childproof gate.

"How did we not know this?" he whispered. "The audacity. He knows what's at risk. He knows what forces he's taunting."

"Quinn," I murmured. "Anything?"

"It's all going on at once," Quinn said, grimacing. "Then and now and next is happening at once. It's like someone screaming in my face."

"He'll know we're here," Lord Hierophant said. "He would have felt his barrier fall."

"Then we move quickly," I said.

I had an idea in mind, but before I could put it into motion, Lady World pushed to the edge of the group, facing the far end of the ship. I saw what she saw a moment later—a winter banshee coming toward us with haggard, floating steps.

The difference was that, now, we were armed. We had our sigils and our instruments of office.

She touched a bracelet around her wrist, then held out her arms. Twisting funnels of water rose from the sea. The water streamed around her hands and formed greenish, giant spheres that shuddered with miniature ocean waves. She bent her arms behind her, and flung the water at the banshee. They hit the creature in a splash that, instead of falling to the ground, writhed and twisted into an envelope.

The moment the envelope was sealed, Lady World jerked her hands in a sharp twist. Plumes of oxygen bubbled. The water grew dense with deep-sea pressure. Within the span of a second—before the banshee had any hopes of a death keel—the monster imploded in a froth of reddish water. Lady World jerked her hands again, and water and viscera splattered the ship decks.

I looked away from the sight in time to see Lord Hierophant monkeying with his Clarity again. I let my own slip for just a heartbeat. The world dimmed into a darker pallet of colors. Down the length of the main deck, I saw a fireball hit the catapulted plane like a rocket.

Drawing on my willpower, I took the tendrils of Clarity that linked me to Lord Hierophant, and wove it around him like a straightjacket. He didn't even seem aware of what I did; he just shook his head and stared in horror at the rest of us.

"These are actual tears in time," he said. "I'm sorry, Lord Sun. I know the lives of people you care about are at stake, but we must take action. We must sink this vessel."

I'm not entirely sure what happened next. He looked like he was moving to the stairwell ahead of him—not far from where I'd once seen two ghosts share a cigarette—but he lost his footing, tripped forward, and slammed into the bulkhead. He hit his head hard and collapsed into a blinking heap.

I took the win.

"There's no time," I said. "Lady World, would you stay with Lord Hierophant? He seems to require a Healing spell."

"We should find the firing controls," Quinn said suddenly, and nudged between Lord Tower and me. "There are two places they can fire missiles from. Up there in the bridge place. And down below."

Then he turned and gave me a half wink.

I made a deliberate choice not to look at Addam, who may or may not be realizing how well Quinn was getting at lying for our sake. "Quinn, will you release another Clarity spell, and anchor it to Lady World? Lady World, the bridge is in that main tower. Just there." I pointed. "I've been below deck before. I'll go there."

"We'll need to stay in touch," Lord Tower said, though, oddly, while staring hard at Brand.

"Easily done," Lady World said. She'd knelt by Lord Hierophant, who had a nasty cut along his forehead, but was conscious. She reached into her pocket and pulled a handful of green stones from them. There were enough to go around, and afterward she released a sigil spell that created a momentary web of green light around us before fading from sight. "It will open an audio channel, when you close your hand around it. An hour's worth of energy. But Lord Sun? We don't have an hour. You understand that?"

"We'll find the kids," I said. "We'll find the Hanged Man. This is ending. Stay in touch."

I stalked away from them without seeing who fell in line. Only after I turned a corner in the direction of the hatch that led to the eating galleys did I sneak a quick look. I was happy to see that Lady Death and Lord Tower had joined the group, along with Ciaran and the others. There'd be even less chance now that Lord Judgment would get trigger happy.

"Down there," I said, pointing to the hatch. "Keep your Clarity active."

"These are emeralds," Max said, staring at the green gemstone in his hands. "I think it's an actual emerald. Do we get to keep these?"

"Move," Brand said, tapping the back of Max's head, which was rather cheeky since I'd already seen him smiling appreciatively at his own gem.

I shook my wrist, loosening my sabre. The warm metal slid into hilt form, comfortable in my palm. I covered the others while they went down the steep, narrow metal stairs.

Lord Tower and Brand were last. Lord Tower blocked the path, and turned to stare at Brand. Brand got busy looking elsewhere.

"Brandon," the Tower said. "Let me be clear. I will cover for you, but this cancels out every favor, every debt, every shred of capital you've earned with me. Are we understood?"

To my surprise, Brand only mumbled, "Yes, sir."

As Lord Tower turned to climb down the stairs, I yanked on Brand's non-throwing arm. "What the hell?" I asked.

"Okay, see," Brand said, "if you look at it from a certain perspective, someone *might* think that it was my ankle Lord Hierophant accidentally tripped over."

I slapped a hand over my eyes.

"But I didn't push him," Brand said seriously, as if this was a compelling point.

"Godsdamnit. I'll still take the win," I said, and grabbed the overhead bar to guide myself down the steps.

* * *

There were all sorts of things to focus on downstairs.

Lady Death had dropped her Clarity against my advice and was staring at the small chapel in the corner of the mess hall. Quinn and Addam were arguing. Ciaran was standing between them with a vial of clear liquid.

"What are the risks associated with it?" Addam demanded. "Do you know? Or are you guessing?"

"It's the only way," Quinn insisted.

"What is?" I asked. Behind me, Brand clambered down the steps.

"This will counter the medicine we've been preparing for Quinn," Ciaran said.

"The one that doesn't work very well and makes him sick," Max added, glaring at Addam.

"And that is another discussion we will be having soon," Addam said. "The only thing that makes me feel more awful about that is the fact that the truth was kept from me."

Quinn begged me with a look. "The antidote will help. I'll see clearer. We don't have time to search the ship."

"It's Addam's decision," I said, and like a bastard, I knew exactly what I wanted Addam to decide, because I wasn't sure what other corners we had time to cut.

"Do you know if there are risks?" Addam asked Ciaran. "With absolute honesty?"

"It will not harm him," Ciaran said. "It will negate the influence of the medicine he's been taking. The only risk is the risk we've always known—that Quinn's gifts are too powerful for a normal mind. But Quinn is far from normal, and I mean that in the best way possible. I think we have been underestimating him."

"He's a seer," Lady Death said, shaking off the memories she'd been entranced by. She saw the look Lord Tower gave her, and spread her fingers with a shrug gesture. "I can be discreet. This is a matter for Rune's court."

"Addam," Quinn begged. *They are children.*

Addam took the vial from Ciaran's hand and held it out to Quinn.

Quinn gave him a look of naked relief, unscrewed the top of the vial, and drank it in one long sip. His face immediately contorted, which just about sent Addam climbing the walls, until Quinn said, "Anise. Bleh."

Then blood began to trickle out of both nostrils, and Addam really started freaking out. "I'm fine," Quinn said, putting a palm on Addam's chest to keep him away. There was a look in his eye, an actual gleam, I'd never seen before.

"I'm fine," he repeated. "There's just a . . . certain . . . rebound effect. It's all so clear. And there's no time. We're going to get lost in it, as it is." He looked around him with those surreally clear eyes. "So many paths. We don't like that way, it wastes minutes . . . So much there and there, and Anna and Corrine are there, and close by, there, a fat spider in thick hemp thread, and I know *exactly* what that image means." Quinn turned and faced toward the back of the ship, toward the big compartment past the galleys with the post office and general store. "Corbie. There. You always feel better when we find him first."

"Good gods," Lady Death breathed. "He's seeing probabilities. I haven't been paying very close attention, have I?"

The look on Addam's face matched mine, a sort of fear that would quickly become an aggressive defense. But Lady Death laughed and patted a dark hand against Quinn's cheek. "You've got a bright future ahead of you, kiddo. Let me know if Rune doesn't treat you right."

"Thank you, but he does. Except when he tries to cook. He doesn't understand what paprika is, and substitutes." Quinn started to wipe the blood from under his nose, but Addam grabbed his hand and put a clean handkerchief in it. Quinn smiled at him, wiped away the blood with practiced strokes, and led us out of the galley.

We walked through the compartments leading toward the store concourse. Lord Tower may have followed the same path I did, for all that the mix of old ruin and preserved death affected him. Lady Death wasn't nearly as calm about it, nor, for that matter, Ciaran. As we walked through the room where I'd seen frantic sailors trying to hide from whatever stalked them, tears filled Ciaran's eyes, and Lady Death gasped.

"What is this?" she whispered.

I forced Clarity on both her and Ciaran, but hesitated on locking it down. "You should keep the spell active. It gets worse," I warned them.

"How was there any question of a raid? How have we not acted sooner? If the human world saw this . . ." Lady Death shook her head. She pulled the emerald out of her pocket and closed her hand around it. As she spoke, I felt the stone in my own pocket turn into a pinpoint of heat. "This is Death. Nothing is at rest here. The psychic damage is . . . I've never seen worse. This vessel must be sanctified. I'll need to partner with Lady Priestess. This is a matter between her court and mine now, and I will not brook opposition. *We cannot sink this ship.* Am I clear?"

I quickly wrapped a hand around my own emerald. I heard Lord Hierophant start to speak in the open channel, but Lady World's voice overrode his. "We're seeing much the same up here," she said. "I am in agreement. We own this disgrace—all of us. We will make amends. I strongly suggest, though, that if scuttling the ship is off the table, we find the Hanged Man, and fast."

"There's still time," Quinn whispered.

"Ending transmission," Lady Death said, and pocketed the stone

"That way," Quinn said, pointing. "Corbie is there, alone, in a barber's chair. The hemp spider wanted to separate Corbie from Anna. He's not sure which one is the principality."

Oh shit.

And, again, as I sometimes did, I repeated in my head: *Oh shit.*

I looked at Lord Tower, Lady Death, and Ciaran. They were staring at Quinn, though trying very hard not to show how much Quinn had struck their interest.

But this Quinn—the Quinn who was very much in control of his ability—noticed. There was nothing absent-minded about his attention span now. He narrowed his eyes at the powerful men and woman in front of him and said, primly, "You will leave Anna alone. It will never end well if you interfere. It will give her an axe to grind, and the only thing worse than the times she's an angry Lady Sun are when she's an angry Lady Tower."

And with that second and hopefully last *oh shit* bomb, he turned and headed toward the barber's compartment. I hurried after him. On our way, we passed the small grated post office, and I took pains not to look at the closed safe inside it.

The short corridor opened into a cramped stairwell landing ringed by the utility shops I'd seen earlier, including the barber. I ran a thumb along my gold ring, releasing Fire. It itched to fill my palms, but I held it at bay, ready to attack anything guarding Corbie.

The barber shop had an actual door instead of a hatch, with a glass pane for a top panel. I saw, in the middle barber shop chair, a small huddled form. No one or nothing else.

Quinn tried the door handle first, but it wouldn't open. I was about to blast it off its hinges when Quinn tapped a sigil on his belt, and rotated his palm above the locking mechanism. The Opening spell released the lock with a click. Clever boy, our prophet.

I flung the door open and rushed over to the chair. Only the shiny cap of black hair told me it was Corbie. He was entirely drawn into a tight, hurting ball.

"Corbitant Dawncreek," I said gently. "This is as far from an ice-cream shop as you can get. We'll have to fix that soon."

I heard a snot-filled sniff, and Corbie raised his face.

His expression was empty. He was dangerously in shock. Dried blood completely covered his jaw. He had a tooth in his palm, and I could see that he was missing at least two others from his now-silent smile.

The rage that always lived inside me reared. It was an almost physical pain, like nails against flesh. But I had taken Lady Death's lesson to heart. I would not have the world react to my power; I wanted the world to react to *me*.

With that attempt at control came calm. My rage was washed clean into purpose. My anger was tempered by responsibilities. Reaction hardened into strategy—into every step I needed to take to end the Hanged Man's life.

Corbie blinked at me, recognition fighting to rise through the batting of trauma. He sniffed again and said, in a dazed voice, "I tried to put it back in, but it won't stay. Will I always look like this? I'll look so funny."

"No, honey," I whispered, picking him up. I'm not sure I'd ever picked a child up in my life, and it was awkward, but I figured it was okay to be clumsy about things like this.

The only thing that mattered was pulling him out of this room. Festeringly bad things had been done here, and they pushed at the edge of my spell. I forced Clarity over Corbie to keep him from seeing anything that would deepen his shock.

He said, "I want Auntie Corinne."

"I'm going to her now," I said, tightening my arms around him. His own small arms finally moved on their own and locked around my neck.

I looked back at the party in the doorway. I calmly calculated the people gathered on the landing, and their use in my endgame. Lady Death or Ciaran. Strong and momentarily dispensable. I had no friendship yet with Lady Death, though. She would not willingly leave.

"Ciaran, will you take him away from here?" I asked.

"Didn't I watch over the hostages last time?" Ciaran said with only the smallest bit of asperity. "I'm always missing the good bits."

"This is a precious request," I said. "Please. He's endured enough. Take him to his brother Layne, at New Saints."

Ciaran huffed and came forward, holding out his arms. I transferred Corbie to him, who made only a small noise. Ciaran looked down at the mop of hair, and closed his eyes. I felt a drowsy spark of power as a sigil spell released. Corbie sighed and said, "I smell strawberry." Then his head sagged against Ciaran's shoulder.

"Sweet dreams, little one," Ciaran said "Your part in this is done."

"You have a clear path if you go now. Right now, Ciaran," Quinn said. "*Hurry.* It's all about to start."

Ciaran, who'd known Quinn longer than I had, didn't hesitate for a second. He swept away, vanishing into the concourse.

"Wait a few seconds," Quinn said in a shush. "The footsteps bring it, and we'll need to distract its attention to keep it from going after Ciaran. Oh. There. Now you know something is coming. That shaves a few seconds off . . . Lady Death, will you ready Invisibility?"

"How do you know—" Lady Death stopped herself from stating the obvious.

"Why Invisibility?" Lord Tower asked.

"So we don't destroy the universe," Quinn said. "Rune, you should go first. You already figured out a way to fight the monsters, and the boy already saw you. That'll make sense soon."

"More icicle screams?" I asked him, pushing through the crowd.

"Yes," Quinn said. "Now. Go. *Go, Rune!*"

I ran down the corridor toward the concourse, back the way we'd come. Just as I breached the larger room, a winter banshee came through an open hatchway in its bizarre, staggering float.

My Fire rose to my hands. It was a spell that could power fantastic offensive abilities over the course of at least twenty minutes; and was truly devastating when expended in a single burst.

I lifted my arm and threw the entire spell in a single jet of superheated flame. The banshee's neck and vocal cords bubbled into liquid and hardened into char. The flames spread along its already-falling corpse, licking down the brown robes.

Something went wrong.

The world tipped into gray, as if my Clarity spell had died. In another moment, the colors returned, brightening into too-sharp distinction, an intense, aural migraine of reality.

The banshee corpse was gone. The old wreckage was gone. Tables were upright, littered with scattered cards and dinner trays. In the corner of the room, a sailor was staring at me in horror. And in the hatchway leading back to the first galley's chapel—

I saw me. Me, but ghostly and insubstantial. I saw me, staring at me. Or me staring at what I thought was a sailor with a flamethrower.

Quinn said something, and magic, like cold water, trickled from crown to toe. The lock of hair in front of my right eye vanished. My extended arm vanished. Invisibility removed me from normal eyesight.

The ghostly image I'd seen of myself was gone. The sailor who'd watched flames bursting from my hand shook his head and covered his eyes, not sure what he'd seen. He'd been caught in a nightmare for a while, after all. He scrambled away from the corner and ran down a passageway, away from the monster hunting him.

"This is real?" Lady Death asked. "We've truly passed through time?"

"Why?" Lord Tower added. "What's changed? This didn't happen to me before. Rune?"

"This is new," I agreed.

"The Hanged Man is doing something," Quinn said. "I'm not sure what. He's not on the ship anymore—not really. But whatever he's doing is reacting badly with the time and stasis magic on the ship."

"He's not here?" Lady Death repeated.

"Sort of. Rune knows. He's guessed where we were going since we set foot on the ship. I told you that you need to pay more attention to him. There's a reason he's *virsa pulcrra*."

That meant *beautiful man* in Atlantean, which made no sense unless it was related to a phenomenally irritating prophecy spoken over my crib. Nice of Quinn to leave a little confusion for me in a statement that confused everyone else entirely.

Quinn added, in tone that sounded flagging and weary, "We need to move. Listen to Lord Tower's warning now. He knows time magic best."

"An unfortunate phrasing," Lord Tower said. "I'd stress my knowledge is only theoretical."

"Sorry," Quinn said. "You still know more than I do. And you are about to warn us. But then we need to hurry. There are only a few tears in time that can take us home. And if we try to make our own, we may create a door that . . . other things can walk through."

I heard rustling, as if someone had moved positions. "Nothing more," Lord Tower said in a hushed voice. At first, I didn't understand the emotion infusing the words, because I'd never, once, in my entire life, heard the Tower scared.

Quinn said, "I know. I understand."

I did not like not knowing where people were standing, or the expressions on their face. So I jumped when Lord Tower said, from right next to me, "Listen closely. Time is essentially fixed. It is very, very difficult to create a paradox, but not impossible. We risk *everything* if we create one. Do not intervene. Do not interfere. These poor men are already dead. Remember that."

In the distance, someone screamed. And screamed again, although now longer, and with genuine injury. The sound ended with unnatural immediacy.

"Jesus," Brand breathed.

"It's okay," Quinn said. "We won't be here long, not if we find the right tear."

"Which way?" Lord Tower asked.

"It's hard to explain. We'll be moving forward and backwards. Time doesn't want us to be here. It's already so broken. But go that way."

"Quinn," I heard Addam say gently. "Are you pointing?"

"Oh. Sorry, you can't see that. We go portside, down the other side of the ship."

That was the direction I knew we'd head in. It also lay in the path of some of the ship's worst massacres.

Before we moved, someone released a sigil spell, and the noise around us—the metal aching of a ship at sea, the distant sounds of people running—faded. Lord Tower said, "We're now silent to them, and unseen even to ourselves, but we remain physical. Be careful."

He had everyone line up in twos, with a hand on the shoulder of the person in front of them. We headed out along the portside of the ship, opposite the galleys we'd entered through. It was the original path Brand, Addam, and I had taken, during our first visit.

Any confusion about what Quinn meant about moving *backwards and forward* was soon answered. Time leapt and jerked around us, each shift accompanied by a panicky second where our bodies moved in slow motion. We flitted along the narrative the Hanged Man had forced on the *Declaration.* The period of seagoing order before his arrival; the initial mystery of vanishing crew; the cat-and-mouse game as sailors were openly hunted; and the final hopeless stands.

One moment we'd be surrounded by shattered skeletons. The next a bleeding crew member would run screaming by us.

As we walked through the first series of galleries that preceded some of the berths ahead, time sent us through dinnertime, before the hunt started. Someone—Max, I think—accidentally stepped into the path of a sailor and sent his tray flying. The sailor started swearing, and then time went sluggish, emptying the room and setting a body down in front of us. This new sailor's blood had painted the walls. He had a letter clasped in his hand written in purple ink, smelling of a woman's perfume.

"This is an abomination," Lady Death said in a grim voice.

"It's really bad ahead," I said. "Or it could be. There's a room with a movie projector. I think it's the first time the Hanged Man attacked openly. In the present, it's just full of bleached bones."

"My grandmother wanted me to marry him," Max said.

I looked over my shoulder, alarmed by his shocky tone, but of course I couldn't see him. "Okay, Max?"

Nothing for a second. Then he blurted, "Sorry, I nodded." He sounded happy I'd asked though, and stronger for it.

Time shifted around us, that slow wash of grayish energy. Ahead, I saw the flicker of a movie projector's light, and heard the crisp dialog of bantering men.

"We'll need to hurry," Quinn said. "The tear we need is ahead."

"Stay along the edges of the room," I said. "On the other side are sleeping berths. If we don't hit the tear then, keep moving portside. There's a long corridor that will take us to the medical wing. That's where this ends."

"How do you know?" Brand asked. And then, before I could speak, he clicked his tongue. "Of course that's where he's holed up."

"And I have a key," I said with satisfaction. "Grab each other, form a line. I'll take the rear. Let's go."

I'm not sure what order we were in—I'm not even sure whose hand I was grabbing—but we linked together and hurried into the next compartment. I looked behind me and saw the sailors watching a black-and-white movie, hollering good-naturedly. The very last sight I had of it, a man rose in the front row, blocking the screen. He raised his arms, and what was a uniform was now a black cloak, which unfurled, wider and wider, until it seemed to fill the universe. The last thing I heard was his laugh as the sailors went quiet, knowing, without really knowing, that something awful was happening.

The hand holding mine tugged hard, jerking me out of the compartment. I felt callouses and impatience. Of course it was Brand.

Time shifted again as we rushed through the soldiers' berths. I tried not to look—we were now suddenly later in the narrative. The rusty stains I'd seen before on the mattresses were bright red. A sailor was stretched out on one, his hands pressed over a bleeding gut wound. He turned his head and coughed, and I felt warm drops patter against my hand.

"There!" Quinn shouted, and the next thing I knew I was passing through a black-and-white world that brightened into what I knew to be the present. My skin prickled and warmed, and faded in reverse, as Lady Death dropped our Invisibility. Lord Tower also disengaged our Silence.

My shoulder throbbed with the tension I'd been carrying in it. I started to stretch out the kink, when Anna screamed.

Ahead of me, from an unseen compartment, Corinne Dawn-creek was hurled across the corridor into the opposing bulkhead with a bone-breaking crash. She sank into a heap. Anna shouted again and ran into sight, throwing herself to Corinne's side.

"You get the boy, I'll handle them," someone ordered from inside the room.

Lord Tower strode ahead of us. Without a single hitch in his step, he walked up to Anna, turned, and vanished into the compartment where the women had been held. There was a single cry of surprise, and then just the sound of bodies hitting the ground, one after the other.

I ran up, glanced in long enough to see that four of the Hanged Man's guards were down, and knelt by Corinne. She was dazed. She had an arm injury, judging from the way she held it; and I didn't like the knock her head had taken.

"Heal her," Anna begged me.

"I can't, Anna. We need to get her to the hospital."

"Why—why not?" Anna demanded. She reared back as if she wanted to hit me. I noticed that she'd made a knife holster with canvas from an old mattress, and a blade made from a metal bedspring.

"We can't heal humans unless they're bonded to us," I said.

"She's a *Companion*," Anna argued.

"But your dad is gone. Her scion is gone. I'm so sorry. We'll get her help, we—"

"Heart," Corinne gasped.

I looked down. And just knew. Knew she hadn't broken her arm after all. She was holding her right side because she was having a heart attack.

"Been—coming," she gasped. "For. While."

"No. No no no no," Anna said frantically.

Corinne grabbed at my sleeve with her left hand. It took two tries to connect. I took the hand in my own and held it. She was in too much pain to speak properly, but she was able to gasp, "Yours. Now. Please."

"They," I said, and forced through hesitation and guilt, because this moment was not about me. I swallowed and said, "They are under my protection."

"More," she said.

"They will be cared for. They will have a home."

"*Love!*" she panted angrily.

My eyes burned. "They will be loved. All of them. Anna, Corbie, and Layne will be loved."

Corinne turned her head toward Anna with a wince. She moved her left hand to the girl's face, pushing aside the fall of hair that normally hid her burn scars. She cupped the cheek and whispered, "Love you."

Furious tears spilled down Anna's cheeks. Her mouth was open in a silent, low scream. She shook her head.

"Love you," Corinne repeated. "Proud."

Anna lowered her face, breathing hard.

And then her head snapped up. Her irises brightened with amber light. She looked at me, then her eyes tracked left to Brand. She looked at the Tower, and her head jerked to the right, eyes narrowed, following an invisible line. With that quick, bird-like movement—

and now, here, I hear the sound of massive wings, and know beyond all plausibility that we are not on a ship, but flying through the sky, surrounded by birds made of thunder

—she looked back at Corinne. She pressed Corinne's hand against her cheek with one hand, and put her free hand on Corinne's own cheek.

The next thing I knew I was flying backwards, buffeted by the release of energy.

I ended up on the ground with Addam's arms around me. Everyone else except the Tower had been knocked off balance. He stood in the hatchway and stared at Anna with hungry eyes.

Anna looked straight at me and said, "*Heal her.*"

"I don't . . . we can't . . ."

Brand understood first. "She made Corinne her Companion," he said in a hushed tone.

"That's not possible," Lady Death said.

But it was. I knew it. It was. Anna had seen—had *traced*—the bond between the two Companion pairings before her. Yet another example of the gorgeous metaphor and mimicry I'd seen her capable of. And she glowed. She godsdamn glowed like a lightning bolt amid candle flames. Her Aspect was breathtaking.

"Addam," I said quickly. "Addam, I used my Healing spell. You have some. Please!"

Addam touched one of the platinum discs along his waist. He pushed me aside gently and went to Corinne, placing a hand between her breasts. Corinne moaned as the Healing magic went to work on her failing body. After a second, Addam slapped at another sigil, releasing the power of a second Healing.

"This is not truth," Lady Death said in a shaky voice. "That . . . *She* is a principality, and no child. Who dared rejuvenate a principality to the form of a prepubescent? That is an outrage."

"She's a child," I said.

"She is *not*, because no child can manifest an Aspect, let alone use the—" Lady Death clamped her mouth shut. She stared at me with angry eyes.

If I had to guess, I'd say that Anna had manifested this ability no one had seen fit to tell me about.

"She's a child," I repeated. The next words tumbled out—a hurried bid to shield Anna from circling sharks, including the friendly ones. "She is my heir. By my voice and will, I name Annawan Dawncreek my Heir Scion. You promised discretion regarding my court matters, Lady Death, and I *will* hold you to it."

"I've lost track of the things I must be discreet about," Lady Death said, shaking her head disbelievingly.

I felt a spark of heat in my pocket. I startled, then realized Lord Hierophant and Lady World were attempting to communicate. I pulled the emerald from my pocket, a movement mimicked by Lady Death and Lord Tower, and heard Lord Hierophant speaking. "—slaved the controls to my command. The ship's batteries shouldn't fire, unless the Hanged

Man fights his way to the controls himself. I'm not putting anything past him, not after what I've seen. Have you found him?"

"Yes," I said.

"Yes?" Addam said, glancing back at me. He'd pulled his own emerald out of his pocket. Behind him, Anna was hugging Corinne, who was unconscious but breathing evenly.

"Yes. He's right ahead of us, in a manner. He's retreated into a pocket dimension he's anchored to the ship. And I have the wardstone that will let me in. It's time to end this."

It took little effort to find where the pocket dimension was set. I'd known already it was in the area of the marine compartments and medical suites. It turned out to be attached to a wall in a small, closet-sized darkroom used for ship photography and X-rays. Preserved in a functional state, a machine showed the outline of a human skull with graphic wounds that looked less like fractures than bite marks. I turned my back on it and faced the opposing wall.

None of us were sure how many people the wardstone key—the one I'd found at the Dawncreeks days ago—would let in. We expected four or maybe five. I stood in front, with Brand grabbing the back of my shirt, Lady Death grabbing the back of his, and Addam grabbing the back of hers. Lord Tower, who'd stepped back for a moment to make a phone call, seemed fairly convinced he could force the door open for anyone else with only minimal delay.

Max and Quinn would not enter. I'd made them swear to it on their names. By that point, Quinn barely had the stamina to stand. His visions had not come without cost.

"How many spells can you balance at once?" Lady Death asked me.

I didn't want to explain to her that I only had eight sigils, and had already burned through two. "Five or six for now."

"Admirable," she said. "Elemental? Fire and Wind?"

"Fire and Frost," I said.

She *tskked*. "Overlap. I'll cover Water and Earth, plus Frost of course. Shields up, Lord Sun. Let's take him down without all the bad guy soliloquy he seems so fond of."

"That's what I always say!" I said.

"Rune," Brand said.

"Right." I pulled the bronze wardstone out of my pocket. "Let's go."

"That's a button," Brand sighed.

I looked down at the corduroy button in my hand. The one the dream sprites had given me. "Huh," I said. "Still just a button." I pocketed it and pulled out the wardstone.

I felt the layered release of sigil magic behind me as Lady Death armed herself. My own hands slid from sigil to sigil, releasing four of my last spells: a second Fire, along with Frost, one Shield, and Telekinesis. They were all easy spells to store, and I'd had limited time in the hospital's public sanctum.

I kept a final spell, Exodus, as a backup. I wasn't sure what effect it would have in a pocket dimension.

With the hilt of my sabre primed for firing, I reached up with the wardstone and walked through the wall.

Everything went black for a split second. I met resistance—as if a narrow hurricane, the width of a pane of glass, wanted to push me back into reality. I lowered my head into it and bulled forward.

We broke through into a brightly lit room.

I immediately slid left. Brand broke through and slid right. I ignored the others coming through—I had Brand, and that had always been enough. Holding my sabre in a two-handed grip, I swept the point in a W, covering potential ceiling-, chest-, and floor-level threats.

The room was a large circle. It was straight out of an old Arabian story—gauzy silk curtains, people-sized throw pillows, gold tassels and gold filigree and gold incense burners. But interspersed with the decadence were crueler reminders of the dimension's ownership. Manacles. Leather whips. A simple metal table in the center of the room, sitting in an empty fountain basin. So very utilitarian. Easily cleaned and drained.

"Shit," Brand said. "Close quarter combat."

"Dust and debris," I agreed. Damn my sigil guesses. Wind would have been handier.

Lady Death made a sharp sound, an intake of breath.

I turned and saw that she stood in front of the portal. She was holding a hand. An actual hand. The neatly severed stump began to bleed.

"Addam," I said dumbly. That was Addam's hand.

"Focus, Rune, we're on our own," Brand said sharply. He had throwing knives and an axe he'd stolen from fallen guarda at the Convocation building; no reliable ranged weapon.

I wasn't sure what I was more horrified with. That Brand was the only human in a room of Arcana, or Addam's injury. Or maybe what horrified me most was the voice whispering in the back of my head, clinically reminding me that Addam had a sigil on him that I very, very much needed.

"Focus," Brand repeated.

"I don't see him," Lady Death said.

"He's here," I said. I threw up a full Shield in front of all of us, cutting off our edge of the circle. "Lady Death, Addam's . . . hand, can you . . .?"

Ice crept along the fingers of the severed hand, inching across the palm. The fingernails glistened like pearl as Lady Death gently set the preserved hand on the ground to the side of the portal entrance. She straightened, and surveyed the room through fresh eyes, finally raising a finger to point. "Cyrillic magic."

I followed the point. On a rounded portion of the wall opposite us, using what may have been a simple black marker, was an intricate square of words. Or, no, not a square. The writing ran at angles, literally a maze. I knew it. The main spell followed a simple line, with appositive phrases branching off to dead ends.

But there were hollow spaces in the inscribed maze. Unused dead ends. No clear center. The spell was unfinished.

"You got so close," I said in a loud, appreciative voice. "Clever idea. Re-anchoring the pocket dimension. Tricky magic. Were you hoping to retreat to your arctic compound?"

The air in front of the magical graffiti wavered, resolving into Lord Hanged Man. At his feet, bleeding and bruised, was John. Pretty Boy. I'd forgotten about that loose end, too. But I suppose it was symmetry, since he was the reason Lord Hanged Man had set eyes on the battleship in the first place.

"It's over," Lady Death said. "You know that. With the things we've seen . . . You must know that the entire Arcanum will turn hand against you. I will give you precisely one chance to yield. One."

I bit back a reply, because I hadn't been prepared to offer even that.

Lord Hanged Man's hypothermic features—the Aspect of a dead, frozen man—eased into a smile. The hemp rope he wore around his neck hung free. Sigil, I thought. Mass sigil. I almost turned Lady Death to tell her, but the Hanged Man finally spoke. He said, "You stand on my ground."

"This is not a dialog. One chance," she repeated.

"If I were you, I'd be more worried about the people you left behind. Even as I speak, my houses rise. They will descend on this ship with fresh force."

"No," Brand said. "They won't. The Companions of Atlantis have a score to settle with you. All of your supporters are penned in by now. I don't care how fucking *fresh* they are, they're not going to last against us."

Mayan, I thought.

The Hanged Man stared at Brand for a very long second, and nodded. He clapped a hand over the hemp rope around his neck and released its spell.

He spoke a word of necromantic magic so powerful that it raked lines up the flesh on his throat, leaving behind bloodless furrows. The magic flew at my Shield and created shining, translucent fissures. Just as it burst, I saw Brand drop and roll to his left; Lady Death stagger;

and then I was entirely lost in the slice across my gut that burned like a guillotine blade.

I lost my grip on Shield for a moment. Just a single moment. But enough time for Brand to leap up and charge the Hanged Man.

Nothing had prepared me for that moment—for the sight of my human Companion charging an Arcana.

And nothing had prepared me for the fact that Brand had obviously spent a great, great deal of time figuring out how he'd survive hand-to-hand combat with a master spell-caster.

With the one-handed axe, he made a single swipe, cutting open the front of the Hanged Man's black shirt, and then immediately followed it with a slap. He did this in a blur of metal—a devastating blow followed by a kick at the Hanged Man's ankle, or a stiff-fingered jab to a joint. None of the weaponless attacks did actual damage—until I realized they weren't meant to. It took concentration to use magic and access sigils, and Brand was keeping the Hanged Man off-balance with attacks that were almost insults. He played on the Hanged Man's pride.

He was buying me time. Lady Death had a massive cut along her arm, bleeding heavily. My gut wound was furiously painful, but at least I wasn't spilling intestines. I leapt up. The Hanged Man saw me coming, and moved his body behind Brand. It was a gift. I fired seven firebolts into the unblocked wall, bolstering them with my Fire spell. The elaborate Cyrillic magic, so carefully constructed, shriveled into flickers of flame.

"No escape now," I said. "You gain nothing by fighting us."

The Hanged Man gave the wall a quick look. "I gain nothing by surrendering," he said.

He pushed out with his hands and an unseen wave of energy blasted Brand off his feet.

What happened next was just what you'd expect in close quarter combat, let alone with spell-casters of our caliber. There were glorious arcs of lightning, and plumes of flame, and sheets of liquid ice. But the effect was completely lost in what happened when all that power collided in a cramped space. Scalding steam; dust and debris from damaged ceilings and walls; chips of ice like tiny pub darts.

I tried to move around the room to flank the Hanged Man, sensing that Brand was doing the same. I couldn't see Lady Death, but the frost attacks marked her as the frontal assault.

"Fine, then!" I heard Lady Death shout. "You want a fight? See now why I'm the youngest Arcana to seize the Death Throne!"

A barely visible wave of energy rolled from her, meeting one from the Hanged Man himself, in the middle of the room. All the smoke and steam was swept clear. Brand and I, along with the human John, were slammed back against the wall.

I experienced a moment of déjà vu, until remembering I'd seen something like this between Lord Tower and the lich Rurik. A simple contest of willpower, only now I knew why it didn't seem to be powered by sigil magic.

I was entirely outclassed. Brand was on the other side of the room. I fought against the pressure keeping me pinned, forcing my arm straight so I could fire at the Hanged Man. My firebolts vanished like sparks as they encountered the torrent of energy linking Lady Death and Lord Hanged Man. One bolt found its way into the wall above the Hanged Man's head.

Opportunity. Gaps. I began circling the room, continuing my flanking. So did Brand. He had lost his axe. He was using a throwing knife as a hand blade, trying to inch toward the Hanged Man.

The Hanged Man saw our approach and started to laugh, but it turned into a cough. He swung his gaze to Lady Death, hands still pouring out the torrent of energy. "You'll beat me. You're good. But you're not experienced enough to multitask, you little bitch."

The Hanged Man cocked his head and whispered something.

The manacles around the room spun into the air like startled birds. One thick, rusted metal bracelet cracked against my cheekbone; another fastened around my arm. I looked over and saw that Lady Death had been knocked down, her magical attack ended.

I pressed a hand against my white gold ring to unleash Exodus. Nothing happened. These bracelets were like the ones at the Convocation—they dampened my abilities. Worse. I reached for my Aspect, but it slipped from my grip. My sabre was dead too.

Brand was the only one standing. He pulled a throwing knife into his second hand.

"No," I shouted. "No, Brand. No. Stand down."

Brand was staring at the Hanged Man. He braced his front leg for a throw.

"Let him kill, if he wants to kill," the Hanged Man said. He closed his hand into a fist. One of the rings he wore released a sigil spell. Brand's entire body stiffened as he jerked upright.

"I have spent *lifetimes* entertaining myself with human puppets," the Hanged Man said. "Why would you possibly bring one before me? Bad tactics, Sun." He flicked a finger at Brand. "Brand, is it? Let's start small, to see how weak you are. We'll save your scion's throat for later." He turned in a searching circle, breathing a little hard, looking for something.

There are personal horrors that I keep to myself. Things I speak of to no one. Brand being mentally controlled by another individual? That was one of my deepest fears.

The Hanged Man's eyes settled on John. "Do you still want to die, my pretty boy?"

The old man, who was half hidden behind a chaise lounge, rose to his feet. He nodded.

"Kill this man, Companion."

Brand lowered his face a little, eyes up, and smiled. He looked about him, seemed to consider the axe he'd dropped, but shook his head and settled on a short sword still in its sheaf around his waist. Brand did not use swords. He did not kill neatly with them.

He said, "Come here, John."

John stepped forward with eager, shaky steps. Brand watched his approach. As John crossed in front of the Hanged Man, Brand said, "You really want to die, John?"

"Yes," he whispered.

Brand leapt and rammed the sword point forward. He pierced John's gut. The blade went through John and out his back. Brand threw all his weight on the hilt, forcing John backwards in a movement so quick that the Hanged Man didn't realize he'd been speared until he looked down at the sword point in his own gut.

He laughed. "This . . . you think . . . this will kill me?"

"I followed orders," Brand said.

He spun around, scooped up the axe, and ran at Lady Death. Lord Hanged Man shouted, "Stop!", just as the blade severed the manacle. Brand dropped to his knees and froze.

Lady Death didn't showboat. She brought up both arms and launched a fresh wave of force at the Hanged Man. The Hanged Man returned the assault.

Behind her, I saw the wall begin to shimmer.

Addam strode through it.

I had never seen him in a rage before. One arm was pressed against his side, wrapped in a bloody bandage. He had a gold disc in his extended hand. His pants and shirt flickered into ghostly plate mail as his Aspect rose. Braided hair now hung free, blowing behind him as he stormed forward.

He released the spell from the mass sigil he'd borrowed from Lady Diana.

Golden light flooded the room. Healing magic from a normal sigil required touch; but powered by a mass sigil? It rushed over all of us like a storm front. The cut on my stomach vanished. My shoulder stopped hurting. Smaller slashes of heat covered my body as wounds healed.

I watched, with immense satisfaction, as the Hanged Man's face locked in fear.

His Aspect—the visage of a frozen man—vanished into the plain features of a brown-haired man with wide brown eyes.

Behind Lady Death, Lord Tower stepped into the room. He took position next to Lady Death, raised his arms, and launched his own torrent of magic.

The Hanged Man tried to hold them both off, but within seconds was thrown against the wall behind him with a sharp, audible crack that may have been his spine.

Lady Death and Lord Tower both stopped. The pressure of their attack vanished, and I felt thirty pounds lighter. I looked at my sabre hilt and, with a flicker of willpower, watched it boil upwards into a garnet dagger.

I went over to the Hanged Man, who stared at me with frantic eyes and made no effort to attack.

"It's kind of ironic," I said. "I got this idea from Layne. Who you kidnapped, bringing him to my attention. He uses death magic to protect himself, too. It's too bad none of us have time to study how you use your own necromancy to power your Aspect."

"We will have time," he whispered, and made a game attempt at grinning. "I will be questioned. I will be punished. I will, at length, find a way free, and we will enjoy a continuation of this match."

"Will we," I said.

"There are rules."

"You mean if you formally yield?"

"Yes," he said.

So I cut his throat.

"This is a strange moment," Lady Death finally said, a good minute later, as we all stood around and watched a man die.

"It really is," I agreed. "Did I just break any Arcana rules, by the way? I mean, he didn't *formally* yield. And my raid was authorized."

"I'm sure his loss will not be keenly felt," Lord Tower said. He bent down and picked up Addam's frozen hand. "I would like to get my godson to a healer."

"Shit," I said. "I was really worried about you the first time I saw your hand! I said something then!"

"Of course you did, Hero," Addam said. He wasn't in pain—*none* of us were in pain, after the healing magic he'd used. But he was still missing a hand. "You are a very good boyfriend. I will step out now. Quinn is most upset by this," he added, waving his arm. He walked back through the portal Lord Tower had forced open.

Lady Death walked across to the bodies in the room. Calm assessment of the Hanged Man's twitching corpse; a bit of unsure sympathy for the old man once called Pretty Boy.

"How did you do it?" she asked, and turned to Brand.

"Do what?" he asked as he walked over to me. While I tried to bat his hands away, he began poking at the various tears in my shirt, to make sure the skin behind it was whole.

"Subvert the Hanged Man's control," she said.

"I didn't. I did exactly what he said, and then some. Do you have any fucking idea what it's like to share a bond with this one? I spend half my time figuring out how he's using wordplay to lie to me."

"What does he lie about?" Lady Death asked, amused.

"Don't," I said, just as Brand replied, "Snack foods, the amount of training he did, the amount of sleep he had, whether he's actually scouting haunted houses or whether he found a nice comfy sofa to sit on."

"You're embarrassing me in front of our new big sister," I said.

Lady Death laughed at that, but Brand caught the *our*, and instead of an eye roll I got a very rare wink.

EPILOG

Addam lost his hand.

Of everything that happened over the next forty-eight hours, that destroyed me the most.

The mass Healing spell he used had effectively cauterized his stump. In a display of cosmic irony, it repaired the nerve endings and torn flesh as if he'd never had a hand to begin with, and made reattachment impossible. Even worse—though he evaded the subject—I suspect he'd known it was a possibility before storming into the pocket dimension. But instead of staying away, or handing the mass sigil spell to Lord Tower, he did exactly what an Addam would always do in an instance like that: he'd ridden to my rescue. There was a reason his Atlantean Aspect looked like a medieval knight.

Dozens of others things also happened, all at once, spinning past me like a hijacked merry-go-round.

Lord Judgment insisted on planning a city-wide ceremony this coming spring to acknowledge my ascension. He wouldn't take *no* for an answer. The Arcanum hadn't had a reason for a party like this since Lady Death assumed her mother's throne at the end of the Atlantean World War.

I made global headlines. Or at least, I made one global headline, before deactivating all the news feeds on my phone. From what I understood, the articles slanted in my favor. I'm not sure that would last if they knew the entire story, and how an Arcana had stolen a World War II battleship and slaughtered its crew.

Regarding that, Lady Death and Lady Priestess formed an alliance to sanctify the *Declaration*. The dead soldiers would be laid to rest. I joined them on their first walkthrough, as they drew up plans to bless the haunted metal corridors. I'd brought a Soul Bind spell with me and, with their acquiescence, used the magic on the sealed mailroom safe. I wasn't sure the memory of it, though, would as easily be forgotten.

The Hanged Man had been buried in an unmarked grave at his Westlands compound. The division of his court would be decided soon. It was widely assumed that the Gallows was finished. The Hanged Man had no heirs, and his death left no appreciable power vacuum. In other words, there was little worth preserving, including his memory. It was a sad statement on what an Arcana should have meant to the city.

For now, the Dawncreeks would be staying in a condo unit Addam owned in his building. Since he hadn't told me he owned a *third* unit, I didn't put it past him to have bought it on the spot. Because, once again, that was the sort of thing an Addam would do.

Corinne, stabilized, would soon be facing a lengthy rejuvenation treatment. Now that she was once again bonded to an Atlantean, such magic would work on her. She had agreed to be brought back to her thirtieth birthday. In human terms, given the slower Atlantean and bonded Companion aging process, it would be the body of a twenty-five-year-old. She would maintain that age through a sequence of near-term rejuvenations until Anna caught up with her.

And Anna? My new heir? None of the Arcana had spilled her secret just yet. The cat was still in the bag—even if the bag was in arm's reach of too many people who wanted to shake it and peer inside.

Which led me to now—the morning of the third day—when I received a message summoning me to the Iconsgison.

The guard, Anaïca, met me at the checkpoint to the Arcanum's floor. She was dressed in a new uniform, and still smelled strongly of soap.

"Lord Sun," she said, with a little bow. "You can pass right through."

"With my weapons?" I asked in surprise.

"The Arcanum isn't in session. It's just Lord Tower, my lord."

My stomach bottomed. Lord Tower? *Just* Lord Tower? "So he has his weapons too?" I asked.

She smiled at that, and held open a gate. Before I moved, though, she seemed to hesitate on saying something, then blurted, "And congratulations. On . . . everything. And thank you."

"Thank me?" I said in surprise. "I was a bit of prick to you, wasn't I?"

"You and Lady Death gave me a field promotion to head captain. And you avenged my friends. The ones who died. That means something to me."

"I had a lot of help," I said awkwardly. "And Lady Death wouldn't have given you that field promotion if you didn't meet her approval. She's scary competent, too, so I suppose that says a lot about anyone who gets her approval. Captain Anaïca . . ." I trailed off for a second. "Maybe you could help me with something? I've been waiting for the right moment."

"Of course, my lord."

I pulled a folded bundle papers from the inside of my black leather jacket. One of them was a list of names I'd torn from a lined notebook. I stared at the names for a second longer than I needed to, and then handed the list to her.

Anaïca's yellow eyes ran down the names, widening a bit. "These are them. The guarda who died fighting the banshee and the Hanged Man's people." She tapped one name. "Him?"

"He was guarda, too. Assigned to a public park near my house. He died helping me protect my ward, Matthias. Do you have a way of reaching the family of these people?"

"I do, Lord Sun."

"Could you . . . Well, there are things I can't say, of course, but these men and women were heroes. They died stopping a monster. If their families and loved ones want to hear that, they can reach out to me. I'll tell them. They deserve to hear it from someone on the Arcanum."

Anaïca stared at me for a long beat. "Of course, Lord Sun. It will be my honor. And not to hurry you, but I think Lord Tower is waiting."

I sighed, but followed the marble throat-like corridor to the Arcanum's chamber. As I rounded the last corner, I spotted Mayan. He was standing at parade rest in front of the closed Iconsgison doors.

"Should I be nervous about this?" I asked him when we were in easy earshot.

"Should you ever not be nervous about something like this?" Mayan countered.

"Point. And thank you, by the way. I never got to say that. I heard that you and the other Companions locked down the Hanged Man's houses while we fought him."

"He didn't have many houses left. Wasn't much of a challenge."

I stopped and gave Mayan a thoughtful look, as much because of what I wanted to say as because I wanted to stall. "I need to tell you something, but I'm not sure I'll phrase it well."

Mayan smiled. He smiled a lot more than Brand or Corinne did. That didn't necessarily mean it was a real smile—just a practiced flick of muscle.

"I'm starting to think there's a lot I don't know about Companions," I said. "Now I've got two of them in my court."

"And you'd like me to explain what you don't know," Mayan said neutrally.

"Oh, no. You'd never tell me. I'd never ask. I just want you to know that Companions . . . I trust them. They're Brand, aren't they? And I trust him more than anyone."

"I'm not exactly sure what you're saying, Lord Sun."

I took a few seconds to put words together in my head. As I usually did in situations like this, when what I needed to say was too important to screw up, I retreated to formality. "I'm saying that I consider the Companions of Atlantis an ally. Now and forward, I will stand with them against trouble. My shield is their shield. They are welcome in my court."

The only thing more rewarding than catching Mayan off guard was catching his boss by surprise. It's the small things that make life fun.

"Better not keep him waiting," I said, and nodded my chin at the massive doors behind him.

Mayan, still surprised, moved quickly to grab the door handle for me. He paused in the act, and said, "Eve."

"Excuse me?"

"Eve. Christian Saint Nicholas's Companion. Rejuvenation treatments leave a Companion in a strange body, so they need new training regimens. I think Eve would be an excellent partner for Corinne."

"I'll ask her. Thanks for the advice."

He nodded and opened the door.

I walked into the Iconsgison as the giant door swung shut on its pneumatic hinges. The room was exactly as I'd remembered it, sans people. Only Lord Tower waited. His back was toward me, and he was staring at the Hanged Man's empty seat.

"Ciaran says we'll need to rename the room," I said. "Iconsgison is a word for a twenty-two-sided polygon, isn't it?"

"It is," Lord Tower said. "We haven't been that for a while now. The Lovers. The Hanged Man. They will not rise again. It's very unlikely the Emperor's throne will be claimed, and the Empress has given no indication that she'll return to the island for anything short her own funeral."

"Eighteen, then," I said. "What's that?"

"An octadecagon."

He still hadn't turned to look at me. I swallowed—wholly unnecessary, since my throat was dry—and said, "Did I break something between us that can't be fixed?"

Now he turned, and gave me a small smile. "No, Rune."

I let out a breath.

"You were worried about that," Lord Tower said.

"Excessively. You asked me to stand down, and I didn't."

"Maybe I was wrong."

I laughed. I mean, honestly.

He sat down on the edge of the dais and gave me a wry look. "I do admit I'm wrong occasionally. Or at the very least, I'll admit I don't always appreciate all the potential avenues toward a solution. You did what you thought was right. And you saved not only Matthias but the Dawncreek family as well. *That said*," he emphasized, "I wasn't aware of

Anna Dawncreek. That would have changed my plans somewhat dramatically."

I sat down near him. Almost next to him, but not exactly. "I wasn't aware of her either, back when we had brunch. Quinn spotted her . . . talent not long after." I rubbed my eyelids and said, "She's so *young*."

"Others will covet her."

I cut him a look.

"Yes. Myself included. But I respect the Sun Throne's sovereignty in this. Although Rune . . . Raising a child like that? A power like hers is generational. Maybe centennial. She must be raised well. You won't get a second chance at it. So make no mistake: I will be paying attention."

"You caught what Quinn said, right? About her maybe being your heir instead of mine?"

"I'm not quite sure he framed that as a compliment. And I'm old enough to appreciate that raising children is . . . not one of my specialties."

It was a remarkable statement, considering the whitewater rapids that flowed under *that* bridge. One of his two children, Dalton, had not been kind to me. An awful episode with him had nearly fractured my relationship with Lord Tower, and left Brand with scars on his back.

But in a way, I'd moved past that. So I examined what he said at face value and was able to spot the tiny flicker of hurt inside it. I said, "I don't know. You did pretty well with me, didn't you?"

Lord Tower gave me a slow, real smile. Just for a second. Then, before it got sappy, he brushed his hands together and stood up. "Look at this room. Such wrecked formality." He pronounced wrecked as they did in Old Atlantean: *wreck-ked*. "One of the burdens we bear as Arcana. So much pomp and circumstance expected of us. I can't wait to see what your court looks like, when you start holding it."

"Why did you make that sound like a verb?"

"Holding court. Formal court sessions."

"Oh, yeah, no. That doesn't sound like me at all."

Lord Tower gave me a much more familiar smile: patronizing amusement. "You'll have people. They will have grievances. They will want to appear before you, to have you decide on their behalf."

"Hell they will!" I barked out before I could stop myself. "Godsdamnit. Are you telling me I'll need to have *office hours?*"

"Rune Sun, you are about to drown in administrivia. You really must put some thought into this. It's one of the reasons I called you here. We have a rather urgent matter before us."

"No! We're going to the beach. The party? You're invited. I'm going *to the beach*," I implored.

"As you say. But first I need your input on the division of the Hanged Man's estate."

I let that settle. "Oh."

"You initiated the raid. While it was most unusual, in its execution, it was still a raid. Several thrones were involved. You could assert your claim to the spoils, as your evidence spurred our action. That said, Lady Death arguably took the greatest damage, between summoning the ghost steeds and the sustained Majeure battle with the Hanged Man. Or you could acknowledge that Lord Judgment—"

"I want the smallest share," I interrupted.

Lord Tower stared at me.

I shrugged. "Maybe you agree, maybe you'd do it differently. You've got a good mind for things like that. But this was my debut. I want to show deference to people who I can learn a lot from. I'll take the smallest share, give Lady Death the largest, and then let her decide the rest of the shares. She really did the heavy lifting—you're right."

Lord Tower kept staring another moment, then nodded his approval.

Since I couldn't help myself, I asked, "Would you have done it differently?"

He pretended to think it over, one of his really-I'm-only-human tricks. "I might have claimed everything and offered only large gifts in gratitude. But we walk different roads. Don't doubt your choice."

I didn't. It was a strange feeling, this confidence.

"There are two other reasons I wanted to see you this morning," he added. "One more pressing than the other."

"Okay."

"It will take time to educate you. On matters that only the Arcanum is privy to. But there is one we must discuss now. All of us—all Arcana, and most Principalities—understand the nature of the Arcana Majeure. As a matter of survival."

"Ah," I said. My lungs felt heavy all of the sudden—the air had weight, the way it did right before you knew you were being told something very, very important.

I had a lot of questions. Only one was essential. "You told me I could hurt Brand by using it."

"You *have* hurt Brand by using it, Rune. You have hurt yourself. Irredeemably."

"I need to know more."

The Tower dipped his chin in agreement. "It is a closely guarded secret. You must talk about it to no one other than Brand. Not even Addam."

"But I can tell Brand."

"Companions are often the exception to the rule. I'm not sure you could keep it from him. Nor should you when the damage applies to him as well."

"What damage?"

The Tower turned to face me. "How have I always appeared to you?"

"How . . . what? I don't understand."

"My appearance."

"Are you fishing for compliments?"

He didn't say anything, as he often didn't when I cracked a joke.

"Okay," I said uncomfortably. "You appear as a man in his mid-forties. By human standards. Hard to tell with our aging—some people hold that look longer than others, even well into their sixties. I don't often see you younger or older."

"Have you never wondered why?"

"There is literally no end to the list of questions I have about your *whys*. But I suppose I thought you just liked this age. It makes you look old enough to be wise, but young enough to be strong."

"True. But wrong. I always rejuvenate to my youngest age."

"Your—" I bit down on the sentence. It made too little sense to be anything but a significant, significant fact.

"I *cannot* rejuvenate any further. I've used the Arcana Majeure too much over the course of my life."

My intuition drew lines, and realization sparked along them, as quick as instinct.

My sabre.

My own life force powered my sabre's magic. A weapons master had once told me that every firebolt took a second off my life. I was literally its battery, and there was no replacing the energy I used to wield it.

I closed my eyes and said, "The Arcana Majeure . . . it's like a sigil, isn't it? It's like using your body as a sigil, only it all happens at once—there's no meditation, no storing of spells. Your life force powers the spell."

"Yes. And that cost becomes very pronounced during rejuvenation. It is why you must be sparing in its use. It is a seductive ability, and there is no undoing its damage."

"And my rejuvenation is Brand's rejuvenation."

"Exactly."

"Are there other limitations?" I asked uneasily.

"Some. No one knows where the magic comes from—we suspect it's genetic. By convention it's what marks an Arcana or Principality. It's a measure of considerable power. You can rapidly deplete your ability to use it, and it takes a while to . . . I suppose the word is *recharge*."

"Why is it such a secret?"

He gave me his schoolmaster smile. "What question did you just ask a moment ago?"

I thought back. "Limitations. You don't want to promote its limitations. You like the fact that the average Atlantean sees you doing these completely inexplicably powerful things, but you don't want them to know it comes with a finite limitation. It could be used against us."

"As you say."

I thought more about it. "What I've done . . . Do you have any idea how much of my life I've used? Is there, like, an equation or something?"

"Would that there were. But your use of the Arcana Majeure is still in its infancy. I would not be overly worried about the cost. Yet."

This line of thinking led to another unpleasant thought. I remembered Lady Death summoning the ghost steeds, telling me I better be worth the gray hair. "Lady Death used the Arcana Majeure. For me."

"Quite a bit of it, yes. It was her choice. You can't shoulder that blame. But . . . Yes. She will pay a price for it."

"Damn. Did you say before we had two things to talk about? Please tell me it's not more existential dread."

"I'm afraid I can't promise that. But still—Yes. I have a gift for you. Another secret. Freely offered." He met my eyes and said, with clear pronunciation, *"Virsa pulcrra."*

I blinked, surprised. "That's what Quinn called me. On the ship. It means beautiful man in Old Atlantean. Is this about that stupid prophecy?"

"It is about your misinterpretation of the prophecy. I'm afraid you may be quite mad about what I'm going to tell you. Bear with me, and I'll explain."

". . . Okay."

"The seer who made that prophecy—of you being the most beautiful man of your generation—was very old. It was during a gala at Sun Estate not long after you were born. Before, even, Brand was brought to you. Wine flowed and I believe the seer overindulged. She was rather indiscreet, in my opinion, in speaking the prophecy while others were around her."

"You were there?"

"I was. Your father was my closest friend." Lord Tower's gaze unfocused for a beat or two, then he shook his head. "I miss him. Now that you have your throne, we'll need to speak more of him. But for now, the rest of the story: The seer was ancient. She'd spent centuries living in a time where Old Atlantean was the *only* Atlantean dialect. In modern Atlantean, *virsa* means man. As it did then. But *pulcrra*? Modern Atlantean translates it as *beautiful*. Old Atlantean translated it as *compelling*."

My breath caught. My thoughts froze. That damn prophecy had hounded me my entire life. I didn't know what he was saying.

"The seer, Rune, saw that you would be the most compelling man of your generation. More importantly, you need to understand that the whole of the word *compelling* had a larger meaning, once upon a time. Especially to a far-seer."

"What are you saying?"

"That while you are a very handsome young man, the prophecy had nothing to do with your physical appearance. It meant that you will play a deeply profound role in this generation."

"Why . . ." I looked down at my hands, which I'd knit together so hard that I could see blue veins through pale flesh. "Why wouldn't you tell me this before now? Do you have any idea how often I've been mocked for that? My entire life?"

"Because it's a heavy secret, Rune. And you've spent enough time with Quinn to understand that telling people their future can often times change it. Sometimes, to ensure the best possible outcome, one must be left alone to fumble through the dark. I apologize if I made a mistake— really, Rune, I do—but I felt you weren't ready to know the whole truth."

"Why tell me now, then?"

"Because I heard what you told the Hanged Man. In this very room."

I knew exactly what he meant. I hadn't known I was overheard, though. I'd said: *And think on this. I know a lot of prophets. I am hip-fucking-deep in prophecies about my future. Are you? Are there any prophecies about your future?*

Slowly, I unclasped my hands, and shook the blood flow back into my fingers. "I think I get it," I said.

"I suspect you do. I suspect it's why you made the decision you did. Claiming the throne wasn't a spontaneous decision. You did it because you knew dangerous events were spinning closer and closer around you."

"Something is coming, isn't it?"

"Yes. I believe so, yes."

"You know a lot more than you're going to tell me, don't you?"

"Smart boy," he said softly. "You must fumble through this dark. This is your generation, not mine. This is your story."

Before the gravity of that sank too deeply on my shoulders, Lord Tower added, "But when the moment comes, I promise, I will walk by your side."

The truth of the words passed by me like feathers, a manifestation of a vow. I blinked my eyes—which felt suddenly gritty—and managed a single nod.

Brand, Anna, and I joined a security team from the Crusader Throne, which was sifting through the ashes of the Dawncreek house.

Addam—of course—had loaned the security team to me, with his mother's explicitly neutral approval. More surprising was that almost all of the guards were from the original team, which had lost two of their number in the explosion. I wasn't sure if they were loyal to Addam, or just furiously determined about their losses, but Addam had made a few oblique comments about hiring them away from his mother.

Which led back to the consuming Question of the Day: hire them to *what?*

Could Sun Estate be saved? Where would I build my court? How would I *finance* that court? Even Corbie knew enough to tell me, point blank, "You're a superhero. You need a *lair.*"

"That," Brand said, and pointed at my face.

"What?"

"That look. That's the reason the guards have come over twice asking if you needed them to find you a bathroom."

"I'm just thinking," I said defensively.

"You're obsessing. And it can wait. Let's just get this over with and head to the Enclave. We deserve a few days off."

The *this* we needed to get over was a task I'd only described to Brand in general terms. There was something I needed to find here. Corbie and Anna had both insisted on coming, but in the end, I thought it'd be too much on the youngest. I tried to pull the same line with Anna, but she neatly responded with, "You wouldn't tell your heir to stay behind. So I'm not your heir?"

It had become a theme. Last night I asked her if she had a bedtime, like normal kids. *So I'm not your heir?* This morning she wanted Brand to train her in using a knife, which I'd objected to. *So I'm not your heir?*

But in this, at least, she was right. If she was powerful enough to be my heir, she needed to be strong enough to deal with the sight of her burned house. I couldn't keep her a kid any more than I could make the sun rise in the west. The Universe simply had other plans for her.

She was standing near the smoking ruins of her living room, well out of earshot. Her face was . . . Not blank. Not empty. There were so many emotions that the whole bundle of them had become a colorless gray. But she wanted this moment to herself, so I gave it to her.

"Okay," I said to Brand. "A few days off. You're right, we deserve it. And then when that's done, we'll need to figure out how the hell I'm going to support a court."

"Because you shot Plan A in the gut," he added, not helpfully.

Brand hadn't been very happy with my decision to take the smallest piece of the Hanged Man's spoils.

"Because I shot Plan A in the gut," I agreed.

Brand settled into a grumbling simmer. It wouldn't last long. He had something to say—I'd felt it move along our bond in a hesitant stop-start dance for a while now.

A minute later, he finally said, "Why didn't you tell me your plan?"

"About taking the throne?"

"Yes, Rune. About taking the throne."

"Because . . . Where do I start? Because I wasn't sure myself, until the very last moment? Because I didn't want even a whisper of it to reach the Hanged Man, who had ears everywhere? Because . . . Well, it was a bit, you know . . . embarrassing."

"*Embarrassing?*"

"Yeah. I mean. Grrrrrr, I am the Sun of Atlantis." I shook my head. "That's the sort of pageantry we always make fun of."

Brand stared at me for a bit, then shook his own head. "Humans don't usually feel magic. Even Companions. We feel the *effect* of it, especially when you're setting us on fire or stabbing us in the stomach with stalactites. But we don't . . . sense it. The closest I'd ever come before this week was when I once pissed off Lord Tower and saw his Aspect." Brand went a little pale at the memory. I didn't blame him.

"Until this week?" I prompted.

"Until you. Until that moment, in the Arcanum, when you claimed your throne. I *felt* you. Not through our bond. I *felt you.* So don't . . . Don't *demean* the moment. Don't take it away from all of us who watched it. Because it was fucking glorious."

I swallowed and cleared my throat, and had to blink a few times. When I was sure my voice was steady, I said, "I like you."

"I like you too."

And then . . . there it was. Right in front of me. The moment I'd been waiting for. The discussion I knew needed to happen.

I thought I'd be a lot more scared to talk about it, but that's the funny thing about secrets. When they finally come out, they move too quickly to spare energy on anything except the momentum of unburdening them.

"There's something I need to tell you," I said.

He started staring at me again.

"I'm sorry I haven't told you before, but . . . It's not easy. It's hard. It's so hard to talk about what happened. About . . . that night. The night our court fell."

His face had grown increasingly upset as I spoke. "Rune, no. Fuck, you're so sad right now. I can feel it. You don't have to—"

"You know about my apartment in LeperCon," I blurted.

He stopped talking.

"The phone." I patted my pocket absentmindedly. "You told me the other day you track me on my phone. That means you know about the apartment I have in LeperCon, right?"

There was a blue-collar area of the city called LeperCon. A sort of bastardized play on a translocated section of Boston's old criminal Combat Zone, and the city's deep Irish roots. A long-past client had transferred a rent-controlled lease in lieu of an unpaid bill. I'd thought, until a few days ago, that it was a secret from Brand.

"I'm not angry about that," Brand said, carefully, not sure where I was leading.

"Why do you think I go there?"

"To get away from me."

"Never."

"Bullshit. I can be a bastard. You deserve a night off every now and then."

I'd been a bastard to him, back at the Green Docks, when I was talking about his own nights off. He hadn't thrown this back in my face, though. I didn't deserve him.

I took a quick breath and said, "It's where I store all the evidence I've gathered. About my father's murder. The death of our people. The fall of our court. My . . . rape. The rapes."

He waited, the wrinkles around his eyes as hard as steel wire. He knew there was more.

"Brand . . . Ashton was one of the rapists."

"*What?*" he hissed.

"I didn't know until the very end. That's . . . why I killed him." It wasn't. Not really. But that is the lie I needed to tell right now. And I repeat in my brain, for the sake of our Companion bond: *This is the lie I need to tell right now, and that statement is true.*

"Why didn't you tell me?" he demanded.

"Because I wasn't ready. I'm still not ready. Please, Brand, I promise—*promised.* I've promised you before that if I ever go after the people that hurt me, I wouldn't leave you behind. But . . . I'm not ready. Not even to talk about it."

"I don't know what to say."

"Don't be mad. Please don't be mad."

"I would never be mad about this," he whispered, and shifted forward so that he was standing directly in front of me, locked in eye contact. "But . . . Rune, you don't need to face this alone. You *can't* face this alone."

"I know."

He continued to search my face for confirmation. "Why tell me this now?" When I didn't answer right away, he added, "Is it because you can use the Arcanum to help you find out what happened that night?"

I slowly shook my head. In a way, it was the perfect question for him to ask, because anger is armor. I felt it creep over my skin, cold and impenetrable. "It's because whatever happened that night couldn't have happened without the complicity of at least one Arcana. So, yes, other Arcana may help me. But when I was in the Iconsgison? I didn't forget for one second that there may have been someone in that room who killed my father and my people. Who hurt me. Not for one second."

Brand gaped at me. I'm not sure I'd ever shocked him, statement for statement, with such affect.

"They treated me like prey," I said. "They probably still think I'm weak and impulsive. But they—whoever they are—don't know I've spent twenty years circling around to flank them. I will know what happened. I will bring an accounting."

"We," Brand said.

I smiled at him.

"We," I agreed.

I heard a ragged cheer from the ruins of the house. Two of the guards emerged from behind a chimney, carrying a soot-stained object between them.

It had survived. I knew it was likely to have survived the flames.

Anna joined us, curiously, as we met the guards. They set the massive seal on the ground—the one with the Sun emblem, that had been stored in the upstairs linen closet—and backed away respectfully. One of them pulled out a handkerchief and handed it to me, which I thought was a rather nice gesture.

"Do you remember what I said about this?" I asked Anna. I began to clean the surface of the emblem with the cloth.

"It still hums," she murmured, running her eyes along it.

"What does the seal do?" I quizzed.

"It identifies you."

"It identifies the bloodline of my house," I corrected. "Can you be very brave for me? I need a drop of your blood. If you want, we can—"

The thirteen-year-old girl gave me a derisive look, pulled a godsdamn steak knife from the back of her waistband, and sliced her thumb. Even Brand's eyes went a little wide.

"*Anna*," I said firmly.

"Am I not your heir?" she demanded. "Wouldn't your heir be armed?"

"That—Annawan Dawncreek, we need *rules*."

"Now? Because I'm bleeding," she said, and held up her dripping thumb like it was a middle finger.

I sighed and said, "Here. Right here." I gently touched her wrist, and guided her hand to the emblem.

A drop of her blood fell onto the stylized sun.

Beneath the patina of soot, the metal began to warm and glow. Amber light fell upwards, coating our faces.

"But . . ." she said, and now her own eyes were as wide as saucers.

"We're kin, Anna," I said softly.

"You knew that?"

"I suspected it. You're very, very special. I don't think you realize how special you are. The same blood that runs in my veins? That ran in my father's veins? It runs in you, too, cousin."

"Cousin," she whispered.

"Cousin," I agreed. "Kin. And for now, yes, you are my heir. It's the best way I can think to protect you. One day, though, you'll have a choice. I'll always make sure you have a choice. You can lead whatever life you want—you can be whoever you want to be. You are strong, and talented, and clever. You're the best mix of a Companion and an Atlantean, and I can't think of a more amazing blend than that."

She edged closer to me, until our knees touched. I realized a second later that she wanted a hug. It wasn't a request that came easily to her, so I had to spend another second blinking my eyes, and then pulled her into an embrace.

"Cousin," she said against my shoulder.

It only lasted a few seconds—like she had only that much childhood left to spare. She pushed away and rubbed her sleeve over her eyes. "So I really am your heir? For now?"

"Yes."

"Okay."

"We can work out the details next week. Let's have a few days to relax, and then we'll enroll you."

She lowered her brow. "Enroll?"

"In Magnus Academy. You're my heir. You're well past homeschooling age."

"School? You're putting me *in school?*" she demanded.

"Absolutely."

Ten seconds later, she was done telling me what she thought about that, which cost her about every quarter in her pocket.

I'm not sure formal invitations were sent out—though we had a Queenie, so there appeared to be structure around the entire operation—but the Sun suite at the Enclave was slowly filling with people to celebrate our victory.

The Enclave was a swank private beach club on the western end of Nazaca Road, the priciest real estate on the island. A global ley line ran under it, bolstering the monarch-level defenses of the building.

Once, it had been a ruined resort in Cambodia called Bokor Hill. The jungle's rust-red moss still clung to some of the outer stonework, giving it a decrepit allure. Each Arcana was portioned suites, even the poorer courts like mine. It was a tradition as old as the Unsettlement of Nantucket.

Addam, apparently, showed up very early with Quinn, and joined me in the master bedroom. I didn't hear him arrive. One moment I was dreaming of a fight, the next he was pressing around the curve of my body and stealing half my pillow. I started to wake, but he shushed me, and I sank back into a peaceful sleep while the palm of his hand slid over my stomach. The last thing I remember was smelling his new cologne— amber and sandalwood.

I woke before him. There was a period where my brain didn't fully engage. It was the most peaceful few minutes I'd spent in weeks. I saw the sunlight slowly crawl across the golden hairs on Addam's arm. Felt his heartbeat where my elbow was pressed into his chest.

Then my brain turned on, and I spent some time thinking. So many thoughts, all with question marks—either because they were genuine questions, or because I didn't understand my luck.

Was he really that handsome? Did he really want to build a court with me? Are you supposed to stare at people when they're sleeping, even when you're in a relationship with them? Would I be able to give him more of myself—physically share more of myself with him? Was I being fair to him? Was—

"Perhaps drink a glass of water," Addam murmured. "Then come back to bed."

Fair enough. I went to the bathroom, fought my bedhead with a cheap black comb, and returned to the master bedroom.

In the interim, Addam had woken up. In every sense of the word. He sat, naked, under a single sheet that pooled over his lap. He had his back against the headboard.

"This is a very disappointing start," he sighed. "I am wearing no clothes, and yet you stare at my hand."

I felt the color rise to my cheeks. "I haven't seen your . . . new hand. It's very bright."

Addam held up his hand—his metal hand, the color of new brass.

And . . .

"Godsdamn," I whispered, and rushed to the edge of the bed. I held my fingers over the metal, barely touching the surface. "That's a *sigil*."

"It is, Hero."

"You don't do anything by half, do you?" I said in absolute astonishment. "I don't think I've ever seen something like this before."

Addam turned the hand in a partial gripping gesture. He grimaced. "Not quite as articulate as a real hand. And please don't mention I said that. This is a gift from Quinn, and I am very, very sore about it."

"You're mad that he found you a sigil to replace your bloody hand?"

"I'm frustrated that my mother let him plunder his trust fund to buy it. Do you have any idea how expensive rare sigils like this are? He should not have spent the money."

I marveled at that. Addam had a razor worth six figures. How much had this sigil-hand cost, to be considered too expensive?

I sat down on the end of the mattress. "You knew."

"Excuse me?"

"You knew you'd lose your hand. Didn't you?"

Addam met my stare, and finally raised a bare shoulder in a subtle shrug.

"It's too much. I can't . . ." My voice dropped to a whisper. "Addam, you can't be sacrificing yourself like that. I don't think I could bear it."

Now he smiled, and there was nothing subtle about a smile from a man like Addam. It reached up to make his burgundy eyes crinkle and shine; it made his cheek cave into a small dimple. "My Rune. The other day, at the hospital? I said that, through you, I would be able to serve my city."

"That doesn't mean you have to lose body parts to do it."

"There are times I wish I could look into your head, the way that Brandon does. I wish I could understand why you have such difficulty accepting that others may need to sacrifice themselves for the greater good, while being so casual about your own role in matters. Why must it all rest on your shoulders? Why don't *you* shrug off this burden?"

I didn't answer. I'm not sure I could, without sounding like an asshole. Getting up, I went over to the gauzy curtains that were closed against a liquid blue sky. I parted the cloth and looked at ocean and air. Too high up to see the narrow beach; just ocean and air.

"It's fine, Rune," he said from behind me. "You don't need to answer. I think I do understand. I suppose, if I were honest, I understand much of what hasn't been said between us. You must not consider me so fragile. I can handle such truths. For instance, I know that I will never be the love of your life."

I froze. Turned. Stared at him.

He smiled at me, a little sadly. "What you share with Brand? I could spend a lifetime chasing it, and it will always be decades out of my reach. How could I possibly offer something to compare to that which you've always known? He isn't simply a lifelong friend. He is irrevocably linked to your very concept of safety and protection. And I can understand that, because I raised Quinn. Quinn is an emotion for me, too."

"Addam . . ."

"We are a people that share our love. I am very Atlantean in that regard. So I do not ask for more than you offer. I know I have a place, and I am happy with that, Lord Sun."

"No, don't—not you."

"Apologies. I didn't mean it critically. I am very, very proud of you." His Russian accent rose with the *R*'s, and his eyes got misty.

He brought up one knee, which made the sheet slide off his leg. After a moment, he smiled, because he knew I was no longer looking at his hand.

"What is your favorite part of my body, Hero?" he asked quietly.

I thought about all the ways that question could go wrong and said, slowly, "Your heart."

He barked out a laugh. "Rune."

"Your legs," I admitted.

"My legs," he repeated, and stretched out a bare leg. "That was a rather certain answer. Do you often think of my legs?"

"Well. I mean. You're so damn tall. Most tall people have skinny legs, but yours are . . . sort of . . . perfect."

His smile widened. He turned and reached down into a duffle bag by the bed, which made his abdomen do all sorts of interesting things. When he resurfaced, he had a length of silk cloth in his hands.

Before I had time to ruin the moment by deconstructing it, he'd tied the silk around his head, effectively blindfolding himself.

He leaned back into the bed and seemed to be enjoying my stunned silence.

"I want you to look at me," he said. "Without feeling judged by my own gaze. Without being able to look to me for approval. I want your attention, and I want your touch. I want this moment to be yours. I will do whatever you want. The only I thing I will not do gladly is to end this moment before we even give it a chance."

I went over to the mattress and sat down on the edge of it again.

My fingers spoke for me.

I touched the arch of his foot, and trailed upwards along his hard shin—lightly scarred from a lifetime of activity. I circled my fingers in, to the inside of his thigh, palest of all his skin. Brushed quickly to his abdomen and its hard muscles.

He sat beneath me and just breathed. Trusting me. Wanting me. Wanting this. Knowing that the best way to give me control was to yield all of his.

And I thought, *But I do like his heart best.*

"I love you, Addam," I said, and then kissed his smile before he could answer back.

Hours and hours later, I found Max in one of the three guest suites.

The windows faced the ocean, and Max was watching Addam and Quinn. Addam had crawled out of bed minutes before I did, grabbed a bagel, and headed to the beach. Now, he and Quinn had separated from the herd, and appeared to be taking turns putting each other in a head-lock.

"That needs to stop before they give Brand ideas," I said, joining Max at the window.

Max smiled at me. "Addam started training Quinn. In self-defense."

I hadn't known, and was surprised at my surprise. I knew we'd been heading in this direction. But seeing it? It filled me with carbonated emo-tions—flickering hisses of guilt and pride and worry and apprehension.

"Do you think Quinn has it in him?" I asked honestly. "To fight?"

"I think Quinn has a million different ways *not* to fight," Max said, rather wisely. "And that's sort of going to be his fighting style. Plus, he'll have me." Max cut his eyes at me, uncertain. "I can learn."

Now I smiled at him. "You're going to have the shoulders of a line-backer, Max. You're going to be a ferocious fighter."

"So you'll let me train with Brand? Really train?"

I thought of the conversation we needed to have. Now. Soon. No, now. There were things between Max and me that needed to be said.

Predictably, I stalled.

"Of course you can train with Brand," I said.

"The real moves? Not the fake Companion moves he pretends to teach me?"

"Technically, those are still self-defense moves, he just flowers up the terminology to make eye gouging and nut kicking sound pretty. I'm sure they'll teach you the same sort of moves at Magnus."

Max went still. "Magnus Academy?"

"Yes. I've decided to punish you for stealing the boat by giving you a world-class education."

"Rune," Max whispered, horrified. "No. You can't."

"It won't be as bad as it sounds."

"It's a school for scions. It's expensive. I can't ask you to do that for me."

"You make it sound like facing the Hanged Man in a battle to the death is cheaper than a semester there. It's really not."

It was a joke, and landed badly, because Max's eyes filled with tears. "That's my point. I'm costing you too much. So much."

"I accept that cost. We all do. Letting people into your life is never without a cost. You do it because, in the end, you've got people in your life. That's what I've learned recently, at least."

I heard a commotion outside. I looked out the window and saw the rarely unsmiling Quinn had crossed his arms and was stomping his foot. He and Addam shouted some things at each other. Quinn kicked sand at Addam, spun around, and stormed away.

"Oooh," I said. "He just found out he's going to Magnus Academy too." I smiled at the look on Max's face—that despair now edged with something like hope. "What? You thought he was getting a pass on stealing the boat? Oh, no. Both of you—and Anna—are being enrolled. It's perfect. It's a punishment, an investment in the future, and also a way to get even with the fat-headed administrators at Magnus. They don't know what's about to hit them. You will tear that place *down*."

Max just stared at me.

"And, you know, get an education in the process," I added half-heartedly. "Are you at least a little excited?"

He turned and walked over to the bed, and dropped roughly onto the mattress. He stared down at his hands, cradled loosely in his lap.

"Max," I said. "Talk to me."

He chewed on that for a moment, and swallowed the pieces of a dozen replies. Finally, after a long minute, he said, "I remember the moment I realized I wasn't special."

"Max—"

"No. I mean, really. It happened. You've got to understand that when I was young, very young, I *was* special. My grandmother doted on me. Lady Lovers. She said I was going to be a great man. She spent so much time with me. She tried to train me. But . . . I just . . . never had it. Never had what you have. What other heirs have. And one day she stopped training me. She stopped calling for me. She just . . . vanished from my life. And . . . and she . . . I was given to my uncle. To be trained for a marital alliance. To . . ."

I went over and sat next to him. "I am not about to base my decisions on the thoughts of a failed Arcana. What happened to Elena says just about everything you need to know about her."

"But still, I'm—"

"You're mine. And you've been special to me from the day you entered my home."

"Brand put my head in a toilet," he reminded me.

"Well, the next day. The very next day."

His brief smile faltered. "You made a deal with her. You didn't have a choice. She tricked you. She gave you a sigil, but tricked you into watching me until I turned twenty-one. You didn't ask for any of this."

"That," I sighed. I reached up with both hands and fumbled with a clasp behind my neck. It took a second, but then the chain sagged into my hands. I pooled the cameo pendant in my palms and held it out to Max.

He shook his head at me, not understanding.

"I'm not about to give you the emerald ring she gave me. I don't want you to keep a single thing from that family. You get this. My mother's cameo. It's a bit . . . well, you know . . . weird. But it means a lot to me."

"I don't . . .What?"

"This sigil is now your sigil," I said. "Its will is now your will."

And the magic spun between us. I felt the loss of it like a cool shiver, and then it stretched to Max and settled on him. Goosebumps rose along his arms.

"Rune," he whispered.

"You'll need to learn sigil magic," I said. "It's far past time. And I don't want you to think I'm raising you because of Elena's ring."

"But . . . if you give up the sigil, you'll have no reason to keep me. I don't—"

"Shhh," I said, and put the necklace in his limp hands. "Listen to me. A few days ago, on the ship, we thought Corinne was dying. And she made me promise to make a home for Corbie, Anna, and Layne. To protect them. To love them. And it was so *important* to her—that last bit. It makes me think I've been stupid for not saying it more often when I mean it in my own life. Max, you have a home. You are under my protection. And I love you. Brand and I? We love you, Max."

He closed his eyes as the first tear ran down the side of his nose.

"Listen to me," I said again. "When this all started—with the Hanged Man—I was hard on you. I came down so hard on you. And what did you do? You didn't complain. You didn't protest. You stepped into the background and waited for the chance to help. And you've just been standing there, quiet, since, letting us take the lead. Which is so good of you. And you've gone off and done this amazing work, both before and after. *You* found the entry to the attic on Sun Estate. *You* figured out a way to interpret Quinn's visions in a truly astonishing manner. *You* got us vital intel on the mushroom farm."

He shook his head, and more tears fell.

"So I don't want you to worry about being *special.* I want you to know you already *are.* I want to see what comes *next.*" I put my hand on his head, which shook as the young man tried to hold in his emotions. "I want you to be brilliant, Max. I want you to shine. I want you to see your potential like I see it, like Brand sees it—and I want you to share it with everyone who has the good fortune to cross your amazing path. And if you need a turning point? If you need a starting point for this change? Then it happens now, and where we stand. Will you enter my house? Not just my court. My house. Will you enter Sun House, and be as kin?"

The door to the room opened. Brand stepped in. Max blinked tears at him, and watched as he crossed behind us and slipped onto the mattress, so that we were all close. The two stared at each other until Brand said, "You've fucking met Rune, right? He's going to get all formal and insist you say the words out loud."

"I . . ." Max whispered.

"Matthias Saint Valentine, will you join my house?" I said.

"I will. I will, please. I will." Then he started crying in earnest.

He buried his face in his hands and leaned into us, partially against Brand, partially against me, so that we both supported his weight.

"Then you are no longer Matthias Saint Valentine," I said. "You are my kin. You are Matthias Saint John, and the Sun Court stands with you."

Eventually, it came to *now*, that moment of the evening when I could slip away and steal a minute of quiet for myself.

Max had picked up my hosting slack. He was meeting new Enclave guests at the door—people who either had been invited or were curious. He seemed excited about trying out his new name, which was cute, and also couched in a display of rather stunning manners.

I went out to the beach, until the party was behind me. It cast faint light and noise along the sand like a northern aura. I dragged a chair near the edge of the rising tide, and told myself I'd go back inside when the water reached my toes.

Time passed, and after a while, I wasn't alone anymore.

Brand had a plain manila folder in his hand, which he threw on the sand between us while throwing himself down with a grunt. I waited a second until he found a proper insult, because, well, Brand.

"It would have fucking killed you to haul over two chairs?" he asked.

I smiled at the black sky and shook my head. "And you can keep that bloody folder to yourself. Nothing good ever happens when you come at me with one of those."

"No?" he said. "There's money in it."

I squirmed around in the chair so that I was facing him. "Our money?"

"*Our* is a strong word. I'll let you look at it, at least. And for the fucking record, nothing good happens when you come at me with a folder, either. Why did you leave that stupid old folder on my bed?"

I'd left him what I'd found in Sun Estate's attic. I didn't want it. I didn't trust myself with it. Either Brand knew everything in the folder, or he didn't. It was wrong of me to make the decision for him.

Brand watched all this play across my face. "We still need to talk about this?"

"No," I said too quickly.

His jaw went mulish. "They're in South Boston. Still. This address is old, but they've been there since I was born. They've been there for generations. I'm Irish, by the way. American Irish. Do you want me to care about this? What would you say if I wanted to go?"

"Go?" I echoed dumbly.

"Will you allow it? If I want to move there, get to know them?"

There was still oxygen in the world. I knew that, rationally. It just felt otherwise. So I pretended I didn't need to breathe fake oxygen to settle my fake panic because everything was fine. This was fine.

"It'd be fine," I said slowly. "They need mercenaries in Boston, right? Or something like mercenaries? That's a skill you can take anywhere. So . . . It's your decision. To move or not."

I've never felt his gaze so heavy on me. He stared at me for another few beats, then shrugged and nodded. He dropped his head and kicked at the sand with the heel of a bare foot.

"I mean," I added, "there are other things I could do, if the mercenary thing didn't work out for us. I could work as a barista. They have lots of barista jobs in America, right? We could find a huge loft, like all those poor young people in American sitcoms live in. We'd be fine."

His eyes shot back to me. The tightness around them melted into a small smile.

"What?" I said.

"Idiot," he whispered.

I sunk back into my chair and wondered why I was an idiot. And why was he so damned relieved? It's not as if—

"Oh!" I shouted, and stabbed a finger at him. "You were asking if you could *leave me*."

"Fuck off," he said.

"No. Oh, no, you are *so stupid*. We are going to grow old and die together. And then? Then we'll get rejuvenated and grow old and die together again. And again. And again. Leave me? Move to Boston without me? Are you mental?"

I think he may have laughed—literally, actually laughed—which he hid behind the brusque motion of slapping the manila folder into my lap. "Look," he said.

I opened the folder. There were a few scary-looking documents with the Arcanum seal on them, along with a check. I picked up the check. I stared at one zero. And then another. And another and another and another and another. Lead by the number four.

"Four million dollars?" I said hoarsely. "Is this a check for four million dollars?"

"Yes. And be careful with it—I want to memorize Lady Death's signature later."

"Lady Death is giving us four million dollars?" I asked.

"Spoils of war. Did you get a nice look at it? Good." He plucked it out of my hands, folded it, put it in his breast pocket.

"We're rich," I said. "I want to see it again."

"No. We need it as a down payment. It's as good as spent."

"What the *holy fuck* are you thinking, and stop thinking it *right now*," I demanded.

His expression tightened. "You're an Arcana, Rune. You're at the top of hill. Know what that means? Everyone is going to want to push you off. You need a compound. We need to rehabilitate Sun Estate."

"Oh."

"Four million dollars seems like a lot, but you know how much damage that place took."

"Oh, we are so poor again," I said.

"Not to mention," he added. "It appears we'll need a very, very big back yard."

I didn't like the way he said that, so I pretended to be interested in a particular big wave that broke in front of us.

"Because remember Plan A?" he continued. "When you had the chance to divide the spoils yourself? Remember that? Remember when you gave Lady Death the job? Well, turns out she has a sense of humor. Open the folder. Go on."

I pinched the edge of the folder and slowly drew it open. The check had been sitting on a document with the Arcanum seal. I started reading what looked like a laundry list of items awarded to the Sun Throne in action against the Gallows. Including . . .

"A dinosaur?" I sucked in a breath. "She's giving us the Hanged Man's dinosaur?"

"You killed the ifrit, its master. And it's not just a dinosaur. It's an *old* dinosaur. They had a healer look at it. It has arthritis. We own a dinosaur with arthritis. Do you want to imagine what the fucking vet bills will be like?"

"Did she give us anything else I need to know about?"

"You mean like a World War II battleship?"

"That's not funny."

"And yet."

"She did *not* give us the battleship. The battleship could cause global retaliation. It's haunted and needs a ton of spell-work. She would *not* give it to me."

"Put like that, you're right—it's amazing she didn't keep it for herself."

I slammed back into my chair and slapped a hand over my eyes. We were silent for many, many waves. There was much to think about.

Finally, I said, in an almost excited whisper, "I own a dinosaur."

And Brand whispered back, "I own five-story battleship guns."

We reached out at the same time and banged fists.

ACKNOWLEDGMENTS

So many more acknowledgments to add this time around. The thing I never expected? Was how damn cool it would be to share New Atlantis with readers. The joy and support and learning they've given me in return has been nothing short of life-changing.

Many, many thanks to Kathy Shin and her art and music playlist; *Run Boy Run* played nonstop while Rune battled among the skyscrapers. Thank you Vic Grey, who shared artwork and Twitter love; their drawing of Rune and the nine animal masks was especially chilling. (They helped name the ninth mask for me, too: the Owl. And have you seen their representation of Lady Death and the Wheel of Fortune on Twitter? Exceptional.) Kathy and Vic join several other wonderful people who drew images inspired by *Tarot*, which was why the free novelette, *The Sunken Mall* (set between *The Last Sun* and *Hanged Man*) was dedicated to them. You can find links to the story and their artwork on my Twitter account.

Thank you to Ben and Keith from the podcast *TG Geeks*. I had my first author podcast interview with them, and they spoiled me for every experience I had after that. They sound like radio gods; I could listen to them all day. Thank you for the wonderful experiences and unflagging support, guys.

And contest winners! Thank you @becausebenjamin for naming the ifrit in a Twitter challenge. And thank you to Grace Craumer and Fabricio Toms who won a contest in Ms. Patricia Jackson's class at Central York High School. Together they named Anaïca, a guarda captain who tried to refuse Rune entry in the Arcanum. *She has an eye tattooed on her wrist, the same color as her irises, and smells strong of clean, plain soap.* Hosting that contest with Central York was one of the coolest things I've ever done. (And every class should have a teacher like Ms. Jackson.)

Thank you Britny Herzog for creating my sequined cloak of many-rainbow-colors for World Pride in NYC in July 2019. Marching with the

Barnes & Noble float during Pride was another Life Highpoint. Words can't even describe how surreal and magnificent it was. Britny made it even more special with that glittery cloak.

Thank you to the folk who run the *Battleship North Carolina*. The battleship museum was, of course, a massive inspiration for this novel. I've spent many, many hours there. You can literally track Rune's progress through the boat on a real floorplan. War is never pretty, not even as a clean museum preservation, but it's a part of our past, and, wow, I wish we would start to learn from it. At the very least, we shouldn't forget.

Thank you Sara Megibow of KT Literary—agent extraordinaire, voice of reason, constant supporter. Thank you Rene Sears, the best editor in the multiverse. Thank you Micah Epstein for the stunning cover; and Audible and Josh Hurley for the exceptional voice narration. Thank you to Kim Yau of Paradigm Talent Agency for representing my Hollywood interests (and for giving me the chance to casually drop a phrase like that into conversation, ever); and to Logan and PL for the fascinating, in-depth talks about what the TV world looks like. And thanks to all the other talented, amazing folk at Pyr: Jennifer Do, Samantha Lien, Marianna Vertullo, Hailey Dezort, Dana Kaye, and Jarred Weisfeld.

Thank you to all of you who follow me on Twitter. (Except family and coworkers. I have banned you, if for no other reason than to keep you from seeing me in a sequined cloak.) I never thought I'd be a social media person, but here I am, loving Twitter and my Twitter friends. Thanks for letting me share snippets and scenes with you in advance.

And thank you to the Writer's Cramp—my longtime writing group. Blakely, Scott, Paige, Christie-Sue, Emmalea, Ali, Kwame, Taylor, York . . . Y'all are my guiding star. But particular thanks to the authors Christie-Sue Cheely and Scott R. Reintgen, who were there until the bitter end, and read the final stretch of *Hanged Man* within hours of it being written. I love you guys.

And you. Seriously: you. Thanks for joining me on this ride. More to come. I promise.

ABOUT THE AUTHOR

K.D. lives and writes in North Carolina, but has spent time in Massachusetts, Maine, Colorado, New Hampshire, Montana, and Washington State. (Common theme until NC: Snow. So, so much snow. And now? Heat. So, so much heat.) Mercifully short careers in food service, interactive television, corporate banking, retail management, and bariatric furniture has led to a much less short career in higher education. *The Last Sun* and *The Hanged Man* are the first two novels in his debut series, The Tarot Sequence. K.D. is represented by Sara Megibow at kt literary, and Kim Yau at Paradigm for media rights.

1/20